DAGGER'S DESTINY

The Destiny Series

KAREN MUIR

Dagger's Destiny

Copyright © 2016 by Karen Muir

2nd Edition 2019

Published by Karen Muir

www.karen-muir.com

ISBN: 978-0-9971914-4-8

Printed in the United States

Dedication

It is my pleasure to dedicate my book to
my amazing husband, Peter,
who has always believed in me.
To my wonderful sons and the special women in their lives
who inspire me.
To my deceased parents, Bill and Estelle,
who instilled in all their children
a passionate nature and a love of life.
To my supportive family, friends, and co-workers
who readily listen to my constant chatter
about characters and stories.
And a special thanks to my beta reader, Judith,
who pushed me to follow my dreams.

~Chapter One~

England – 1354

Please, God!

Gasping for air, Lady Katherine de Grey mouthed the silent plea as she darted between bushes and trees. Her mantle flapped behind, tangling on sharp branches that reached out like talons from the wooded depths.

"Halt, girl!" ordered one of the three men in pursuit, as he crashed headlong through the underbrush.

Katherine dared not. She lifted her surcoat and kirtle out of the way and ran as if a pack of hounds snapped at her heels. Her vision clouded with pain from the jagged twigs slashing the backs of her bare hands.

"Slow down. We will'na hurt you," one man pledged.

A roar of laughter erupted from his friends, disputing the truth of his words.

Katherine instinctively headed toward home, then quickly changed course. She couldn't return to Rosemont. Her father and brother were dead; her beloved castle no longer offered sanctuary. As of yesterday, Lord Seton, their murderer, was the new lord and master.

I can't go back. Not yet. Not until I can claim my revenge.

She gulped a mouthful of cool morning air that burned a trail to her lungs. The men were a good distance away, but with every passing minute, the ground between them lessened. Her legs screamed for relief, and her heart beat so wildly the sound pounded in her ears. After a sleepless night, it was only a matter of time before she could go on no farther.

The branches ahead parted, exposing a rugged deer path up a steep incline. With a small burst of strength, she pushed herself up the climb. At the top, she scanned the woods below. They were gaining on her. She'd have to hide.

Through the muted morning haze, her eyes locked on an old fallen tree covered with new growth, partly embedded in the forest floor.

She raced down the hill, scrambled over the felled rotting oak, and stretched out on her side along its length. Her ragged breath came in gasps and her chest rose and fell in short, quick waves.

Just pass me by, echoed in her head as she burrowed against the damp, rough bark. Hopefully, the foliage would conceal her long enough for her assailants to tire of their chase.

How foolish I am.

Her lack of judgment this morning was disheartening. If she had paid better attention to her surroundings, these wretched ruffians wouldn't be on the hunt. More than one form of danger awaited a lone woman in the midst of nowhere. She should've been more vigilant after escaping Lord Seton's imprisonment the previous night. If grief over the recent loss of her family hadn't jumbled her wits, she would never have wandered into the cold camp, drawing the notice of a man only half-asleep.

Katherine closed her eyes. *Just breathe.*

Branches snapped in the distance. Her body tensed. She sucked in a deep gulp of air that caught painfully in her dry, scratchy throat. Her trembling fingers wrapped in a death grip around the hilt of her mother's dagger attached at her waist. The small weapon was the only possession rescued from her home Slowly, she drew the blade from its sheath.

For a brief moment, she imagined a whisper of her mother's long-departed spirit brush against the back of her neck, but in the next instant, the sensation was gone.

A small crevice in the crumbling bark of the decaying tree provided an odd-shaped opening. She peered through the hole and held her breath when her assailants charged over the hill. With their prey missing, the three quickly split up and vanished from her sight. She exhaled slowly and sank deeper into the crumbling pulp of the wood.

As suspected, these were not Lord Seton's hirelings. From their tattered tunics, torn hose, snarled hair, and Scottish brogue, they were likely thieves and outlaws. Dangerous men to be sure. If caught, she didn't doubt they would ravish and kill her.

"Where'd that whore get off tae?" a breathless male voice yelled.

"Hiding, I'd wager. Come out, girl. We've something for ye!"

Unable to see her enemies, she focused on their sounds as they stomped through the thick brush.

"Ye better show yourself right now if ye know what's good for ye," one bellowed in the distance.

"Ye're warned, lass. Come out, or it'll go bad for ye."

Katherine swallowed hard. Their blatant threats wouldn't be enough to convince her to reveal herself. They wanted to hurt her either way. She wouldn't give up that easily. If the outlaws wanted her, they would have to find her.

"Show ye self. It will'na hurt but a wee bit. We can teach ye a thing or two about men."

Loud guffaws, from different directions, reverberated off the trees.

A vivid image of their foul unwashed bodies pressing against her naked flesh flashed before her eyes. She bit down on her quivering lower lip. The taste of warm blood prompted her to stop. She needed a miracle.

An outlaw nearby shushed the others into a deadly silence. The bright new greenery sprouting around her hiding spot failed to do its job.

He found me.

The musty smell of decomposing timber mixed with fear caused a wave of nausea to turn her stomach. With her dagger clutched against the curve of her breast, she steeled herself for the assault.

Even forewarned, she still startled when cruel fingers clamped onto her shoulders.

"Unhand me!" she cried, as the ruffian yanked her from her shelter and into the air. In flight, she struggled to bring her dagger out from under her mantle, but the weapon became entangled in the folds of her cloak.

When he slammed Katherine's back onto the ground, the air forced from her lungs lodged like a cork in her throat before bursting forth in one big whoosh. As she inhaled again, the outlaw's rank breath accosted her senses, causing her to gag. Her nose wrinkled in disgust. She turned her head to ward off the stink, but in that scant moment, he pinned down her forearms and straddled her thighs. Fully restrained, she writhed in pain, his weight crushing her legs.

"Ye were warned to show yourself. Now ye'll pay," he snarled, his leather-skinned face only inches away.

"I am Lady Katherine de Grey. Leave me be, or I will have you sliced into small pieces before you are put to death," she shrieked as she thrashed under his weight. The bite from the man's handhold on her upper arms penetrated layers of clothing. She blinked back tears obstructing her vision.

The man shouted to his friends, "See here, I caught me a lady dressed as a serving wench."

Narrowing her gaze, she clenched her jaw. "I demand you release me this instant!"

"Ye want me ta let ye go?" he huffed. "Now that would'na be much fun."

A wave of despair swelled in her chest. Had God abandoned her? She shook her head to dispel the devastating loss of hope threatening to suffocate her.

God would never forsake her. She didn't deserve such torment after what she'd been through yesterday. How dare these men intend her harm.

Katherine's anger began as a small knot of outrage forming in the pit of her stomach. Then a tight bundle of barely restrained fury grew to a volatile force in the center of her chest. Unable to hold back the building of her deep-rooted pain and raw emotions from the ungrieved loss of her family, she took a deep breath, opened her mouth, and let loose an ear-piercing scream.

Her eyes widened in surprise, for the savage sound belonged in another world. The man hovering over her must have thought so too because he loosened his grip. Seeing her chance, she heaved her shoulder against his hold on her forearm, causing him to let go. Able to regain movement in her arm, she brought her dagger out from under her mantle.

The double-edge blade reflected a beam of sunlight as the weapon jabbed at his chest. The outlaw, taken back by the sight of steel, jerked away and scooted toward her feet. As she pressed forward, he retreated even farther until she was free from his weight.

Katherine continued to advance and moved to an upright position on her knees. She faced her assailant with her brandished dagger and warned him off with the sharp tip. Out of the corner of her eye, she glimpsed the other two curs rushing forward. She watched them warily, expecting them to overpower her with their numbers, but the outlaws were content to remain out of arm's reach.

"Are ye going to let the little girl best ye?" one taunted.

"Come on, Hugh. Get her. Ye can do it. Ye can take her," another cheered.

With bolstered courage, the man tried a frontal assault. Her blade whizzed through the air and found its mark on the big man's forearm, cutting a deep gash.

He yelped in pain and pulled back. Blood oozed between his fingers as he held tight to his injured arm. Hatred blazed in his eyes.

She met his heated stare without blinking.

"Ye little whore, ye'll pay for this," he ranted.

Ready to battle again, Katherine struggled to rise from her knees. The material from her gowns caught beneath her feet, making her attempt to stand impossible. She fixed her gaze at her adversary. Her hand quaked as she pointed the wet blade at his middle.

A vicious smile twisted the man's chapped lips and his cold, murky eyes shone dull with evil intentions, well aware of her plight.

Where was her miracle?

***

As Sir Richard Weston traveled toward Lord de Grey's holding, the easy tempo of his horse's gait lulled him into a state of tranquility. Titan's massive hooves pounded rhythmically upon the dirt road and the animal's black mane swayed with each bob of the head.

While he rode, Richard constantly scanned the woods on either side of the dirt road. Since the end of the plague, the byways had been safer for a lone knight to travel without a heavily armed escort. Honest work was plentiful for those so inclined. Any outlaws roaming the lands would be smart to give a well-trained knight a wide berth, but still, he remained wary.

In a few hours, he would arrive at the gates of Rosemont to deliver his father's missive. Hopefully, by this time tomorrow, he'd be well on his way north to Lockhart Manor. The sooner he made an offer to lease Lord Marten's estate, the better. Since King Edward approved the acquisition, there was little doubt about the outcome. Once he secured his own holding, he would return to London and ask for Lady Alice's hand in marriage.

She bore an uncanny resemblance to his best friend's wife. Although he barely knew the woman, with her by his side, he was guaranteed a good life, just like William had found with Lady Elizabeth.

As with everything Richard did, he had carefully considered the benefits of a union with Lady Alice, and they were not based on her looks alone. Her father was a powerful lord and in the good graces of King Edward and the nobles.

Marriage to Lady Alice would form a strategic alliance between their families and would ensure protection if needed.

Titan lifted his head and snorted. Well-toned muscles rippled down the curve of the animal's neck. As the stallion danced beneath him, Richard laid a hand on the hilt of his sword and listened carefully. In the distance, birds took flight and small animals scurried for cover.

"Is something amiss, my friend?"

At the sound of a woman's shrill scream, he gritted his teeth. Without hesitation, he reined his horse toward the cry for help and urged his charger forward.

Titan left the dirt road and raced through the forest. Branches swiped at Richard's clothes. He wore no heavy armor, just a layer of fine-linked chainmail under his leather tunic, but he always carried his sword. As he rode, he unsheathed the sharp blade from the scabbard attached to his hip. The power of the animal beneath him surged through his veins and made them one. Over the years, the two of them had joined forces in many battles, trusting one another, working together to stay alive.

As Titan crested the peak of a hill, Richard slowed his mount and took in the scene below. The foliage was thick, but from his vantage point he made out three men taunting a young woman who held them off with a small dagger.

Not able to stomach such injustice, he charged down the slope while sounding a deep roar.

The two men standing shoulder to shoulder shifted uneasily as they unsheathed their swords.

Richard appraised their strength. Neither wore armor and their weapons were ancient. He guided Titan directly toward them.

The closest man brought back his weapon. As Richard rode by, the man pointed the tip of his blade at his torso and jabbed with force. A clang of steel rang out as Richard deflected the lunge with his own weapon. Hardening his arm against the vibration, he pushed forward, sending the smaller man reeling in the opposite direction until the outlaw landed on his backside.

The second man rushed forth, holding his heavy sword in one hand out to the side. With all his might, the man swung the sharp blade in a wide arc. Richard anticipated the move and hooked the man's sword with his own, causing the weapon to fly out of the man's hand and land a fair distance away. He spun his horse around and urged his charger forward until Titan's massive chest slammed into the surprised man, knocking him off balance. As his assailant teetered backward, Richard squeezed his thighs and yanked on the reins.

At Richard's command, Titan drew back on his haunches, rose on his hind legs and struck out with his front hooves. A gigantic hoof smacked against the man's head with a sickening whack. A garbled sound escaped the outlaw's mouth before he fell in death.

A noise from behind caught Richard's attention. He reined his horse in a tight circle and barely missed a wild blow from the first man, who had regained his senses. As his attacker made an awkward attempt to move the weighty sword in a defensive position, Richard plunged the tip of his blade into the man's chest. His opponent's squeal of agony ended when Richard withdrew the blade and the man's lifeless body dropped to the ground.

The third man rushed forward with his sword held high and stabbed at Titan's unprotected chest. Richard whirled his stallion out of danger and brought his sword down so hard on the outlaw's blade that the clash sent a pulsing current through the hilt of the men's swords.

His opponent cried out from the sting and dropped his weapon. Defenseless, the man rushed to the woman a few feet away who struggled to rise from her knees.

"Behind you," Richard shouted.

The woman was too busy righting herself to react. The man came up from behind, seized the small dagger from her hand, and wrapped a thick arm around her throat. Pure panic crossed her face. She tried to pry away the unwanted limb, but it never budged.

"Behave, or I'll snap yer neck," the man barked in her ear.

At her assailant's warning, the young woman grew still. The man yanked her off her knees and onto her feet with a quick jerk. He dragged her backside against the length of his body and placed the tip of the dagger against the curve of her neck. The outlaw's eyes burned with anger when he surveyed the bloodied bodies of his two friends lying motionless in the dried leaves.

Richard considered his options. The woman's blue eyes silently pleaded for help. He urged Titan forward.

"Halt or I will slit her throat!" the man threatened, his voice cracking with apprehension.

Richard sat deep in the saddle. Titan stilled.

The man watched warily.

Richard swung a leg over his mount's neck and let his bulk slide down the side of his horse until his feet hit solid ground. The outlaw knew the woman was the only thing keeping him alive and wouldn't be foolish enough to dispose of her without good reason.

Pointing his hefty sword toward the ground, Richard studied the pair with calculated disinterest before he spoke.

"You may kill the girl before I have a chance to stop you, but your small dagger is no match against my sword. In no time, I will cut you down, just as I have done your friends." He dipped his head in the direction of the dead bodies to validate the truth of his words. "Drop the dagger, unhand the girl, and I will give you a chance to retrieve your sword. Who knows, fate may be on your side this day."

Richard offered the man a chance. Not much of a chance, but a chance, nonetheless. He hated men who treated women poorly.

"Ye'll let me retrieve my sword?" The man's eyes narrowed with suspicion.

"By my word," he promised.

Beads of sweat dripped down the outlaw's face. He stared at the sword on the ground, only a few feet away.

Richard had his answer.

Good, he will fight.

The young woman scanned her surroundings, preparing to take charge of her escape. Richard sensed her fear but admired her resolve. She displayed courage. He liked that.

Her stained and tattered clothes spoke of a lowly position, but her manner said otherwise. The woman had wavy, golden hair cascading down her back in total disarray. Yes, she was a beauty, even with leaves, twigs, and pieces of dirt hidden throughout her sun-kissed tresses. Thick, dark lashes framed clear blue eyes. Eyes that no longer pleaded but were now unwavering, preoccupied with a purpose.

The man shoved the young lady aside onto a pile of leaves and tossed away the dagger.

Richard cleared his mind for the task at hand. He remained planted in his spot, allowing the outlaw time to retrieve the old, dented sword. When the man held the weapon in a double-handed grasp, Richard let his sword come alive in one swift motion.

Out of the corner of his eye, he caught a glimpse of the young lady as she picked herself off the ground, reclaimed her dagger and headed into the woods. He exhaled a deep breath of relief. She remained unharmed.

Richard stood at his full height and turned his attention to his adversary. Legs braced apart, he let his arms tense with the weight of his long sword. As he pressed forward, he fixed a stare into the man's dark, frightened eyes. The coward would pay. He would never harm a woman again.

When metal hit metal, Richard ignored the familiar jolt traveling up his arm. The man was not well-trained and displayed little tolerance for battle. Soon the outlaw's breath was heavy with exertion. He had no real power behind his blows, and his movements were choppy, not fluid. The outlaw's stance was all wrong; if Richard hit him just right, the man would topple over.

Richard's opening came soon enough. With a forward lunge, he shoved the sharp tip of the blade through the man's skin and then into the dense bone over his heart. His opponent crumpled to the ground with a grunt, finding his eternal sleep.

Richard heaved a loud sigh that sounded odd in the noiseless forest. He did his duty by answering the woman's plea for help, but now he was obliged to escort the young lady out of harm's way. Although unscathed, she would not remain safe if she continued to travel alone.

He crouched down and cleaned the sticky blade on the sleeve of the man's shirt. The outlaw chose his fate. He wasted no second thoughts on the dead man lying at his feet, instead, he marked the spot where the woman went into the woods.

He would have to follow her. He had no choice.

~Chapter Two~

With a wide swing of her arm, Katherine swept aside the leafy branches blocking her path as she scurried away from the fight. Small droplets of sweat beaded on her brow, threatening to obscure her vision. She wiped them away with her fingertips.

If only she had time to remove a few layers of bulky clothing so the fresh morning air could dry her damp skin. Last night she dressed like a servant so as not to draw attention, but now she regretted her decision. The coarse linen kirtle and woolen surcoat were much warmer than her own gowns. She sighed heavily, resigned to her misery.

Behind her, steel clashed against steel. The sharp sound churned her stomach. No matter the outcome, she intended to be far away when the battle ended. The victor might still pursue her.

She clenched her small dagger and quickened her steps.

Up ahead, the fast-moving water roared as it rushed over jagged rocks. Although thunderous, she welcomed the calming effect the sound had on her nerves. When there was no longer a threat, she'd stop for a drink. Imagining the cool liquid sliding down her throat made her lick her dry lips.

When she reached the water's edge, she'd follow the river as it snaked through the forest. Eventually, she would make her way to Lord Weston, her father's best friend. Only under his protection would she be safe from Lord Seton or anyone else who wished her harm.

Fraught with fatigue, she moved her feet without much thought. Suddenly, the pointed toe of one of her leather boots caught a gnarled root. In mid-stride, her body fell forward. Her arms waved wildly in a futile attempt to regain her balance. When her hands and knees impacted the hard ground, her dagger flew from her grip.

It was over. With no strength left to fight off the exhaustion weighing on her like a cloak of chainmail, she rounded her back and hung her head. Her eyes welled with tears.

Why go on? My father is dead. The life I know is gone.

From behind, powerful hands grabbed under her arms and lifted her off the ground. While her feet dangled as if she was no more than a child, she clawed at the man's thick fingers and kicked her legs madly, but the more she fought, the tighter his hold. Only a few feet away, she spotted her precious dagger resting atop a pile of rotting debris, no use to her now.

"Unhand me, or you shall feel my wrath," she rasped, attempting to keep the fright from her voice.

"Easy, my lady," a deep, strong voice replied.

Immediately she knew who had won the battle; the knight had a unique masculine tone. She stopped her struggle and let her body relax. As expected, the man sensed her yield and set her down, releasing his hold.

Once freed, Katherine rushed forward and scooped up her dagger. She spun in her tracks and faced the big, brawny knight with the weapon held in her trembling hand. Pointing the sharp tip in the direction of his midriff, she willed her shaking arms to still.

No one could be trusted, except Lord Weston, especially an unknown knight.

The man cocked his head to one side and placed his hands on his hips. His crystal blue eyes twinkled with amusement. He had no right to find merriment in her feeble attempt to protect herself. It was daft to threaten a knight and he clearly thought so too, but she wouldn't withdraw. She raised her chin and straightened her shoulders, refusing to quake with the fear lying just beneath the surface.

"A lady, you say. And what, pray tell, makes you believe I am a lady? Who do you believe me to be?" Her voice grew stronger with her inquiry.

Her newly acquired mistrust of men, noble or not, was warranted. When Lord Seton discovered her gone, a search would begin. Perhaps he had already sent this man to retrieve her.

The knight made no attempt to move toward her and stood stone still. "I assure you. I can spot a high-born lady without much difficulty, no matter what form of dress she chooses. You are no exception. I don't know who you are, but I'm curious as to why you travel alone, clothed as you are, without the protection of your family."

He raised one of his dark brows, as he awaited her reply.

The man was taller than he first appeared, for he stood at least a foot over Katherine's head. A frown tugged at her mouth; his considerable size would pose a problem during a struggle unless she slowed him down with her dagger. Her gaze dropped to his thick legs, partially covered by high, black leather boots. Outrunning him wasn't an option, as the man was in good form and she was too tired to go far.

He wore a black leather tunic over a thin layer of fine-linked chainmail that added extra bulk to an already large frame. She imagined it would take very little for such a massive man to crush her.

She steeled herself to look upon his face. A quiver of pleasure made her heart flutter. The knight had a well-defined mouth, almost hidden behind a short-cropped beard. He parted his shiny, black hair down the center, and it was swept out of his face by orderly waves that fell short of his shoulders. Excitement rippled in her belly as she gazed at his perfectly sculptured features. She chided herself for such a reaction.

When their gazes met, she gripped her dagger tighter, for his piercing blue eyes chipped away at her composure. She refused to look away, and instead, stared with defiance into their alluring depths. The smug smirk forming at the corners of his mouth made her wince.

Somehow, the knight's confidence, or was it arrogance, seemed oddly familiar, but Katherine had no idea where their paths had crossed. She rarely ventured far from her family's holding.

Maybe he was present at her father's castle during the siege? Or was it elsewhere? She pointed her little dagger toward his stomach and poked the air with the tip of the blade in a threatening manner.

"Sir, I will need to know your name and intentions before I answer any questions."

In return, the knight smiled an unsettling grin so full of light mischief that she almost dropped her guard. He performed an exaggerated bow and said in an eloquent voice more suited for the finer establishments in England than the deep woods, "Of course, my lady. May I have the honor of introducing myself? I am

Sir Richard Weston, second son to Lord Weston of Stamford." His eyes sparkled with a bit of humor. "I believe I'm here to rescue you."

Her eyes grew large and her jaw slackened. She took a step back until she could go no farther, hampered by a small tree. Both arms fell limply to her sides. The once menacing dagger hung loosely from her hand, no longer a threat.

"Richard? Is it really you?" she questioned in a weak whisper. Was her battered mind playing tricks on her? Had God answered her prayers?

Searching his ruggedly handsome face, she recognized the boy she had known as a young girl. His appearance had changed much over the years, especially with the addition of his black beard. Gone was the awkward innocence of youth and in its place stood a fully-grown man. What was he doing so close to Rosemont?

Quizzical bright eyes stared at her. "You know of me?" He stepped forward and removed the dagger dangling from her lifeless hand. "I'd recall if our paths crossed."

"Tis I, Katherine de Grey. Do you not remember me?" She waited patiently for him to consider her closely and piece together long-ago memories.

A familiar, easy smile curled the edges of his mouth. "I'd never have recognized you. Many years have passed, a good ten, and you've changed much. Where is the young girl who sat on the rail to watch us train when my family visited Rosemont each summer? That child appears to have disappeared."

Her cheeks warmed. Those were her favorite memories … him wielding a sword in the training yard. She turned her head so he wouldn't see her discomfiture. When her gaze returned, she noted his raised brows.

"Why are you in the woods without an escort? Your father will be furious by your lack of judgment," he chastised. "It isn't safe for a lady to travel alone. You could've been killed. I'm taking you back right now. I'm sure you will have a lot of explaining to do. It's a good thing my father sent me on an errand to Rosemont. You're fortunate I happened by."

Katherine's jaw tightened. How dare he speak to her in such a manner and reprimand her when her troubles were due to no fault of her own. Richard treated her as if she were still a child. He asked for no explanation and assumed she couldn't make good decisions.

"It would not do you a bit of good to return me to Rosemont. My father and brother are dead." Her voice took on a sharp edge. "There is no one left to care about my welfare, so you need not take me back."

His eyes darkened to midnight blue as he absorbed the significance of her words. An eternity passed before he spoke. "You jest. It cannot be. My father returned to Stamford from a visit with your father just yesterday. Lord de Grey was alive and well."

"I assure you, I tell the truth."

"How does it come about that they are both dead? How did they die?" His voice hardened with anger.

Her insides trembled. She dreaded having to say the words out loud. Averting her eyes, she stared at a small seedling fighting its way out of the ground near her boot.

When she finally found the courage to speak, her voice came out broken and cracked. "Yesterday morning, a group of riders came upon Rosemont and asked for lodging. My father and brother welcomed them in behind our walls. Everyone assembled in the hall for the noon feast. When my father, brother and our men least expected it, the visitors turned on them with their daggers and murdered them without warning, before anyone had time to react. Within a matter of minutes, everyone was dead and they had seized Rosemont."

Katherine gazed at Richard, but his outline was hazy through her misty eyes. She reminded herself to stay standing when her body sagged with weariness.

He reached out and slipped a hand under her elbow for support. "How did you come to be here?"

"I escaped last night with the help of my maid. I journey to Stamford. All I have is the hope that your father will offer me his protection."

"Of course, he will." His lips tightened, and his face grew taut. "Do you know who carried out the attack?"

"The man goes by the name of Lord Seton." She spat out his name as if the words were distasteful in her mouth. "He was of the mind to marry me but was thwarted when one of his men killed our priest. I escaped while he searched for another."

"Was your family friendly with this man before?"

"My brother knew him from his travels, but I had never met him." She brushed a loose piece of hair away from her face. "Do you know of him?"

His eyebrows drew together. "I've had the displeasure of running into him a time or two. He's a dangerous man. Because he didn't hold your father and brother for ransom, I can only assume he wants you. If you were his bride, he would have an easier time claiming Rosemont as his own. Since he's a landless lord, it would be worthwhile for him to acquire a holding through marriage. With your family gone, there is little to stand in his way. If King Edward has no knowledge of Lord Seton's hand in the demise of your family, the king might readily agree to such a union."

Katherine shuddered. It was hard to hear her own thoughts spoken aloud. She swallowed the lump trapped in her throat. It was as she believed. Lord Seton would seek her out. He wouldn't let her go. The prize was too valuable.

"How could he think to get away with such a feat without King Edward finding out?" she asked while leaning heavily against a full-grown elm tree; relief from no longer being alone only added to her fatigue.

"Lord Seton is a cunning man. He would never attempt such an endeavor without some surety it would work in his favor."

"Your image of him is very disturbing." She tugged the ends of her mantle tightly together.

"I didn't mean to alarm you."

"I assure you. I was well enough distressed before you arrived."

"I imagine you were." He glanced over his shoulder. "Those three men were outlaws. Lord Seton would never hire such unskilled men. Let's hope he hasn't discovered you gone yet." His jaw muscles twitched under his short beard.

She rubbed her hands within her cloak as she awaited his thoughts.

"I'll make sure you arrive safely at Stamford," he said with a reassuring look.

"I would be indebted to you." The weight of uncertainty lifted. He would escort her to his father's unharmed. Once there, she would find a way to seek her revenge.

Richard placed her dagger back in the palm of her hand. He closed her fingers around the hilt and gave a heartening squeeze. A tremor traveled up her arm and warmed her innards.

He let out a loud whistle. His charger pushed his way through the foliage and stopped a few paces away. "We must make haste, but first I need a few minutes to cover our tracks. It's better Lord Seton believes you disappeared."

She stepped back and stared at the large black stallion.

"If I remember well, you are skilled with horses. Take Titan to the stream." He tilted his head toward the running water only a short distance away. "Drink your fill and prepare for a rough ride. We will have to travel fast."

He ushered her away from the tree by using his hand on her waist.

"Titan's mouth is extremely sensitive. Don't yank on the reins, or he will rear up and strike out. When you lead him, place a hand under his chin or on his shoulder. He will follow."

Richard was leaving? Her heart drummed in her chest. She didn't want him to leave her alone.

"Are you well?" His face pinched with concern.

Startled from her thoughts, she sputtered, "I…am."

"I'll return shortly."

She had no choice but to watch him disappear into the forest. He was right about removing any signs of a fight. She replaced her dagger in her girdle and nibbled softly on her lower lip. He'd come back for her. He wouldn't let her go it alone; after all, they were friends a long time ago. Surely, one didn't leave a family friend to fend for themselves? He certainly wouldn't leave his horse in her care if he were not coming back.

She shook her head to chase away her tormenting thoughts. He left with every intention of returning posthaste; she was not alone anymore.

When Katherine turned toward the water, she found the stallion observing her with open curiosity. She moved slowly until she stood in front of the regal beast. With one arm outstretched, she offered an upturned palm as a token of friendship. Titan brushed his velvet muzzle over the flat surface and snorted. She stepped closer and stroked the side of his face.

"It seems we are on our own. Let us take your master's advice and get a drink." The destrier snorted again. Her mouth curled up in a weak smile. She held the reins loosely, placed her hand under his jaw and guided the stallion to the nearby stream.

Richard would return. She was sure.

~Chapter Three~

At the river's edge, Katherine knelt on the bank and quenched her thirst. After she was through, she splashed a handful of chilly water on her filth encrusted face. Using the rough bottom of her woolen surcoat, she wiped away the droplets along with a layer of dirt. For the first time in many hours, her racing heart slowed its beat.

The peaceful sound of the whooshing water cleared her head. Awaiting Richard's return, she sat back on the grassy embankment and scanned the woods across the river. Since she saw no signs of imminent danger, she removed pieces of twigs and leaves entwined in her hair. Soon tired of the task, she patted down her disorderly waves, twisted the strands into a loose braid, and tied the end with a strip of cloth she cut from the bottom of her kirtle.

Richard had saved her life. Of all people to come to her aid, she would have chosen him. He'd escort her safely to Stamford.

A vision of her father flashed before her eyes. As she recalled the moment of her father's brutal death, a jolt of pain jabbed her heart. She sucked in a mouthful of air and let out a soft, wretched sob. The jarring sound broke the tranquility around her. She silenced the pitiful noise with her shaky hand.

He's truly gone. Moisture pooled in her eyes.

She envisioned her father's quick, cheerful smiles. He had been such a temperate man. She would never lay eyes on him again. His smiles never again bestowed. A dismal sadness engulfed her.

No good would come from thinking about the past or the future. Every thought one way or the other caused too much pain.

I have to stay in the moment.

Titan's head rose from the stream. Ever watchful, the charger's ears came forward. When he turned his neck to look around, water dribbled out of the sides of his mouth and landed on her head.

"Uhh!" she gasped.

Katherine raised her arms and shielded her hair from the sudden downpour. "Titan, mind your manners. My stench must be foul, but there is no time for a bath," she cried in feigned disgust. The big horse gave her shoulder a playful shove with his head and toppled her onto her side.

"Behave." She righted herself, but he knocked her over once again. A soft chuckle escaped her lips, and she pushed his head away.

Something in the woods caught Titan's attention. His well-defined neck muscles grew stiff as he extended his head as high as it would go and stared in one direction.

The change in his posture alarmed her. She glanced about, her hand reaching for the hilt of her dagger. Titan nickered softly. A second later, Richard pushed his way through the thick underbrush and into the open.

Her chest hammered with excitement. She lifted her skirts and scrambled to her feet. Richard came to stand beside his horse, and she reminded herself to breathe. She never expected the sight of him to cause such a reaction. Ten long years had come and gone, but barely a day passed she hadn't thought of him. Although the image she carried in her heart was of a much younger man, it was Richard alone who occupied her youthful fantasies. Now that he stood before her, she found him even more appealing than her childhood dreams.

He placed a few fond pats on his horse's thick neck. "We can be on our way. I hid the bodies behind a rotted, fallen tree. It should give us some time."

She brushed aside the harsh picture of lifeless bodies pressed against the trunk where she once hid. "How long will it take us to get to your father's?"

Richard knelt at the river's edge and filled his water pouch. He brought the skin to his lips and swallowed with a loud gulp.

"We'll stop at my friend William's castle first. It's out of the way, but he can offer us a safe escort to Stamford. If Lord Seton is determined to find you, he'll have all the roads watched, including the one to my father's castle. We'll do well with some protection." He stood and stroked Titan's nose. "We should arrive tomorrow. Midday, if we make haste."

He stepped forward and without warning grabbed Katherine about her waist. In one swift motion, he lifted her off her feet and placed her none too gently in the front of his saddle.

Surprised by her sudden flight through the air, she waved her arms frantically until her fingers grabbed Titan's long mane.

"Please, sir, warn me before you throw me about so I may prepare myself," she cried.

Richard shrugged. "We have a lot of ground to cover before the sun sets. The greater the distance we put between Lord Seton's men and us, the safer we'll be." He placed his foot in the stirrup and swung up behind. His thick arms encircled her as he leaned heavily against her back to take the reins.

Mortified that her whole backside pressed tightly against the front of his muscular frame, she drew her mantle snugly around herself and sat as far forward as possible.

While Titan walked along, she concentrated on not allowing their upper bodies to touch, but the undertaking seemed almost futile and her efforts became a huge strain. His warm breath brushed across the top of her head and one rock hard forearm rested on her thigh, adding to her troubles.

Soon the task of avoiding his nearness was too daunting. Her eyes, heavy from exhaustion, began a slow dance of closing and opening. As time passed, Titan's measured gait wrapped her in a world of peace. Her head bobbed up and down. Each time it fell forward, she jerked it back, opened her eyes and focused again on her surroundings.

"Katherine, stop being so headstrong. Lean against me and rest. I promise not to let you tumble off," he said.

"Humph," she snorted. How she hated to show weakness, especially in front of him. Even as a young girl she had yearned for his respect. Because she was five years younger, he always treated her like a child. It annoyed her that he continued to regard her in such a way. As a woman full-grown, she could take care of herself. She wanted to remind him that the girl he remembered was long gone, but she held her tongue.

"You're exhausted," he stated.

"I am fine," she retorted a bit crisply.

Katherine at once regretted not taking him up on his offer. She longed to give in and melt against his chest, blanketed in the safekeeping of his embrace. She shook off the desire. How could she accept without appearing feeble?

He nudged her thigh. "Stop your foolishness."

"Maybe you do not care, but I do not think it would be proper," she said stiffly to cover her conflicting emotions.

"Circumstances are what they are, and it's not practical at this time to maintain our distance for the sake of others," he stated. "I assure you. I have no intention of walking to William's. You'll have to resign yourself to the fact that our riding together is not going to change any time soon."

He draped his other arm around her waist. With a tug, he drew her into his wide chest and made her sink fully against him while he enclosed her securely in his arms.

She gasped in protest.

"Go to sleep; you need rest," he insisted as he rested his chin on top of her head.

Katherine's ire rose. He infuriated her with his high-handedness but being enveloped in his strong arms felt so wonderful that any building anger quickly vanished.

Maybe he was right. Why behave so obstinately? After all, she was in desperate need of rest. If she slept for a brief time, maybe the images of her father's and brother's deaths might stop playing over and over in her mind.

Resigned to her fate, her eyes grew heavy and she drifted off into the blessed darkness.

***

Richard loosened his grip when she dozed off. What a stubborn woman. It took nothing on his part to keep her upright. She barely weighed a thing. He didn't mind in the least holding her small, soft body in his arms.

The sweet smell of lavender drifted up from her hair and teased his senses. The aroma stirred pleasant memories of childhood summers spent at Rosemont. Even then she smelled like the flower. The floral scent held a special place in his past.

Thoughts of Rosemont quickly turned to Katherine's brother, Sir David de Grey, who was knighted last year. He had returned home to learn how to run

Rosemont. As Lord de Grey's only son, upon his father's death, David, and then his heirs, would've received his father's title and the small but regal stone castle that sat on the cliffs overlooking the ocean. It was unfortunate David never had a chance to see it so.

Lord de Grey and his father squired together as young men and were as close as brothers. When Katherine's mother passed away during the plague, her father took his wife's death hard and became reclusive. Since Rosemont was far from a well-traveled route, his father was probably one of their only visitors.

Richard studied the top of her head as it rested heavily against his chest. Years had passed since they were last together. Although she was much younger, he had enjoyed her company. She had always been friendly, witty, and willing to do anything the boys were doing. They never tired of having her around. As a young girl, she was not one to complain, and her warm, eager smiles were as contagious as her merriment.

Her mother used to worry she'd never mature into a lady. Obviously growing up a willful child had no adverse effects, because she was certainly a lady. A very competent one. He doubted less than a handful of other noblewomen could have persevered under such circumstances. The ladies he met over the years reminded him of delicate flowers whose petals would fall if treated poorly.

Although Katherine appeared fragile, he didn't doubt her strength.

A few years ago, he heard talk at court that Lord de Grey's daughter suffered a facial injury in a kitchen accident. Now after laying eyes on her, he found no truth in those words. It struck him odd such a story passed from person to person among the nobles. His father said it was just a rumor and encouraged him to call upon Lord de Grey and his daughter during his last visit, but as he was on his way to attend to the king's bidding, he promised to stop by another time.

In thinking back, he found it curious his father always pushed him to stop by Rosemont when he came home. Wondering why, but finding no answers, he gave Titan a nudge to pick up the pace.

As the hours dragged by, Richard became more bothered. He hadn't counted on this unforeseen turn of events. He was only supposed to make a quick stop at Rosemont to deliver a message before moving on to Lockhart Manor. Now everything had changed.

Although a mere knight, he had gained enough wealth and permission from King Edward to manage his own lands. He looked forward to marrying Lady

Alice Cromwell. She hadn't yet agreed, but she would. A picture of dark hair, flawless skin, a mysterious smile, and exotic eyes flashed in his mind. Her resemblance to William's wife, Elizabeth, was truly incredible.

With the right woman, he would find the life William now enjoyed. It was time he settled down.

Now that he had to retrace some of his steps, go out of his way to William's and then return to Stamford, the whole trip would easily set him back five days. He hated changing his course, but he had a duty to make sure she arrived at his father's safely. He would have to accept this necessary delay and hope for the best.

~Chapter Four~

"Time to wake."

Katherine only faintly heard the faraway words Richard breathed in her ear. A gentle shake drew her out of a peaceful slumber. Through cat-eyed slits, she peered out over her surroundings with growing curiosity.

"Where are we? What are we doing here?" she mumbled, as she rubbed hours of sleep from her eyes.

A neglected cottage and half-standing fence sat forlornly in a clearing near the river's edge. As Richard dismounted, she grabbed Titan's mane and leaned heavily to the opposite side. Left alone, without his warmth, she trembled from a damp chill as dusk endeavored to engulf them in its smoky veil.

"We'll spend the night at Sir Walter Prescott's home. He was once a knight in King Edward's army. When too old for service, he chose to live out the remainder of his days alone in these woods. William and I came across this place years ago. It's only a few hours from Hammerstead. Sir Walter shared some great tales of yesteryear during our frequent visits."

"Does he live here still?"

Richard's brows furrowed. "He's since died."

"I am sorry for your loss."

"No need to fret. He lived a good life. Come, there's not much light left, and we'll have no fire tonight." Strong hands encircled her waist and lifted her from the saddle.

Prepared this time for assistance, she rested her hands on his shoulders. The muscles beneath her touch grew taut as he effortlessly settled her on the ground. She struggled with the stirrings his nearness conjured and quickly asked the question foremost in her mind.

"If we are close to your friend's estate, why do we not continue until we reach his castle?"

"Darkness is coming fast. We'll be safer behind walls with a roof over our heads for the night."

He strolled toward the broken-down cottage, unsheathed his sword, and climbed the few stairs onto the decaying porch. When he opened the half-closed door, he disturbed a flock of birds resting inside. The swallows flew out through a hole in the roof, fluttering their wings as they soared away.

In the yard, Katherine crossed her arms under her maid's well-worn mantle. She stared at the open doorway and listened closely to his rummaging around inside. A few moments passed before a family of squirrels escaped through the same opening as the birds and jumped from the roof onto an overhanging branch. They ran up the tree and appeared none too happy at being chased out. One, in particular, spun in his tracks and chirped loudly at Richard when he descended the front steps.

She covered her mouth to stifle a giggle. "I guess they are not pleased you have banished them from their home."

He made his way across the yard to her side and looked up into the branches as the last of the squirrels disappeared into the cover of leaves. "I wouldn't mind so much sharing my sleeping quarters, but something tells me you might be opposed," he said with a touch of humor, softening his voice.

"I think you may be right." She couldn't help but return his warm smile. His easy company reminded her of their long-ago friendship. There was comfort in his nearness until a painful image of her father trespassed on her peace. She pushed aside her sadness, took a deep breath, and willed the aching memories from her mind.

Richard replaced his sword and returned to his horse.

She, still fatigued from the long journey, sat on the wooden steps. To pass the time, she untwisted her braid, freeing the strands from the tangled mess. Picking out the short twigs and pieces of dried leaves buried in her curls turned out to be a laborious task. As she worked, she watched Richard unsaddle his mount.

Never had she set eyes on such a handsome animal. She studied the blacker than midnight destrier as he munched on new blades of grass and let her eyes casually roam over his resplendent outline. The animal's long, glistening mane moved eerily in the light wind. Well-defined muscles traveled over the stallion's thick, rounded neck, across a wide-barreled chest and down powerful legs. As Richard rubbed his charger down from head to tail, she admired the care he showed his steed.

"Why must one go gently when Titan has the bit in his mouth?" she asked.

Richard stopped his labor and glanced up from his work. "My friend here was sorely abused by his last master. His mouth was in a very sorry state." He gave his horse's neck a fond pat. "We came to an understanding. If I didn't tug on his mouth, he wouldn't toss me on my backside."

The image of Richard landing none too softly on the ground whilst his horse stood over him with laughing eyes, curled her lips in a soft smile.

A glint of mischief danced in his blue eyes. "Now that he's healed, if you pull back on his reins he will rear up and strike out. A very useful ruse when one is assaulted by another rider or even by a man on the ground."

"I cannot imagine why anyone would give up such a fine animal."

"The man died." Richard rose to his full height, his face as hard as stone. "Very suddenly."

She drew in a deep breath and changed the subject. "How did you happen to come to my rescue? Your father told us you were in London."

"I left a few days ago." He relaxed his stance. "My men and I made our way to Stamford to visit my father. Since he was still at Rosemont, we awaited his return. When he arrived, I told him I intended to head up North to meet with a man. He gave me a letter he needed delivered to your father."

His gaze dropped to the leather satchel next to his saddle as if to check on the safety of his missive. "My men were tired of travel. At my father's insistence, I left them to rest at Stamford. I doubted I would find much danger along the way. The roads remain quiet of late." He picked up a hoof to clean it out. "I heard your scream from the road."

Katherine shivered, not from a chill, but from the memory he stirred. It amazed her how loud she could cry out when provoked.

"It's a good thing I never made it to Rosemont. I don't believe Lord Seton would've given me a warm welcome. I might've shared your family's fate, had our paths not crossed in the woods."

She turned her head and looked unseeing into the darkening forest. *Richard would've been killed.*

"Your father and brother were good men. My father will be deeply troubled by the news."

Katherine offered him a weak smile. Sadness wrapped around her like a wet, heavy quilt. She fought through the numbness and welcomed the heat of her fury when her temper grew. "I hate Lord Seton and the man who gave him his orders."

She stared at the tip of her leather boot peeking out from the dirty hem of her ragged surcoat. Pulling her foot back, she kicked a small rock with all her might, sending it bouncing into the yard. "I will avenge my family, even if it is the last thing I do."

When she looked up, she caught Richard staring at her with a narrowed gaze. Something she said didn't sit well. She braced herself for the storm of words she knew would soon follow.

"In the first place, it's not your duty to avenge your family, and secondly, what do you mean when you say, 'the man who gave him his orders'? What makes you think Lord Seton didn't act alone?"

"I know he did not," she stated. "After his treachery, a man came to the hall and gave Lord Seton more orders."

She shuddered and tugged her mantle tighter across her shoulders.

"Did you know this man? Would you remember his face if you saw him again?"

"He wore a hood over his head and took great lengths to conceal himself in the shadows. I never glanced upon his face." She closed her eyes and pictured the eerie outline of a dark-clothed man, whose features were a blur. She searched into the recesses of her mind for something that made him stand out.

When she opened her eyes, Richard stared at her expectantly. It suddenly came to her. "He had a strange laugh. A very cruel, high-pitched one. I would recognize the sound if I heard it again."

Richard tugged on his short-cropped beard. He wasn't overly impressed with her small piece of memory.

"What did they discuss?"

"I heard only a little. The man was angry one of Lord Seton's men killed our priest. He wanted another to be found quickly so vows could be exchanged. He said the king would not readily challenge a marriage blessed by the church."

She winced at the thought of being forced to spend her life with such a vile man. "I have reason to believe that this man gave orders for other holdings to be taken over in the same way. Families murdered and unwed daughters made to marry men of his choosing."

Richard scowled.

A lump formed in her throat. She was the cause of her family's demise. Flustered, she pleaded, "Please, I beg you, let us not speak of this at the moment."

"As you wish." His face softened, and he returned his attention to his horse.

She heard the touch of annoyance in his voice. He wanted to hear more, but she couldn't continue. Leaning her shoulder heavily against a porch timber, she let her mind sink into darkness. When she finally found a thin thread of peace, she resumed her quiet scrutiny of Richard as he cleaned the rest of Titan's hooves.

Katherine knew him well. Knew everything he had done over the years. She made a point to keep track of his whereabouts through his father. Afraid her warm feelings would be discovered, she always asked about his brothers, Garrett, Tristan and Bryce, first, saving Richard for last. For years, her stomach fluttered each time she remembered the occasions they spent together as children. He had made a lasting impression, and she was pleased with the man he had become.

"Why did you choose to travel alone? Once you escaped, was there no one outside your father's gates you could've asked for help?" His deep voice brought her back to the present.

"I considered asking for assistance, especially when I made my way through the black of night, but I was too afraid Lord Seton would punish those who offered me protection, along with their families. I did not wish anyone harm, so I thought to follow the river until I found my way to the Copper Stallion Inn. Once there, I knew I could find someone to take me the rest of the way to your father's castle."

He gazed at her as if seeing her in a new light.

"May I go down to the water before the dark settles around us?" She stood, ignoring a shooting pain radiating across her back, patted down her woolen surcoat, and adjusted the girdle holding her dagger beneath her cloak.

"Do not wander far from the path."

***

Richard couldn't take his eyes off her as she strolled by him, her mantle rippling behind. Her unbound hair, free of debris, cascaded like a waterfall over narrow shoulders and down her straight back. He stood in awe, mouth open, as he admired the picture she presented of a woodland nymph. Aware of his boyish behavior, he snapped his jaw shut and turned his attention back to Titan, who stared at him with inquisitive deep brown eyes.

"Don't look at me that way. Blind, I'm not."

He gave his horse one last pat before he headed for the empty cottage. Once inside, he found a rope bed lying on its side. He crossed the room in a few easy strides and righted it. An old straw pallet lay crumpled in a dry corner. He arranged the padding on top of the frame. After removing his heavy mantle, he laid the thick garment over the mattress. An old chair, upside down in the middle of the room, was placed next to the door.

Katherine returned a few minutes later. "Will you tie Titan up or at least put him behind the fence?" she asked, her voice pitched with concern.

"He'll not wander off," he said in good humor. "We have an understanding."

"What sort of understanding?"

"As you're aware, I don't like to walk if I don't have to. He remains close, so I may ride."

"I am not sure I understand why he does not wander off," she said with a hint of amusement in her tone.

"Don't worry. He'll be around in the morning. You'll not have to walk the many miles to Hammerstead." Richard smiled to himself; he liked to keep her guessing. He handed her a piece of dried beef.

She took a seat on the edge of the bed. After giving him a quick nod of thanks, she munched hungrily on the chewy morsel. "I fixed you a place to lie down."

She glanced at his mantle, fur side up, spread out on the pallet beneath her. "I could curl up on a bed of spikes and fall right to sleep," she teased, as she stroked the soft fur with one hand. "But I am glad I will not have to."

It pleased him that she found pleasure in the small comfort he offered. "Get some rest. We leave early." When he turned toward the door, he caught a glimpse of fear on her face in the diminishing light.

"Where will you spend the night?" she asked uneasily, as if afraid to be alone.

Richard pointed to the chair. "I'll be guarding the door. Now, close your eyes. I'll be right back." He grabbed his water pouch and left the cottage.

Richard returned to find Katherine tucked into a small ball on the bed. Her blonde curls fanned around her in a protective circle. He grabbed the back of the chair and positioned it in a way that let him scan the whole clearing from the opening. After leaning his crossbow and extra arrows against the door frame, he then laid his sword across his lap.

It would be a long night with no sleep, but it suited him to be cautious. As he reclined onto the hard surface, he watched the darkness encroach upon their abode. His vision grew accustomed to the shadows, and he listened for sounds out of place in the forest. Although relaxed, he could be ready in an instant. Titan munched on grass not too far from the cottage and would also warn of advancing danger.

As the hours slowly passed, the only incident was when one of the squirrels climbed back down through the hole in the roof. Concerned about waking Katherine, he tried to quietly herd the squirrel out through the opening. His attempt at not creating a disturbance was to no avail. The vermin protested loudly at being chased from his home, yet again. After the commotion subsided, he glanced back at the bed. His worries were unwarranted. She was so exhausted she never stirred.

Close to dawn, he heard soft moaning coming from the bed. In a troubled sleep, she had tangled herself in her cloak. Her movements turned frenzied, and her pitiful moans grew louder. "No!" she pleaded over and over again.

He stood at her side and tapped her arm gently.

She didn't respond.

Her thrashing increased and her "No!" became more desperate. He grabbed her slender shoulders and gave her a powerful shake. When she didn't react, he called her name.

***

Katherine stood frozen as a sheer mound of white smoke swirled around her feet. She fought to move, but something sinister held her back. A few feet away, Lord Seton stood next to her father with a knife to his throat.

"Please, Katherine, please help me. Save me!" her father pleaded.

She tried to go to him but couldn't move her legs. Her arms were as heavy as lead, and with no strength to pick them up, they hung limply at her sides.

Lord Seton cajoled her to take a step. He would let her father live, only if she reached them in time. She struggled with all her might but was unable to move.

A high-pitched laugh escaped Lord Seton's throat. He knew she would never be able to save her beloved father.

"No! No! Please, no!" she begged, as a stream of hot tears rolled down her cheeks.

Then Katherine heard a male voice from far away. It was familiar, but not of this place. She didn't want to listen. She had to save her father.

His deep voice cut through her reserve.

He called her name. She had no choice but to go to him.

As soon as she turned her back on her father's plight, she knew the voice was Richard's.

He called her name and she went to him.

***

Katherine opened her eyes. She immediately knew where she was and what had happened.

In the moonlight shining down through the holes in the roof, she caught a glimpse of worry softly outlined on Richard's handsome face.

"Are you all right?" he asked.

She prayed the semi-darkness would hide her wet and heated face.

"I am fine. No need for concern," she whispered hoarsely. "You may release me now," she added when his powerful grip tightened upon her shoulders.

He let her go. "Are you sure? I had a hard time waking you."

When he tried to get a good look at her face in the darkness, she turned her head. "Would you fetch me a drink of water? I think it will help."

He removed the water pouch from the back of his chair.

While out of his sight, she wiped away a trail of tears with her fingertips. Perched on the edge of the bed, she wrapped herself in her cloak. When he returned, she accepted the pouch and took a few swallows of the cool water. When finished, she breathed a sigh of relief, surprised it, actually helped.

"A drink was exactly what I needed." She handed the pouch back.

"You should try to get more sleep while you can. It's not quite light yet."

To appease him, she snuggled back onto the soft fur of his mantle and shut her eyes, but with them closed her unease grew…afraid the vivid scenes would return. A burst of restlessness overcame her and she spent many minutes tossing and turning, looking for comfort.

Richard must've taken pity on her, for he finally spoke. "My favorite childhood recollections include those summers spent at Rosemont. My mother enjoyed your mother's company so much I wasn't sure who was in a bigger rush to get to Rosemont, my father, my mother, or my brothers and I," he said in a husky voice that broke through the serene quiet of the wee hours of the morning.

Wrapped in a cocoon of wool and fur, she stopped thrashing. Lying on her back, she stared at the stars through the hole in the ceiling and listened to his words, letting the memories return.

"We welcomed your visits. They were always the best time of the year," she said softly.

"For us, also."

"It was so long ago." Her voice sounded far away. "I remember the last time you visited. On the very last day, our parents were out in the bailey overseeing the packing of the wagons, and the six of us were in the Great Hall. We were very impatient because we knew your visit was at an end."

"I remember that day well. David thought it would be fun to catch you as you stepped off the edge of the open stairway leading to the upper floors," Richard recalled.

"I did not realize how bad the idea was at the time," she said with mild distaste.

"The way your brother explained how it worked made me think you two had done it before. When David demonstrated the first few steps, it seemed easy enough. You weighed near to nothing," he reflected.

"The first few stairs were not too bad. Although stepping off the edge became scarier the farther up I went."

"I have to admit, the higher you went after each jump, the more challenging it was to catch you."

"You handled me easily enough, even when I was way over your head," she added appreciatively.

"My apologies for dropping you."

"It was not your fault your mother entered the hall, took one look at what we were doing and screamed in fright. When I was falling through the air, I saw David bump into you in his hurry to get away. I was so high up, there was nothing else to do but fall right on top of you. If he had not panicked, you would have caught me well enough, and I would not have broken my arm."

"Our parents were furious we put you in harm's way. We should've known better." He noticeably cringed in the dim light.

"Father and Mother fussed over my arm and did not reprimand me. I am not sure breaking my arm was worth getting out of trouble, though. My arm throbbed for days and I had to stay in bed for weeks until it healed."

"You never cried."

"I kept my tears to myself. I did not want anyone to know how much it hurt."

"We never spent another summer at Rosemont after that year. My mother passed away the following spring," he stated flatly.

"Summers were never the same."

A few minutes went by as they reflected on long ago memories. Richard broke the silence first. "Dawn is not far off. Since it appears you're not going back to sleep anytime soon, what do you say we start out early and begin the journey to William's?"

"Let us be on our way," she agreed.

~Chapter Five~

The early morning darkness drifted away, only to be replaced by bright sunlight. Katherine rode in front of Richard in companionable silence, enjoying Titan's fast-moving pace. At the river's fork, they followed a smaller stream as it snaked through the lush forest. Not long thereafter, the narrow waterway brought them to the edge of the woods and out onto a well-traveled road.

Upon Richard's command, Titan slowed his steps.

She inhaled a deep breath and stared in awe at a majestic castle sitting grandly in the distance. A vision to behold, the stronghold sat on top of a small, green knoll. A curtain of rock, close to thirty feet tall, rose out of the ground with circular towers, softening all four corners. The rounded blocks of stone were spotted with narrow archer openings, their black lines bold against the grayish-brown background. Battlements emerged from fortified walls, presenting a commanding sight.

The land was cleared from the woods to the moat, except for a small village situated outside the fortress, not far from the drawbridge. In the distance, peasants moved about the village, worked in the fields, and herded animals along well-worn paths.

"William's Hammerstead Castle. Formidable, is it not?" he said, as Titan's hooves hit the dirt road leading to the drawbridge.

"Very grand, indeed." In her travels, she had never laid eyes on a castle as beautiful as this one.

Over the years, she seldom ventured far from Rosemont. After her mother's death, her father refused to send her away to be a lady-in-waiting. Instead, he kept her close to home, under his watchful eye.

Once a year, he escorted her to Lord Weston's estate. The first and last night of their journey they lodged at the Copper Stallion Inn, halfway between the two estates. There she marveled at the goings-on in the little town.

New places stirred her senses. The excitement of laying eyes on Hammerstead Castle rose in her belly and she endeavored to absorb all the sights and sounds.

"Since becoming Lord Huntington, William has labored hard to return Hammerstead to its former glory. When he inherited his family's holdings from his brothers, the property was in poor condition. The people were oppressed. Walls crumbled in disrepair. The grounds were overgrown."

Richard prodded Titan to pick up a faster pace. "William is a third son. He never imagined he'd inherit his father's title and estates. After we were knighted, we traveled the countryside on a quest to line our purses. Less than two years ago, William received word his father had died and his oldest brother was the new heir. Not six months later, we received word his oldest brother had died and his other brother was the new lord." He paused before continuing, "Then four months later, that brother died."

"What happened to them?" she asked.

"All of them murdered."

"Murdered? Did Lord Huntington ever find out who killed them?"

"He did. And the killers were not the same person. Unfortunately, the story will have to wait."

Titan was halfway over the drawbridge. Two guards standing below the raised portcullis challenged their entry.

She expelled a deep sigh. How she wished to hear more about Lord Huntington's unexpected rise to his new position. As Richard addressed the guards, she vowed to someday remind him to reward her with an ending.

The gatekeepers granted entrance and Titan moved forward to the inner bailey. As they rode past knights and men-at-arms, many recognized Richard and called out words of welcome.

Titan halted at the limestone steps leading to the double oak doors of the keep. The heavy doors flew open and a huge man strode through the entryway and planted his feet firmly on the top landing. With hands on his hips, he gave Richard a big smile framed by bright white teeth.

"Back so soon?" the man's voice boomed. "Did you miss our company so much you needed to quickly return?" He let out a cheerful laugh and bounded down the stairs.

"William, you surely jest. When I leave here, I'm glad to put your ugly face behind me." Richard chuckled. He dismounted in one swift motion and took a few steps forward to meet his friend.

She winced when the big man engulfed Richard in an all-powerful hug that lifted him clear off the ground. Once his feet were again settled upon the earth, he punched his friend in the chest and received an equally hard blow in return.

Sitting back on Titan, she observed the men with great interest. Lord Huntington was anything but ugly. He was a tall man, towering a few inches over Richard. Built like a tree, he was wide, sturdy, and strong. Dark brown hair hung just below his ears, no part, but his hair stopped above his brows and swept to one side. A short-cropped beard emphasized prominent cheekbones. When the man smiled, his whole face lit up like a flash of golden light.

For a moment, a quick stab of longing pierced her heart. To have such a friend, but alas; she was never afforded such a blessing.

Movement at the top of the stairs caught her eye. She broke her scrutiny of William. There above her stood a regal lady with her hands clasped at her waist. Her face glowed with flawless beauty as she gazed lovingly at the men. Long dark lashes framed deep brown, almost midnight eyes. Some of her neatly braided black hair circled the top of her head like a crown; the rest flowed down her back to the top of her long legs.

Next to the woman stood a young girl with short curly hair and William's muddy-brown eyes. At first, the child stood perfectly still, watching the men's silliness, but then her small hand covered an escaping giggle.

The lady softly cleared her throat and waited for the men's audience. When she gained their full attention, she presented them with a sparkling smile. Richard hurried up the steps two at a time. The lady held out her hand. He placed a gentle kiss on top before letting her hand drop.

"Welcome, Sir Richard," the lady said fondly.

William, who had followed his friend up the stairs, took his place next to the woman who Katherine assumed was his wife.

"I never tire of your company, Lady Elizabeth," Richard said loud enough for Katherine to overhear.

He stepped aside, knelt on one knee in front of the little girl, and said in a soft voice, "Nor do I ever tire of yours, Emma."

When he stroked the child under her chin, a shy smile formed on the little girl's face.

Katherine watched the exchange. These people shared a deep affection. She did not belong in their circle. Her hands fiddled with the edges of her borrowed, ragged mantle and she wrapped the wool closer about her body. She wished she had insisted upon taking a moment to wash the dirt from her face before they arrived.

Having caught Lady Elizabeth's notice, Katherine found herself being observed for the first time. A look of surprise crossed the woman's exquisite features, making Katherine contemplate crawling into a deep, dark hole.

Instead of giving in to her insecurities, Katherine sat taller in the saddle and boldly stared back.

The lady turned to the two men who had returned to their game of elbowing each other. "You two should be ashamed of yourselves," Lady Elizabeth chastised in a calm, quiet voice.

The two men gazed at the black-haired woman in wonder, not sure what to make of her rebuke.

Lady Elizabeth turned to her husband and chided, "It's your responsibility to see our guests are well cared for, and you have been sorely careless in your duties."

"But we always welcome each other like this." William gaped at his wife in total confusion. He gave his friend a half-smile and loud pat on the back.

Lady Elizabeth's attention turned to Richard. "I am truly appalled."

Richard shifted his weight uneasily.

The lady glanced at Katherine. "To leave a lady sitting on top of that monster of a horse, obviously weary from a long journey, while you two men have at it like children is not very chivalrous."

A mutual understanding crossed both male faces at the same time. Together, they turned and looked at Katherine. When the men's wits returned, they could not reach her fast enough. Both shoved each other aside to be the first to help her down, scaring Titan in the process.

Katherine peeked at Lady Elizabeth during all the excitement and received a sly smile. Immediately, Katherine's tight muscles relaxed.

Richard won the right to help her dismount, although it took a lot of jostling on his part, as his friend was very determined to win back his wife's favor. Once her feet hit the ground, the chaos abated and the men remained statue-still at her side.

Lady Elizabeth floated gracefully down the front steps wearing an emerald green velvet surcoat with long slits up the sides showing off a light green kirtle beneath. Hanging from the short, tight sleeves of her surcoat, long tippets flowed from her arms and moved like flags in the light breeze. Elaborate gold embroidery danced along her deeply rounded neckline. A beautifully adorned girdle holding the lady's ornate dagger pressed against the side of her hip.

When Lady Elizabeth stood before Katherine, her eyes twinkled with pleasure. She executed a perfect curtsy. "I am sorry about our poor manners. Please, forgive us. My name is Lady Elizabeth and this is my husband, Lord William Huntington."

Katherine curtsied in return and nodded at one and then the other.

Eager to set things right, William hastily took up her hand and pressed his lips to her bare skin. "Welcome to Hammerstead, my lady." He tilted his head in the direction of the little girl. "My sister, Emma."

The child presented Katherine with a well-practiced bob, so she smiled and did the same.

William cleared his throat. "I regret I didn't see to your needs right away. Please, forgive me." He stole a quick glance at his wife to make sure he behaved appropriately. Rewarded with a diminutive smile, she assured him of his return to her good graces.

Katherine had to hold back her smile when William dropped her hand abruptly and nearly beamed with delight at his wife.

"No remorse necessary. I am Lady Katherine de Grey, Lord de Grey's daughter from Rosemont. I am afraid I found myself in peril, and Sir Richard was good enough to come to my rescue." She caught Richard's eye and silently pleaded with him to give the details.

He stepped closer to Katherine. When he spoke, his voice took on a grave tone. "A few days ago, Lord Seton seized Rosemont after killing Lady Katherine's father, her brother, and most, if not all of their men. She escaped on foot into the forest, where our paths crossed. Our families have known each other for years, and it's nothing short of a miracle I came upon her when I did."

He placed a gentle hand on the small of her back.

She bid him wordless thanks.

He locked eyes with William. "As we speak, Lord Seton is more than likely turning the country inside out looking for her, as he intended they married. You know how he doesn't like to be thwarted. Good news, though, I believe we are ahead of anyone looking for her. You haven't come across any of his men, have you?"

William remained solemn. "No strangers have arrived in the past few days. Ever since we had those problems with my departed brother's band of pillaging knights, I keep a sharp eye out for anything amiss. As yet, the guards have reported nothing out of the ordinary."

"My gut tells me Lord Seton won't stop until he finds her. We should consider doubling the men-at-arms on the battlements," Richard said.

"I agree; extra men are in order," William replied.

"I also need to send a message to my father. He must be informed. An armed escort should accompany the messenger to ward off any trouble."

Before the men said another word, Lady Elizabeth held up a hand to stop their talk and addressed Katherine. "Please come with me. I intend to find you a comfortable chair by the fire and furnish you with a meal."

Lady Elizabeth took Katherine's arm and drew her up the stairs.

When the ladies were on the top landing, Lady Elizabeth turned to the men. "We will leave you to your affairs. Please join us in the hall when you are free."

The men bobbed their heads in unison, retrieved Titan, and headed for the stables, with little Emma following in their stead.

"Please, call me Katherine."

"And you may call me Elizabeth."

"As you wish."

"It saddens me to hear about your family." Elizabeth drew Katherine closer.

"Thank you for your kind words. The past few days do not seem real." She welcomed the comfort of the freely offered gesture.

Once inside the Great Hall, Elizabeth instructed her servants of their duties, and people scurried in all directions. Servants were to bring food; two guest rooms were to be readied, and water was to be carried upstairs for baths.

Elizabeth escorted Katherine to a set of cushioned chairs gathered around a low burning fire at one end of the hall. When she sat, her tired body melted into the overstuffed chair.

Elizabeth took a seat across the way. "My apologies for leaving you to sit atop Titan for so long; I am afraid I did not notice you right away. The men go through this ritual every time Richard comes to visit and the scene is so wonderful to watch, I get caught up in their play."

"I also found myself engrossed by their back-slapping and banter. What surprised me the most was their reaction when they thought you were displeased and how badly they wanted to get back into your good graces."

Elizabeth grinned.

"Did you see the way Richard elbowed your husband in the stomach during their race down the stairs? Your husband's face turned so white I feared for his health."

The women covered their mouths to curb their giggles.

Katherine dropped her hand to her lap. "When they finally reached me, I was afraid for them to help me down. I thought they would grab me from the stallion's back, throw me over their shoulders, race up the steps two at a time and dump me at your feet." She had trouble muffling her growing mirth.

"I am sorry," Elizabeth said brokenly, holding back a snicker. "I meant you no harm. I did not know they would treat the task like a competition each was bent on winning."

The moment she made eye contact with Elizabeth, they both burst out in a peal of laughter.

"Please, Elizabeth, no more. I do not think I can hear another word." She clutched her sore stomach.

It took a few minutes and a great deal of strength to regain control. When their laughter subsided, Elizabeth said, "I cannot remember the last time I laughed so hard."

"Neither can I." She pushed aside a twinge of guilt that surfaced for being cheerful when those she held dear had recently suffered.

"May I ask how you met up with Richard? He was headed to London with his men the last time he parted our company."

Katherine did not mind sharing. Too worn out, she offered a brief, dry accounting and finished with, "So, I travel to my father's only friend to beg for protection. What comes of my life from then on is not quite certain."

"Everything will work out fine. The worst is over. You are in good hands now. Richard will see that you arrive at Stamford safely." Elizabeth smiled broadly.

"I hope so." She prayed the worst was behind her.

"I like you, Lady Katherine de Grey. We are kindred spirits. If you do not mind, I would be honored to consider you a friend. Of course, such status would mean that if you need assistance or a place to live, you would only have to ask and I would give you what you desired without hesitation."

Katherine didn't know what to say; she was taken aback by such an offer. The knowledge that she was not entirely alone in the world made her stomach quake. Not sure what else to do, but wanting to show her gratitude, she leaned forward and rewarded her new friend with an affectionate hug.

Unshed tears welled behind her long lashes. When she straightened, she had difficulty seeing through the haze. "Oh, thank you. You have no idea how much your offer means to me," she gushed and brought her hand up to wipe her wet eyes.

"I do understand," Elizabeth murmured. "Unfortunately, my story is somewhat similar to yours, for I too found myself alone, away from the comfort of my home or family, and without a friend in the world. My parents had provided me with a quiet life under their protection, and they left me ill-prepared for the uncertainties and loneliness I faced after their passing." She smiled brightly as she squeezed Katherine's hands.

Katherine grinned. "My luck must be changing."

Platters of food and drinks arrived and were set upon the low table in front of the women. The servants placed a basin of water and a towel on the table. She washed her face and hands; filthy after her long journey.

The aromas thrilled her senses, and her stomach growled loudly. Mortified, her eyes shot a quick peek at Elizabeth, who had also heard the rumblings. Her new friend hid a big smile behind her hand.

"I guess I might be a bit hungry," she admitted.

"As you should be. I imagine you have not had a good meal in days."

"It seems like weeks."

As soon as the servants finished arranging the food, Katherine waited for Elizabeth to give her permission to start. When she received the subtle nod, she made quick work of a piece of bread and bowl of chicken stew, taking a sip of mead between bites.

When the men returned with Emma, they took their seats next to the fire. William's little sister remained half-leaning, half-standing against Richard's chair, but he didn't appear to mind the timid little girl's proximity.

Elizabeth invited Richard to sample the feast laid before him, so he fixed a heaping plate. When William raised a questioning eyebrow, Richard protested, "What? I'm starving. A knight can really work up an appetite rescuing damsels in distress."

Katherine looked up from her food in time to see a silly smirk painted on his face and couldn't help but giggle at his light-hearted banter. He gave her an even broader grin, and her stomach churned, not from her meal, but from the delight at being in his company.

William reached over to load his plate. "Well, I better get my fill too. Who knows when I might have to do some damsel rescuing." He chuckled and followed suit by bestowing on his wife a captivating smile, making everybody laugh.

A servant girl came down the steps from the second floor. "Milady, the guest bedchambers are readied and a bath prepared."

"Very good, Anna." Elizabeth turned to Katherine, who swallowed her last bite. "Could I entice you with a warm bath and a fresh set of clothes?"

"That sounds wonderful." She pushed away her empty bowl and rose to follow Elizabeth.

"You no longer need your cloak. Give the garment to Anna. She will take care of it."

Katherine welcomed removing the heavy mantle after sitting so close to the warm fire and handed the dreaded thing to the maid. She turned away from the men and followed Elizabeth up the first few steps.

"Katherine!" Richard roared. His loud, jagged voice echoed off the walls and broke the silence in the hall.

Servant's footsteps slapped against the stone floor as they hurried from the room.

She flinched at the piercing sound and stopped short.

Immediately, she understood his outcry and regretted letting her guard down. After being so careful, it only took a moment to forget that once her cloak was removed, the shameful whip marks on her back would be revealed. Although the wounds were bandaged, she had sensed early on during her escape and then after her rescue, that the gashes had opened, bled and dried, a time or two.

Ever since she joined him, she had a nagging feeling the blood had seeped through the thin material of her peasant gowns and would be visible without her cloak to cover them. She took care not to remove her wrap until now.

Katherine looked up at Elizabeth, who was one step ahead of her on the stairs. William's wife reacted to Richard's biting tone by glancing over her shoulder and giving him a pointed glare.

"Richard, what is the matter with you?" Elizabeth chastised.

"She knows exactly what I'm about," he stated, undoubtedly upset. "Why didn't you tell me?" he asked, his voice softening.

Katherine offered her friend a reassuring nod and slowly faced him as he stood at the bottom of the stairs. Deep concern etched across his handsome face.

When her uncloaked back came into Elizabeth's view, the woman let out a surprised gasp. Her muscles tensed at the sound, but she didn't waver.

She owed him an explanation. "I did not tell you everything that happened because if I shared about the whipping, I thought the discomfort might go away." Katherine took a deep breath. "I want the wounds to throb and burn. The pain reminds me that I am still alive."

Moisture filled her eyes, but her voice stayed strong and sure. "As long as I live, I will find a way to avenge my family's murders and make those responsible pay dearly for what they have done. I fear that without the pain I will go numb and die too. Then all will be for naught."

She turned around listlessly, her movements sluggish as she grabbed onto the railing. Elizabeth steadied her and the two women walked without a word to the upper floor, arm in arm.

***

At a loss for words, Richard returned to the chair across from William and tried to absorb what had come to pass. When he first saw the three bloody lines dried into the material of her gown, crisscrossing her small, narrow back, it was as if a fist slammed into his chest. The air caught in his throat and only by roaring her name had his breath returned.

She purposely hid her pain from him.

Her behavior now made sense. Always wrapped in her cloak, hiding the truth.

"Emma, go outside and find Alex," William said, sending his sister away.

Richard shifted uncomfortably in his seat. He swept his fingers through his hair. Leaning forward, he rested his elbows on his thighs and squeezed his head.

The injustice of her suffering gnawed at his insides. It vexed him that she didn't tell him of her hurt, not trusting him enough to share in her agony. He was furious at Lord Seton and upset she had endured such torment. Her words haunted him; *the pain reminds me I am still alive.*

"Can you believe her? She must've been suffering, but she didn't trouble herself to tell me. I had no idea. Every time I touched her; she must've wanted to cry out in misery." He looked to William for understanding.

"You had no way of knowing you were hurting her."

"Why do you think she kept the whipping to herself? Why didn't she tell me? I want to help her, but how can I if she's unwilling to share with me what happened? It makes me wonder what else she's keeping to herself."

"Maybe not sharing helps her forget that two days ago she lost her entire family."

"Perhaps you're right."

"You should still ask her to tell you everything, no matter how painful," William said.

"The problem is I might not be able to stomach what she tells me. Just thinking about such a whipping makes me beyond angry."

William nodded.

"My father will be crushed when he hears the news. He has strong feelings for her. Whenever I go home, she's all he ever talks about. Now, I'm wholly responsible for her welfare, and I need to get her safely to Stamford, as soon as possible. I don't think she deserves any more torment."

"Lord Seton can't get away with what he did," William said.

"I had been on a different course before I encountered Katherine. That will have to wait. Now I want to make certain the man pays for his vicious deeds," he countered.

William pounded his fist into an open hand. "I'd like a piece of him."

"We'll not have long to wait. The message is on its way to my father as we speak. He'll begin preparations and won't let Lord Seton get away with this brutality. He'll want to avenge his friends' death."

Richard reached for a tankard of ale and brought the rim to his lips. Katherine would get her revenge, and he would get the satisfaction of seeing the man dead.

With nothing else to occupy their minds, the men quietly returned to picking absently at their meals, each deep in their own thoughts.

***

Upstairs, Elizabeth led Katherine into a guest room and directed the maid standing in the doorway to retrieve some binding material and salve.

Katherine gawked at the bedchamber in wide-eyed wonder. A big room by any standard, it boasted high ceilings and wide-board wooden floors. Bold colored tapestries adorned the stone walls. Two tall windows, framing thick opaque glass, selectively filtered in the daylight. On the carpet in front of the massive hearth stood a tall wooden tub set-up with linen draped over the sides. She gazed longingly at the canopied mattress while being led to a small wood chair by the tub.

"I see you eyeing the bed." Elizabeth smiled when Katherine tried to hide her guilt. "I am afraid you will have to wait until we take care of some of your other pressing needs, such as bathing, binding your wounds, and getting you into clean clothes."

The maid returned with a basket full of the items requested.

"That will be all," Elizabeth said.

The maid closed the door lightly on her way out.

Elizabeth took the basket to Katherine and pulled up a chair. "I will try to be gentle, but the cleaning might hurt a bit."

"I know," she replied.

Slowly, Katherine unfastened her decorated girdle attached to her waist and removed her dagger from its sheath. After she laid the girdle on the floor next to her chair, she let her hands lovingly stroke the jeweled dagger in her lap.

Reassured that her only possession was in good order, she handed the dagger to Elizabeth. "You may use my mother's dagger to slice away the loose material. I keep the blade sharp."

Katherine leaned forward and rested her elbows on her knees to give Elizabeth a flat surface to work on.

"Tis a beautiful piece," Elizabeth said admiringly.

"My mother gave her dagger to me right before she died. Good fortune was on my side when my maid found a way to return the blade to me before I fled."

"Or was it the dagger's destiny to return to you? I believe some things or even people are destined to be together. Since the knife is something you hold dear, maybe it was not meant to be parted from your side, and so the dagger found a way to return."

"I never thought of it like that. Somehow having the blade near always gives me comfort."

Elizabeth slit a hole in Katherine's layers of clothes and cut away any material, including the underlying wrapping, not stuck to her back.

"The wounds appear as if they opened, bled, and dried a few times." Elizabeth worked slowly and gently until the rest of Katherine's clothing was completely unobstructed and could be easily removed.

"I felt them open when I climbed over the cliff rocks and when I struggled with the outlaw who wanted to do me harm."

"Sounds like you had a horrible time of it, but that's all behind you. Now we need to get you out of those clothes and into the tub. The warm water will help loosen the material still stuck to your back. We'll peel it off later."

She unlaced her leather ankle boots and removed the garters holding up her silk stockings. Elizabeth helped her out of her woolen peasants' surcoat, linen kirtle, and chemise.

When testing the water, a little moan escaped her lips as the fairly hot water brushed across her bare hand. She stepped into the warmth and sank slowly into the water's depths. At first contact, her injuries stung but as the water saturated the small amount of remaining material covering the wounds, her pain eased. With her eyes closed, she let the soothing liquid work its magic over her sore muscles.

Elizabeth gathered the remnants of her clothes and whispered, "I will be back in a little while to help you with your hair. I need to find you a few things to wear. Relax and enjoy." Silently, she left the room.

Katherine sat back and rested her neck on the edge of the tub. Her thoughts drifted off and visions of her father and brother came to mind, but when the images became too painful she shut them out and instead inserted blessed nothingness.

A knock sounded on the door and Elizabeth floated in with an armful of clothing. "I found a few things I think we can have taken in and hemmed to fit you. I am sure you will be delighted to be rid of those roughly woven garments."

"Oh, yes, I never want to see those clothes again. I have a new appreciation for women who wear them. They are warm and sturdy, but not very comfortable."

Elizabeth put down her bundle and took a chair next to the tub. "Let me help you clean your hair, and then we will pull the softened material away from your skin and dress those wounds."

She gave way to Elizabeth's easy take-charge manner.

After Elizabeth washed her hair, Katherine wrapped herself in a thin linen sheet and sat on a stool by the fire. She enjoyed the heat of the hearth, while Elizabeth combed out her tangled hair.

William's wife made a point not to ask her about the whipping but instead shared entertaining stories. It thrilled her to have another lady's companionship, and she listened eagerly while her friend chatted about Richard, William, and Emma.

Finished with Katherine's hair, Elizabeth focused on the task of pulling away the material stuck to her wounds.

"The gashes look painful, but appear to be healing well, and do not require stitches to keep them closed. I put some salve on them and will wrap them firmly to prevent them from opening again." Elizabeth yanked the bandage tight.

"Go easy, I do have to breathe," she exclaimed in jest when the binding squeezed uncomfortably.

"Forgive me. I will loosen the wrap a little. We don't want you to stop breathing altogether, do we?" Elizabeth teased, her eyes twinkling. "I guess that would defeat the purpose."

"I am very fond of breathing," she quietly chuckled.

Elizabeth handed Katherine a white linen chemise and helped her into the silky cloth. Elizabeth then held up two changes of wardrobe; each front lacing surcoat had a matching kirtle in a lighter shade.

Katherine had never laid eyes on such exquisite finery. "Oh, Elizabeth, I cannot accept these, the gowns are far too nice." She reached out and stroked the blue set, reveling in the rich velvet that was soft to the touch.

"I will not let you say nay. I have far too many and have little need for them all," Elizabeth insisted. "When I lived at court, the queen wanted me to dress in elegant gowns and strut about like a peacock to attract the attention of the nobles needing a wife."

Katherine smiled at the thought of her friend having trouble attracting a man. "Is that how you came to be married to William? He laid eyes on you all dressed up and could not let you go?"

"Not at all. The only men I attracted at court were rich old nobles who wanted me only for the picture I would present hanging on their arm or undesirable young nobles who wanted my wealth to elevate their position. I had dozens of marriage proposals and refused to accept any of them."

Katherine had only dreamed about a man asking for her hand in marriage, and her friend had dozens of men interested in her.

Elizabeth's voice softened as if to share a secret. "To tell you the truth, people whispered behind my back and called me the 'Ice Princess'. They said I could turn a man's heart cold with just one stare."

Elizabeth seemed not at all offended by the rumors.

She smiled at her friend's story, unable to believe a word of such a tale. A warmer and more endearing person she had never met.

"King Edward was not happy with my objections of those who offered for me, but out of respect for my father, and at the urging of Queen Philippa, he agreed early on to let me choose my own husband, with his consent, of course."

"King Edward became your guardian and let you choose?"

"He only agreed because my father was one of his favorite nobles and he felt bad I had lost both my parents at the same time. When I found out William was the new Lord Huntington of Hammerstead, I quickly made my choice, knowing King Edward would be agreeable to such a match after I refused so many others. William was taken aback; one minute he was a mere knight and the next he was a married noble. I told you how alone I was in the world. I knew my marriage was going to be the one thing that would define the rest of my life, and I wanted my life back. William was the man I chose. Life at Hammerstead was not easy at first. My husband did not know how much he needed me. I have no regrets."

Katherine inhaled deeply, processing all she heard.

Elizabeth smiled sweetly. "You are alone now, so I will give you some advice. If you want someone to share your life, you will have to be strong and fight for the life you want. In my experience, men do not always know what they want."

Elizabeth walked Katherine to the bed and drew back the covers. She hastily climbed in and laid her head on the pillow. When the covers reached her neck, she said, "I am blessed to have met you, Lady Elizabeth Huntington. You have given me hope. I no longer feel numb and no longer need pain to remind me I am alive."

"It pleases me that I could help." Elizabeth walked to the chair and picked up the pile of gowns.

At the door, she glanced back over her shoulder. "I will have these taken in before you awaken. Have a good sleep."

***

Unable to stay seated, Richard paced back and forth across the bottom of the stairs. Every so often, he looked at William but was met each time with a scowl.

"Richard, you are causing my head to spin. Sit before I make you sit," William said.

"What's taking so long? Perhaps, I should go find out." He put his foot on the first riser.

"Let the women be. My wife will keep us informed," William said, halting his progress.

He caught sight of Elizabeth at the top of the landing. "How is she?"

"Katherine will be fine," Elizabeth assured him, as she made her way down the stairs.

Richard hovered at the bottom. "How bad are the wounds?"

"Three deep slices cross her back. There was no sign of a fever. Whoever dressed and wrapped the wounds when they were fresh did well keeping them clean."

He sighed softly, and his shoulders dropped in exhaustion.

Elizabeth laid a hand on his arm. "She rests quietly. Now that you filled your belly, go to your room and enjoy the bath I sent up for you. You should also find some rest, for it appears as if you had little, if any, sleep last night."

"I had none." He placed a big hand over hers and gave it a few small pats. "I think I'll take you up on your offer. Call me down for the evening meal."

His face lit up mischievously. "After all, I have to keep up my strength for rescuing damsels in distress," he said teasingly.

On his way up the stairs, he heard Elizabeth laugh softly at his jest. From above, he watched her stroll over to William who reached for her delicate hand and gently brought her knuckles to his lips.

One day, he too would feel the same about a woman he called his wife. If all went well, she'd have the same blackened hair and beautifully shaped eyes as Elizabeth, but he'd call her Alice.

Very soon, his desires would come true.

~Chapter Six~

Richard spent the afternoon soaking in a warm bath and catching a few hours of much-needed sleep. When he awoke, he felt refreshed. He would take a short reprieve from the more serious business of deliberating Katherine's plight. An evening of friendly conversation in the company of good friends awaited him downstairs, and he welcomed the distraction.

With a determined step, he left his room.

As he approached Katherine's bedchamber, he slowed his pace. If she was awake, he'd ask her to accompany him to the Great Hall for the evening meal. Elizabeth's assurances that Katherine's injuries would heal lightened his mood, but he wanted to see for himself how she fared.

Muffled sounds passed through her door. He leaned close to the wooden portal and vaguely heard her saying "No!" as if warding off an unwanted visitor.

His stomach tightened.

He tested the handle while he unsheathed his dagger. A foreboding came upon him. Finding the door unlocked, he weighed the wiser action; to barge in quickly or to slip in noiselessly? He opted for the quiet entry and readied himself for whatever awaited on the other side.

Little by little, Richard opened the heavy door and was thankful when the hinges didn't creak in protest. He slipped noiselessly through the narrow space. The room was cast in darkness, the thick drapes closed to ward off the late afternoon's light. Only a soft glow spilled forth from the remaining embers in the fireplace. His eyes strained to adjust to the dimness of the room.

He made out the vague outline of Katherine's small body molded under a blanket in the massive bed. She thrashed about as she repeated the word "No!"

over and over. With every muted sound, his heart raced faster. He prepared himself for a direct assault and moved toward the bed with silent stealth, but there was no danger, just another bad dream.

Richard heaved a sigh of relief, keenly aware of his overreaction. He replaced his dagger, strode to the windows, pulled back the drapes, and cracked a hinged window. Daylight and a sudden flow of fresh air entered the room.

He returned to the edge of the bed and leaned over Katherine.

She was lying on her back with the blanket bunched about her waist. Sweat beaded on her forehead. Some of her unruly blonde curls were plastered along the sides of her angelic face while she flailed side to side. Dark long lashes moist with unshed tears rested against flawless skin.

Never had he laid eyes on a woman lovelier than the one before him. Her thin white linen chemise draped over rounded curves and pressed tautly against full breasts. His breath fell shallowly as he brushed aside a wave of desire. Guilt plagued him as he reminded himself of his vow to keep her safe.

Richard knew from experience what to do. He grabbed the top of her shoulders and gave a gentle shake. He called her name until she worked her way through the fog.

With a self-satisfied smile, he waited patiently until she began her journey back.

***

Katherine opened her eyes to Richard's handsome face mere inches away. His sweet breath mingled with her own. Her confusion quickly abated as she came to full understanding. A surge of heat washed over her. She rolled onto her side and clutched a pillow.

"You had another bad dream. You've been through too much and it'll take time to heal," he said in a low voice.

"I want my nightmares to stop. I do not want to relive my father and brother's deaths every time I close my eyes. I want to stop feeling guilty I did not save them," she wailed.

Richard swept a wet curl from the side of her face. "You have to accept what happened. Unfortunately, some events are predetermined by God and no matter what one does, the end remains the same."

He filled a cup with water from the clay pitcher on the bedside table.

She considered his words. Was he right and no matter what she might've done, her family still would have died? What if she had never left her bedchamber? Would her father and his men have been so unaware of the danger if they had not watched her come down the stairs…dressed so purposefully to catch every man's eye? Wasn't she to blame for their demise?

Richard didn't seem to blame her.

Maybe if she accepted that the past couldn't be changed, the nightmares would end. She propped herself up on one arm and took the cup.

Richard's demeanor abruptly changed while she drank. His eyes narrowed and he frowned. "Why didn't you tell me? How can I be of service to you if you keep secrets? I need to know all that has happened."

Katherine knew he spoke of the whipping. "At the time, I did not feel you needed every little detail." She set the cup down on the wooden table.

"Let me be the judge of what I think is important and what is not," he said a bit harshly.

"As you wish." Ire laced her tone.

Because of her small stature, people often treated her like a child. He just made that mistake. She pressed her lips together and hugged a pillow to her chest. If he wanted a better account, he would have to ask nicely.

After a few moments of silence, he must've caught onto her game because he ran his fingers through his thick hair before he coaxed, "I beg you. Please tell me everything. What you say may be of great importance."

"I doubt it," Katherine said under her breath. She wanted to avoid the uncomfortable topic and hoped he would back off, but he continued to wait expectantly.

"Please," he urged.

She sighed loudly and clutched the pillow even tighter.

"I was in my room when the men arrived." Her voice rang out sharp and tinged with a touch of annoyance, as she relived her recent pain. "My maid told me my father requested my presence in the Great Hall as guests were staying for the afternoon meal. I was told at least one was a titled nobleman. I readied myself and made my way to the upstairs landing. When the room full of men noticed my presence, they stood and watched me come down the stairs. As I reached the bottom step, Lord Seton let out a whistle, put his dagger to my father's throat and killed him without hesitation. At the same time, his men did the same to David, our knights, and men-at-arms."

She swallowed hard. Tears welled in her burning eyes, threatening to overflow.

"It took me a moment to realize what happened. There was no warning. My family never had a chance. When I looked at Lord Seton, his mouth was turned up in a sneer and his eyes were cold and taunting. I do not know what came over me. I rushed forward, withdrew my dagger and flew across the table at him. I wanted to slice the smile off his face."

"He never expected such a reaction and was slow to protect himself. My dagger cut him across the left side of his face, from ear to mouth. He howled in pain as his men grabbed me and took away my dagger. Our priest tried to come to my rescue, but in the chaos of the moment, Lord Seton's men killed him."

She paused and focused on a rich-colored tapestry hanging on the wall depicting a hunting scene. The hues were vivid and easily distracting. She had to remind herself to return to her painful story.

"Lord Seton was enraged that I dared to strike him." She locked eyes with Richard. "I didn't care. Hurting him gave me a great deal of satisfaction. He ordered his men to bind my wrists, then they hoisted my arms over my head using a hook on the wall. One of his men sewed his face back together. When the man finished, Lord Seton called for his whip. After the first few blows, I thought for sure my end was near. Then the man he worked for, the man in the hood I told you about, came into the hall and gave him orders to stop. Lord Seton would have killed me otherwise. The man said Lord Seton needed me alive for the marriage ceremony and what he did with me after was no concern of his."

She trembled. "His men cut me down and carried me to my bedchamber, where my maid, Mary, tended my wounds. That night, after everyone fell asleep, Mary drugged the guard and helped me to escape. The rest you know."

***

Richard's anger rose to near explosion. He used all the constraint he could muster to keep his fury under control. It drove him crazy to imagine her hanging from a hook, her body jerking from the taste of the whip. He inhaled harshly to slow his rampaging heartbeat.

"I'll make sure my father gets a full accounting of the events that took place. We leave at first light," he said, his voice flat and restrained.

"I will be ready when you are." She burrowed her chin in her pillow.

He noticed her dejection at his lack of response. She wasn't fully aware of how her suffering affected him. If she knew, she'd be frightened. Inwardly, he seethed with barely controlled fury. He wanted to kill Lord Seton.

No, I want more than that.

Richard wanted to watch the man writhe in agony and bleed out slowly. A bloodthirsty rage was brewing and Richard wanted to spare her that side of him.

"You showed great courage. Your father would be proud."

She gave him a slight nod as she accepted his words. Her sky-blue eyes sparkled with the compliment.

"I'm on my way down for the evening meal. Would you care to join me?" he asked, remembering why he came to her door in the first place.

"No, I think I will rest. I am not yet myself."

He rose from his seat on the edge of the bed and headed toward the door. "I'll have a plate sent up for you later."

"That would be nice."

***

Katherine woke before dawn. She hopped out of bed and scurried across the room to stoke the dying embers. Somewhere in a faraway memory, she recalled Anna coming in during the night to add logs to the fire. She found herself well-rested and anxious to be on her way to Stamford. Lord Weston was the one person who could understand the magnitude of her loss and share in her grief.

It was still dark outside but the flames from the fire cast enough light for her to make out the stack of new clothes on the seat of a high-back chair. There were two full sets including kirtles, surcoats, and stockings.

With great appreciation, Katherine ran her fingertips over the soft sable lining of the new black mantle. She chose the blue outfit to wear and held the cloth up to the curves of her body. The pieces were altered to fit. She closed her eyes and silently thanked Elizabeth for her generosity.

She dressed within the flame's circle of warmth. Finding an ivory comb in her pile of new clothes, she dragged the teeth through her golden locks. She braided her hair in a single long strand and used an embroidered ribbon to tie off the end.

Richard said he wanted to leave at first light. Katherine hurried along so as to not keep him waiting. She stuffed the extra outfit in a linen bag provided, threw her new cloak over one arm, and headed out the door toward the Great Hall.

When she reached the top of the stairs, she eagerly scanned the room below. Her lips formed a slight frown, for no one from the family or even Richard was in attendance. Only a few servants roamed the hall as they busied themselves with their morning duties.

At the bottom of the steps, she stopped a young boy who walked by with a clean bucket of water. "Will the family be breaking their fast soon?"

"Aye, milady. Anna is helping Lady Elizabeth get ready as we speak and Lord Huntington is in the yard with his men, making the day's preparations."

The boy's answer pleased her. There was still time before everyone gathered. "Would the family chapel be available for guests?"

"Aye, milady, follow me." He put down his water buckets and directed her to a wooden door leading from the hall. "In there would be the family chapel, milady."

She nodded her thanks and turned her attention to the ornately carved door. After lifting the latch, she gave the ash planks a big push and the solid door opened wide enough for her to squeeze through the doorway.

When she stepped into the chapel, she was taken aback by the beautiful decor. The room was graced with high beamed ceilings, decorated moldings, and facing the altar were six hand-carved wooden benches. The stained-glass window let in colorful beams of light from the morning's sun. Unlit candles hung all along the walls in decorative holders.

Reverently, she stepped farther into the chamber and held her breath when a sudden peacefulness passed over her. This is what she needed to heal her wounded heart. On the closest bench, she set down her bundle. With her hands clasped together, she walked down the aisle to the altar. After a moment of respect, she made the sign of the cross, knelt on the low step, bowed her head, closed her eyes, and quietly recited her prayers.

***

Richard was on his way down the stairs when William strode in from outside.

"Good morning," William boomed when he caught sight of Richard. "Are you finding your bed so comfortable you have to lay in it all day long?"

"Are you talking about that lumpy old thing you call a bed? I had to sleep in a chair because the pallet pained me so," he replied, returning a broad smile.

"If you slept in a chair, it's because you're getting too old to find the bed," William thundered back, causing them both to laugh.

He joined William at the bottom of the steps and, together, they walked to the thick oak table on the dais and took their seats. The men's conversation turned serious as they discussed their upcoming tactics while awaiting their morning meal.

Elizabeth arrived and sat in a chair next to her husband.

Richard exchanged a quick good morning and then asked, "Have you seen Katherine this morning? I stopped by her bedchamber, but the room was empty. I assumed she was breaking her fast."

"Anna told me she was in the chapel. I wanted to give her a moment alone," Elizabeth replied.

***

A few minutes later, Elizabeth spotted the chapel door opening. Katherine stepped into the Great Hall carrying the linen bag under her arm. When Katherine noticed Elizabeth, she made her way to the family table and bestowed on Elizabeth a warm and generous smile. To the men, she gave each a friendly nod in passing.

Elizabeth noticed the men could do nothing but stare, both speechless. Katherine was quite a vision in her form-fitting, contrasting shades of blue kirtle and surcoat. Her decorated girdle and dagger hung low on well-rounded hips. Hair rich in golden rays curled playfully about her head only to be tamed slightly by her long braid. Clear jewel-like eyes sparkled with friendliness. For a small woman, she stood tall and proud, carrying herself with confidence as she moved easily across the room.

"I visited your chapel. I hope you do not mind," Katherine said cheerfully, unmindful of the effect she had on the men seated at the table.

"Not at all. I see you woke well-rested this morning," Elizabeth replied, intrigued by the other woman's unawareness.

"Oh, indeed. I feel much better than yesterday. The past few days took a toll on me."

"Your new clothes fit you well. I guessed right that those varying shades of blue would be good colors on you. They match your eyes. You look wonderful." Elizabeth looked at the men who appeared taken back by her friend's appearance.

Katherine lovingly stroked the sable fur on the inside of the cloak hung over her arm. "The clothes are perfect and I adore this mantle. The cloak will keep me very warm indeed. I am forever in your debt."

"I am happy to share with you." Elizabeth gave the men another sideward glance. Their mouths still slackened in wonder.

Elizabeth smiled to herself. When she met Katherine for the first time yesterday, Elizabeth could easily tell that physical and emotional fatigue weighed heavily on the young lady, but beneath the worn-out appearance, Elizabeth knew what attributes her friend was blessed with. Now well-rested, well-fed, and well-garbed, Katherine showed a definite transformation.

She gestured for Katherine to take a seat next to her. "Please join us and break your fast before you go. You need to keep up your strength."

Katherine placed her parcel and cloak on the edge of the table and took a chair next to her.

A servant girl made haste to present a morning plate.

The men resumed their meals, both preoccupied with their own thoughts.

When Richard finished, he stood and addressed Katherine warily, "The horses and men await your arrival outside. Whenever you are ready, we'll be on our way."

He moved to the end of the table, grabbed her bundle, and hastily left the room with William following close behind.

"Did I do something wrong? Richard seemed unhappy with me. He would not look me in the eye and was deliberately ignoring me," Katherine said perplexed.

"I believe Richard and William are trying to adjust to how different you are today than you were yesterday," she said.

Katherine picked up a loaf of bread and tore off a piece. "I am not sure I understand."

"The men were not prepared for a real lady to come through the door of the chapel. They are not at ease in the presence of a woman of standing. For all of their show of unswerving confidence, the men are just simple knights and not very comfortable in courtly ways."

"I am the same as I was yesterday. They did not appear to have too much difficulty in my company then." Katherine buttered her bread.

Elizabeth placed a hand on Katherine's upper arm. "Yesterday, you were a young, innocent lady, vulnerable and needing protection. The men were in control and thrive on protecting those in need. Today, you are not what they expected, as you are confident and capable of making your own decisions. Worst of all, they realized you are beautiful. You scare them."

"I cannot imagine anything scaring those two."

"Nothing scares them more than a beautiful lady. You should have seen William when we were first married. He was so terrified of me he practically shook in his boots whenever I came near."

Katherine giggled.

She gave Katherine her most wicked grin.

They took a few minutes to finish their morning meals. When finished they left the table and walked to the double doors with some reluctance.

"I am sorry you have to go so soon, for it seems like you only just arrived," Elizabeth said, already feeling the loss. "I suppose you are anxious to get to Stamford."

"I must make my way to Lord Weston. He's a good friend of my family, and I need to tell him in my own words what happened. My fate is still unknown."

"As I mentioned yesterday, I am sure things will work out in your favor. Do what I did and figure out what you want and go after it until it is yours."

"That may be much easier said than done."

On the top of the steps leading down into the yard, Elizabeth grabbed onto Katherine's arm and stepped in front of her. "Remember, my offer still stands, our home is always open to you. You will have a place with us if you find yourself in need."

Katherine placed her arms around Elizabeth's shoulders and gave her a big hug as she whispered in her ear, "I will keep your offer in mind. Have faith, my friend, this is not the last time we will be in one another's company."

Elizabeth hugged Katherine back. "We will see each other again, soon."

"I will hold you to your promise," Katherine replied, as they broke their embrace.

***

Katherine descended the stairs while drawing her new mantle about her shoulders to ward off the chill in the air. Richard stood next to Titan, waiting for her at the bottom of the steps. He was more than handsome this morning in newly cleaned clothes, freshly washed hair, and recently trimmed beard. Gone were yesterday's signs of lack of sleep.

A little surprised she didn't get a horse of her own, she raised an eyebrow at her tall escort.

"You are riding with me today. It'll be safer," he replied, as if able to read her mind.

Standing next to Titan, she patted the horse on his muzzle. The massive stallion snorted and rubbed his glistening black head against her shoulder, sending her flying backward.

Richard reached out in time to prevent her from falling.

After she had steadied herself, he grabbed about her waist and lifted her off the ground to place her on the front of the saddle, then mounted behind.

"William, I will send word if I need you," Richard called out.

"And I will come," William replied.

He swept his arm to the side and said fondly, "Lady Elizabeth, as always, thank you for your fine hospitality."

From the top landing, Elizabeth bestowed on him a dignified wave with a slight bob of her head. The merriment in her eyes contradicted her stoic façade and her true deep affection for the knight shone brightly.

Katherine finished adjusting her skirts and mantle and waved a warm goodbye to the couple now standing together.

Richard wrapped his arms around her, surrounding her in a familiar blanket of strength, and urged Titan forward through the gates of Hammerstead with four of William's mounted knights following in their wake.

~Chapter Seven~

The pace was quick as the group of riders made their way along a well-traveled road that twisted through woods and fields toward Stamford. Two mounted knights held positions in front of Titan, while the other two brought up the rear. Katherine suspected the seasoned men sensed trouble. On alert, they constantly scanned the sides of the road for danger as their chargers walked briskly along.

The morning chill was on its way out and the sun's rays teased her face with intermittent warmth. After a good night's sleep, she found herself filled with unbridled excitement. Being in the company of well-trained knights provided a sense of freedom from fear which allowed her to enjoy the journey.

With a hungry eye, she looked about like a curious child whenever the riders passed a cottage or small village. From a distance, she observed farmers tilling their fields or tending their animals. Women and children worked closer to home as they cooked over outdoor fires, fed clucking chickens, and labored in newly turned gardens. Scattered travelers moved slowly along the rutted dirt roads, but they always made way for their formidable group of mounted riders.

Being encircled in Richard's powerful embrace let Katherine withdraw into a cocoon of security. No longer awkward with his nearness, her body melted against his chest, and she basked in the comfort of his arms. Titan's fast-paced gait was beautifully smooth and rhythmic, adding to her pleasure.

An easy silence occupied their travels, but she soon yearned for some distracting conversation, for every step toward Lord Weston was a step away from the closeness and familiarity she presently enjoyed.

When they arrived at Stamford, things would change. She would no longer need Richard to see to her safety. He would no longer be in charge of her welfare.

"I noticed you know Lord Huntington's knights quite well," she said to break the silence.

"As well as I do my brothers."

"That well? How did you happen to come to know Lord Huntington and his knights?"

"You're full of questions this fine morning. If I'm not mistaken, this is how you usually draw a story out of an unsuspecting person. What's the matter? Are you finding our journey too quiet for your liking?" he teased.

"If you are inclined to gift me with a tale or two, I would not mind." she smiled softly, for his husky voice stirred something unfamiliar in the pit of her stomach. It pleased her that he knew her well after so many years.

He chuckled. "A story it is then. Let me see, where should I start? You already guessed that William and I have known each other for years. We squired together under Lord Beckett. He was a good man. If death had not taken him, we would've sworn our fealty to him alone. Alas, fate was not on his side, and he died during a land dispute. When his son claimed his title and holdings, we had no reason to stay. Since we were knighted, William and I chose to remain together and try our hand at earning our own keep."

"Is that when you started to enter tournaments?"

"Who's telling this story, you or me?" He laughed.

"You are. Please continue." A smile played at the corners of her lips. She liked hearing him laugh; there was something very agreeable in the deep sound.

"As I was saying," he gave her a playful squeeze about her waist, "we found out about a big tournament up north. The purse was one of the richest in years. Lord Beckett took us to a few tournaments each year, so we were familiar with the preparations. We signed up, full of youthful expectations. We entered the jousting competition. Both of us unseated our opponents and in doing so, we won their horses and armor."

She glanced up and over her shoulder. His eyes gleamed with pride.

"Marcus, the older knight," he gestured to the knight in the lead, "was one of those men. Never unseated before, Marcus didn't expect to lose, so he competed on his best horse. When he lost the animal to William, he was beside himself with the desire to get his charger back. We needed a few good men, so William offered him a deal. If he wanted his horse back, he'd have to join us. He readily agreed. We gave the same terms to the man I unseated. His name is Peter. You'll meet him at Stamford. The two of them have ridden with us ever since."

She stared at the knight in the lead. Dressed impressively in full armor, his back was as straight as his sword, his manner commanding. He rode a high-stepping bay stallion, and she wondered if the animal was the same beloved destrier that made him attach himself so hastily to men he didn't know. Taller and broader than the other knights, his height and width rivaled Richard's own. Locks of slightly graying hair crept out from under his helmet, conveying his passing years. A well-groomed, short-cropped, gray-speckled beard gave the older knight an air of distinction.

"The other knights are Miles, Godfrey, and Owen." Richard pointed them out. "They were also chosen along the way. All come from noble households. We took on knights skilled in battle, trustworthy and loyal. Most of our men have ridden with us for years. In between tournaments and providing service to King Edward, we also hired out our swords for a price. The work was hard, but the money was good."

"So, when you and William separated, some of the men stayed with you and some went with him?"

"That's the truth. Half of our knights were tired of wandering the roadways, never sleeping in the same bed twice. Those who wanted a life of leisure followed William, and those who were not ready to settle down followed me," he explained.

"What about you? Are you still content to travel the countryside hiring out your sword arm and entering tournaments?"

"Actually, I returned home to talk to my father about a new course. I no longer enjoy moving around and have considered leasing Lord Marten's manor and property up north. While in London, a rumor circled that he was in financial ruin. It seems while at court, he stopped paying attention to his holdings. His steward took advantage of his lack of interest and robbed him of his wealth. I was told he might accept money for leasing out one of his estates. King Edward gave me permission. I wanted to try managing my own lands."

She was delighted he considered working his own holding. "I know you can make any estate under your care flourish."

"Well, with my oldest brother getting married soon and producing heirs of his own, it's unlikely I'll ever inherit my father's title or lands. I need to find another way to acquire holdings of my own."

"Your father told me…" She stopped mid-sentence. Richard's muscles tightened unexpectedly, squeezing her firmly about her waist. Titan pranced beneath them with barely contained energy as tension thickened the air. They were in the middle of the forest, no longer near a village or open land. The road was well-worn but narrow. Ahead of Marcus and Owen, she noticed a group of riders approaching.

Marcus looked over his shoulder at Richard to receive wordless orders.

Richard turned to the knights behind them and then back. He breathed in her ear, "Put your hood up, tuck in your hair, keep your eyes down, and don't look at them when they pass. Maybe they'll ride on by."

"Do you think these are Lord Seton's men?" she whispered as she put up her hood and bit nervously on her bottom lip.

"Possibly. I count five mounted knights, dressed in full." He paused and then continued, "I want you to bring this leg," he tapped her leg, "over to this side."

With his help, she quickly moved her leg over Titan's neck, so they rested on the same side. After readjusting herself in a more comfortable position, she gazed at him from under her hood. His face was taut, and she could tell he was concerned for her well-being.

"If these are Lord Seton's men, they may attack without provocation. If I give the word, I want you to wrap your arms around my waist, press fully against my chest, and close your eyes. All you have to do is move when I do."

He flashed her a big, reassuring smile.

She nodded.

"I'll not let you be harmed." He lifted her chin and stared deeply in her eyes. "Trust me."

"I do," she said passionately without doubt.

***

Not prepared for such a forthright response, Richard immediately turned his head. For a moment, his breath caught in his throat. Her unwavering belief in him knocked him off guard. When he brought himself back to the present, he realized the mounted knights were almost upon them. He adjusted his mantle out of the way, rested a hand on the butt of his sword and protectively encircled Katherine with his arm while holding a loose rein.

Because of the narrow road, the riders passed in single file. They sized up the riders opposite as they rode next to each one. William's seasoned knights were skilled in the art of deception and projected an air of indifference to the strangers.

Unfortunately, their stoic features were not enough to dissuade the other men.

When the opposing knight in the lead took one look at Richard holding a woman, the thrill in his eyes could not be mistaken. The second knight in line could also barely contain his enthusiasm.

Richard knew what would come next; before the third knight rode up alongside, he roared, "Now!"

***

Katherine didn't hesitate to do what Richard asked. At his order, she turned her body, grabbed his waist, and with all her might plastered herself against him, resting her cheek upon his padded chest.

With one swoop, he unsheathed his sword and pressed his mount forward.

She shut her eyes. All around, the shrill clatter of battle blared. Men grunted and groaned with exertion. The piercing sound of metal hitting metal echoed through the woods.

She concentrated on Richard's movements, letting him move her at will.

When the first blow landed on his sword, shock coursed through her body. Then, an impenetrable wall of steel kept hitting steel again and again; sending powerful jolts slamming into her every time.

As Richard warded off multiple blows, his men nearby did the same. Titan danced beneath them as the animal worked with his master to push back their attacker.

In the distance, someone cried out in pain, a horse squealed, and a man shouted a warning.

Visions of a blade slicing through her tender flesh festered in her mind. Her stomach churned. Panic pounded in her chest.

A moan of death registered nearby, and a horse raced away with another galloping after it.

Yet their assailant kept striking at them. Richard, she remembered, was not in full armor, only light chainmail, and his leather tunic. In her ragged mind, she pictured him maimed or killed. A building urge to grab onto her mother's dagger to help protect him became unbearable.

Katherine repressed the impulse and instead latched onto him even tighter. She would do as he asked. She would trust him.

His arm tightened around her back as he yanked hard on the reins, urging his warhorse forward at the same time. Titan reared. She felt the quick jerks of the stallion striking out with his front hooves. The other horse squealed in pain. Richard shot forward with a tremendous thrust and then pulled back just as quickly. She heard a body hit the ground and a horse dart away.

Beneath them, Titan danced with excitement, yet no more blows fell their way.

Richard belted out orders. "Godfrey, help Owen with the one that ran off. Make sure he doesn't get away. We don't want Lord Seton to know where Lady Katherine is."

Katherine opened her eyes and untangled herself from his hard body. She twisted around to take in her surroundings. The sights awaiting her were disturbing. Scattered upon the ground were the dead bodies of their attackers. In spots, blood mixed with the dirt of the road, turning the soil the color of rust. The smell of death hung in the air. With her recent encounter of fatality so fresh in her mind, her stomach knotted painfully, and bile rose in her throat.

Desperate to break free from Richard's arms, she pushed frantically on his steel-like limbs while she half-ordered, half-begged, "Let me down! Please, let me down!"

He steadied Titan and set her upon the road.

Katherine raced forward to the closest tree. She threw a shaky arm around its width and clung fiercely to the damp bark as she leaned her hip heavily against the solid wood. To quiet the flutter in the pit of her stomach, she placed an open hand over her belly. With closed eyes, she rested a cheek on the cool, rough surface of the tree and prayed that she would not embarrass herself further.

In the distance, she heard the riders return. All must have gone well; no one gave a call of alarm. Richard's strong voice ordered the knights to hide the bodies. Men dismounted and set themselves to the task. Sapling branches snapped and leaves stirred as William's men dragged the dead away.

Her legs trembled. She hung onto the tree to keep from toppling over. The battle was too intense, her emotions too out of control.

She brought her shaky hand up from her stomach to brush loose tendrils from her face. What had she felt? Fear, worry and yes, even exhilaration.

"Are you all right?" Richard's deep voice only a few inches away cut through her pensive thoughts.

At the unexpected sound, she startled, scratching her cheek on a sharp edge of the bark. "Oww!" she cried out, slapping her hand over the wound to lessen the sting.

She turned toward him, "Shame on you for coming upon me as quiet as a cat."

He placed a hand under her chin and lifted her head. With his other hand, he removed her fingers from the scratch. He gently glided his thumb over the welt to assess the damage and teased, "Oh, stop complaining; you broke no skin. The wound isn't that bad."

"Of course not. It did not happen to you," she shot back, brushing his arm away. Her anger quickly disappeared when she gazed into his warm blue eyes.

"Are you well enough to ride or do you need more time?" he asked.

"I will be fine. I am much better now," she replied. His nearness had a calming effect on her nausea and she no longer wished to be alone.

"Come then, let us deliver you to Stamford as soon as possible. I have worked up an appetite from rescuing you yet again," he said lightheartedly while bestowing on her a smile that lit up his handsome face.

He whistled sharply, summoning Titan to appear at their side. Once he settled her in the saddle, he found the stirrup and hauled himself up behind.

She took a moment to assess the mounted knights surrounding them, worried they might have received an injury. Although their armor was banged up, the men didn't appear to be in any real discomfort.

Marcus rode up beside them, considered her for a moment and gave her a silent nod of approval before he moved away to take up his position in the lead.

His odd behavior baffled her, and she raised an eyebrow in puzzlement as Titan fell in behind.

~Chapter Eight~

The late afternoon sun hid behind a cloud as Katherine and the other mounted riders crossed Stamford's wooden drawbridge. Their horses' hooves struck the weathered planks in unison, alerting the castle folk to approaching visitors. When the group reached the massive portcullis suspended above the castle entrance, the guards on duty called out a welcome to Richard and let them enter through the gates.

As the riders made their way up a gradual incline to the keep, they passed the training fields. Katherine noticed they attracted the attention of over two dozen knights and men-at-arms practicing the art of war with their swords, javelins, and crossbows. All instructions ceased when shouts of greetings cried out as the on-lookers fell in line, following the newcomers to the inner bailey. Once the knights in her party dismounted, the group was quickly set upon by those eager to hear news from Hammerstead.

Richard dropped to the ground.

From her perch on the back of Titan, she caught the welcome sight of Lord Weston passing through the double doors of the keep. The weight of her recent sadness lifted with a glimpse of her father's friend. She raised her arm to get his attention but halted when an impatient hand brushed against her leg. She glanced down at Richard standing by her side.

With a smirk, he said, "I have done the impossible and have delivered you safely to my father's door." A flicker of warmth burned in the depth of his gaze. Reaching up, he grabbed her waist and settled her next to his mount.

"As I knew you would," she replied breathlessly.

He gave her a cocksure smile before turning to speak with a fellow knight, eager for an audience.

With her feet firmly on solid ground, she again scanned the yard for Lord Weston. Her efforts were in vain, for she found herself surrounded by a few massive horses and a wall of giant men. Try as she might, she couldn't see past the men's chests, never mind over their heads. Those mingling around paid her no heed as they were too preoccupied with welcoming William's knights. She searched for an opening in the crowd, but her labor proved fruitless; she found none.

A wave of unease washed over her; the crush was too much.

In the distance, Lord Weston called her name.

"I am here," she cried in a voice that failed to carry over the noise.

She was not the only one ill at ease. Troubled by all the commotion, Titan stamped a gigantic hoof and threw his head up and down in protest, but the men were so caught up in their own pastime, they ignored his complaints. His enormous body moved sideways in his impatience, pressing her deeper into the throng.

Panic rose in her chest and stuck in her throat. She took a deep breath to calm her racing heart. Her eyes darted to Richard, but he conversed with an older knight and he didn't notice her plight. Annoyed with him and his steed, she shoved Titan's rump to reclaim a bit of her precious space, but the stubborn horse never shifted his weight.

***

Richard took a moment from his discussion with Peter, his knight-in-charge, to glance in Katherine's direction. What he saw terrified him. The woman seemed oblivious to the fact she was in jeopardy of being trampled by his mount. A sudden rush of alarm slammed like a fist into his stomach. He knew exactly what Titan could do to a man underfoot, and visions of her mangled body caused him to react swiftly.

In two big strides, he was at her side. He scooped her up into his arms and carried her through the crowd, leaving his high-strung stallion behind.

He hadn't spent the last few days rescuing her, just to have his contrary horse do her in.

***

Surprised by her flight through the air, Katherine grabbed frantically to the first thing her arms latched onto; Richard's thick neck. When her senses returned, she realized the noise quieted, all eyes were upon them, and the wall of men parted easily, giving them a path out.

She buried her face in his broad shoulder as she tried to hide from those who bore witness to her helplessness. Out of the corner of her eye, she caught sight of Lord Weston standing at the opening Her tense muscles immediately relaxed.

"Katherine, my dear, are you hurt?" Lord Weston's face tightened with concern.

"Only my pride, since your son considers me to be no more than a sack of stones and throws me about at will," she reassured him good-naturedly.

Lord Weston chuckled.

"Is that all the thanks I get for saving you from being trampled? Come to think of it. I believe I've rescued you yet again." Richard smiled smugly. "It's turning out to be quite a task to keep you safe."

Katherine let out an offended snort.

He set her down in front of his father.

"I will have you know I was doing just fine without you. I am perfectly capable of taking care of myself."

Richard rolled his eyes and grunted.

Dismissing him with the toss of her head, she turned to Lord Weston and smiled with all the tenderness she could muster. His presence was a pillar of comfort and strength. She studied his familiar face with his short-cropped salt and pepper beard and well-known smile. He stood a foot taller than she and was broad of the chest like his son. He cared deeply for her; the affection shone brightly in his gray-blue eyes.

Lord Weston leaned down, wrapped his thick arms around her in a loving embrace and picked her up off the ground for a big hug. At her wince of pain, Richard frowned and took a step forward to stop his father's rough welcome.

With the sweep of her hand, she gestured him to be still, for she would not ruin Lord Weston's joyful moment.

When her feet touched the ground, she quickly hid her discomfort behind a mask of pleasure.

"Let me look at you, lass." Lord Weston held her shoulders at arm's length. "No worse for the wear, I see. A little tired perhaps, but all-in-all, still in one piece. Well done, son," he proclaimed, nodding his approval.

"As I said earlier, not an easy task," Richard drawled while sending a sly, sideward glance in her direction.

She rolled her eyes in feigned disgust.

Lord Weston stepped closer, wrapped an arm around her shoulders, and gave a gentle squeeze.

"I heard about your father and David. We'll put things aright. They were good men and sit with God now. Let's not be sad. Instead, we should toast their eternal life."

Katherine laid a cheek against his chest. He was right. As a deeply religious man, her father would be disappointed if she suffered unduly from grief.

Lord Weston released his hold and tipped her chin. "In the meantime, I've sent a letter off to the king. As a young noblewoman without family, he's your guardian now. I wanted to keep him informed."

As Lord Weston's hand dropped away, she considered his statement. *The king is my guardian.* She frowned with concern, remembering Lady Elizabeth's situation.

"Don't worry, lass; I have things well in control." Lord Weston gave her a gentle pat on her shoulder.

A servant stepped beside them carrying her parcel. "Milord, where shall I put Lady Katherine's belongings?"

"Place her things in the last bedchamber at the end of the hall." Lord Weston turned to Katherine. "The room shall be yours for as long as you wish."

When her few meager belongings disappeared, a wave of melancholy washed over her. Life as she knew it was gone.

***

A commotion in the yard drew Richard's attention. Titan was rearing up on his hind legs and striking out at a frightened groom tugging on his reins.

"You better handle that brute of yours before I lose one of my men," his father said with a ragged edge of concern.

"Titan will tear him to pieces," Richard said under his breath. He strode across the yard toward his destrier. The yard full of men stood in a wide circle around the high-strung animal and watched as the young groom tried desperately to maintain control, without much luck.

He walked calmly between the seemingly distraught man and his stallion and slowly raised an arm. "Easy, boy," he said in a soothing, deep voice, while he took the reins from the terrified young man and let them slacken.

Titan immediately quieted.

Richard closed the gap and stood in front of his horse, who settled his considerable head against his chest in total submission.

Applause erupted from the circle of men. With comical pomposity, he bowed, causing them fits of laughter. He scratched Titan behind an ear, spoke a few gentle words of affection, and led his horse off toward the stable.

At the entrance, he stopped. In the distance, his father walked arm in arm with Katherine. Deep in conversation, the two made their way to a stone bench next to the flower garden bursting with color. His father offered her a seat and knelt on one knee so he could gaze into her eyes as he spoke. His father then stood, cradled her head between his large hands, and placed a gentle kiss on her forehead. Seeing them so friendly didn't sit well. He wasn't sure why it bothered him, but it did.

Richard knew his father discussed her family's deaths and was only comforting her. Annoyance ate at him anyway. He turned his back on them; she wasn't his problem anymore. She no longer needed his protection. His father would care for her now. Richard's future was set in stone. The sooner he finished what he started and made Lord Seton pay with his life, the better. After that, he would be free to follow his own course.

Titan, annoyed at Richard for standing in the doorway when food and water waited in the stall, nudged his chest, bringing him out of his thoughts.

"What's the matter, boy, have you also worked up an appetite after rescuing her?" The massive beast seemed to understand and softly nickered in response.

"Come, my friend," he said, patting the big black head before leading the stallion into his stall.

***

On his way out of the stables, Richard noticed the men had scattered and returned to the training fields. With the excitement over, the castle people resumed their daily chores and paid him no mind. He expected to find Katherine and his father still in the garden. Surprisingly, they were already gone.

Richard made his way to the training fields to join his men. He'd speak to his father later.

A half-hour later, Richard walked into the Great Hall and sat down on a padded chair by the warm fire. He caught a scent of fresh-baked bread and instructed a young servant girl to fetch him a loaf, a pitcher of ale, and two mugs. His father hadn't yet made an appearance, and he found himself impatient with the wait. Surely Katherine would see fit to leave out most of her story, but he was determined to give his father a full accounting. He was also eager to hear his father's thoughts on seeking revenge on Lord Seton.

After Richard had had a few drinks and a full belly, his mood improved considerably. He was in better spirits when his father finally arrived and joined him.

His father grabbed the pitcher and poured a mug of ale. "Katherine filled me in on what happened over the past few days, including this morning's attack."

"Did she tell you everything? She has a habit of leaving out important information."

"Do you mean did she tell me about the whipping?" His father struggled with the words as if a bitter taste stuck in his mouth. "She did. I sent Flora to tend her back. You remember Flora; she's skilled in the art of healing."

"Oh, yes, I remember the woman. It was clever the way she stopped Garrett and me from stealing pies from the baker. If I'm not mistaken, she put something in the last pie we stole that made us vomit for hours." He shook his head at the painful memory.

His father chuckled. "Well, the baker was very upset with your mischief and wanted to teach you a lesson. She enlisted Flora's help, and they came to me for approval."

"I always knew you had a hand in our punishment. You walked by while we were spilling our insides, smiled cheerfully, and continued on your way as if you never noticed anything amiss."

"She assured me that no real harm would come to you."

"What do you mean no real harm? To this day, I can't bear to look upon a berry pie, never mind having a bite. You, with the help of Flora, have ruined me for all time," Richard whined in good fun.

"I guess it was a lesson well-learned." His father laughed heartily.

Richard missed the old man's agreeable company.

"Well, Father, what should we do about Lord Seton? I can tell you, I'm not at all pleased about how the attack on Henry de Grey came about. It was cowardly and unacceptable to present oneself in friendship and then cut a man's throat at his table. Lord Seton went against the code."

"I agree with you. I have struggled with the circumstances of Henry's death. He was my oldest and dearest friend. I don't intend to let his, and his son's deaths go unpunished. There was nothing honorable in Lord Seton's actions. Ever since your letter arrived, I have thought long and hard about what we should do in retribution."

He gave Richard an inquiring look. "What would you do?"

What if William had died from such treachery?

"I wouldn't hesitate. I would act immediately before Lord Seton, or the man he works for has time to send for reinforcements. Half his men are searching for Katherine as we speak. He has no way of knowing if she found refuge. They probably believe she's still wandering the woods or hiding in a villager's cottage. He wouldn't expect a full-scale attack so soon. I doubt Lord Seton understands the depth of our alliance with the de Greys. It's not common knowledge outside a small circle of friends. He probably reasoned that if he killed Lord de Grey and David, and then married Katherine, no one would dispute his claim to Rosemont, and no one would question how he came about his acquisition. If I were in charge, I would send a full garrison of mounted knights and men-at-arms to Rosemont as soon as possible. I would first attempt to go in unawares, maybe cause a diversion and slip a few men in undercover to take over the gatehouse. If discovered, I would make a stand outside the walls and wait him out."

"Go in quickly before he gets reinforcements. Use the element of surprise to unbalance him and his men," his father summarized Richard's proposed tactics and then stared unseeing at the tapestry hanging on the wall. "I wonder if I could add something. Katherine told me how she escaped through a secret passage leading out to the cliffs. If you and your men were to find the opening and use the tunnels to get into the keep, you would indeed surprise Lord Seton and his men. While some of your men are busy fighting in the hall, the others could take control of the gatehouse and let in the rest. The battle could be over in a matter of minutes, with minimum casualties."

"How do you know about these secret passages? Katherine never told me about them."

"Well, son, they're called secret passages for a reason," he leaned over and whispered, "They're secret." He chuckled.

"Hmm. Your tactic would work, as long as the opening can be found in the dark." He took a swig of his ale.

"Indeed."

"Will you be leading us, Father?"

"Oh, no. Not me. I would be no good to anyone. My gout is too bad." His father leaned down and rubbed his foot. "I can barely walk, never mind sit a horse. You'll have to go in my place."

Richard cocked an eyebrow. His father had always been strong and sturdy and showed no outward signs of discomfort or pain earlier. He pursed his lips and tried to recollect if his father limped when he made his way down the stairs. The man appeared fine.

"Ale helps quite a bit." His father lifted his half-empty mug to his mouth and took a big gulp.

"What about Garrett? I haven't laid eyes on him since I arrived; will he be joining me?"

"I sent your brother on an errand, and he won't be back in time." A quick look of guilt washed over his father's face.

Richard scowled; something wasn't right, but he couldn't figure it out.

His father raised his cup. "I'm counting on you to lead the assault and avenge my friend's death. Of course, you'll have at your command my men, your knights, some of Garrett's men, and I believe William's knights would also insist on joining you. I'm sure you'll have enough men and supplies at your disposal for a successful outcome."

Richard rose from his chair. "I need to find Peter and Marcus to discuss our preparations. Would you like to join me?"

"Oh, no, my gout is too bad." His father rubbed his ankle before struggling to place his foot on the low table in front of the chair. "I think I'll leave everything in your capable hands."

Richard expelled a loud breath. "Father, I do believe a few minutes ago you said the pain was in your other foot."

"Be off with you now. You must have better things to do than to be standing over me watching my every move. If you need anything, I'll be sitting right here by the fire, resting both my feet. Of course, as long as that's fine with you?" His father lifted his drink again to his lips.

"As you wish." Richard found his father's behavior puzzling and wondered if maybe the old man's brain was addled with age. As he strode from the Great Hall, he shook his head in bewilderment.

***

Two hours later, Richard returned to the keep. The afternoon had turned out fruitful, and preparations for a full assault were underway. He had years of experience in warfare, as did his men. The supplies they needed were easily found in his father's well-stocked storehouses.

He made his way to the hearth and found his father dozing peacefully in the cushioned chair, an empty mug clutched in his hand. As he stood over the gray-haired man, he smiled to himself. Give the man a few pints of ale next to a warm fire and he falls asleep as if all's well in the world. Now that Garrett had taken over most of the day to day affairs of Stamford, his father had few worries.

Richard took the seat next to him. He picked up a full mug of warm ale and quietly observed the hall filling with knights and men-at-arms eager for the evening meal. The crowd was in good spirits while they found their places on the benches surrounding the long wooden tables positioned about the room.

A troupe of minstrels arrived carrying their instruments. The players chose to sit at a short table close to the small stage directly across from the head table. Serving girls hurried to set plates, bring out mugs of ale and skirt away from wayward hands.

William's knights intermingled good-heartedly with Richard's men. He wished William had accompanied him to Stamford, yet he understood why his friend chose to stay at Hammerstead. William remained behind to protect his family in case Lord Seton's men came to his door. Since William married, his priority was the safety of his wife, Lady Elizabeth, and his sister.

Richard didn't like to admit it, but he envied William's loyalty and devotion to his family. It wasn't a coincidence, Lady Alice, the woman he had chosen to one day marry, had so many physical characteristics in common with Lady Elizabeth. Both were tall, dark-haired beauties. He hoped to find the same happiness William had found. Once he avenged the de Grey family, he would continue on the path already cast. He would start a new life with the one woman in England who reminded him of Lady Elizabeth.

At the top of the stairs, movement caught his eye. Katherine stood at the rail. He admired how perfect she looked in her soft blue kirtle and darker matching surcoat that snuggly caressed her womanly curves. A thick braid wrapped around her head, tamed her blonde curls, giving her a soft glow of maturity. Her ever watchful bright eyes swept the hall below and sparkled when they rested on him and his father by the hearth.

He poked his father awake as Katherine joined them.

"Good evening, Lord Weston. Richard." Katherine gave each man a nod and a dainty bow.

His father sprung up spryly from his seat, belying any infirmities. He grabbed onto her hand and pressed a gentle kiss on the top. "I must say, my dear, you look lovely tonight."

Richard noticed she appeared uncomfortable with his father's praise. Her cheeks grew a rosy red. He made a point to lazily scrutinize her from head to toe. She nibbled nervously on her bottom lip, keenly aware of his perusal.

Not one to let an opportunity to tease pass by, he presented her with an amused smile and said in an unusually exaggerated tone, "I must agree with my father; you look absolutely radiant."

She clearly didn't believe his candor. Her cheeks reddened, and she shot him a fierce glare that would've sent a weaker man running for the nearest drink.

He chuckled to himself.

***

"Let's put all the bad things behind us tonight and have a nice meal." Lord Weston took Katherine by the arm and led her to the head table on the dais. "I have a special treat. We are fortunate enough to have in our midst a very talented traveling minstrel. I think he will impress you with his gifts, as he has a magnificent voice and plays the lute beautifully." He tapped her arm, affectionately. "I can honestly say I've never heard better."

Katherine couldn't help but smile at the man who tried so hard to make her feel welcome. She took the seat offered on Lord Weston's right, and Richard took the seat to the left.

Once Lord Weston sat down, the servants began passing out the first course of delicacies and continued to bring out dish after dish. Soon the hall full of men quieted while they busied themselves with devouring the platters of stuffed pheasants, mutton stew, and loaves of fresh-baked bread placed before them. When the crowd was fully sated, the noise level in the hall grew again, as pretty serving girls regularly refilled the tall mugs.

When she finished her last bite, Lord Weston caught the watchful eye of the minstrel and with a nod, bid him to start the entertainment. The gaily dressed man smiled broadly and took his place on a chair in the middle of a raised platform. A hush fell over the hall. The minstrel positioned his lute on his lap and strummed the first note. Pleased with the crowd's attention, the entertainer smiled broadly and made a point to lock eyes with Katherine. He plucked at the strings with expert precision and sang her a song, rejoicing in her beauty.

Hearing such words of praise, she placed her fingers over her mouth to hide her distress.

She turned away but was drawn back to the man's piercing brown eyes and the range of his mystical voice.

Strangely moved, she found herself lulled into a state of peacefulness and accepted the tribute given.

***

Richard observed Katherine responding to the music. Suddenly, he was very annoyed with this minstrel who sang of her feminine attributes. The men in the room stared at her with newfound curiosity. From deep within him, rose a strong urge to shield her from view and throw a few overly eager men across the room. Since such behavior wouldn't be fitting, he opted for distraction instead.

Before the song ended, Richard bellowed from his seat, "Well done, my man, but now can you play something with a quicker beat so my men can tap in time?"

A roar of approval echoed in the hall as the men looked from one to another in anticipation. The other musicians joined the lute player on the elevated platform with their tambour, shawm, and recorder.

Richard glanced at Katherine. His father placed his large hand over her small one and gave her a reassuring pat. She offered his father a sweet smile as the pair exchanged unspoken words.

The two of them shared a strong bond. Never had his father acted this way with a woman. Another disturbing twinge burrowed in his chest. He had no time to question the odd sensation, for a half a dozen men grabbed a few willing serving girls and boisterously led them around the hall in a whirlwind of dance, most of the men trying without success to keep time to the music. He found himself drawn into their merriment and laughed at their drunken efforts. When the song ended, he looked over to see how Katherine fared but was surprised to find an empty chair next to his father.

"Katherine retired to her room. I don't think she's in much of a mood for festivities tonight," his father supplied.

"I suppose you're right." He turned back to the entertainment at hand, but his thoughts were not far from Katherine for the rest of the evening.

~Chapter Nine~

Lord Weston paced back and forth in front of the master bedchamber's stone hearth. He stopped abruptly and gazed unseeing into the leaping flames. The king's messenger had finally arrived. After reading the king's message, he found himself in a quandary.

How should I proceed?

Any decision made tonight would change Katherine's life forever.

He let out a deep troubled sigh. If his grown sons ever found out how fond he was of the young woman, they'd call him an old fool, and he'd have to agree. Since her family was gone, it was up to him to see to her future. He owed her that.

Over the years, Katherine had become the daughter he never had. She was the softness in his hard world. Henry didn't mind sharing his only daughter's company. On his frequent visits to Rosemont, the men would sit by the hearth and enjoy her softness. They teased her in fun, and she rewarded them with smiles and laughter. Her easy rapport brought them peace and contentment. She deserved to feel safe and secure and to be happy.

She deserves my son.

He couldn't ignore that some sort of fate had brought Richard and Katherine together after so many years apart. There was a comfortable familiarity between the pair as the couple exchanged friendly jesting. He'd noticed the deep concern etched on Richard's face when they discussed Katherine's well-being, and his son couldn't hide his irritation when other men noticed her beauty.

Lord Weston made his decision. He would shade the truth. The king wanted to join him and Katherine in marriage.

How absurd.

How could he marry a woman he considered a daughter? The marriage would never work. She deserved better. He was an old man, his life almost over, but his son's life was just beginning. They would make a good pair. They were well-suited.

Now he needed to figure out how to approach Richard.

His son wouldn't take what he had to say favorably. Ever since he was a small child, Richard never liked to be told what to do. He didn't take orders well. Out of all four of his sons, it was with Richard that Lord Weston had to hold his tongue or, at times, even turn to sneaky methods to steer his son's way of thinking.

Clasping his hands behind his back, he returned to his pacing. Richard had been summoned and would soon stand before him. Lord Weston had to choose his words carefully. If he didn't, his son would refuse to listen to reason.

Much depended on the right words.

A few hard raps sounded on the thick oak door. He stopped short. "Enter."

The portal opened with a loud creak. "Father, you summoned me? Will you be joining us tomorrow? The hour grows late. Preparations will have to…" Richard trailed off when their eyes met.

"No, son. I haven't changed my mind. I wish to discuss something else." He offered Richard a seat and watched his son stiffen before he made his way to the chair and stood behind it. Richard was already on the defensive, but, no matter, there was no going back.

"I've received a message from King Edward. As you know, due to Katherine's noble standing and not having the protection of a living relative, the king is her guardian. As such, he is in charge of her welfare. The king believes she's in grave danger and doesn't want her to fall into the hands of Lord Seton or men like him. He suggests the only way to protect her is to join her in a favorable marriage to a man of honor, courage, and strength. One who's loyal to the crown. He wants a man who can regain her family's holdings and keep her safe from those who would use her as a pawn. He offers Rosemont as the prize."

Lord Weston paused to let Richard take in his words. So far, his son remained calm on the outside, but he could tell there was a storm brewing beneath the surface.

"Richard, the king believes a wedded match between the Westons and the de Greys would be in the best interest of both families."

Lord Weston wanted to say he agreed. Instead, he kept his tongue quiet and his opinion to himself. Better not to voice his thoughts. He didn't need his son's anger pointed in his direction.

Richard's jaw clenched.

Good, he didn't have to disclose the real truth of the king's message. Just the right words flowed over his tongue to convince his son that the king wanted Richard to marry Katherine.

A long moment of silence hung awkwardly in the air. His son stepped from behind the chair and paced the room like a caged animal. Each time he strode past Lord Weston, Richard glared at him with icy blue eyes, until he finally found a voice for his thoughts.

"This was not my set course. I have chosen a different path. I came home to tell you I intended to run my own estate and marry Lady Alice Cromwell. That's my desire." His son's voice held an angry edge.

Lord Weston knew Richard didn't like to be thwarted. He took pity on his proud son.

Richard continued marching past him.

Leaning against the hearth with his arms folded across his chest, Lord Weston let the anger bounce off him. He was surprised to learn of Richard's intent to marry another. He was aware his son wanted to lease land but had no idea he considered marriage.

Well, no matter, such could be undone.

"I might've rescued Katherine from certain death, but that doesn't mean I have to be chained to her forever. She's a child, a woman-child." Richard's loud tirade continued, his voice laced with fury. "I won't do it. I've always been a loyal servant to King Edward. The king has no right to change a loyal subject's set course to suit his own."

Once the words were spoken, Richard looked away sheepishly, well aware of his ridiculous rant. "I told Lady Alice I'd return to London. I can't break my promise."

"Have you already spoken for her hand in marriage?" Lord Weston questioned, curious about his son's relationship with this other woman.

"I didn't actually ask for her hand. I wanted to settle some particulars before a formal proposal. It was loosely implied. I have a set course in mind. I know what I want and where my path leads. I have given my future a lot of thought." Richard grew even more irate.

Lord Weston continued to listen and smiled inwardly.

Good news. Nothing bound his son to Lady Alice. With this new information, he was confident Richard would come to the conclusion that a marriage to Katherine would take place. As Richard noted, he was a loyal servant of the king and as such he wouldn't forsake what he believed to be his king's desires.

Richard clasped the back of the chair with both hands as if it was the only thing holding him back from going into battle.

"I vow to you, on my honor, and in the presence of God, that I will take Lady Katherine de Grey for my wife, but bed her and consummate our vows, I will not," Richard proclaimed.

Lord Weston's stomach churned.

"I will avenge her family's deaths and keep her safe from Lord Seton, but I promised Lady Alice I would return to London, and I will. When I present myself to her, if I find I still feel as strongly about her as I do now, I will petition the king to dissolve our marriage and the king will have no choice but to find a more willing suitor for his ward. It has been done before for Lord Malloy when he wed Lady Celia to protect her from her devious relatives. The king dissolved their marriage when he found it was not a good match. He can do the same for me when he realizes I would suit better with Lady Alice. I know he will. He has shown me favor before," Richard said with conviction.

Lord Weston shook his head and stared into the flames. Oh, to be young and headstrong. Since Richard had declared such a vow, his son wouldn't take his promise lightly.

Richard was an honorable man. That would be his downfall. The words passing over his lips sealed his fate. His journey would be harder than it had to be.

God be with him.

***

A few hours ago, Katherine left the Great Hall by making an excuse about being too weary to enjoy the entertainment. She tried to convince herself her haste to her bedchamber was due to fatigue, but the real reason was Richard had hurt her feelings. At first, she was uncomfortable as the minstrel sang of her beauty, but soon she longed for the words to be true.

Obviously, Richard didn't hold the same sentiment as he called for the man to hurry up and play a different tune. It wounded her that he found no truth in the pretty words, and she found herself yearning to hide in the comfort of her bedchamber.

Once she was alone in her room, it offered little reprieve as the emptiness reminded her of how lonely she was without her father and David. She wished she hadn't let Richard's slight bother her.

Undressing down to her chemise, she wrapped herself in a blanket and made her way to the chair by the fire. She stared at the flames as they crackled and popped until her eyelids grew heavy.

While curled in a ball under a finely embroidered quilt, she struggled to push aside all the painful memories associated with the loss of her family and instead focused on the blessed nothingness that had recently become her friend.

A loud, booming knock on what she thought was her door startled her out of a light sleep. She untangled her legs and made her way to the wooden portal. Opening the door a sliver, she peeked out in time to see Richard, silhouetted by a lit wall sconce, enter his father's bedchamber.

Curious as to why Richard visited his father at this hour, she wrapped the quilt tighter around her shoulders and stepped out of her room. Barefoot and without a candle, she made her way down the murky hallway. Cloaked in darkness, she stood against the wall outside the master bedchamber.

She heard Lord Weston's muffled voice on the other side of the door. It sent a twinge of guilt tumbling in her stomach. She shouldn't be here. She whirled around to leave, then overheard her name which piqued her interest. Changing her mind, she pressed her ear to the door.

After a brief silence, Richard's raised angry voice came through loud and clear. She leaned heavily on the wall for support when the meaning of his words broke her heart. Richard didn't want her. He thought of her as a child. He wanted another. As she scurried back to her room, her world crashed down around her.

Katherine burrowed deep under her bedcovers to protect herself from all the hurt she endured after being so thoroughly discarded. She wanted to cry, but no drops flowed. If Richard cared naught for her, she wouldn't waste her tears.

***

In the early morning hour, a knock on Katherine's door woke her from a restless sleep. She sat with her back against the headboard and pulled her covers up to her chin. "Enter."

The door opened, and Lord Weston crossed the threshold. There were circles under his eyes, and his eyebrows were drawn together.

"My dear, prepare yourself, for I have good news. I received a message from King Edward, your guardian, and he had a fine idea. He thought it would be in your best interest if the Weston and de Grey families were united through a bond of marriage. If you married Richard, posthaste, you'd be out of Lord Seton's reach."

She stared blankly at him.

Lord Weston applied a fake smile. "What a wonderful idea. He decreed you may marry right away. He and the cardinal have permitted you to forego waiting for your banns of marriage to be posted. Your safety is their main concern. If your father were alive today, he'd be delighted."

Lord Weston couldn't fool Katherine; he was trying miserably to be cheerful. He waited for her to absorb the news and watched closely for her reaction. When he noticed her lack of excitement, he frowned.

"My dear, what's the matter? I thought the news would please you. Is it because I spoke of your father?" He sat down on the edge of her bed.

"No, it helps to speak of him with someone who knew him so well. I suppose I am a bit overwhelmed. My head is spinning."

"Is this turn of events not as you wished?"

"Of course, the news pleases me. Any woman would consider herself fortunate indeed to be Richard's wife." She painted on a pretend smile to go with her merry voice, then the guise fell away when she added in a more depressed tone, "But, I do not believe him to be so thrilled with the news."

"Of course, he is." Lord Weston assured her. "He makes preparations to have a priest bless your union this morning."

"This morning! So soon? What is the hurry? I am perfectly safe right now." She nervously swiped loose tendrils from her face. The idea of marrying a man who didn't want her weighed heavily on her mind.

"Richard leaves directly after mass on a quest to get Rosemont back. He imagines he'll be more successful if he catches Lord Seton by surprise. No one will gainsay him if he acts as a husband bent on regaining his wife's property, especially with King Edward's blessing. Lord Seton will have few allies if the siege is long and drawn out."

Katherine wrapped both arms around her knees and drew them into her chest. The weight of his words hit her. She was expected to promptly marry Richard, a man who didn't want her. She would be essentially left at the altar, so he, as her husband, could go into battle to reclaim her family estates, maybe dying in the process.

"I cannot let him do that for me. He has done enough already. I know marrying me was never his intent, nor possibly losing his life on my behalf." Her voice came out a high-pitched wail. Knots tugged uncomfortably in her belly.

Lord Weston patted her arm. "My dear, let me be honest with you. In the first place, Richard will battle Lord Seton, no matter, it's a given. That's what he does. It's what he does well. We couldn't stop him if we wanted to. He has his mind set on this course. Second, you're right, Richard isn't pleased about getting married, but his aversion has nothing to do with you. My son has a real distaste for being told what to do. He is a leader of men because he's not good at being led. He's incapable right now of realizing what benefits a marriage to you may produce. All he sees is that a marriage between the two of you was not of his choosing. Such an arrangement makes him angry and resentful."

Her eyes welled with unshed tears.

"I'm aware you've held him in your heart for years."

She looked away.

"You were right to choose him. He's a good man, a strong man, but he's also very stubborn. Right now, his judgment is skewed. I believe fate has brought you together for a reason. You were meant to be united."

She hung on his every word.

Lord Weston leaned close and placed a hand on her bent knees. "Because this union isn't of his choosing, he'll build up walls to protect himself from feeling anything for you. He'll convince himself that any entanglement with you is wrong because he was ordered into it. He'll blame you for his circumstances. He'll try to keep you out of his affections. You'll need to chip away at his defenses."

"How am I supposed to do this when I am left behind after we … marry?" her voice came out hoarse with emotion.

"Well, if you tell me you truly want him as your husband, I'll make sure you're not left behind. It may be dangerous, but I can persuade him to take you with him on his journey. He'll protect you. Granted, he'll not be happy with your company, but it will give him time to accept the marriage." Lord Weston smiled at her, his eyes now twinkling with intrigue.

"I do not know how to make him like me," she declared. Then added shyly, "or want me for a wife."

"My dear, be yourself and he'll have no choice. If he is mean, chastise him. If he's rude, rebuke him. If pleasant, smile at him. If he teases you, tease him back. All you have to do is make sure you are constantly in his thoughts."

She nodded in understanding.

"It saddens me that your father won't be here to see you marry my son."

"I miss them and feel guilty for their deaths."

"Do not. It's not your burden to bear."

She wiped away a lone tear. "I would be honored if you would take my father's place by my side. I think he would be pleased. I know I would."

"Consider it so." Lord Weston leaned forward and kissed her on the forehead.

Hope pushed its way through her despair. She made a silent vow to see things through to the end. Elizabeth's words came to mind, *if you want someone to share your life, you will have to be strong and fight for the life you want.* She had always wanted a life with Richard. For years, he had been all she dreamed of until finally their coming together seemed too far out of reach.

Now she had hope.

"I will do anything I have to do to make this work," she said, sealing her fate.

"Good, I prayed you would agree." Lord Weston gave her an affectionate pat on her shoulder.

"Now, where do we start?" she asked breathlessly.

~Chapter Ten~

An hour later, Lord Weston retrieved Katherine from her room and escorted her beyond the castle walls. They walked at a brisk pace in complete silence, both too nervous for friendly banter. More than anything, she was thankful for the elder's company, his presence was reassuring.

Her vows to Richard would be exchanged on the steps of the little stone church in the village where Lord Weston married his wife, Lady Sarah.

There was no need for her mantle this morning, as the sun's sparkling rays sent kisses of warmth upon her skin. She wore Elizabeth's burgundy velvet surcoat, with a light pink kirtle peeking out from beneath. The gown's scooped neckline flaunted the rounded curves of her breasts. She prayed the bold style drew attention to her womanliness, for she didn't want Richard to think of her as a child.

On her hips sat her decorated girdle, and from the belt, her mother's jeweled dagger hung from its sheath against her side. Her hair was swept up in a graceful style, courtesy of Flora, who had a knack with disorderly locks. She dared not imagine what kind of rosy glow must be illuminating her delicate features; her cheeks were aflame.

Outside Stamford's gates, William's knights and Sir Peter stood at the bottom of the church steps. Villagers gawked, curious about the ceremony they were not invited to attend. The priest's robes settled tautly around his girth as he stood on the top landing in front of the thick wooden door, waiting for Katherine to cross the yard on Lord Weston's arm.

She hadn't laid eyes on or spoken to Richard since last night's meal. The betrothal contracts were signed with only Lord Weston as a witness. She wasn't sure how her future husband would receive her.

As the church rose before her, she spotted him leaning against the handrail, on the top step. A quiver of panic surged through her veins. Her confident demeanor almost faltered.

Richard glanced her way and ran stiff fingers through his dark, wavy locks. Dressed in his black leather surcoat and high thigh boots, he struck a commanding stance. She studied his handsome profile.

Her heart skipped a beat; here was a man who stood above the rest. Marriage to him was what she dreamed of, had wished for as long as she could remember.

Lord Weston guided her up the risers to join her hand in Richard's. She presented her soon-to-wed husband with a gentle smile, but he would have none of it. In return, he gave her an icy glare attached to frosty indifference that sent shivers down her spine.

Obviously, he didn't share her pleasure. He held her small hand coldly in his larger one and stared straight ahead at the priest, avoiding any more eye contact.

Katherine concentrated on the priest's words. Away from the hostility radiating from her future husband. She wanted this union to work with all her heart, but doubted her ability to change a man who now held her in such low regard.

She closed her eyes. *God, please bless this marriage.*

***

Richard was in a foul mood to be sure. He hadn't been in his right mind since he rescued Katherine in the woods. His whole life changed because of one small woman-child.

Who was she to upset the course he had so carefully laid? As his own man, he always made his own decisions. Then, she calls out for help, and everything changes. His traitorous horse was all over her. He's ordered into an unwanted marriage. William's men go against his wishes and come to witness the ceremony. Then, Peter also shows up for this mockery.

Damn her!

Damn her for appearing so at ease and satisfied with this turn of events. She probably intended this all the time. How he resented marrying her, just to keep her safe. Damn her for looking so pleasing to the eye…all dressed up in her finery, every bit, the lady.

The sooner he reclaimed Rosemont, the sooner he could travel to London and have this farce dissolved.

The priest jolted him out of his thoughts when the man cleared his throat, looking for a response. He regained his wit and returned to the task at hand.

"I receive you as mine, so you become my wife and I your husband," he said in a clear, dispassionate voice.

"And I receive you as mine, so you become my husband and I your wife," she countered in an emotionally charged tone, her voice soft and feminine.

He cringed inwardly when the musical words passed over her tongue. Her long dark lashes floated lazily over bright blue eyes. His throat constricted, making it hard to breathe. A sense of dread pressed in around him.

The priest held up the Weston family ring and blessed the wide jeweled band. Richard took his mother's ring from the short, rotund priest and held Katherine's fine-boned hand in front of him.

He placed the ring on her thumb and said, "In the name of the Father," slid the band off and placed it on her next finger, "in the name of the Son," removed the ring yet again and placed onto her middle finger, "and of the Holy Spirit, Amen."

A tight knot formed in the center of his stomach.

***

Katherine watched Richard carefully, wishing for a morsel of encouragement, just some small gesture showing hope of a good life together.

When none was forthcoming, a slow, disappointed breath escaped her slightly parted lips.

At the end of the ceremony, the small party climbed the stairs and entered the church. The couple stood under a canopy while the priest performed the nuptial mass.

She received no comforting looks from Richard, but Lord Weston, who stood at her side, was generous with his. More than once the older man squeezed her arm reassuringly.

The priest's words sounded far away. She fingered the beautiful jeweled ring, newly positioned on her hand, and prayed she'd be as happy in marriage as Lady Sarah. She mused over her parents' marriage. Without a doubt, she knew they found love. That was the reason her father clung to her so strongly after her mother died, he was afraid to lose her, too.

She spared a sideway peek at Richard. His brows were furrowed. His face a mask of stone.

Close to the end of mass, she noted the priest neglected to transfer the Kiss of Peace to the groom, who would've transferred it onto the bride at the appointed time. The little round priest appeared uncomfortable about the slight. Wringing his hands, he gaped at Richard questioningly. It seems, her new husband asked to leave out a few elements of their marriage ceremony.

She heaved a deep sigh of resignation.

After the nuptial mass, Lord Weston placed a hand upon Richard's shoulder. "I need to speak to you before you depart. Will you wait for me on the steps?"

"As you wish," Richard replied. He eyed his father suspiciously before he exited, leaving her behind.

Lord Weston grabbed her clenched hands. "Katherine, my dear, I want to welcome you to the family, daughter."

"I hope I can make you proud."

"Oh, my dear. I'm already proud, and I'm sure your father would be also. Not too many women would've been able to bear my son's hostility quite so well." Lord Weston's tone was filled with awe and respect.

"Well, I must say, he can be a bit intimidating."

"Unfortunately, his anger may get worse before it gets better. He's known to hold a grudge for a long time." Lord Weston shook his head. "I want you to hurry to the stables. There's a pretty little spotted-gray mare waiting for you. I purchased her from a man in the next village. He swears she has a great heart and is thoroughly sound. She runs like the wind. I planned to give her to you as a gift on my next visit, since your sweet Molly passed away. Now she's my wedding present to you on this special day."

"Oh, thank you. What a wonderful gift." She opened her arms wide and hugged him.

"I wish I could do more. I had your things packed and brought to the stables. There's an extra set of clothes stuffed in your bag, the ones we discussed. I'll inform Richard he has to take you with him on his journey. He'll not be happy, so don't expect much. You better be on your horse and ready to leave when he storms over to the stables. The ride will be brutal. Look to Sir Marcus and

William's men for support. They've shown by their actions today that they hold you in high regard and don't care if they provoke Richard's displeasure. William's men will keep you safe."

Lord Weston lifted her chin. "Remember, if something goes awry, and I pray nothing does, you will always have a home here with me."

"Thank you."

He grabbed her head between his big wrinkled hands and placed a kiss on her forehead. "God be with you."

She mustered a hopeful smile. "And also with you."

Katherine spun about and hurried down the aisle toward the open door. When she stepped out on the landing, she raised a hand to block out the bright morning sun.

Richard stood at the bottom of the stairs waiting impatiently for his father. His face was stiff and taut. He had his arms crossed over his expansive chest as he leaned against the rail. A bent leg rested on a step, while his boot tapped incessantly on the stone riser.

She stroked her mother's dagger, took a deep breath of courage, lowered her gaze, and raced past him down the stairs. Afraid he would question her destination, she dared no more than a sidelong peek. Once she was safely by, she made haste toward the stables, knowing she left a perplexed husband behind.

***

"There is no other way," Lord Weston said.

"You have to be mad. I'm not taking her with me. This is not an afternoon ride. This is a siege. A battle will likely ensue. People will die," Richard growled.

Lord Weston went nose to nose with his son and didn't back down. "Exactly. What I suggest will keep the death toll at a minimum. Katherine is the only one who can lead you directly to the opening of the passage."

"I won't do it. I refuse to take her with me. She's just a child. I can't be responsible for her welfare. She belongs here with you," Richard bellowed.

"You're wrong, she's a woman full-grown and capable of performing this task. Stop letting your pride cloud your senses. Don't risk the lives of your men because you don't want to be burdened. I thought you were a better man than that." He shook his head in feigned disappointment.

Lord Weston knew his last words cut deep. His son considered himself a good man, always putting the lives of his men first. Richard would question the truth of the words spoken.

"Ugh!" Richard grabbed his head and squeezed.

Relief surged through Lord Weston's body; he took a cleansing breath.

"I don't like this one bit." Richard dropped his arms to his sides. "She better keep up. I won't show her extra courtesies. She'll have to tough it out."

Lord Weston nodded in agreement. He had won this battle; he also knew more battles were to come. At some level, he felt sorry for his son; the poor boy couldn't yet fathom what last night's impassioned vow, of not consummating his marriage, would cost.

He smiled smugly to himself as he headed to the stables to let Katherine in on the good news. Richard didn't have a chance.

***

Katherine had no trouble finding her wedding present in the stables. Her new palfrey was in a stall, tacked with a new hand-carved leather saddle and bridle. Her bags, mantle, and water flask were already attached.

The young gray had a sweet personality and affectionately mouthed the palm of her hand. The mare's muzzle was as soft as velvet. Katherine fell in love with the horse instantly. She ran her hands along the animal's sleek lines, over the dainty legs, and through her silky, dark gray mane. The horse was bred for speed.

She wished she had time to take her out for a fast run. Instead, she led the animal outside to a small box, stepped on top and climbed onto the saddle.

A mounted Marcus gave her an inquiring look. She shrugged and smiled innocently, causing Marcus to roll his eyes and shake his head. His dark green orbs twinkled with merriment as his face brightened into a broad, white-toothed grin.

"This should be an interesting journey. I'm glad I was not made to miss it," Marcus said with a chuckle of pleasure.

She shot him what she hoped was an impish look.

Lord Weston came to stand next to her mare and patted the palfrey's neck. "Everything is set. Are you sure you're ready to go through with this?"

"As ready as I will ever be." She trembled when the weight of his question hit her.

"How do you like your wedding present?"

"Oh, I love her. She is the most beautiful animal I have ever laid eyes on. I cannot wait to get her out in an open field and give her some freedom. I bet she can fly."

"All in due time, my dear," Lord Weston chortled. He grabbed her small hand in his larger one and gently kissed the top. "Good luck, Lady Katherine Weston. Be safe."

When Lord Weston retreated, some of her bravado disappeared, especially when she spotted Richard heading in her direction with nostrils flaring. Lord Weston's prophecy was correct; Richard's mood was foul, and he was furious.

Being forewarned, she prepared herself to withstand his disapproval.

Richard's jaw tightened. His sapphire eyes narrowed into angry slits when he saw her sitting atop her new mount.

"A gift from your father," she offered, leaving out the word *wedding* so as to not irritate him further.

Richard stood at her horse's side. He glared at her. "I will tell you now; I am not pleased. I do not want you along, nor will I let you slow us down. Keep up, or I'll leave you behind."

"I will be no trouble," she promised.

Richard let out a loud snort of disbelief as he strode to his stallion. He grabbed Titan by the mane and effortlessly swung himself into his saddle. He galloped to the front of the group, turned to the mounted knights and men-at-arms waiting in the yard, unsheathed his sword, pointed the blade to the heavens and shouted, "We ride!"

The men let out a unified cheer, raised their weapons high above their heads, and fell in behind as he led them in a canter over the drawbridge and down the road.

Katherine was not asked to ride at Richard's side, where a wife would've been positioned. Instead, she found herself behind his personal knights, eating their dust, well aware of the meaningful slight. William's knights, Marcus, Owen, Miles, and Godfrey, chose to ride with her, one in front, one in back and one on each side.

For their company, she was thankful, and although the men said little as they rode, their presence alone was comforting. Richard was right about their pace being fast. Her young palfrey had to step lively to keep up with the huge warhorses.

Their journey began on the dirt road, but before long the whole party headed into the woods. When she asked Marcus about their change of course, he explained that an army of men such as theirs would draw too much attention on the road and alert Lord Seton to their approach. By traveling under the cover of the woods, their journey was slower, but they could maintain their element of surprise. The carts carrying their supplies took the road with a few men for protection and would meet them at nightfall.

A little after noon the warm sun vanished behind dark clouds. She donned her fur-lined mantle to ward off the nip in the air. Soon thereafter, a light mist spilled down upon the travelers. She pulled on her hood, grateful for its protection. As the early afternoon progressed, the rain fell faster. The wind blew. Her palfrey had a hard time finding firm footing. The massive chargers ahead of her horse tore up the ground, and once the dirt mixed with pooling water, the path turned into mud.

Still, she did her best to urge her mare on, too afraid to fall behind.

Then the unthinkable happened. While crossing a shallow but wide stream, her horse's small hooves sucked deep in the churned-up bottom. As her mare squealed in terror and fought to pull her slender legs out of the muck, Katherine jumped off, landing knee-deep in the cold running water.

Ignoring the rushing current swirling her garments around her legs, she reached out to soothe the frightened animal, afraid her mare might panic and break a leg. Marcus and Miles joined her in the stream. They worked together to help the animal out of the deep mud.

After they had freed her mare, Miles led her horse up a grassy bank on the other side while Marcus wrapped his arm around her waist and made sure she traveled through the water safely. Owen went to halt the riders ahead.

As Marcus held her horse still, she inspected the animal for injuries. Expertly, she ran frozen hands over her mare's fine-boned, mud-covered legs. When she came to the right front fetlock, she applied pressure and wasn't surprised when her horse pushed her away. The tender area was already swollen. She grabbed the reins, patted the animal's silky neck and whispered soothing words into her mare's ear.

Marcus took his turn examining her palfrey. When he laid his big hands around the swelling, the mare stamped her foot in protest. He straightened. "Lead her around, so we can tell how bad the injury is."

She led her horse in a wide circle around Marcus.

"Your horse appears only slightly lame. I wouldn't ride her for the rest of the day. She'd heal better if she carried no weight, but the saddle on her back. We still have a way to go before we stop for the night."

Katherine let out a quick sigh of relief. There would be no lasting damage.

"Sir Marcus," she said timidly, "would you see her well-tended to? I hold her dear and I would not care to see her injured further."

"I would be honored, my lady."

Branches snapped as Richard and Titan pushed their way through the brush. "What's going on here? Why have you stopped?"

Katherine stared up at him through the driving rain. She opened her mouth to explain, but Marcus cut her off.

"Your wife's mare's front legs sunk in the mud after the warhorses stirred up the stream. If she had been at your side, such wouldn't have happened." Marcus's green eyes blazed with disapproval. "Now the animal is lame and shouldn't be ridden."

The two men stared at each other without so much as a word between them until Richard finally turned away.

Without warning, Marcus grabbed Katherine gently about her waist and lifted her up to sit in front of Richard. "Lady Katherine rides with you now." His tone left no room for argument.

The giant man turned and grabbed the mare's reins. While leading the young animal back to his horse, he said over his shoulder, "I'll take charge of your horse's healing."

Marcus had left Richard no other course but to return to the head of the group, newly burdened with her, his unwanted passenger.

~Chapter Eleven~

Katherine huddled deeper into her wool mantle. Richard's displeasure with being forced to ride double was obvious. A painful silence formed like a wall between them. She assumed nothing she could say would ease his annoyance, so she said nothing at all. Arms that once held her kindly were distant and tense, offering no warmth. On the occasion when his chest brushed against her back, it was hard and unyielding, a stark contrast to her own softness.

To protect her bare skin from the driving rain, she lowered her head and pulled her hood down over her face. She tucked her arms beneath her cloak and rubbed her numb hands and fingers against the soft fur lining.

Because she had plunged knee-deep into the cold water, her ankle boots were soaked through to her feet. The bottoms of her gowns and cloak had received the same fate and were heavily weighted. Sitting astride as she was, the sodden materials followed a frosty path to her thighs. Her stockings were like icicles against her legs. Under her mantle, she hugged her arms tighter to her chest.

I've never been so cold.

As the miles sped by, she willed herself not to complain. Even though utterly chilled, she refused to show her new husband weakness. She wouldn't validate his belief that she should've been left behind. Instead, she passed the time praying they would stop and light a fire. She planned to warm herself in front of the flames and could only imagine how wonderful the heat would feel against her icy face.

Before dusk, a horse trotted up beside them.

"When do you intend to stop for the night? The men are grumbling." Marcus's deep voice barely cut through the endless pelts of rain.

"We'll stop when I say," Richard snapped and urged his horse forward at a faster pace.

Katherine glanced up to take note of Marcus's reaction to Richard's tone, and her hood slid back, partially uncovering her face. Marcus studied her for a moment. A look of pure rage distorted the older man's features.

Surprised by such fury, she recoiled against Richard's chest and bit down hard on her trembling lower lip. The knight's anger stunned her so much she allowed herself to shiver.

***

Richard was taken aback when Marcus kicked his destrier forward and reined the animal sharply into Titan's path. Forced to halt, his horse threw his head in protest.

"What's the matter with you?" he shouted while calming his mount.

"It's I who should ask the same question of you. Are you so cold-hearted you do nothing when your wife is freezing? Look at her. Do you not see her lips are blue and her teeth chatter? Are you so determined to get out of your marriage that you would let Lady Katherine die?"

What was Marcus talking about? Die? Granted, Richard deliberately pushed on to make her uncomfortable. He wanted to punish her for coming along and interfering in his future. It never occurred to him that her life could be in danger. She gave him no sign of trouble. No complaints.

Richard peered at the top of her covered head. He grabbed the front of her hood and yanked the wool back, uncovering her golden hair. With the tips of his fingers, he tilted her chin up and gazed down at his new wife's face.

A ragged breath caught in his throat. Marcus's observation was correct. Her lips were blue, teeth were clacking, and gray rings circled sunken eyes, making her pale skin as colorless as ash.

Her glassy blue eyes glared at him defiantly before she swatted his hand away. He let his arm drop heavily to his side.

"I am fine," she said in a raspy voice. "A little cold. With a bit of warmth from tonight's fire, all will be well."

He stared wide-eyed at Marcus.

She pulled her hood back over her head with mud-dried hands and looked straight ahead. "Nothing to be concerned about."

"I didn't know. I was blinded by my anger," Richard said softly to Marcus. He took up the sides of his mantle and wrapped his arms protectively around her small body.

"What will you do, my friend?" Marcus asked.

"The warmth from an outside fire won't be enough. The Copper Stallion Inn is only a few miles away. I'll take Owen, Godfrey, and Miles; we'll find rooms for the night. Call them forward." He turned Titan around and scanned the column of men who had halted behind them.

Marcus signaled William's knights forward. "Peter and I will set up camp in that clearing ahead."

"We'll meet you tomorrow. Don't wait for our return. We'll find you."

William's knights joined them at the front of the line.

"We ride!" Richard bellowed as he reined Titan away from the main body of men and led the three knights through the dense underbrush at a ground-eating gallop. Since Katherine voiced no complaints, he guessed she was in full agreement.

The riders arrived at the small village in no time. As they made their way to the inn situated in the center of town, the group slowed their pace to a brisk walk. William's knights formed a half-circle around Titan, the palms of their hands resting on the hilts of their swords.

He halted in front of the Copper Stallion Inn. It was a large, two-story, timber and clay building with a tightly thatched roof. A crooked sign hung over the entrance beckoning weary travelers to step inside. Two horses tethered to a nearby post appeared miserable in the driving rain and stood quietly with their heads hung low.

Katherine's body trembled in his arms. He hoped for a quick trip to a bedchamber with heat. "Owen, see that we'll not be in the company of Lord Seton's men."

Owen alighted from his destrier and went inside. A moment later, the knight returned to the open doorway. "All clear."

Richard cradled Katherine in his arms and dismounted in one swift motion.

"Put me down. I can walk on my own," she said through clicking teeth.

"No," he said, climbing the stone steps.

"I said, put me down." His wife squirmed in his arms. "I will not allow you to carry me in there like a child. I will not stand for it."

Richard held her tighter, ignoring her protest. On the landing, he turned back to Miles who stood at the bottom of the steps holding their mounts' reins. He tilted his head toward the stable next door. "See the horses bedded down for the night." He whirled around and stepped through the doorway.

Katherine kicked her legs in midair. "Did you hear me? I said put me down."

"No," he said sharply. "You'll be carried. You're to stay hidden under your hood and not say a word. Do you understand?"

"Yes," she replied, her body relaxing in his arms.

"Good, I don't care to discuss this again." He alone was responsible for her welfare and would see her safe, whether she liked it or not.

Owen moved farther into the darkened inn, Richard followed, and Godfrey brought up the rear. On such a dreary night, the lantern-lit room was filled with travelers and villagers taking respite near the big open hearth. As a friendly serving girl refilled ale mugs, her peals of laughter rang out, setting a cheery tone. The aromas of simmering chicken stew and fresh-baked loaves of bread watered his mouth, and his stomach grumbled in anticipation.

Suddenly, the mood in the room turned somber. The friendly din quieted. Curious heads turned to consider the three large knights walking through the gloomy tavern. The crowd's reaction was expected. With such a formidable group of strangers in their midst, an air of distrust swirled around the taproom, but the trepidation worked in his favor; it kept the patrons at a wary distance.

He spied the innkeeper standing behind the serving bar and headed his way. "Good sir, we require two rooms, side by side, preferably one with a fire already burning, as my wife is overly chilled."

"Is she not well?" the innkeeper questioned. The man pitched forward to get a better look but quickly backed off when met with three sets of glaring eyes.

"Just cold."

"I have two rooms upstairs at the end of the hall on the right. The last bedchamber's fire throws heat as we speak." The innkeeper took two lit lanterns off the bar top and handed one to Owen and one to Godfrey.

"Those rooms will do us well," he said. Then added, "We'll require a meal, with pitchers of ale and mead."

Owen went up the stairs first, carrying one of the lanterns. Richard followed on his heels, then stopped at the bottom step and hailed the innkeeper. "I'll also need the services of a servant girl to take care of our wet garments."

"I'll see it done, milord," the innkeeper replied, obviously hoping for a big reward at the end of their stay.

Richard took the stairs two at a time, unburdened by the weight of his wife in his arms. He followed Owen to the last room at the end of the hall and waited outside the door as the knight entered the bedchamber, set the lantern down on the bedside table, and returned to the hallway.

He faced his men. "Two men rest and one stays on a chair outside our doors. Relieve each other every three hours."

"Yes, sir," the knights responded in unison.

"And don't drink too much ale," he added with a hint of good humor.

"Oh, don't ruin it for me. Food, ale, bed, and a warm fire. What more could one want on a wet night such as this?" Owen interjected lightheartedly.

"I think you're getting soft, my friend. It must be your easy living with William," Richard teased, causing the men to chuckle. He made his way into his bedchamber and shut the door with his foot.

"You can put me down now," Katherine chattered.

"If you insist." Richard placed her gently on a soft chair. He hung his mantle on a peg by the door and made his way to the hearth. By adding a few logs and poking the embers, he coaxed the flames to a good height.

"Come, warm yourself by the fire," he beckoned.

Katherine took down her hood and struggled to stand. Once upright, she shuffled to the hearth at a slow pace, her legs moving as if she had lead weights attached to her ankles. When she was close to the heat, she held her fingers over the flames and rubbed them together in a frenzied fashion. Her teeth clacked non-stop. The more she fought to control the chatter, the louder they clicked.

He didn't like the way she hovered over the fire, her face pale and drawn.

"Get out of those wet clothes and wrap up in this." He yanked a blanket off the bed and laid the coverlet over the back of the chair. "I'll take your garments when you're done and have the maid dry them out. I'm off to see to our meal and will return shortly." He gave her his back and left the room.

***

Katherine stood in front of the fire, too afraid to move far from its warmth. She pressed her jaws tightly closed and toiled at untying the soaked cords on her cloak. No matter how hard she tried, her numb fingers fumbled unsuccessfully with the knot, failing to undo the braided strands.

Overwhelmed by the task, she placed her hands on the stone ledge above the hearth and laid her forehead on top of them. Propped in such a position, she stood helplessly immobile while she savored the heat of the flames against the front of her body.

"What's the matter? I thought you'd be further along," Richard said.

She startled at his voice. Her head jerked around toward the door.

He placed food and drinks on a small table.

"I cannot untie my mantle," she whispered.

"Is that all?" Richard came to stand by her side. He turned her from the hearth, retrieved her short dagger from her girdle and cut the braid next to the knot, releasing the strands from their hold against her neck.

"Oh, no," she cried, grabbing the severed end. "How will I tie the cords tomorrow?"

He shrugged. "I'll have the maid sew the braid back on."

"I cannot…believe…you did that," she exclaimed, shocked by his brashness. A shiver wracked her body. She took the mantle off her shoulders and tossed the heavy, wet garment onto a nearby chair.

"It's off, is it not?" His eyes twinkled as he held the dagger menacingly in the air. "Now, is there something else you would like me to help you with?"

She crossed her arms over her chest, protecting her new clothes. "I do not think your help will be necessary. I can manage myself."

"Then stop tarrying and finish undressing. The sooner you get out of those soaked clothes, the sooner you can get warmed, and the sooner I can work on getting them dry."

She straightened her back. "I would move quicker without you gawking at me."

He laid her dagger on the top of the ledge and devoured her with his eyes. "Milady, you have much more to worry about than me gawking at you. If you don't get a move on, and I don't see you put a little more effort into the task, I may be tempted to see the job well done."

Her cheeks burned at his suggestion that he would unclothe her right then and there until she noticed the smirk forming on his lips. He was just having fun.

"Look here, see how well I am doing on my own. I will not need any help from the likes of you." She quickly used her numb fingers to undo her girdle and placed the weighted belt on the back of the chair.

"As you wish. I could've been a great help, had you but asked," he said, his eyes bright with mischief.

"No need to trouble yourself." She stepped behind the high-backed chair.

Richard scooped up their mantles. "I'll deliver these to the maid and get you a few more quilts. The way your teeth keep chattering I think you'll need them."

At the door, he turned. "Just a warning, if your soaked clothes are not removed and you are not wrapped in that blanket when I return, you will have left me no choice but to assist you."

He shut the heavy door with too much force, causing a loud bang.

Katherine glared at the closed door. Finally, he was gone. How dare he goad her into action when all she wanted to do was rest in a bubble of heat in front of the flames.

Her heart sped up a few beats. The memory of his veiled warning sent a wave of warmth pulsing through her body, depositing a ball of fire in the pit of her stomach. When a noisy sigh escaped her lips, she realized she longed for something she knew nothing about. Worried he would return too soon and catch her at an awkward moment, she made haste to do his bidding.

She loosened the cords on her burgundy surcoat until the weighted garment dropped like a sack of potatoes to the floor. Her pink kirtle was next; she had to undo more laces before she could pull her arms out of the tight-fitting sleeves. Once the undergarment was free of her shoulders, she dropped it so it landed in a heap on top of the first gown. Next, she doffed her soft linen chemise and let it plummet with the rest of her clothing onto the rough wooden boards. Finally, she unpinned her damp hair, shook her head and her locks cascaded to her waist.

Afraid to be caught unaware by Richard's return, she grabbed the blanket and wrapped it around her body. She needed more than a blanket warmth. She hauled the chair as close to the flames as she dared and perched on the edge of the seat. In this position, she was able to untie her garters and roll her silk stockings down to her ankles. The wet, cold skin on her legs prickled from the warm air. She sat back into the chair and brought each leg up to rest on the edge.

Once situated, she reached forward to untie her short leather ankle boots, but the sodden leather cord made the task impossible. Exhausted, she tugged the blanket tight around her body, laid her head against the back of the padded chair, and closed her eyes in surrender.

***

Richard walked into the bedchamber to find Katherine curled in a ball on a chair by the fire with the coverlet bound tightly about her small frame. Her teeth persistently clacked. A few feet away, her drenched garments were heaped in a pile. He spied her shoes peeking out from under the blanket.

When he gazed upon her face, his breath caught in his throat. He'd never seen anything so lovely. Her glorious, golden hair that had been pinned so perfectly atop her head earlier in the day was now loose and flowing, making her appear strikingly beautiful in the light of the fire's flames.

It took a great deal of self-control to stop staring at his wife. He raked his fingers through his hair. It was up to him to take care of her. He made his way to the table and poured a cup of mead.

When he brought her the drink, her lashes opened slowly. She stared at him with dull, hollow eyes. He experienced an uncomfortable pang of guilt. Squatting down, he put the cup in an open hand lying in her lap.

"Drink this; you'll feel better." He helped guide the rim to her trembling lips. Big jewel-like eyes, framed by long black lashes, studied him warily as she gulped the warm sweet-smelling liquid. When the contents were gone, he reclaimed the empty cup. With the side of his thumb, he gently brushed away a drop of mead from her lips.

"Do I dare ask why you're still wearing your boots?"

"I could not get them off. The laces are knotted."

"Let me take a look." Richard pulled up the other chair, situated it across from her, and took a seat. He put her sopping wet boots and cold legs in his lap. His clumsy oversized fingers groped at the swollen cords, but he had no luck loosening the knots. "They're good and stuck."

She watched him with rapt attention while swaddled like an infant in her blanket.

"I'll have to cut the knot to get them off," he said.

She nodded, obviously too worn out to voice any discord.

He took his dagger from its sheath and sliced a lace on each boot. Once the knot was gone, the boots were removed with little difficulty. Next, he rolled down the drenched stockings. Finding her skin cold, moist and clammy, he rubbed vigorously, in an attempt to bring back some warmth.

She had beautiful legs, muscular, but proportioned to her size. The task was very pleasurable, especially when she wiggled with troubled unease. Not willing to break his vow, he quickly released her legs to tuck under the blanket.

"Would you like something to eat? We have chicken stew and bread," he offered.

"I just want to lie down," she whispered, her eyes were glazed with drink and her lids were heavy with exhaustion.

"I want you near the fire tonight." Richard stepped behind her chair and dragged her away from the hearth. He was quick to note her disgruntled look when her heat was taken away but dismissed her annoyance. What he had in mind would eventually add to her comfort.

He went around the room and gathered her discarded clothes, including her shoes and stockings. He stacked the pile of wet clothing by the door. Moving to the bed, he hauled the feather tick mattress off the rope bed frame and laid the pallet on the floor in front of the flames. On top of the mattress, he threw goose feather pillows and a few wool blankets.

"Now, you'll have all the heat you desire," he promised.

She granted him a small smile of gratitude. Enveloped from neck to toes in her blanket, she walked with cautious tiny steps to the over-stuffed mattress. Once she stood at the foot of the newly made bed, she bent her knees and let her body fall like a log onto the soft pallet. Facing the flames, she adjusted the pillow under her head and curled up into a small ball.

"I apologize for causing you such trouble," she said through trembling lips. "I never intended to be a burden. Thank you for your assistance."

Her soft-spoken words of apology made his stomach sour. He was well aware of how poorly he had treated her today. The only reason she was in this perilous situation was because of his actions. He behaved no better than Lord Seton. He purposefully caused her pain.

Perhaps he didn't use a whip, but he did try to hurt her through harsh words, anger, indifference, and hardship. He was ashamed of himself for trying to make her suffer for marrying him. He could've accidentally killed her. Had Marcus not spoken up, things might have turned out much differently.

"Get some rest." He took extra quilts and threw them over his new wife, tucking them in around her.

A timid knock sounded on the door. He opened it to the young maid he had spoken to earlier. She bowed and waited to do his bidding.

"Can you have these garments dried by tomorrow morning?" He gathered Katherine's clothes and handed the young girl the bundle.

"Yes, m'lord. Even if I have ta stay up all night turning them," she replied, keeping her eyes downcast.

"Very good. You'll be well rewarded."

The maid bowed and left the room.

Richard stuck his head out in the hall. Owen sat upon a wooden chair outside their bedchamber. He nodded a quick goodnight to the knight and closed the door. A loud growl from his stomach reminded him that he had not broken his fast in many hours. He went to the table and helped himself to a bowl of stew and a few mugs of ale.

Since the fire was dying, he stacked on more logs. The flames grew to a roaring height. With one good blow, he extinguished the lantern and undressed by the light from the hearth, then hung his clothes near the fire to dry. He positioned his sword and dagger on the floor within easy reach.

Richard sat down next to the small mound of blankets covering his wife from head to toe and stretched out lengthwise. As he lay on his side, facing her back, he grabbed the top blanket and pulled the wool over his nakedness.

Up on one elbow, he leaned over her shoulder and inspected her closely. She was fast asleep. Her breathing was rhythmic but heavy. No more chattering teeth. The coverings were tucked under her chin. He swept a damp tendril from her heated face. Long dark lashes rested lazily against the newly rose-colored skin. He rearranged her hair and slipped a big arm under her head. His other arm wrapped around her little body and he drew her close to benefit from his warmth.

Then he prayed.

He prayed to God that she would sustain no ill effects from her chill and berated himself for his foolishness. When his mind finally found peace, he fell asleep with the sweet scent of lavender tickling his nose.

~Chapter Twelve~

Katherine awoke in a mindless fog. With the back of her hand, she rubbed the sleep from her eyes and sat up slowly from the soft pallet on the floor in front of the hearth. Vaguely, she remembered the weight of Richard's brawny arm draped over the curve of her waist, but couldn't decide if the pleasurable memory was real, or just a dream. The fire had burned down to a mound of glowing embers, though the room, thankfully, still held its warmth.

It took a moment to sort out why she found herself on the floor in a strange room. When last night's memories returned, she quickly glanced around to make sure she was indeed alone. Relief soon turned to horror when she noticed the quilt fanning out around her only scantly covered her naked body. Arms, legs, and much more were fully exposed. A wave a heat washed over her skin and she rearranged the blankets to hide her more closely guarded parts.

Oh, what a picture she must have presented in her sleep. She quickly brushed aside her humiliation and reminded herself that Richard was now her husband and well within his right to gaze upon her in such a state.

A flash of light drew her attention to the thick gold ring sitting heavily on a slender finger, reminding her of yesterday's events. She lovingly fingered the jeweled piece, admiring the beauty of Lady Sarah's ring. Many times as a child she had watched the gems sparkle in the sunlight and marveled at their brilliance.

The ring was not freely given. A stab of guilt pressed deeply against her heart for having accepted the ring when a less worthy one would've sufficed. Things hadn't gone as well as she had hoped. This was far from the wedding and marriage of her dreams. She couldn't help but be disappointed their first night as man and wife was not as it should've been.

A timid knock made her pull the quilt to her chin. "Enter."

A young maid opened the door and stepped inside. She bowed, her arms burdened by the weight of Katherine's clothes. "M'lady, yer husband sent me ta help ye with yer morning dressing. If ye wish, I can bring up a bowl of warm water so ye may freshen up."

"I would be very grateful," Katherine said.

The servant girl laid the garments on the chair and left.

Because she didn't know if Richard might barge in without warning, she wrapped the blanket loosely around her nakedness before she slowly rose. In the pile of clean, dry clothes, she found her linen chemise and withdrew the garment. Not wanting anyone to catch sight of the binding still wrapped under her breasts and around her back, she slipped the thin material over her head before she discarded her covering.

The light filtering through the hazy windowpanes drew her notice and she stood in front of the window. The rain had stopped, and the early morning sun peeked out expectantly from behind a wayward cloud, its brightness, a welcome sight. Today would be a good day. Her spirits soared.

A soft knock announced the maid's return. The girl set the washbasin on the table with some clean cloths. Katherine hastily plunged her hands into the soapy water and removed a thin layer of grime coating her skin from the day before.

"May I have your name?" she asked.

"Rebecca, m'lady," the girl supplied with a nervous little bow.

"You have a pretty name," she stated, trying to put the girl at ease.

"Thank ye, m'lady. Would ye like me ta help ye with the rest of yer clothes?"

"I would welcome your assistance. I am moving a little slower than usual this morning,"

In a matter of a few minutes, Rebecca helped her dress.

"Well done." Katherine ran her hand down the soft velvet of her surcoat. Affectionately, she readjusted her dagger on a rounded hip. "You did a fine job drying my gowns and shoes. I cannot begin to tell you how uncomfortable I was yesterday in wet clothes."

"My pleasure, m'lady. Yer husband asked me ta give them extra care, making sure yer clothes were completely dried before I returned them."

Her eyes widened in wonder. Richard was concerned about her clothing? Yesterday, she could've sworn he wanted her uncomfortable and miserable. It astounded her that he had shown consideration amid his recent displeasure.

She patted down her wild curls. "I guess the only thing left is to tame my unruly hair."

"Oh, no, m'lady. I've never seen the likes of it before. It's so thick and wavy, like a waterfall of honey. I think your hair 'tis lovely," Rebecca gushed.

"You honor me with your compliment."

Rebecca beamed. "If ye would like, I could braid it fer ye. I thought ta bring a comb." The girl stared at her feet and added, "Just in case."

"I do not know if I have time. My husband probably waits as we speak."

"Yer husband and two of his knights are breaking their fast downstairs in the common room. Another knight waits outside yer door. They don't look ta be in a rush."

"Then maybe it will be fine if we hurry. Something simple." Katherine didn't want to take too long. She didn't want to give Richard any excuse to be angry with her again.

Rebecca made quick work of untangling Katherine's tresses. After smoothing down the curls, the girl parted Katherine's hair down the center, separated each section into a smaller portion, braided each part, one on either side, and joined them together behind her head where the maid then made one long braid down her back, letting the rest of her hair fall free.

When the maid finished, Katherine touched the hair with her fingers.

"Oh, thank you. Now I will not have to worry about my hair flying in my eyes." As an afterthought, she continued, "I wish I had something to give you…to show you how pleased I am, but I have nothing."

Rebecca's face turned various shades of red. "Thank ye, milady, yer husband has been more than generous with me. He wanted me ta make sure ye had everything ye needed."

The girl's statement surprised and pleased Katherine at the same time.

"If that is so, I should be on my way and not keep him waiting."

Rebecca placed the newly dried mantle over Katherine's narrow shoulders. The maid had sewn the cord back on, so Katherine had no problem tying the braids at her neck. She bestowed a warm smile on the servant girl and tipped her head in gratitude before leaving the room.

She almost bumped into Miles, who stood guard outside the door but quickly recovered.

"Good morning, Lady Katherine," the knight said.

"Good morning to you, Sir Miles." She gave him a slight tilt of her head and an amiable smile.

"You look like you're feeling much better this morning."

"Thank you, kind sir. I do feel better."

"Your husband, Owen, and Godfrey are downstairs in the common room awaiting your arrival. The horses are saddled. Ready for our journey. Richard would like you to put up your hood and keep your head down when we walk through the inn. We don't want any attention drawn your way, as we don't want anyone to be able to say "yea" you were here."

Katherine made haste to tuck her loose hair and braid inside the back of her cloak. She pulled her hood over her head and let the drooping sides hide her face.

Satisfied that she was properly covered, Miles escorted her down the stairs. As they reached the main floor, the door to the inn swung open and hit the wall with a loud bang. Into the common room walked two big knights. The men were dressed in full armor, except for their helmets, which they held under their arms.

"Innkeeper. Bring us some food and ale. Now!" one of the knights bellowed while dropping into a wooden chair at a table near the door.

Miles turned to shield her from view and guided her to a seat next to Richard. Miles took his place across from her in full view of the newcomers. She kept her head down, but stole a quick glance at Godfrey and Owen, who gave her slight nods in greeting, then continued to present masks of indifference.

When Richard placed food and mead in front of her, she stared into his sparkling blue eyes. Between his warm manner and diverting smile, she nearly melted under his gaze, until her presence of mind returned and she recognized the seriousness of the moment.

Her hand shook as she brought her mug up to her lips. She sampled a sip of mead. The sweet taste helped to relieve some of her apprehension. More than likely these knights were Lord Seton's men.

A swallow stuck in her throat.

If the knights discovered their prey was within arm's reach, a fight would break out. If something happened to the men in her party because they tried to protect her, she would never forgive herself. Too many had already died.

***

Richard watched the servant girl come out of the backroom carrying a tankard of ale and two mugs. She placed the knights' drinks down on the plank table and hurried away. When she returned with their food, one of the knights blocked her path.

"Girl, we're looking for a yellow-haired lady. No bigger than this tall." The man raised his arm. "She has blue eyes and is fair of face. We'll pay for information. Have you seen her?"

"None around h're like that." The serving girl's expression remained blank. She placed the food on the table and started to walk away, but was stopped short again when the other knight grabbed her wrist and yanked her to him. "What about that woman over there? The one all covered up?" he demanded boldly.

The maid glanced swiftly toward Richard's table and then back at the knight before she spoke. "The lady tis married ta the knight dressed in black. I don't know his name. The woman has dark brown hair and covers her head with her hood to hide a scarred face. She's not the one ye seek." The serving girl tugged at her imprisoned hand and begged, "Please, sir, let me go?"

The knight pushed her away, then warned, "Keep the ale flowing or you'll be sorry."

Richard said to Katherine in a low voice, "As soon as you're through with breaking your fast, we will be on our way."

Her eyes were wide with fright, so he smiled slightly to reassure her.

To Owen and Godfrey, he said loudly, "Stay and drink your fill. Meet us later."

He took a few coins out of his pouch and slid them across the table. His unspoken words and real meaning weren't lost on them. His men nodded in silent understanding.

When she finished her buttered bread and drink, he stood and pulled out her chair. Using his bulk, he took care to shield her from the other knights' prying eyes. Draping a firm arm across her back, he guided her out the front door. Miles followed closely behind.

When they arrived at Titan's side, he grabbed her about her waist, placed her gently onto the back of his horse and hoisted himself up behind. As she positioned herself in the saddle, he noticed she took care to keep her head down and hood in place.

Miles swung up on his horse. Together, the mounted riders walked their steeds out of the village, their pace leisurely.

Once they reached the outskirts, Richard spoke. "You can take your hood down now."

"Do you believe the knights recognized me?" Katherine uncovered her head.

"No, the maid did well covering for you." He couldn't help wondering why. The girl appeared as though she feared her own shadow, then lied bravely to two very dangerous men to protect his wife.

"You do not think Lord Seton's men will change their minds and follow us, do you? Should we make haste?"

"Owen and Godfrey will watch our backs. Those men won't come after us, nor will they tell anyone of our whereabouts. We don't have to worry about them."

***

Katherine marveled at how Richard was so sure of himself. She wanted to question him further, then it dawned on her.

Lord Seton's men were going to die.

More of her innocence drifted away. A clear picture of the men who accompanied her was brought to light. These knights showed no weakness, no mercy when warranted. It's kill or be killed. They draw their swords and defend themselves and their purpose every step of the way. They yielded: power, strength, honor, and when needed… fierceness.

Considering the knights in her company in those terms made her breathless. With them, she was safe and protected.

Silently, she wished her father and brother could've had a few more of their traits. Maybe if they had been different men, their lives wouldn't have ended so soon. If they had been on guard against treachery, they would have still been alive. If they were powerful men, they wouldn't have been targeted. Neither one of them were fighters. Both preferred an oversized chair next to the hearth over a battle. David went to tournaments but seldom participated. Her brother instead socialized with his friends. Even King Edward used him for errands when it was time to pay his dues. They were good men, although not strong or fierce men. She couldn't have changed who they were.

Noiselessly, she let out a soft sigh of defeat.

***

Richard felt Katherine's body mold itself into his chest. "You appear well-rested this morning."

"Oh, do you refer to the fact that I can speak without my teeth chattering?" she said with a hint of amusement. "I have never been so chilled before. I had my doubts I would ever be warm again. Thankfully, I was wrong. It amazes me what a roaring fire and dry clothes can do for a person."

It pleased him that she hadn't lost her ability to make light of potentially serious situations. Her condition yesterday could've easily turned grave had he not acted quickly. It was a good decision to take her to the Copper Stallion Inn, even though exposing her to people put her in danger of being discovered by Lord Seton's men.

Again, he received an uncomfortable stab of guilt for all the hardship he put her through.

As they rode along in silence, his thoughts drifted to this morning in the inn. He'd awoke to find her clutching his muscled arm and pulling it against her soft womanly curves. Her naked legs were intertwined with his, sending quivers of yearning throughout his body. Her ripe lips parted slightly every time she breathed out, and her cheeks were a rosy red from the heat of the fire. Her silky, golden hair lay in disarray around them, releasing subtle hints of a flowery scent. Blankets tossed about in abandon left little to his imagination, and it became quite clear to him his father was right; Katherine was a woman full-grown.

With a keen eye, he had assessed her feminine form and found no imperfections. She was soft, well-rounded, and proportioned ever so perfectly.

He enjoyed waking up with such a beautiful and courageous woman in his arms.

Richard had never experienced this reaction before. Usually, he preferred to sleep alone. His women consisted of camp followers or eager castle servants. He harbored no attachments to those women in his past. No one had stirred his blood longer than a night or two.

He had little knowledge of high-born ladies. As a general rule, noble ladies were trouble, and he avoided them like the plague. That is until he met Lady Alice with her black…or was it brown hair?

It didn't matter. All that mattered is from the moment he set eyes on the young noblewoman's untouched beauty, so like William's wife's loveliness, he knew she was the one he wanted to have by his side. Although Lady Alice didn't seem overly interested at first, she soon changed her mind and was more affable when he mentioned his desire to lease Lord Marten's estate. He wouldn't obtain his father's title, but he had made a good name for himself over the years. With his name and enough wealth, her family wouldn't refuse his advances for a third daughter, especially if he acquired his own estates to run with the king's blessing.

This morning, when Katherine aroused in him a desire he had no intention of feeling, he made haste to untangle himself from her clutches, grabbed his clothes, donned them in a rush, and left the room without delay.

He found himself in jeopardy of losing control. He had to remind himself of Lady Alice, who awaited his return, and his vow to God and his father to not consummate the marriage. Once he arrived in London, he would seek out Lady Alice to confirm his true course and then ask the king to dissolve his rushed union to Katherine. Others petitioned the king in the past. It could be done again.

To see it so, he just had to keep his distance from Katherine. As long as the two of them were in the company of other people, he could maintain good control. That would be his goal, always to make sure someone else was near.

It shouldn't be too hard.

A slight breeze stirred the air and a pleasant scent of lavender drifted on the wind to torment his senses.

Not too hard at all.

He passed a gloved hand below his nose to chase away the aroma. Suddenly, he became acutely aware that his reined hand lay upon a lithe thigh and the rest of her soft curves contoured perfectly against his frame.

He looked up at the forested canopy overhead.

Please, God, give me strength.

The day's light shone down through the newly opening leaves. Closing his eyes, he let the warm rays kiss his face in a hopeful reply.

As they continued, the good weather aided their progress. In no time, the two horses had covered the distance between the village and his men.

As ordered, Peter and Marcus had disbanded their camp and set out in the early morning hours. He rode directly to the front of the long line of men armed for battle and settled in next to his men-in-charge.

"Any trouble?" he inquired.

"None," Peter responded. "We have riders around our main body and the guards report all is quiet. We've seen not a soul."

"We ran into two of Lord Seton's knights this morning at the Copper Stallion Inn. Owen and Godfrey stayed behind to take care of them. As far as I can tell, we remain undetected."

Marcus and Peter nodded.

***

"Lady Katherine, I see you are no worse for the wear," Marcus said cheerfully.

Katherine hung her head and blushed. "I am much better, Sir Marcus."

She spotted her little gray mare on the other side of Marcus's stallion. The muscle-bound charger showed off for her palfrey with a high-stepping prance that had his rider fighting to steady him.

"How does my mare fare? Has the swelling gone down? Will she bear my weight?"

Marcus chuckled. "She's healing nicely. Last night I rubbed her leg down with cold compresses, covered her fetlock in salve, and wrapped the leg. The swelling has receded." He gave Richard a haughty look. "But I still wouldn't recommend you ride her today."

She heard Richard's snort of skepticism.

"Oh," she responded, disappointedly. "I suppose if she is healing nicely, I would not want to chance damaging her further."

"I'll make sure she is well cared for, and as soon as I think she's ready for your weight, I'll let you know. I only hope you are comfortable enough riding with your *husband* until then." Marcus emphasized *husband*, and she knew at once he did it to irritate Richard.

"I will be fine," she assured him. "Please accept my gratitude. I am indebted to you for the care you have taken with my palfrey. You have done a fine job. I am much pleased."

Marcus beamed as he accepted her praise.

Horses cantered up from behind. Men in the ranks called out loud welcomes to the returning Owen and Godfrey. She twisted in the saddle and leaned heavily to one side while she craned her neck around Richard's wide chest to make sure the two knights were unharmed. With his arm held tight against her waist, she had no fear of tumbling to the ground.

She sighed with relief. They looked intact.

"Things went well. No problems," Owen offered, moving his horse beside Titan.

"And the young maid?" Richard asked.

His question provoked her curiosity, and she stared at Owen. Why would her husband ask about Rebecca?

"I tried to give her the extra coins for protecting Lady Katherine, but she didn't want payment. She said she was happy to lie, so no harm would befall such a lady." Owen looked down at Katherine. "She told me to tell you *Godspeed.*"

"How nice."

"And," Richard waited impatiently for Owen to continue.

"And then I insisted she take the coins. I gave her no choice."

"Good." Richard kicked Titan to lengthen his animal's stride.

~Chapter Thirteen~

"Let me help," Richard said, as Katherine wiggled back and forth in front of him on the saddle, pulling the edges of her mantle out from beneath her thighs. Without waiting for a reply, he untied the cord against the curve of her neck, grabbed hold of the opening, and freed the cloak from her shoulders.

Yesterday's chill was long gone and so was his unreasonable umbrage and desire to make her miserable. With barely a whisper of a wind, there was no need for such a heavy garment. He gave the mantle to Marcus to attach to her palfrey's saddle.

As they continued their journey, the distance between Rosemont and his band of men narrowed with every step. Richard had much on his mind, not to say the least were the soft mounds of flesh bulging over the low neckline of her velvet gown. He reminded himself not to look down, but the soft curves of her well-rounded breasts caught his attention time and again and his gaze was drawn to them often.

To keep himself diverted, he reviewed practical courses of action for the upcoming siege but found he was unable to focus on such things. Instead, he tried to picture Lady Alice. A clear image of her was just out of his grasp. Blue eyes and blonde hair came to mind, but he was sure those weren't her colors, yet he couldn't recall the correct ones with any amount of clarity.

Frustrated with himself for his weakening resolve, he urged Titan to pick up the pace so he could finish his task and get to London as quickly as possible.

When the sun sat directly overhead, he halted his group of riders in a large grassy meadow, next to a fast-running stream. Men were sent to scout the tree line for possible danger. Once the area was deemed safe, he stationed guards around their borders. Orders were given to water, feed, and rest the horses.

Richard jumped from Titan and reached for Katherine. She placed the palms of her hands on his shoulders as he helped her down. Sweat broke out on his forehead and his jaw slackened when he found himself face first, inches away from the soft mounds that had taunted him all morning. Quickly, he put her on the ground as if touched by fire.

Marcus let out a loud chuckle, well aware of his plight.

He sent a dirty look in the knight's direction.

"I will be just a moment," he heard his wife say from a good distance away.

He spun in his tracks in time to see her heading toward where the meadow met the edge of the woods. She was looking for privacy. Not wanting to leave her unattended with a whole legion of men less than a hundred feet away, he grudgingly followed at a distance.

Women didn't belong amid men going into battle. Females were too much of a distraction when a man's mind should focus on other things. She disappeared into a thicket, so he halted not too far off. Turning to face his men, he crossed his arms over his chest, spread his legs and dared anyone to venture too close.

A few moments later, the bushes rustled behind him.

"Don't wander too far from me," he stated, gruffer than intended.

Her surprised intake of breath alerted him to the fact she had no idea he was there. Without glancing back, he strode toward his horse, giving her no choice except to follow at a quick pace.

When he reached Titan's side, he loosened the girth, grabbed a sack off the back of the saddle, and let his charger graze on the new shoots of grass with the other horses. He claimed one of the trees by the water's edge and leaned peacefully against the hard bark as he shared his water flask and the food he bought at the inn with his new wife.

***

While Katherine ate, she gazed out over the swiftly moving stream. How she missed her father and David. Visions of fun times with her family on the beach below the castle came to mind. A branch floated by, caught up in the fast-moving current. As the wood ebbed and flowed in the wild water, she brushed aside the rush of emptiness that washed over her.

To chase away her melancholy, she checked on the welfare of her little gray mare, munching on grass close by. She ran her hands up and down the mare's legs, examining her palfrey for injuries, but found none. Her horse stamped her foot with annoyance for being disturbed while she ate, so she patted the animal on the neck and returned to her husband's side.

He ignored her, and she found his behavior frustrating. Marcus and Peter joined Richard after finishing their midday meals. Their talk soon turned to their line-of-attack. Seated on the soft moss under the shade of the tree, she listened while the men openly discussed their ideas.

Finally, she could be silent no more. "Excuse me."

All heads turned her way.

She cringed when Richard glared at her in annoyance. She raised her chin and looked him in the eye. "I could not help overhearing your exchange. I think I might be able to propose a thing or two."

Richard sent her a daunting look. When she didn't back down, he surrendered. "By all means, share your thoughts," he said as if he didn't expect her to say anything worthwhile.

Katherine was up for the challenge. She knew her land better than anyone. Richard extended his hand and she let him help her stand. She swiped her leather boot back and forth over a bare spot on the ground, making a smooth surface and removed her dagger from her girdle. Squatting down, she used the sharp tip to draw a quick map of Rosemont in the soft dirt.

As she spoke, she pointed to various spots on the map. "The castle stands here…situated on the edge of the cliffs. Here…is the village and the tree line. Here…are the fields. The main road runs this direction, away from the cliffs."

She glanced up to find Marcus and Peter engrossed in her demonstration. Richard, on the other hand, appeared preoccupied, his eyes upon her chest.

A wave of warmth heated her skin, but she refused to let him cause her any disquiet and quickly proceeded. "If I understand correctly, we have to find a place to wait out the night. Somewhere we will not be detected, yet close enough to surprise those inside the gates before dawn."

Marcus and Peter nodded.

She turned her attention back to her map. "Secluded a little way from the castle in the woods, fairly close to the cliffs, live the Connor brothers and their families. The twins supply the castle and village with chopped and dried wood. Their homes are situated here." She pointed to a new location.

"They have a big enough clearing next to their cottages for your men and their horses. No one goes out there. They are off any well-used paths and keep to themselves. They were always loyal to my father. If we cross the stream here, sweep around and come in from behind," she said, pointing with the tip of her dagger, "we could make it here…undetected. There is enough room to wait out the night. We would be close, but also, far enough away. 'Tis only a short walk to the cliffs."

She locked eyes with Richard. "I can find the opening and lead your men into the castle unnoticed. If you station half the men here…," she pointed to a spot next to the gate, "and the other half here…, when the gates open, your men-at-arms can be inside in a matter of minutes."

Marcus and Peter stared down at her curiously. She could tell they were considering her idea. Richard would probably try to discredit it in some way.

His jaw tensed and his posture grew rigid. He placed his hands on his tapered hips as he towered over her. She braced herself for one of his tongue lashings.

"What are you talking about?" he roared. "You're not going to lead anybody into the castle. Nobody said you were coming with us. You're just going to point the way. That's all. You'll stand at the side of the cliff and point in the direction of the opening. Leave the fighting to the men."

***

Richard was livid. He couldn't believe it. Is this how Katherine lived her life, always on the edge of danger? Had she no sense? Did she have a death wish? From the moment he rescued her, it seemed as if he had spent almost every other moment protecting her from herself.

His heated words drew forth her ire. She stood with her back straight, her slender hands cupped around her narrow waist, mimicking his posture.

"Did you not hear my idea about taking respite at the Connors? Did you not hear how you could get close to Rosemont without being detected?"

"I believe Lady Katherine has a good proposal. She knows her lands. Our assault hinges on positioning ourselves as close as possible to Rosemont's gates without being detected. I think following her lead will see us successful," Marcus stated.

"I have to agree with Marcus. If what Lady Katherine says is true, it's a firm course of action. We'll have an opportunity to rest the men and horses before we attack. We'll be in a good position," Peter said.

Richard shook his head in disgust at how easily his new wife won over these hardened knights. He glared at her, only to receive a self-satisfied smirk before she sat on the grass. Stretching her legs out in front of her, she arranged her skirts and leaned back on extended arms, displaying her womanly figure to its best advantage.

He scowled; obviously, she waited for him to admit she was right.

Richard wanted to raise his voice in argument if just to release his frustration, but he owed it to his men to weigh her suggestions. He swallowed a hard ball of distaste and put aside his infuriation with his wife. He reviewed her map and paid close attention to each detail. Unfortunately, he liked what she proposed, yet had a hard time admitting her idea was a good one.

The more he thought about it, the more he realized the strategy could work.

All except the part where she put herself in danger. Danger from the rocks on the cliffs. Danger from sneaking through darkened secret passages. Danger from fierce hand-to-hand combat and danger from Lord Seton.

"It's settled. We find the Connors' cottages and wait there until before dawn." He looked at his wife, who was inordinately absorbed in watching the water race by, playing at innocence.

He knew better.

"As for you…" she turned slowly to face him, "…you'll only point the way to the opening, and then be left with the Connors. You'll stay there until all is clear."

"As you wish," she said.

His stomach twisted in a knot. She was far too agreeable. Somehow, he didn't believe her for a moment. He stared at her suspiciously.

She smiled back amiably.

An apprehensive shudder traveled through his body, a silent premonition of things to come.

~Chapter Fourteen~

It was late afternoon when the travelers arrived at the Connor cottages. The two dwellings stood side-by-side in a clearing, dwarfed by a fortress of soaring trees. Richard found Katherine to be true to her word. She had guided his group the long way around, off any well-worn road.

As far as he knew, no one from Rosemont was aware of their presence. In their travels, they didn't cross paths with any of Lord Seton's men. Richard held out hope that most of them were far away, still scouring the countryside for their wayward lady.

Once the mounted riders reached the cottages, they were met by two almost identical, big, brawny men emerging from the stables. Each brother carried a long-handled axe against his shoulder. Their weathered faces hardened with concern when they noticed Katherine sitting in front of him, but soon softened when they realized she was in no danger.

"To whom do I speak?" Richard questioned.

One of the men swung his axe off his shoulder and rested the heavy head upon the ground. "I'm Timothy Connor and this is my brother, Thomas."

"I'm Sir Richard Weston. My wife, Lady Katherine, believes you and your brother would be willing to aid us in reclaiming Rosemont from Lord Seton. Is what she says true?"

Timothy smiled broadly. "Aye, Sir Richard. If Lady Katherine said it's true, it would be so."

"Then you will allow us to rest in your clearing before we continue our quest?"

"By all means. We'll do all we can to champion your cause," Thomas assured him.

"Very well." Richard swung his leg over Titan's back and alighted. He reached for Katherine, and with little effort, placed her feet on the ground. When he motioned to his men, they dismounted, also.

Thomas stepped forward. "Lady Katherine, it's good to see you well. We were worried about your welfare. We didn't know what happened. There was talk Lord Seton wanted to make you his wife. Most of his men are out searching for you."

"Thankfully, I am fine. He can no longer make that claim. No need to fear." She adjusted her gown.

His curiosity was piqued. "If what you say is true, then his defenses are low. We need to get a good count of how many men he has left."

"I could deliver firewood to the castle," Thomas volunteered. "Their reserves must be almost depleted. We haven't dared to return since the attack. We hear there is much to fear within Rosemont's walls. The castle would welcome a delivery, allowing me to move about easily."

"That would work. I need to know how many fighting men he has on the ramparts and behind his walls before I send my men into battle." He gave Titan's neck a quick pat.

"If I left soon, I could return by nightfall," Thomas said.

Richard spied an empty wood cart in the yard. "My men will load your wagon, so you can be on your way."

He directed a few of his men-at-arms to fill the cart with the already split, chopped, and dried wood stacked against the stable wall. Leading Titan, he headed toward Marcus and Peter and gestured the brothers to follow. There was much to discuss.

***

Katherine noticed the men's families huddled in one of the cottage doorways. She knew the Connors well. Thomas was married to Helen and Timothy to Isabel. Both had young children who peeked out from behind their mother's skirts as they stared wide-eyed at the gathering of big men, many in full armor, moving around their yard.

Isabel's two youngest boys, who were born three winters ago, held a special place in her heart. The twins were each blessed with a crop of yellow hair and big beautiful dimples.

She made her way toward the women, pleased to recognize their familiar faces. The ladies met her halfway with their broods following closely behind.

Helen bowed in greeting. "Lady Katherine, when we heard you escaped, we prayed no harm would come to you. It's good to see you well."

"Thank you, Helen. I had a few very difficult days, but I am much better now."

Isabel bowed extremely low, weighted down by a twin in her arms. "My lady, men came looking for you. They threatened us, yet we knew nothing. Even if we did know your whereabouts, we would never have told them. We didn't find out what happened until later. I'm so sorry about your family."

Katherine hung her head for a moment then glanced at Richard, who was in deep conversation with his men. When he returned her gaze, she gave him a slight smile.

"My husband and I will make sure Lord Seton pays for his actions."

The women were eager to share stories from the past few days. She listened to the miserable tales of Lord Seton's reign over Rosemont, and her heart sank, burdened by the heavy load.

While the women talked, the children's boldness soared, and they ventured farther from their mothers' circle of security. With all the commotion in the yard, the little ones' restlessness began to build.

Out of the corner of her eye, she noticed one of Richard's men leading Titan close to the group of women. A twin grabbed onto her skirts and squealed in delight as one of his siblings chased after him in fun. The little boy made a tight circle around her legs, trying to hide from his brother. She patted the top of his golden head. When the lad scurried off behind her, alarm registered in the back of her mind.

Katherine spun around in time to see the twin, giggling in merriment, run in front of Titan's massive legs. Too excited by his brother's game, he was oblivious to any danger.

She watched in horror as the man leading the stallion jerked hard on the warhorse's mouth to stop him from advancing. Titan sat back on his haunches. Without thinking, she lunged forward, and, with a swoop of her arm, she lifted the child off the ground and brought him to her chest.

Isabel screamed as the destrier reared up and struck out.

Spinning swiftly, Katherine moved the little one away from Titan's deadly reach. She blew out her held breath and handed the baby over to the child's mother.

Isabel kissed her bewildered son none too gently as tears of relief flowed down her face.

Helen ushered a weeping Isabel and all the children into the nearest cottage for their safety.

In shock, Katherine stood alone in the front yard. She hugged herself to stop her body from trembling. A few feet away, the nervous stallion pranced in place, while the terrified man struggled to regain control.

Suddenly, her shoulders were grabbed from behind.

Richard whirled her around and gave her a quick shake. "What's the matter with you? Are you trying to kill yourself? How dare you get near my horse like that! Have you no sense at all? Titan can kill in one quick blow! Do you not value your life? You must be simple-minded!"

She stared at him blankly. His angry words stung her ears. Unshed tears pooled in her eyes. Her face flamed from her husband's public tongue lashing, given freely in front of his men.

"Unhand me," she said in a low, icy tone.

Richard dropped a hold of her shoulders.

She glared at him and rasped under her breath, "How dare you speak to me in such a manner?"

A strong desire to leave him gnawed in her belly. Turning away abruptly, she marched into the empty cottage and slammed the door with a deafening bang.

Once inside, Katherine leaned heavily against the closed door.

How could he embarrass her so?

Her husband's hurtful words repeated in her head. He thought her simple-minded, stupid, and unworthy. He also made sure everyone else thought of her the same way.

Her mortification was complete.

She stifled a sniffle and plodded to the table in the middle of the room where she sat down hard on the edge of a bench. Weak and drained, she laid her arm across the well-worn wood and slumped in defeat.

A soft knock sounded on the door.

She wiped her eyes with the back of her hand.

Helen entered the cottage, shut the door, and made her way to the table where she crouched down next to Katherine.

"It was a brave and unselfish act you performed, my lady. Had you not risked your life; my little nephew would surely have died. We'll be forever grateful to you for your courage and eternally in your debt."

Katherine wiped her eyes again.

"Please don't take what your husband said to heart." Helen leaned in a bit closer as if sharing a secret. "He just overreacted when you put yourself in harm's way. I think your husband feels responsible because it was his stallion misbehaving."

Helen placed her fingers over Katherine's hand. "A husband only reacts that way when he cares about his wife."

"Are you certain?" She stared at Helen, searching for the truth of her words.

Helen's face lit up with an all-knowing smile. "Of that, I'm sure. Only a husband who cares about his lady would've spoken so harshly. I myself have been talked to rather unkindly on more than one occasion when my husband believed circumstances were out of his control and he was concerned for my safety."

"You do not think he hates me?"

Helen shook her head. "Not at all."

More than anything, she hoped Helen was right. "Thank you. I appreciate you telling me this."

"Now you need to show me where that hoof clipped you." Helen patted Katherine's hand.

"You know?" She said incredulously.

"I read the pain in your eyes when you turned with the baby. I understand why you kept the injury to yourself when your husband stood over you. It's not good to let our men think they're right."

Katherine grabbed onto her left upper arm. "Titan only grazed me with the edge of his hoof. He was reacting to the pressure placed on his mouth. He would never harm me on purpose."

"Let me look at the damage." Helen ran her hand down the front of Katherine's arm.

She flinched with pain when pressure was put on a specific spot.

"I don't believe anything is broken. We need to get you out of your surcoat, so we can take a better look. Don't worry. No one will bother us. Isabel is taking care of the children in her cottage and my husband is leaving for Rosemont as we speak."

Katherine stood and removed her girdle and dagger, placing them on the edge of the table. Helen untied Katherine's velvet gown, helped her out, and then loosened the laces on her kirtle and chemise so the low necklines could be pulled over her shoulder to bare her upper arm.

She sat back down on the bench.

Helen found a purplish mound and lightly ran her fingers over the swelling. "A lump is already forming. We'll place some cold cloths on the injury and perhaps we can lessen the pain."

"Sounds like a good idea."

Helen brought a basin of water and cloths to the table. She made a cold compress and placed the wet material on Katherine's upper arm. Satisfied all was as it should be, Helen busied herself with stirring the stew simmering in a cookpot hanging over the fire.

Without warning, the cottage door flew open, making both women startle in fright.

Richard filled the doorway. His dark blue eyes landed on Helen. "Leave us."

Helen gave Katherine a sympathetic look, then closed the door behind her.

Richard took up a great deal of space in the little cottage. He folded his arms over his wide chest and towered over her.

She shivered.

"Why did you not tell me?" His tone was laced with unexpected gentleness. *He knew.*

Katherine was ashamed of herself for hiding things from him…things he always found out about anyway. She shrugged, only to grimace in pain. "You were mad enough already."

"How bad is it?"

"Just sore, I will be fine." She pressed the cloth tighter to her upper arm.

Richard closed the gap between them. He positioned a chair next to her injured arm. First, he took the cold compress from against her skin. Then, he lightly ran his thick fingers along the lump, feeling its contour. She relaxed her arm as he lifted it up and down, noting when she winced in pain. He dipped the cloth in cold water, wrung the compress out, and then pressed it back on her arm. His other hand rested against the back of her neck, under her hair.

"Katherine…," he began, leaning so close his breath brushed upon her bare skin.

She interrupted him. "I do not want to fight anymore." She willed herself to ignore the rough fingers molded around the curves of her neck, setting her skin on fire.

"I don't want to fight. I wanted to say I'm sorry I yelled at you. The thought of Titan killing you was too much for me to bear." His voice sounded hoarse.

"I did the right thing. Even if I had been hurt worse, I know in my heart I did the right thing and would do the same again. There is no way I would let a child die, any child die if I could stop it. I make no apologies for my actions."

"I know."

"How did you find out?"

"The man who held Titan's reins thought the animal connected with something. He wasn't sure because it happened so fast. Knowing you as I do, I figured, rightly, that the beast had struck you."

"Titan just swiped my arm with the edge of his hoof, nothing more. In a few days, all will be as it was." Katherine brushed a tendril of hair away from her face using her uninjured arm and stuffed it behind her ear. She wasn't used to him touching her or sitting so close.

He ran his hand along her bare skin from the nape of her neck, over the curve of her shoulder, to the wet compress. Gently, he held her arm between his two big hands. "Is this the arm you broke as a child?"

She shuddered involuntarily as heat pulsated over the area he touched on his journey down her arm. When she replied, she tried to sound calm, but inside her heart pounded like a herd of wild horses racing across a meadow. "The very same. I suppose I was lucky to not break it again."

"Very lucky, indeed," he said smoothly.

It made her uneasy to have him so attentive and pliant. It was time to broach a subject she'd skirted around these past few days.

With some trepidation, she began, "I realize our getting married was not of your choosing. You have made your feelings clear. I want you to remember I was forced into this marriage the same as you. Or have you forgotten?"

He looked at her with deep skepticism, as if to say it was unfathomable she had not wanted to wed him.

"I also saw a different future. Now, because of the king's edict, everything has changed for me, also." She hoped God wouldn't strike her down for bending the truth a bit.

"What are you saying?" He watched her intently.

She took in a deep breath and surged forward before she lost her confidence. "I am tired of your anger and disdain towards me. I do not want to fight anymore. I do not want your hostility directed my way."

She had his full attention and wanted to get everything out in the open while she still had enough courage. "When you treat me with disrespect in front of your men, they think they can do the same. I do not deserve that from you or them. I am hoping we can have a truce between us. Maybe you can treat me the way you did before we exchanged vows, before you felt animosity towards me. I guess I am looking for some civility until Rosemont is taken back and we have completed what we set out to do. What say you, Richard? Are you willing to work together?"

***

Richard stared blankly into the beautiful blue depths of her sparkling eyes while he pondered her accusatory words.

Had he really treated her so badly? Of course, he had, she could have died yesterday from her chill all because he wanted to punish her.

Had he really been so disrespectful? Most certainly, especially when he refused to let her ride beside him as a wife should.

Was she just an innocent bystander?

Probably.

Richard had to admit he might have let his temper get in his way, a little. He knew himself well enough to know he didn't like being told what to do. And maybe she didn't get what she wanted when she married him. He was a mere knight, not a titled lord.

But then again, she no longer had a dowry, so without the return of Rosemont, her prospects for a good match with a man of her rank were slim.

Maybe she only accepted what she could get.

He could try to be a little nicer; she'd been through a lot lately. To be honest, he did miss the easy banter they had shared before their marriage.

She fidgeted in her seat, awaiting his reply.

He dunked the cloth into the water basin on the table and wrung it out before he reapplied it to her arm. Her gown hung provocatively across her body. He took a moment to appreciate her beautifully sculptured shoulder and creamy soft skin. "Well, I might've been somewhat hard on you recently."

"Humph," she breathed loudly and shot him a disgusted look for minimizing his bad behavior.

He smirked at her response; he liked stroking her temper. "You've borne my foul mood quite well. Better than most actually. I suppose, under the circumstances; I can give you a little respite."

She shook her head in amazement. "I imagine I will have to accept your lame words as a roundabout way of saying that you also desire we get along."

"I guess you will."

Richard grabbed his wife's free hand from her lap and put it on her compress. He rose from the little chair and made his way to the stew simmering over the fire.

"Do you think Thomas's wife will throttle me if I help myself to some of her stew? Their meal smells so good, my belly is growling in anticipation."

***

Katherine chuckled softly at the image of Helen chasing Richard around the kitchen with a broomstick but knowing Helen, that would never happen.

"To tell you the truth, I think she would be pleased and honored to share her meal with you."

"As she should be," her husband stated with cheerful arrogance.

He removed the cookpot from the fire and ladled generous portions of the meat and vegetables into two bowls he took off a shelf. He placed a bowl and spoon in front of her, along with a piece of warm, fresh bread. Her husband then set himself up with the same. When he again sat in the little chair, the aged wood protested with a loud crack under the strain of his great weight.

"You better be careful to not move in that tiny chair or you are apt to find yourself sitting on the floor." She brought a spoonful of steaming food to her mouth.

"This chair wouldn't dare sit me on the ground for fear of eliciting my wrath!" He joked loudly and gave her a wicked smile. "I can be quite formidable when I want to be. Besides, no chair wants to become kindling for the fire, and that's how it would end up."

"If you keep moving around the way you are, the chair will have no choice," she said merrily, pleased with their new arrangement.

Hours had passed since their last meal, so the couple ate with relish in friendly silence. When finished, Richard stacked the dirty dishes.

"I'm going to deliver the stew and loaf of bread to the women and children next door. We'll stay here tonight. Much before dawn, we leave for the cliffs and need to be well-rested." He put the bread under his arm and picked up the pot. "After I finish with my men, I'll retrieve your bag and cloak. Is there anything else you need?"

"Could you check on my mare? I would like to know she is well." The animal was her responsibility and she didn't want anything untoward to happen to Lord Weston's gift.

"I'll see to your wishes, my lady." He playfully tipped his head before he shut the door behind him.

A blissful sigh escaped her lips. The sound was oddly loud in the empty cottage. A rush of pure joy traveled from her head to her toes.

Richard's small acts of kindness and sweet teasing made her giddy with pleasure. He listened to her words and agreed to work on a truce. She held onto hope he might change his mind.

Maybe he could care for her enough to remain by her side and honor his vows.

Full of renewed life, she left the table to prepare herself for their night together. After taking care of her needs, she washed and placed the water basin on a small table next to the bed. Seated on the edge of the wool mattress, she kept her injured arm close to her side as she used the other to undo her hair. With her fingers, she combed through the waves and shook her head to let the soft tresses fall around her. Not sure what to expect regarding a night with her husband, she chose to stay in her loosened light pink kirtle but decided to remove her ankle boots.

While she sat alone in the little room, her mood slowly changed. The flames in the hearth flickered. Staring into the fire, she let a wave of gloom wash over her. Tomorrow, the lives of so many would change. People would die. Just like her father and brother had died.

One minute, they would be alive, and the next they would be nothing but a shell.

She shuddered at the thought.

Katherine could do this. She could steel herself against leniency for the people who killed her family and snatched away her life. She would harden herself from bestowing compassion on those who showed her none. Vengeance would be hers.

Tomorrow would be a day of reckoning.

***

Richard returned sometime later, his arms loaded with his mantle, armor, weapons, and his wife's things. His men were finishing their meal and finding their beds early tonight, as a good night's sleep might mean the difference between life and death during a siege.

He caught sight of Katherine sitting on the edge of the bed, bending down to remove her shoes. His heart thumped erratically. Her gown hung enticingly off a delicate shoulder. When her honey curls enfolded her in their splendor, his manhood hardened and he questioned his sanity. Forgotten too late were his wishes to not be alone with her.

If he intended to get some real rest, he should head to the stables and bed down with his horse.

He laid his burden by the front door, taking enough time to regain his composure. "Let me throw my mantle on top of the bed for you."

If he stayed busy, it would lead to distraction. With his mantle tucked under his arm, he made his way to her side and motioned for her to stand. He tossed the cloak over the bed, letting it float through the air and land fur side up, on top of the mattress. "Now that'll make a fine bed."

"Indeed it will. What would I do without you?" She curtsied and giggled.

"Nothing is too good for a lady," he quipped, passing his arm gallantly in front of him, directing her back onto the soft surface.

***

Before settling down on the freshly made pallet, she wrung out her cloth in the water basin and reapplied it to her arm. In bed, she positioned herself on her uninjured side and situated the cold compress in a way where she didn't have to hold it in place.

With her good hand under her pillow, she had an unobstructed view of Richard as he went about organizing and readying their things for their night-time awakening. For a big man, he moved with ease and grace. The fire was roaring, so the room was warm. After the sun went down, there would be a pleasant glow in the cottage.

When he arrived at the edge of the bed, he had already discarded his black leather tunic, chainmail, and thigh-high boots. He positioned his sword against the side table and placed his dagger on top. The wool mattress sank when he settled on his back next to her on the narrow bed.

"How is my little mare doing?" she questioned, trying to move past her unease.

"Your mare is well. Marcus is tending to her nicely. Everything is in order for tomorrow. Go to sleep. I'll wake you when it's time."

"Goodnight," Katherine said in a soft voice, nervous because of their proximity. She closed her eyes, but sleep didn't come. His strong scent was all over the soft fur of his mantle. She couldn't get enough of the musky aroma and buried her face deeper in the cloak's folds.

As the two of them lay side by side, his masculine essence floated like a protective circle around his body. The power and strength surrounding him, even at rest, was impressive. His nearness was a heady experience.

The minutes passed at a snail's pace as she peeked at him through half-closed lashes, making out his outline. He was more than attractive in his white linen shirt and black hose. His entwined fingers rested on his flat stomach.

Her breath caught in her chest; she had never laid eyes on such a handsome man, nor had she ever experienced such a strong attraction toward one.

Some of his black, lightly curled hair framing his stoic face was still damp. While he was gone, he must have taken time to wash the day's grime off his face and hands. He had a beautifully chiseled nose and nicely trimmed short beard.

She closed her eyes; in her mind, she pictured his charming smile, the one that made his whole face brighten when he was in good spirits.

Again, she opened her eyes a slit and took another peek at the man resting at her side. Her breath came out slowly. The memory from the other night, when he'd rubbed her feet and legs with his big, rough but gentle hands sent quivers racing through her body.

How would it feel if he stroked her elsewhere, like he did when he trailed his fingers over the naked skin of her shoulder and down her arm? That small touch, skin to skin, was so glorious, she wished the moment had lasted forever.

Although they never had a wedding night, she knew exactly what it entailed. Since she lost her mother at an early age, some of her servants were eager to share their own experiences.

Matilda, especially, was very outspoken about her exploits. The woman was a very pretty, well-endowed young serving maid, who had an insatiable appetite for male company. She shared some of her more colorful moments with her friend Rosa while clearing the tables in the Great Hall.

She would be busy with her needlework by the fire as Matilda discussed her amorous adventures. It was a game the women played, knowing it would be inappropriate to share such talk with their lady; they would let her overhear instead.

Katherine's thoughts drifted back to some of those more vivid stories. Her need to experience flesh on flesh grew. She resisted an urge to reach out and touch his hard-muscled arm, wondering what it would feel like to caress his bare skin, ever so lightly, under the sleeve of his shirt and to…

"Katherine," his deep voice sliced through the silence. "Stop staring at me."

She coughed to cover her startle.

"I am not," she lied without shame.

"I can feel your eyes upon me," he said gruffly. "Go to sleep."

She hid her heated face in the fur of his mantle. Embarrassed to the core by her naughty imaginings, she was sure she would never be able to look at him again. How could she?

~Chapter Fifteen~

In the dark, early morning hour, an annoying nudge brought Katherine slowly awake. Her lips parted to voice a protest, but she paused before uttering a word.

Only one person would dare prod her so abruptly, then walk away.

Richard.

Beneath her body, his fur mantle enveloped her in a warm, soft nest. She affectionately ran her hand over the silky surface. His musky, faintly smoky male scent clung to his cloak, and she inhaled his lingering aroma.

Heated memories of the night before returned. Although she had been so sure she could never look at him again, she glanced his way.

He stood in front of the hearth stoking the fire to a roar, spreading a circle of light about the room. Through his thin linen shirt, the outline of his chiseled body shone strikingly against the growing flames, causing an unaccustomed knot to tighten in her stomach.

He looked up from his task. "We ride in a few minutes."

At the sound of his deep husky voice, a wave of pleasure swam through her veins. She sat up slowly and rubbed the sleep from her eyes.

He donned a thick, padded doublet over his long linen shirt.

She scanned the room expectantly.

"Have you no squire to help you dress?" Her father and brother always had squires to help them. She was sure she saw some older boys riding among the men.

"I clothe myself and need no help from others." He picked up his thin chainmail and dragged the armor over his head. The small, finely tooled metal rings clanked together as they slid down over his full form, ending mid-thigh. For his next layer, he donned his black leather tunic. He fastened his wide, decorated belt low on his hips and took a seat on a wooden bench by the door.

She was mesmerized by his graceful movements as he glided his tall boots over thick, muscular legs. When he stood to collect his sword and dagger, her heart pounded and she forgot to exhale.

Richard forced open the door of the cottage, causing the hinges to creak in protest.

"Ready yourself quickly. We'll be waiting." He squeezed through the narrow opening.

When he was gone, she left the bed and raced to retrieve her bag. In the glow of the fire, she dumped the contents onto the table and smiled. Hidden in the folds of her blue outfit was a bundle of squire's clothing.

She held the cherished garments tightly against her chest. *Thank you, Lord Weston.*

Her fingers worked swiftly to remove her kirtle and chemise. In their place, she donned braies that she tied around her waist and mid-thighs, a pair of thick, woolen hoses she attached to the braies, and a white linen shirt. Over everything, she put on a woolen tunic.

Unfortunately, the clothes were not intended to fit someone with a bosom. She struggled to lace the material but managed to pull the cords snug.

Taking her ivory comb from the bag, she passed the teeth through her thick locks. Once her hair was somewhat tamed, she braided the strands into one long rope until it reached below her waist and then tied the ends together with a piece of cloth. She slipped on her ankle boots, placed her girdle around her waist, and sheathed her dagger.

She stole a quick glance at her new outfit. It felt odd that the tunic ended at her knees and not on the ground like her gowns, but she shrugged off the strangeness.

At this moment she couldn't worry about how she looked. What she wore was very sensible for what she planned.

At the cottage door, she halted and took a deep breath. Richard wouldn't be pleased.

Suddenly, her resolve crumbled. She rested her shoulder against the rough, wood door. One look at her manner of dress and his anger would surface.

Maybe, if she was lucky, he wouldn't chastise her too badly in front of his men. Her humiliation would know no bounds if she were given another public tongue-lashing like the one she endured yesterday.

She closed her eyes, touched the dagger resting at her hip, and rubbed her hand lovingly over the smooth jewels embedded in the hilt.

The dagger had been her mother's prized possession. Throughout the years, the decorated blade hung with dignity from Lady de Grey's lavishly embroidered girdle. Her mother's words from her death bed came back with clarity. *May my dagger bring you great strength and courage in a time of need.*

She certainly could use some strength and courage right now.

A jolt of determination rushed forth. She straightened her back. It was time to face her husband's disapproval. She opened the door but much to her dismay, the weathered hinges squeaked in protest, ruining her attempt to go unnoticed.

Richard stood next to Titan and looked over his shoulder at the sound of her arrival. He immediately stiffened.

She smiled innocently and stepped outside the cottage, into the night. As she made her way toward him, he clenched his jaw so hard no doubt his jowl was in jeopardy of snapping in two.

Richard took a few big steps and met her halfway. Without so much as a word, he grabbed her uninjured arm, whirled her around and directed her back into the cottage. He slammed the door shut and released her swiftly.

"Well?" he said with an edge of irritation, his arms crossed over his chest.

She stared at her clasped hands. "I suppose you are not pleased with the way I am dressed."

It was encouraging that he wanted to discuss things in private.

"I have no time for this," he complained, the strain in his voice signaled his building annoyance. "What in the world are you wearing? You are a lady. You can't go around wearing squires' clothing. Whatever made you think you should dress as you are?"

She peered at her husband towering over her. "Your father put them in my bag. He said the climb would be too dangerous maneuvering over sharp rocks in my gowns. He thought this manner of dress would be more appropriate."

"My father packed those for you? He would have you join us in our trek over the rocks? He has become an addled old man, and you should stop listening to his nonsense. You won't need those clothes because you aren't going any farther than the edge of the cliffs, where you'll only point the way."

"I am not sure that is going to work. It is pretty dark tonight, not quite the full moon it was a few days ago. It would be much better if I showed you the opening of the passage. I'm sure I would be able to find the entrance easily enough, having seen it before in the dark."

He stared at her in stubborn silence.

She raised her chin and returned a steady gaze. Her attempt to reason with him was falling on deaf ears. It was time to tell him the truth and plead her case.

"Please, Richard. Please, let me do this. I must. It is my duty to make sure your course goes smoothly. I want…no, I need to be part of avenging my family's deaths. Please do not order me to wait at the Connors', so far away, not involved in any worthy part at all. I will go mad if you make me do that."

She pressed her hands together and begged pitifully. "Please, let me go with you and show you the way into the passages. Let me be of service."

Richard sighed loudly and sent her his best exasperated look. "I don't like this at all."

He turned and opened the door. "Gather your mantle. It will be cold by the water. You'll do exactly as I say. I'll leave you where I choose, and you'll not argue with me."

He stepped through the doorway and never looked back.

Thrilled, she threw the fur-lined wool cloak around her shoulders and ran out after him.

In the torch-lit yard, she saw the seven knights who would accompany them. The men were already mounted. The knights would ride the distance to the cliffs to conserve their energy for the fight.

Peter was in charge of getting the men-at-arms to Rosemont and then positioning them outside the gates. As soon as they won the gatehouse, the drawbridge would be lowered, portcullis raised, thick oak doors opened, and the waiting men would rush into the castle.

In the dim light, Richard glared at the group of knights waiting atop their mounts, daring them to say a word. He lifted her onto Titan's back and swung up behind.

Marcus took a position beside them as the couple started out. The older man gave her husband an all-knowing smirk.

Richard's body hardened.

He must have bestowed on Marcus one of his icy stares because his friend chuckled in return. Her husband urged Titan forward and they moved with haste away from Marcus's perusal and into the darkness of the night.

***

Katherine led the mounted party to the edge of the cliffs, out of sight of Rosemont's guards. While Richard helped her dismount, she breathed in deeply of the familiar salt air, then shut her eyes for a moment. *I'm home.*

A breeze came off the water, the moisture clung to her face. She glanced over her shoulder at her escorts who were finding their footing on the rocky ledge. The knights were dressed in light armor, mostly chainmail. They would need to move unhampered while maneuvering over the sharp rocks. Each man was well-equipped with an array of weaponry in all shapes and sizes.

Only Richard's and William's knights were present. While waiting by the edge of the steep cliffs for the men to ready themselves, she considered why that would be so. Then it came to her, Richard would only reveal the secret of the tunnels to those knights he trusted above all others. Any knowledge of such passages could lead to future vulnerability and open the castle inhabitants to danger. Her husband was a very careful man and left nothing to chance.

Richard came to stand by her side. Together, they looked down at the waves crashing with angry slaps against the impenetrable rocks below.

"Can I take your mantle?"

She pulled her fur-lined cloak closer to ward off the chill. Now that she stood near the water, she had second thoughts about giving up her warmth.

"I think I will keep it on and wrap the bottom around my arm while I climb over the rocks."

"How's your injury?" He placed his hand lightly on her shoulder.

It pleased her that he worried about her welfare. Some of his features were visible in the moonlight and he gazed at her with deep concern.

"'Tis a little sore when I move it, but tolerable. I will be fine as long as I do not reach too high."

He nodded, looked over his shoulder at his men standing behind them, and then turned back to her.

"Lead and we will follow." He extended his palm, so she could place her hand into his larger one. Fiery warmth flowed through their clasped fingers. Her eyes met his in the hazy darkness. She turned her head away to gather her wits and inhaled deeply to quiet her reaction.

With his help, she swept up the fullness of her cloak, threw the wool over her arm, and made her descent onto the jagged rocks. The path chosen needed to be a good one. She concentrated on hand and foot placements. One wrong move could cause a person to tumble down the almost vertical drop to the rocks below, so the pace was slow and movements well thought out.

Richard hovered so close that any slight falter on her part brought forth large hands to grab her waist or elbow; helping her regain her balance. For a big man, he moved with natural agility, but she couldn't say the same for some of his men. Time and time again, she heard curses uttered behind them.

***

Richard's anxiety concerning Katherine's well-being grew as he followed her over the uneven ground. He became painstakingly attentive to her every move. His men were having a difficult time climbing over the rocks, and he was in awe that she had made her way over the same rough path during her escape.

He found it hard to imagine her making this journey alone in the dark, in anguish over her family's deaths, her back in excruciating pain, and her skirts snagging on sharp edges. He gazed at her with admiration.

Was he forever going to be surprised by her seemingly endless courage, determination, and fortitude?

This morning, when she sat atop the bed with her gown hanging off her shoulder, displaying her flawless skin, it took all the strength he could muster to turn away and not break his vow.

Never had his eyes beheld such an angelic vision. And yet, only a few minutes later, he wanted to throttle her for wanting to put herself in danger again.

How could one young lady cause him so much turmoil? What was it about her that burrowed so deep beneath his skin?

Loose rocks crumbled underneath her foot. He laid his hand against her small waist, ready to pull her toward him if need be.

He wasn't about to let anything happen to his wife.

***

Katherine breathed a sigh of relief when she reached the narrow cave opening and stepped onto a flat surface.

Richard's arm halted her progress. He entered the darkness first.

While waiting for him to light a torch, she unwound her cloak from her arm and brought the material around her body to ward off the chill from the ocean's cool breeze.

When the cavern was illuminated in a soft glow, she stepped aside to let the rest of the men file past her and light their own torches.

The head of the tunnel was larger than she remembered. But then again, during her escape, she had only one candle to light her way. A short distance into the cave an iron gate separated the entrance from the passageway.

She moved to the side of the cave and scraped her foot back and forth across the dusty stone floor.

"Katherine, what are you doing?" Richard asked.

"After I locked the gate, the key fell from my grasp. I was in a hurry and could not find it in the dark, so I left it behind. It should be here somewhere."

Suddenly, she spotted the metal key and picked it up. She motioned for Richard to follow with the torch and they walked to the bars. Once there, she fiddled with the lock until the ends gave way. The gate screeched in protest, as they pushed until it opened wide.

Richard's hand came down on Katherine's shoulder to stop her short before she went any farther.

"What will we find at the end of the passage?" he questioned loud enough for all to hear.

"The tunnel gradually gets steeper and steeper as the passage heads up into the castle," she said in a strong voice. "A few hundred feet up, the tunnel will spill out into a small room. From there, it branches off into three different passageways. Two of those tunnels will turn into steps. One goes to my father's bedchamber and one to mine, both on the second floor of the keep. The third tunnel will take you to the family chapel off the Great Hall. At the end of each passage is a door. A lever on the right has to be lifted to release the latch before the concealed doors will open."

Katherine could barely hold back her excitement. She was here with the men who would avenge the deaths of her father and brother. Lord Seton would suffer for what he did to her family.

Richard stepped forward and turned to address his men. "Owen, you are with me. We'll go to the lord's chamber and wake Lord Seton from his slumber. Godfrey, you and James will go to Lady Katherine's bedchamber and quietly make your way through the rest of the rooms on the second floor. Once we're sure the upstairs is clear, we'll meet the others downstairs in the hall. Marcus, I want you and the remaining men to take the passage to the chapel. More than likely, there'll be men sleeping in the hall. Miles, you're in charge of getting to the gatehouse. You'll need to take control of the portcullis and drawbridge so Peter can get in with the rest of the men to battle any men-at-arms on the battlements and in the barracks. We all know what kind of men these are. They're ruthless. I would be surprised if any of them throw down their arms. More than likely, they'll fight to the death. Watch your backs and each other's."

Katherine waited eagerly to learn what her role would be, hoping he wouldn't cast her aside, alone in the bowels of the blackened cave. She pleaded with her eyes, beseeching him not to leave her behind.

He pursed his lips and considered her a moment before he spoke. "You'll stay with me."

She expelled her held breath and gave him a look of gratitude before she eagerly took her spot next to his side. With a gentle hand on her lower back, he steered her through the open gate behind Owen, who took the lead.

Once the men reached the small room, each group took their designated tunnels. The knights' anticipation of the approaching battle charged the air. An aura of strength and power radiated from the seasoned fighters.

As they ascended the steps, Katherine matched Richard's pace to the master bedchamber. With her outstretched hand, she groped her way along the rough, cold stone of the passageway. Vivid memories of a tunnel just like this one came rushing back.

At that time, she descended into blackness with only a stub of a candle to guide her way. All alone with barely any light, she had experienced terror like no other but refused to give in to it. Instead, she clung to her mother's jeweled dagger and surges of strength pulsated from the metal, warding off unwelcome feelings.

Today, under Richard's protection, her fear was kept at bay. She was no longer alone as she moved forward into the eerie darkness. Reaching down, she stroked the bumpy hilt of her dagger, just to reassure herself that the blade remained securely in its place.

Again, a simple touch reminded her of her mother, and with the memory came strength.

On the day of her escape, Mary, her beloved elderly maid, convinced Katherine to seek her freedom. The maid used her invisibility as an old woman to steal back Katherine's mother's dagger, obtain the peasant garments, drug the guard stationed at her bedchamber door, pilfer the key to her chamber, and set forth Katherine's flight through the hidden tunnel.

Mary had refused to accompany Katherine on her journey, insisting instead to stay behind to cover any traces of her ward's disappearance.

According to the older woman, the less Lord Seton knew about the tunnels and her escape, the better. Her elderly maid said that when Katherine was noted to be gone, the drugged guard would eventually admit to a lapse of time when he was asleep, and everyone would assume Katherine snuck out through the door and was hiding in the castle. Time would be wasted searching Rosemont while she was well on her way to Lord Weston's.

A disturbance washed over her. She shuddered inwardly from the coldness. A foreboding surrounded Mary. Something wasn't right, but Katherine couldn't put her finger on what was wrong. Her head throbbed.

She returned her thoughts to the moment and concentrated instead on putting one foot in front of the other as she made her way up the stairs to her father's bedchamber in the hazy light of the torch.

There was no time for apprehension.

~Chapter Sixteen~

Lord Seton was in a foul mood as he made his way back to the enormous four-poster bed in the master bedchamber. His eyes adjusted to the faint moonlight streaming in through the cloudy panes of glass covering the windows overlooking the ocean below. The wee hours of the morning were an unwelcome sight. He'd spent most of the night traveling back and forth, to and from the garderobe.

Fiery pellets scorched his innards. When he recovered, he'd find out who tried to poison him.

The notion of making someone pay with their worthless life made the corners of his mouth curl in a vicious smile. A sharp pain burned along the deep gash running over his cheek, ear to lip. He touched the side of his throbbing face.

His thoughts turned to Lady Katherine de Grey. Bitter bile rose in his throat. Nobody had set eyes on that vile creature for six days. It was as if the earth had swallowed her whole.

He'd dispatched his men in all directions, their mission simple: find the rebellious lady. They should've recaptured her in a matter of hours.

How hard could it be for seasoned men to find one lone woman?

They claimed to have seen no signs of her. Obviously, he employed a bunch of idiots. Some of his men were unaccounted for and he couldn't be sure if they just decided to leave his employment, too afraid to return empty-handed, or if some harm had befallen them.

No matter. Others would take their places. Men had a price. Now that he had found the old lord's hidden coins and jewels, he was a rich man.

Lord Seton sighed heavily. He detested *that little bitch*. Part of him hoped she lay dead in the woods with insects and animals gnawing on her rotting flesh.

Unfortunately, his life would be too complicated if they never found her alive, so he expected to get her back. When he did, he would marry her, then torture her into submission.

Out of the corner of his eye, he caught what looked like a sliver of light out of place in the darkened bedchamber. The three-foot glowing horizontal line shone from where the wall met the floor, on the far side of the room, underneath a richly decorated tapestry.

He squinted and puzzled over why it was so out of context in the darkness.

Suddenly, it made sense. He grabbed his sword and dagger and noiselessly scooted under the bed.

As he lay on the floor, he pushed on the rope slats to make his bulk fit and held his dagger at the ready in a clenched hand. He turned his head toward the paper-thin line of light and watched as it was snuffed out, blackness returning.

He remained perfectly still. Anyone wishing to do him harm would believe he adhered to the codes of chivalry. They would never think to look under the bed. No lord or knight would hide from danger but face it head-on.

His peers always misjudged his underhandedness, as he was not an ordinary man.

Much smarter than other men, he'd throw off his enemies by doing the unexpected. While other knights followed a certain set of high ideals, he was not bound by them. He didn't feel the need to show himself and face his attackers. He would wait them out and let them pass.

After all, he preferred to attack a man's back.

I have plenty of time.

***

Richard caught sight of the end of the passageway and motioned Owen and Katherine to stop. He had memorized the steps to the door and took a mental note of the lever on the wall before he doused the flame.

He took hold of Katherine's hand and gave her fingers a little squeeze. They stood quiet for a few minutes, so their sight could adapt before he guided them forward.

So far, his wife had borne their journey well, displaying a courageous nature and thirst for adventure. Although uneasy over her safety, he was glad he'd not left her behind.

Richard stopped when he reached the door and reluctantly dropped her hand. Finding the lever, he opened the portal with excruciating slowness.

A large tapestry hindered his entry. He carefully pushed the wall hanging aside as he poked his head into the chamber. The lord's bed was empty, so he stepped cautiously into the room.

He held his sword at the ready and gestured Owen to wait with Katherine.

Richard moved swiftly and smoothly, without a sound, around the room and attached garderobe. Through the opaque windows, he caught a glimpse of the tip of the sun rising over the water.

Satisfied that Lord Seton wasn't present, he locked eyes with Owen and shrugged.

Where was the coward?

He led Owen and Katherine into the hall. They left the door open to capture the newly developing daylight.

Godfrey and James met them in the passageway. James shook his head to impart they found no one.

Richard furrowed his brows and whispered, "No Lord Seton. Owen, stay upstairs. If there's trouble, go down the tunnel to the cliffs."

Owen understood his orders. Protect Katherine at all costs. Flee if the battle turned bad.

His knight nodded and placed a big hand on Katherine's shoulder to keep her with him.

Godfrey and James began their descent of the stone steps to the Great Hall.

Richard followed. Every step from her side twisted his gut in painful knots, and he summoned every ounce of grit he had to leave her behind.

At the top of the landing, he halted and looked back at his wife.

She appeared so small and vulnerable standing next to Owen. For the first time in his life, he worried about the outcome of a looming battle. He wasn't concerned for himself or his men but worried about his wife's safety if things didn't go well.

He gave her a reassuring smile.

She returned the favor. One laced with unspoken belief in his abilities. Her unwavering faith unsettled him.

He didn't want to disappoint her.

With a deep breath, he shook off his uneasiness and continued down the open staircase to join his knights.

They were correct in assuming there would be men sleeping on pallets amongst the rushes. It seemed the new lord didn't want to share his rooms upstairs with any of his hired help.

Marcus and his men were across the way, in the doorway of the family chapel, ready for the assault. The rising sun cast a shimmering light upon the hall as a small number of rays found their way through the elevated stained-glass windows.

Richard issued a war cry, loud enough to wake the sleeping men. His knights followed suit and sounded their own roars.

The idea of courtesy was clear. The warning allowed Lord Seton's men an opportunity to defend themselves, which was more than the cowards had done for the former inhabitants of Rosemont.

Lord Seton's men, caught completely unaware, flailed their arms and legs as they tried to protect themselves from the impending onslaught.

***

Katherine's heart hammered loudly in her chest when Richard bellowed his call to arms.

Only a few days ago, she had heard the roar for the first time. She strained against Owens's hold and tried to get closer to the edge overlooking the hall.

"It will not hurt to look below, will it?" Katherine whispered, hope ringing in her voice. She so wanted to see if Lord Seton was, with any luck, under her husband's sword.

Although the tall, lean knight in charge of her safety seemed to want to shield her, he relented to her plea and escorted her to the waist-high stone wall.

Katherine gathered both her cloak and her courage and kneeled on the low wooden bench, attached to the short barrier along the full length of the second-floor landing. She leaned over the edge and watched the scene unfolding beneath.

Owen hovered behind her, his hand resting on her shoulder, ready to pull her away if need be.

She hardened her emotions against the violence and reminded herself these were the men who killed her family and friends without remorse.

From her perch, she noticed her husband and his six knights were outnumbered, but it didn't matter. They were better trained, and surprise was on their side. They worked together against the other knights and men-at-arms.

Richard's men watched each other's backs, leaving no one unprotected. Lord Seton's men were only concerned for themselves. As Richard's knights bore down on the scantily protected men, their opponents slashed with wild abandon.

The noise echoing in the keep was deafening. Fighters grunted and groaned as they wielded heavy swords. Injured men yelled in anguish and pain. Steel clashed against steel and the racket reverberated off the stone walls, creating an eerie sound.

She drew her hood over her head and covered her ears with the palms of her hands.

With swelling pride, she watched Richard brandish his sword in a deadly dance, time after time. His heavy chainmail didn't slow him down. Each movement almost effortless. He was magnificently powerful and commanding, standing out above the rest.

So engrossed in the spectacle, she had to remind herself to breathe.

Suddenly, the hairs on the back of her neck stood straight up. She shuddered when a bone tingling chill penetrated her cloak and seeped into her bones.

Owen's thick fingers dug forcefully into her shoulder and then broke away.

Sensing danger, she whirled around to find the gallant knight stumbling in circles, arms raised, as he tried desperately to place his hands on the back of his bloodied head. Padded and thickly dressed, his bulky arms couldn't bend enough to stem the flow of blood.

Terror jolted her when she saw Lord Seton smugly standing over the wounded man, enjoying the knight's dilemma, while thick, red liquid dripped from the spiked hilt of his sword.

Katherine didn't think, she reacted.

She snatched her dagger from her girdle, jumped on top of the low wooden bench, and using the height to push off, she sailed through the air, landing with a thud on Lord Seton's back. She wrapped her legs around his waist and hooked an arm around his neck. With her dagger held menacingly, she stabbed at his chest, again and again, trying to get the point of her knife through the thick metal links on his hauberk.

Still holding onto the hilt of his sword, Lord Seton tried to claw her arm away from his neck, but since she held him in a death grip, he was unable to break the embrace.

He then attempted to take control of the threatening dagger. She changed her course and sent the razor-sharp edge toward his unprotected face, which caused him to shield his exposed skin instead of seizing her dagger.

To halt her assault, he staggered to the sidewall, within view of the hall below, and rammed his whole body back into the hard stone blocks.

She let out a loud, "Humph."

Attached like a leech, she refused to loosen her grip around the man's neck and returned to hacking away in the same spot on his metal tunic.

Out of the corner of her eye, she saw Owen, woozy from his head injury, totter to the low wall. He dropped to his knees on the low bench, leaned over the stone barrier, and with the last of his strength he shouted, "Richard!" before collapsing.

Lord Seton slammed her once more against the rough, hard surface of the wall. The wind got knocked out of her lungs and she gasped for air.

She looked down at the fight below.

Richard glanced up and for an instant, their eyes locked.

"Katherine!" he bellowed.

Lord Seton, hearing her name, must've finally realized who rode his back.

"You! You brought these knights to my door." With renewed energy, he turned in circles as he tried to pull her off, hatred fueling his determination. "I swear I'll kill you."

She wouldn't relent and kept up her constant assault.

"I will see you dead this day!" she screeched while she plastered one of her cheeks against the side of his chainmail-covered head. Through total perseverance, she bent enough metal links to sink the sharp tip of the blade through his thick skin, partway into his chest.

He yelped in pain.

She took her open hand and slammed it hard onto the top of her dagger's hilt, lodging the weapon deeper.

Lord Seton howled and dropped his heavy sword. A loud clatter rang out when steel hit the stone floor. He used both of his hands to dislodge the blade from his flesh.

Katherine knew she had only a short reprieve and removed her arm from around his neck. With her dagger gone, she had no way to protect herself. She jumped from his back onto the low wooden bench attached to the stone wall and ran down its length, balancing herself on the foot-wide surface.

When she came upon Owen, she leapt over his still body sprawled out across her path. She hoped Lord Seton would no longer see him as a threat.

At the beginning of the steps, she hopped down onto the landing to start her descent to the Great Hall. Abruptly, her long flowing cloak strangled about her neck, stopping her dead in her tracks.

"Where do you think you're going?" Lord Seton snarled.

A ball of dread churned in the pit of her stomach.

Without glancing back, she knew he had captured her mantle. Her air supply constricted as her neck strained heavily against the fastened cords.

"Katherine," Richard shouted.

The sound of his husky voice, deep with emotion, gave her strength.

Looking down the straight drop from the top step into the hall below, she saw him standing beneath, arms raised. Marcus stationed himself at his friend's back, holding her husband's sword.

Richard's dark blue eyes bored into hers.

A silent exchange took place.

She fumbled with the ties at her neck and yanked hard to release the cloak. Without wavering, she stepped off the side of the step into mid-air, as she had done so many years before.

Katherine had no doubt he would catch her as she fell to his open arms.

***

Richard caught Katherine without much effort; unhindered by her usual gowns, she was as light as a feather. He let her slide down the side of his body until her feet touched the ground. He wrapped a possessive arm about her shoulders and tugged her into his chest for a hard squeeze.

Marcus threw him his sword; a look of awe still lingered on the older knight's face. It was clear what Richard had to do next. He guided his wife to the bottom of the stone steps and, with some reluctance, handed her off to Marcus's care.

"See to her welfare," he ordered briskly.

"As you wish," Marcus responded dutifully while he pulled Katherine close to his side, next to the wall, and shielded her body with his bulk.

The hall was jarringly quiet.

Richard scanned the room. Lord Seton's men were dead. Bodies were strewn about haphazardly. Miles and two of Richard's men had already left for the inner bailey, their sights set on getting to the gatehouse. Two knights stayed behind, ready to protect Marcus and Katherine, if necessary.

Richard put on his practiced mask of cold indifference. He took the stone steps two at a time with his sword held high.

How dare Lord Seton harm, Katherine? How dare he fight so cowardly?

Anger mixed with cool restraint flowed through his veins. Years of training taught him self-control, so he stuffed his rage away. It was dangerous to bring emotion onto the battlefield.

Anger was a weakness he could ill afford.

Lord Seton stood at the top of the stairs, watching insolently. He wore a grotesquely arrogant lopsided smile. Having retrieved his sword, the man handled the weapon with confidence.

"Well, well, who do we have here? Sir Richard Weston. Have you come to rescue the fair maiden?" Lord Seton growled, bitterness pulsating in his voice. "I can assure you that your presence isn't needed. I've made the lady an offer of marriage, and I plan on making it so."

Richard halted a few steps away, his heavy sword eager to dance. "You're too late. Lady Katherine is already married…" He pressed forward onto the upper floor as he warded off his opponent's blow. "…to me!"

Shock registered on Lord Seton's disfigured face, and the man's upset turned into uncontrolled fury.

Hitting a nerve, Richard continued to taunt him in between blows.

"Your reign of terror is over. King Edward knows how you cowardly cut down Lord de Grey, his son, and men, and then spinelessly stole Rosemont. He knows about the traitor you are working with. And, above all else, he chose to marry Lady Katherine to me, a mere knight, just to keep her away from the likes of you, a titled but unworthy, Lord."

Lord Seton's face turned bright red with hatred and primal rage.

The man would consider Richard an insolent underling who had no business even suggesting he was the better man.

With Lord Seton's upset came an explosion of power behind his strikes. He swung his sword hard and recklessly. The wild thrashing did nothing more than expend his energy. His body, already damaged by the dagger's sharp blade, began to tire.

Realizing the futility of his angry outburst, Lord Seton stepped back to regain his balance. "Did your pretty little wife tell you what I did to her?"

Richard's jaw tensed and his lips tightened.

Lord Seton struck another blow, but it was easily deflected. The sound of steel bouncing off steel swirled about the hall.

"It was one of my finest moments. You should've been there when my men tied her hands and hung her on a hook like a gutted pig."

Lord Seton smiled with malice, one side of his face swollen and distorted. "They cut away her gowns, leaving the noble lady hanging, feet barely touching the ground, in only a thin chemise. Fine little thing she is, too."

Richard swung with reckless abandon, fury boiling to the surface.

"With the first flick of my wrist, I laid down a nice stream of blood from shoulder blade to waist. It was beautiful the way her little body kicked back when the tip sliced through her soft, delicate flesh."

He jabbed at Lord Seton's waist, yet missed when the man easily stepped aside.

"The second lick of the whip caressed her back once again." Lord Seton's excitement rose with each word.

Richard swung his sword with all his might. The man repelled the blow.

"By the third stroke, she let out a glorious moan," the man cried in triumph. "And her white shift turned a scarlet red."

Seething with umbrage, Richard took another calculated swipe but missed. His desire to avenge Katherine so great he couldn't see straight, his sight clouded by his fury.

"After, as she hung limply from the hook, silent tears poured down her cheeks," Lord Seton bragged, smiling at the memory.

Richard jabbed his blade thoughtlessly, and in a lucky move, his opponent side-stepped, a potentially deadly thrust. When Lord Seton turned, Richard's arm got caught under his.

Lord Seton rammed Richard backward with an explosion of force into a nearby wall.

The hilt of Richard's sword dislodged from his jolted hand.

The weapon flew through the air and hit the stone floor with a loud clang. As he pushed against Lord Seton to throw him off, the man turned like lightning and grabbed the long dagger out of Richard's belt, aiming the blade at his chest.

"Well, well. This has turned around quite nicely. The great knight, Sir Richard Weston, stands before me without even a weapon to keep him safe. I think it's a shame that your new wife is going to be a widow so soon."

Richard shook his head at his foolishness for letting Lord Seton provoke his ire and with it his recklessness. He regained his composure and focused on his situation. A dagger and sword held against him posed a problem, but not a reason to give up. He had practiced hand to weapon combat many times before.

While Lord Seton basked in the light of his assumed victory, Richard slammed the bulk of his body against the man's side before the coward could counter with either weapon.

Caught off guard, Lord Seton teetered backward. As the man righted himself, Richard launched himself into the air and tumbled across the stone floor, coming up on his feet behind his opponent.

Lord Seton whirled around, weapons at the ready. The overconfident man took a determined strike, but the blow was easily side-stepped.

Richard's arm swooped forward from behind his back, holding Katherine's dagger. The one he retrieved unnoticed from the floor during his roll.

"This is for my wife!"

With all his might, he jabbed the sharp blade upward, underneath Lord Seton's jaw.

In a moment of stark understanding, Lord Seton's eyes grew wide with the knowledge he'd been bested. He collapsed instantly and fell with a loud thud to the hard floor.

~Chapter Seventeen~

Katherine leaned heavily against Marcus's arm as he held her back at the bottom of the stairs.

From her vantage point, she only caught glimpses of Richard and Lord Seton battling on the upper floor, but the intensity of the fight was heard with every clash of the men's swords.

How she longed to warn Richard of Lord Seton's fondness for deceit and underhandedness. Richard didn't know his adversary as she knew him.

Her husband was an honorable man, a knight who followed his duties and beliefs, faithfully. How could he win against a man with no morals? A man who used treachery at every turn?

She closed her eyes. *Please, God, keep Richard safe.*

Suddenly, the hall quieted. No more clashing of swords, groans or heaving.

Too afraid to open her eyes, she squeezed them tight as she waited in agony for some sign of victory.

When Marcus loosened his grip, her eyes shot open.

Richard stood at the top of the landing.

A strangled cry caught in her throat. She squeaked out his name as she pushed past Marcus and hurried up the stairs.

***

"Owen's in a bad way. He'll need attention," Richard called down to his men.

His knights reacted swiftly. An onslaught of heavy boots slapped against the stone steps, two at a time, as they passed Katherine in their rush to see to their friend's needs.

Arriving first, Marcus appraised the damage done to Lord Seton. The knight nodded and made his way to Owen. He bent down and checked his breathing.

"He lives," Marcus announced.

Katherine reached the landing, heaving and out of breath, eyes only for him.

Out of the corner of his eye, he watched Marcus, James and Godfrey carry the unconscious man into the nearest bedchamber.

His gaze found hers and he smiled broadly.

Her joyous and unrestrained response, when she saw him unharmed, pleased him. He wanted to sweep her off her feet and encase her in a warm embrace.

Instead, he opted to savor her presence.

In the early morning light, her squire's outfit emphasized her loveliness, and he took pleasure in the sight. Her proximity elicited an inner calm he had long been missing in his life. He inhaled her lavender scent he seemed to forever be searching out and found a moment of contentment.

Unfortunately, his newfound peace was short-lived, for he shuddered when he recalled he'd almost lost her forever. It must've been an act of God that kept her safe while she battled Lord Seton.

Silently, he said a prayer of thanks.

***

"Tell me you are not hurt," Katherine breathlessly insisted, as she stood before Richard, hands on her hips.

Her eyes scanned her husband up and down, to double-check, but still, she needed to hear the words from his lips. His dark, damp hair was plastered to both sides of his handsome face. After such rigorous labor, his breath was heavy, and his body slumped with fatigue.

"Nay, not at all. Are you well?"

"Aye, I am." Her back was sore, but she didn't believe her wounds had opened up, for they were well protected in their bindings. Her injured arm was throbbing, but she brushed aside the pain, just thankful to be alive.

"I will be forever grateful you did not drop me this time," she teased, giddy with emotion now that the fight was over.

"I can assure you, over the years, I've become quite good at catching damsels in distress. I was pleased to be of service in your time of need." He gave her a good-humored bow.

Her face grew warm. She liked their easy banter. "I must confess; I was quite worried you would be harmed."

Mischief shone in his twinkling eyes. "There was naught to fear. Lord Seton was no challenge for a man as skilled as myself," he boasted, with a tinge of playful arrogance in his voice.

She looked down at Lord Seton's lifeless body. His wide vacant eyes stared into nothingness. With satisfaction, she noticed her mother's jeweled dagger was lodged deeply through the bottom of the man's jaw.

"I see you made good use of my dagger. I would like the blade back when you are done with it." Relief filled her body; her family was avenged, and justice meted out.

"Your dagger came in handy," he professed. "I assure you; it'll be returned."

Now that her fret over his welfare had all but subsided, her thoughts turned to William's knight. "How badly is Owen injured? I did not notice where they took him."

She couldn't believe she had forgotten about the wounded knight. She glanced around the landing for a sign of their departure.

"They carried him into your bedchamber." He pointed in the direction of her room.

"Owen will need the healer as soon as possible." She hurried to the short stone wall, leaned over the edge and scanned the dark shadows of the hall below until she found Rosa, hiding in their depths.

She called down, "Rosa, find Arthur and send him straight away to my bedchamber. Make haste."

"Yes, milady," a high-pitched voice replied from a blackened corner. Footsteps rushed forth from the keep.

"Until the healer arrives, let me do what I can," she said.

Richard preceded her into her bedchamber. The knights were removing Owen's chainmail. Unconscious, his lean but large body was flaccid and limp.

"James, go and ensure the healer makes it up here as soon as possible," Richard said, addressing his youngest knight.

As James left the room, Marcus silently beseeched Katherine for help. The troubled expression on the older man's weathered face revealed his fear. He held a piece of blood-soaked cloth tight against the back of Owen's head.

"The wound is wide. There's a lot of blood loss," Marcus said grimly.

She moved to the side of the bed, lifted the cloth, and gave the ugly gash a quick assessment.

"This wound will need to be stitched to stop the blood flow." She placed the cloth back on and let Marcus hold it in place. "Sir Godfrey, I will need you to go to the kitchen and bring up boiling water to clean the wound."

"Yes, milady. I'll see it is done." Godfrey spun around and left.

She glanced at her husband who stood at the foot of the bed. His face was tense with dread. "Use your dagger and cut off his doublet," she ordered.

He moved with great speed, appearing relieved to have a task to perform.

"After you finish, we will sit him in an upright position to slow the blood loss."

When Richard completed his task, she grabbed a few pillows and blankets and stuck them behind Owen's back and head, propping him up. She went through her trunk and removed a stark white linen chemise. She handed the material to Marcus and instructed him to place the clean cloth on the wound.

James returned, followed by Arthur, an anxious little man with bird-like features, who held a bulky wooden box under his arm. Rosa trailed behind the men as they made their way through the doorway.

"I met them coming up the front steps," the knight volunteered.

"What's happening outside the keep?" Richard asked in a rough voice, indicating the welfare of his other men was heavy on his mind.

"Peter and the rest of our men are inside the gates. Lord Seton's men are dead. We're in control of the castle," James said.

Richard nodded at the good news.

Arthur's eyes widened when he first saw her. "Lady Katherine, it's good you are unharmed."

The healer quickly made his way to his patient's side and laid his box on the table next to the bed. Opening the chest, he exposed its contents full of medicinal herbs stored in an array of glass vials and various healing instruments. "What do we have here?"

She reported all she knew about the wound and her attempts to assist. The little man furrowed his forehead as he took over Marcus's spot and viewed the open gash.

The healer looked up. "Rosa, I'll need the hot water as soon as it's ready."

"Aye, Arthur." Rosa spun around and exited.

"How does he fare?" Richard asked hoarsely.

"Your man was lucky; a little deeper and he could've lost his life. I'll clean the wound and sew the edges closed. That should stop the blood loss. Then we'll apply cold compresses to bring down the swelling. Afterward, we'll have to let the man rest and see what comes of it," the healer said.

Richard stood at the foot of the bed, one hand gripping the bedpost. "I would be forever grateful if you would attend to his welfare and do everything in your power to heal him."

"Of course, milord. I'll do what I can to help your man," Arthur said.

"I leave all in your capable hands. If you need anything, ask and it will be yours. Marcus, stay and oversee the stitching while I see to the castle?"

Marcus was hovering over Owen and didn't appear to be in any hurry to leave his friend's side. "I'll keep Godfrey with me when he returns, in case Owen wakes."

Richard locked eyes with Marcus, and in that brief moment, she could tell they exchanged an unspoken hope that their friend would survive. Her husband turned on his heels and left with James following in his footsteps.

A moment later, Godfrey and Rosa returned with the boiling water.

Arthur treated Owens's wound and directed the knights in the positioning of the patient.

Since Katherine was no longer needed, she didn't want to be present during the stitching. She gave Rosa, who was standing nearby, a stack of clean chemises to use for bandages and motioned the servant to stay and be available if needed.

From her wardrobe, she grabbed a clean surcoat, kirtle, and chemise. Without disturbing those present, she made her way across the hall to her father's bedchamber.

The sun rising over the water blanketed the room in bright morning light. Scrutinizing her surroundings, she searched for anything amiss. A shiver of revulsion made her tremble when she noticed Lord Seton's personal belongings strewn about.

She gathered all of his things and piled them outside the door to be taken away. Finding her father's money pouch and jewels amongst Lord Seton's items soured her stomach. Immediately, she returned the valuables to her father's hiding spot inside the wardrobe, where they belonged.

When a wave of deep sorrow flowed over her for the loss of a beloved parent, she fought back the tears.

Lord Seton was dead. The man who cruelly killed her family was finally burning in hell. God would make sure he suffered for all eternity.

Richard had come through with his promise of avenging her family. How fitting to have her mother's dagger deal the final death blow.

She was thankful she was present to witness Lord Seton's demise.

The past few days led up to this moment. Relief flooded her body.

It's over.

The intense hatred for Lord Seton that had driven her on, melted away. The gnawing in the back of her stomach dissipated. She spared no pity for him or his men. She couldn't forgive them for what they did so cold-heartedly. They got what they deserved. She wouldn't waste her sympathy on murderers such as them.

She huddled on the window seat, staring out over the ocean as she relived the earlier battle. Owen could've been killed instead of wounded. Lord Seton could've cut her to pieces, had he recognized her sooner. Only by chance had Owen been able to warn Richard that she was in danger, so he could make it to the stairs in time to catch her. Even worse, Lord Seton could have killed Richard.

She shuddered. *Everything is well.*

Now that all signs of Lord Seton were gone from her father's bedchamber, she doffed her squire clothes, washed up, and put on a pure white kirtle with tight-fitting sleeves. Over the elegant garment, she donned a fine woolen, rose-colored surcoat. The low and richly embellished neckline accentuated her womanliness.

She selected her clothes carefully. In this garment, none could mistake her for a child. She braided the front sections of her hair into two ropes, pulled them together at the back of her head, like a crown, and let the rest of her golden locks cascade down her back. Around her waist, she attached her girdle, minus her dagger.

Their conquest of Rosemont was successful. There wasn't much time before Richard left for London to ask the king to dissolve their marriage.

She couldn't bear the thought of losing him. Her only hope was for him to change his mind and decide to keep her for his wife. Unfortunately, the past few days did nothing to prove to him what a worthy wife she would make. If anything, she made herself look weak, foolish, stubborn, and adversarial.

Richard's opinions of her were wrong. She was no longer the child he remembered, but a woman full-grown and one who would make him a good wife. She had the advantage; she was in her own surroundings and could show him how efficiently she ran Rosemont. Maybe, if she impressed him enough, he wouldn't be able to picture another woman in her place.

Rosemont was his now. Through his acquisition, the king gave him permission to take over as the new Lord of the Manor. He could do with her home as he saw fit.

If he were to cast her aside for another, she would lose her beloved home along with the man of her childhood dreams. She wasn't sure she could handle such a blow to her heart. There was no doubt in her mind. The life she wanted was with him.

Lady Elizabeth's words rang in her ears when she left the bedchamber, *if you want someone to share your life, you will have to be strong and fight for the life you want.*

Determined to get what she wanted, she set out on a quest to find Richard.

Walking by her bedchamber, she slowed her steps. She peered in and found Marcus sitting in a chair on one side of her bed and Arthur sitting in a chair on the other. Rosa pressed cool cloths to the back of Owens's head.

Now it was time to wait and see what would happen to the injured man. Hopefully, Owen would wake with all his faculties intact.

She conveyed an optimistic look to Marcus, who, in return, gave her a tight-lipped smile.

As she left the open doorway, she said a silent prayer for the good and loyal knight.

~Chapter Eighteen~

As Katherine stepped onto the upstairs landing, a caustic taste crept into her mouth. She swallowed hard to push back the bitterness. Lord's Seton's body was gone. The only evidence of the earlier fight was a pool of blood where his body had lain. A befitting end for such an evil man. She lifted her skirts, stepped around the darkened spot, and started down the curved stairway.

In the hall below, the other bodies were also gone. Since there was no sign of Richard, she made her way to the front doors leading to the inner bailey. From the top step, she saw an army of men loading carts with corpses in preparation for burial. A strong stench of death hung in the air, causing her nostrils to flare in disgust.

Scared castle folk peeked out from behind partially opened doors and half-shuttered windows. Her heart went out to them. They were curious, yet afraid. These were her people. She had known them her entire life. After the cruelty they endured under Lord Seton's rule, she wanted to lessen their fears about what kind of man their new lord would be.

She began her descent, determined to put their worries to rest.

After two steps, she halted; Richard stood across the way in front of the stable. Thomas and Timothy must have arrived with the horses. Her husband stroked Titan's neck and scratched the beast behind an ear.

How she wished he bestowed upon her the same warm fondness he showed his great steed.

As he glanced her way, she gave him a shy, flirty smile. With her arms held wide, she silently bid him to notice she was no longer dressed as a squire.

Richard flashed a beautiful white-toothed grin and bowed in playful appreciation.

It was a friendly gesture from a man who didn't want her. Even so, it made her heart soar, nonetheless.

Katherine continued on her way. Halfway down the steps, she caught a glimpse of a thick wooden pole standing erect, out of place, in the middle of the garden. Troubled by the unfamiliar sight, she stopped to get a better look. Upon closer inspection, she realized a body hung limply from the post.

Her stomach knotted. How could anyone do such a vile thing?

She turned away from the revolting display. Then she knew.

Oh, my God! It's Mary. Her dear elderly maid, dead and hung in the garden to feed the birds.

Katherine's world whirled uncontrollably. Numb legs shook violently. Standing became almost impossible. She reached without seeing for the handrail and made her way blindly down the last few steps to the yard. Tears welled in her eyes. She rounded the corner and staggered to the wall of the keep. Clutching her stomach, she doubled over as a wave of dry heaves racked her body.

She knew immediately when Richard took up a position next to her, using his body to shield her from view of those in the yard. He gathered her unbound hair in one hand and stroked her back with the other.

He needn't have bothered keeping her curls away from her face; there was nothing in her belly to expel.

When the contractions subsided, she turned and stared blankly at the ties on his leather tunic. "I should never have left her. I should never have left Mary behind. Look what they did to her."

Tears streamed down her cheeks. She closed her eyes. "I should have stayed and let Lord Seton have me. If I had stayed, she would have been alive right now. Tis my fault. Oh, God, it should have been me!"

"Don't say such." He seized her by her shoulders and gave her a firm shake that snapped her head back.

Her eyes shot open. She gulped a big breath of air and let out a gut-wrenching sob. Anger and guilt fought for the upper hand.

"Leave me be," she cried, as her fists pounded inconsequentially on his padded chest.

It was her fault. Lord Seton killed Mary and paraded her dead body on a pole as if her life meant nothing. Her arms stopped drumming, her legs grew weak, and she slumped toward the ground.

Richard wrapped her in a strong embrace and held her tight against his chest as soft sobs shook her body. He murmured in her ear, "You did right by escaping. Things would've turned out very badly. You may not believe it now, but your maid made a good decision to stay behind. She bought you more time. She gave her life so you could live."

Very softly he added, "She must have loved you very much."

Her breath caught in her throat. His deep voice spoke so tenderly.

Was what he said true? She laid the side of her face against his shoulder and quieted her sobs. His matter-of-fact words comforted her as if he stroked her with a gentle caress.

***

Richard made eye-contact with Peter, who hovered close by, and silently bid him to cut down the old woman's body. Once he saw his man understood his orders, he turned his attention back to his wife. As the weeping subsided, her body relaxed.

"Her death is not your fault. She chose to stay behind. If you're going to blame someone, blame Lord Seton. He killed your maid, not you," he whispered soothingly.

When she was steady enough to bear her weight, he guided her along the length of the building toward a waist-high wall overlooking the ocean. Her distress was so powerful, he found himself plagued with a need to take away her pain.

"Anger directed at yourself when someone you care about dies for you will eventually destroy you. I know. It happened to me. Earlier I told you Lord Beckett died in a land dispute. What I failed to mention was that he died saving my life."

She gazed up at him, her black lashes moist with recent tears.

He brushed away a wayward curl plastered to her wet face. Leaning against the stone wall, he gazed out over the ocean. A slight breeze ruffled his hair as he stared at distant waves.

"I was a young knight. The battle was fierce but over quickly. Men were clearing away the dead, and I was helping." He looked down at her upturned face. Empathy was written on her delicate features. He knew he could entrust her with his painful memories.

"A man who looked dead, yet who was only wounded, brought up his crossbow and aimed the arrow at my heart. Lord Beckett dove in front of the shaft meant for me." He paused and took a deep breath, for with the telling came the long-forgotten raw emotions.

He grabbed her under her arms and hoisted her up to sit on the top of the wide stone wall so the two were almost eye level. His big hands encircled her waist, so she couldn't tumble back to the water below.

"I relived the images over and over again in my mind, trying to piece together if I could've done anything different. The nightmares stayed with me for months."

"What did you do?" she asked.

"His death devastated me. I believed it was my fault the man I admired so much was dead and I was still alive. I hated myself. I threw myself wholly into my training. I became crazed. I wanted to punish myself. Punish others. Guilt drove me. William helped me understand the errors of my ways. My dying slowly through my own self-loathing was never Lord Beckett's intention when he saved my life."

He placed two fingers under his wife's chin and raised her head a notch, so he could gaze in her eyes. "Your maid sacrificed herself for you. Don't let her death eat you up inside. She died so you could live. No regrets. Don't look back. As I told you before, we cannot change the past."

Richard brought his hand back down to her waist. "I'm sorry for your loss, but there are a lot of people here who are alive and scared. They are counting on your direction to get them through this change."

She grabbed the long tippet hanging down from her elbow and brought a corner of the material up to wipe her wet face. "Yes, you are right. I have to think about the people of Rosemont. Mary would never have allowed me to wallow in my guilt, not when there are those who need me."

"Good." He swept some of her thick hair over her shoulder, letting the tendrils fall down her back.

When a throat cleared behind them, Richard instinctively reached for the hilt of his dagger. He glanced over his shoulder only to find a young priest standing reverently a good distance away, wringing his hands nervously.

He gave the man a silent nod to speak.

"Excuse me, milord, I wouldn't normally interrupt, except I believe I can be of service. I have intimate knowledge I believe would comfort Lady Katherine," the priest said.

Richard took a step to the side, giving the priest a full view of his wife, but his arm remained wrapped protectively around her waist. "As you will."

The priest moved a few feet closer. "Lady Katherine, I was present when your maid died. A few days ago, after Lord Seton's men brought me here against my will, Lord Seton escorted me up to your bedchamber to perform a wedding ceremony. I saw your maid courageously rush forth from behind a curtain with her dagger held high, ready to kill Lord Seton's man. The man reacted instantly and put his dagger through her heart. It was over in a second. Your maid suffered naught at all. I believe a quick death is what she planned all along. Lord Seton became enraged that his man killed the only person who knew what happened to you, he slew the man in retaliation. He thought to make an example of your maid and hung her body in the garden for all to see after she was already dead."

The priest took a deep breath, then continued with pride, "I made sure the people were aware of her bravery. I hope my telling comforts you. She did not die in agony, as he would have you believe."

"Did you hear that? She did not suffer and passed quick," Richard reassured his wife. He was extremely relieved the old woman found a swift death and Lord Seton never had the chance to extract information through painful torture.

"I am glad she did not suffer unduly." She managed a weak smile. "Thank you. It does help to put my mind at ease."

The young priest beamed. "I'm at your service, milady." He presented her with a respectful bow.

Richard silently dismissed the priest and turned to Katherine. He seized her about her waist, lifted her off the wall and set her feet upon the ground. Cupping her face in his hands, he ran a thumb across the bottom of each eye, wiping away the remaining dampness. "Are you well?"

"I will manage," she said feebly, placing her hands on his forearms.

"If you want to go into the keep and rest, I'd understand."

"No. I want to finish what I set out to do and introduce you to Rosemont's people."

"Good." He placed his hands on her shoulders. "The morning is still young. There's much to do today. The work would go faster if the people of Rosemont were eager to help."

"We ought to have a big mid-day meal for those helping to set things right. I can put together a noon-time feast," she offered.

"It would be well received." He was pleased with his wife's attempt to move forward.

He stole a glance in the direction of the garden to make sure the maid's body was gone. Peter had removed all traces. He berated himself for not seeing to the task sooner when he first noticed the old woman's body but thought to get rid of the bodies in the keep beforehand.

"Where would you like your maid buried? I'll do the deed myself."

"She was very dear to me. I would have her buried close to the family burial site, up on the cliffs, overlooking the water."

He placed a hand on his wife's waist and turned her in the direction of the keep. "As you wish. I'll see it's done."

"Do you know where my father and brother have been laid to rest?" she asked as they walked along.

"I was told the villagers made sure your father and David were buried in their rightful places, next to your mother."

"'Tis good they saw to them."

Richard guided his wife to the steps leading to the Great Hall. He called out to Peter and Thomas, who were standing together in front of the stable and asked them to gather everyone. Making their way up the stairs, the couple stood before the double doors so everyone in the inner bailey could get a good look at them.

"Are you ready?"

"I will be fine." She patted down her windblown hair and smoothed the front of her gown.

He reached into the top of his thigh boot and removed her jeweled dagger. "I believe I promised to return this to its rightful owner."

"My dagger! I cannot begin to tell you how I have missed my blade."

He placed the knife gently in her outstretched hands.

She ran her fingers lovingly over the jewels embedded in the hilt. "My mother gave me this on her deathbed. It is the most cherished thing I possess."

"Then it's good the dagger is back where it belongs."

She sent him a warm, thankful smile before their attention was drawn to the commotion in the inner bailey.

Doors from the kitchen, bakery, smithy, servant's quarters and stables opened. Castle folk streamed into the yard. A large group of villagers strolled in from the outer bailey and outside the castle walls, curious to meet their new lord.

Peter, asserting his role as the knight-in-charge, climbed half-way up the steps and heralded the assembly of people. "Hear ye, hear ye. I give you Sir Richard Weston, your new Lord of Rosemont."

Shouts rang out from his men, along with the people of Rosemont. The introduction sent a shock wave through him that traveled from his head to his toes.

So concerned he was for Katherine's well-being, he hadn't truly prepared himself. The weight of Peter's words became clear. He would be the new Lord of Rosemont. These people were his responsibility. They would look to him for protection, security, and prosperity.

He was so caught up in seeking revenge against Lord Seton and being saddled with an unwanted wife, he neglected to focus on what rewards he would reap from such a conquest. Rosemont was his now; this would be his home, with the king's blessing. There would be no more talk of leasing an estate from Lord Marten.

Finally, he had acquired the holdings he longed for. Why had he been so blind? Katherine befuddled him so, his thoughts were not clear. Throughout the journey, he always thought of Rosemont as her home and his mission was to get the castle back for her.

His wife stood regally at his side, her hand resting on his forearm, silently showing her support. When she looked up, her eyes twinkled with pride, and a sudden rush of elation passed over him.

He addressed the people in a loud, powerful voice. "Good people of Rosemont, some of you may be familiar with my father, Lord Weston of Stamford, who was a good and loyal friend to Lord de Grey and his family. King Edward has heard about the treachery meted out by Lord Seton and sent me to avenge Lord de Grey's death."

The crowd of onlookers let out a unified cheer.

"To keep Lady Katherine safe from those who would do her harm, we have married." The people of Rosemont clapped boisterously, obviously pleased by the news that their beloved mistress was now the lord's lady.

"What we need to do now is unite and work together. There will be much to do in the next couple of weeks, and we need to move forward for a common end. Today will be a day for getting rid of all traces of Lord Seton's rule and a time to heal."

Another ovation sounded from the assembly of men and women. "We'll require assistance burying the dead. For those willing to help, there will be food and drink in the Great Hall for our mid-day meal."

There was a unified shout of approval from the yard.

"You'll find me a fair man. I look forward to continuing in Lord de Grey's footsteps in making Rosemont a safe and prosperous place to live."

He stood tall as the crowd roared three cheers to the new Lord of Rosemont.

The gathering quickly dispersed as his knights busied themselves with directing the eager castle-dwellers and villagers in various duties.

***

Katherine looked out over her people scattered about the inner bailey. She was glad the introductions had gone so well. The people of Rosemont appeared accepting of their new lord and master. She knew in her heart her father would be pleased one of Lord Weston's sons was the next Lord of Rosemont.

Suddenly, she caught sight of a lone woman hiding in the shadows on the side of the kitchen and recognized Matilda's shape. The young serving maid stood against the wall, purposefully out of the castle people's view.

Curious as to why Matilda concealed herself, Katherine made her way down the front steps and across the yard.

As she got closer, Matilda looked up. The maid's hood fell away from her face.

Katherine's breath caught in her throat when she glimpsed what lay beneath the folds. Matilda's beautiful face, so admired by all, was now black, blue and so swollen that her features were hideously distorted. The young serving maid, who once was overly confident, appeared timid and fragile.

Katherine stood directly in front of the hooded figure and gazed into the brown eyes that were almost swollen shut. Slowly, she reached up and gently removed her maid's head covering, letting the material fall around the young woman's shoulders.

***

Richard followed his wife and stopped a few feet away. When the hood dropped, he recognized the signs of broken facial bones. The maid's tightly clutched arms wrapped protectively around her chest spoke loudly of a ravished body. Without a doubt, Lord Seton's men had badly abused the young woman.

A pang of pity went out to the girl, and he silently cursed the man's name. Amazed, he watched as his wife reached up and, ever so delicately, cupped the girls face with both of her hands. With barely a touch, she glided her fingers over the sore, swollen mounds, as if absorbing the pain.

"I am so sorry for your hardship," she said with heartfelt emotion. Her hands halted when they rested on the woman's shoulders.

The maid's puffed-up eyes filled with unshed tears. "Milady, I know you also suffered at their hands."

"Lord Seton is dead now. His men are dead. They can hurt us no more. Our bodies will heal. We did nothing to deserve our suffering. Let us suffer no more from our bad memories."

Rosa, the young maid who fetched the healer earlier, came over and put an arm around the young woman's shoulders. "I'll see to her, milady."

"You are a good friend," his wife said, as Rosa guided the young woman through the side door into the keep.

"Will she be all right?" he asked.

Katherine joined him and stared at the door the women walked through. "Matilda has always been strong. It breaks my heart to see the violence heaped upon her. It will take time, but I think she will be all right."

She locked eyes with him. "I almost wish Lord Seton was still alive so I could kill him again," she said with venom in her voice. "This time slowly. I think I would unman him and then cut out his taunting eyes."

Richard was stunned by the depth of her violent statement. "There's a real blood-thirsty side of you I wasn't aware of. Remind me not to provoke you or I may have trouble sleeping at night. For I fear I would be too busy watching my back, along with a few other vital parts," he teased.

"You cannot say you were never warned," his wife threw over her shoulder, as she made her way toward the kitchen.

He stared after her, not quite sure if he should take her seriously or not.

~Chapter Nineteen~

Richard stepped lively as he made his way through the double doors of the keep. Hours had passed since he last laid eyes on Katherine, but she was never far from his thoughts.

Some moments were more vivid than others…such as when he nudged her awake before daybreak. The way she stretched so enticingly across his fur mantle made his stomach pitch every time he conjured up the image. After his eyes alighted on such a vision, it took all the strength he possessed to walk out the cottage door.

As he relived other encounters in her company, a powerful charge of excitement rushed through his veins. He remembered every look, word, and touch she bestowed upon him, igniting a burning need to return to her side.

Now that he had seen to all pressing matters, he intended to seek her out before their late-night meal.

He was impressed she was able to collect herself and move forward for the sake of her people after a close call with death, followed by a devastating bout of guilt and grief. Throughout the day, he watched her from afar as she ran Rosemont effortlessly. She displayed a good working rapport with her people and never missed a detail, no matter how small.

After leaving him at the bottom of the stairs in the early hours of the morning, she retreated to the kitchens. Not long thereafter, she emerged, followed by a few serving maids carrying trays and baskets filled with food and drink to break his men's fast. His knights and men-at-arms welcomed her kindness and he was much pleased with her thoughtfulness for their welfare.

As the day wore on, he observed with wonder as men, women, and children scurried to and fro doing his wife's bidding. Smiles graced their faces while they helped her prepare for her promised feast.

At mid-day, Richard, his men, and those who helped returned to the hall. He was amazed by all the work his wife had carried out in such a brief time. The stone floor was scrubbed clean of recent bloodstains. Sweet-smelling rushes were scattered like a thin veil over the hard surface. All broken furniture was repaired or replaced.

No outward signs of the early morning battle remained. The meal itself was fit for a king, with course after course of savory food. Ale flowed readily and everyone partaking in the feast was in high spirits, the earlier violence long forgotten.

When she joined him at the head table for their meal, he was accosted by a heady sweet flowery smell, causing his nostrils to flare with the tease. Pleasant and witty, she talked nonstop as she pointed out certain castle folk and their roles. He couldn't help but give her his undivided attention, so beguiled he was in her company. Her delight at being home was contagious and he found himself swept up in the whirlwind.

Once in a while, though, he glimpsed deep within her brilliantly blue eyes a touch of sadness and knew some of her grief still simmered beneath.

During their meal, he realized his new wife was so more than just ravishing. Although he had caught himself today, on more than one occasion, staring with desire at the tops of her rounded breasts deliciously displayed in her finery, he found himself noticing something more. What he missed earlier was how she radiated warmth and life. He was drawn to her as strongly as he had been to the baker's fresh berry pies when he was but a boy.

As their meal came to a close, he wished the time spent with his wife didn't have to end. With great reluctance, he left the hall to get back to work. There was much to do to fortify the castle and surrounding countryside. Danger still loomed. An unknown number of Lord Seton's men, who were out searching for her, would return soon.

He also didn't know who Lord Seton's accomplice was or how important Rosemont was in their plot to rule England. He would let caution be his guide and sent Miles down the tunnel to lock the gate and make sure the secret passages remained closed and invisible to the eye.

Now, hours later, he scoured his surroundings impatiently for his wife as he strolled into the well-lit hall. When he found no sign of her, his lips drew taut in disappointment.

He went to the second floor and checked on Owen. The big knight was in the center of the ornately carved bed, where they had propped him in a half-sitting position. His eyes were closed. Thick arms rested limply across his waist. The young girl with the broken face stood over him and held a compress to the back of his head.

"How is my man?" he asked.

The young girl flinched in fear.

"I would like to see him well. He's a good friend of mine," his voice came out purposely soft and yielding.

The maid regained her composure but dropped her head to hide her face. "Your man woke a little while ago, and I gave him a sip of water. He fell back to sleep within minutes. There's no sign of a fever as yet. Lady Katherine says I'm to tend him and find her if anything changes."

"Very well. Do you know where she is?" He thought his wife was very shrewd to have this girl care for the welfare of another, rather than focus on her recent hardships.

"Awhile back, milady came by to check on how he fared. She went into the master bedchamber."

Richard hastily turned on his heels and crossed the hallway. He opened the heavy oak door but was instantly disheartened to find the room empty. A large wooden tub sat in front of the hearth, appearing to have recently been used. The strong scent of lavender floated in the air, along with remnants of moisture from the warm bath.

On a nearby chair, stacked neatly, he found a pile of his clothes she must've had delivered.

Frustrated he was no closer to finding his wife, he left the bedchamber with quickened steps as he returned to the hall.

"Have you seen Lady Katherine?" he asked the first serving girl he came upon.

"Yes, milord, she's resting on her father's chair by the fire."

He sent a puzzled look to the grouping of upholstered chairs in front of the richly decorated hearth. Surely, he would've noticed someone sitting by the fire when he strode by earlier. He made his way to the sitting area and walked around to the front of the biggest high-backed chair in the group.

A smile tugged his lips when he found his wife curled up in a ball, snuggled against the padding. Her slender arms wrapped around her bent legs, which were drawn tight against her chest. Damp golden waves of hair encircled her body.

Again, she appeared almost angelic in her exhausted state.

Richard expelled a noisy sigh of disappointment. The day was long. He couldn't fault her for surrendering to her fatigue. As much as he desired to spend time with her, he would let her be.

He bent down, scooped her up in his arms, and let her rose-colored gown and long hair fall around them.

Jostled slightly awake, she reached one arm around his neck and rested her head against his shoulder. Her eyelids, heavy with sleep, opened no more than slits. She shook her head to rouse herself, but her eyes remained almost closed.

"Put me down. I can walk. I am not a child," she whispered.

"That you are not. But neither can you walk, so you'll have to trust me to make sure you find your bed."

"I have a meal to get ready. I have things to do," she protested wearily.

"You've done enough today. Your people will present the meal."

She drifted deeper into sleep as he carried her upstairs. Once they entered the master bedchamber, he brought her to the massive four-poster bed, peeled down the fresh bed linens, and laid her gently on top of a clean coverlet. As she snuggled up to a soft feather pillow, he unlaced and removed her leather ankle boots.

Standing over her slumbering form, he contemplated taking off her surcoat, kirtle, and stockings, then decided against undressing her. She was far too tempting in full dress, never mind with almost nothing on.

Visions of the morning at the inn came back to haunt him. Memories of soft, creamy skin stretching perfectly over well-formed curves taunted him.

Recalling his impassioned vows, he let out a low growl of defeat. He reached for the blankets and dragged them over his sleeping wife.

Tonight, she would sleep fully clothed.

The thought of going to the hall for the late-night dinner no longer appealed to him now that he wouldn't be in the company of his spirited wife. He gazed longingly at the already filled tub beckoning him from its place of honor in front of a low-burning fire. A soak might be just the thing he needed to rid himself of his newfound restlessness.

He stood next to the elaborate man-sized basin and tested the water. As he hoped, the temperature was still tepid. He discarded his clothing, stepped into the tub, and let the water flow over his sore muscles. His eyes closed and his mind wandered wherever it would take him.

Unfortunately, the flowery scent wafting from the perfumed water steered his thoughts toward the lovely woman lying peacefully in his bed. Suddenly, multiple reasons why he should break his vows and consummate his marriage came to mind.

Alas, as an honorable man, it wasn't his practice to take vows lightly. When knighted, he swore an oath before God to uphold the codes of honor. It was important for him to remain faithful to his pledged words, even impulsive ones.

In jeopardy of giving in to temptation, he grabbed the slimy bar of soap sitting on the bottom of the tub and vigorously scrubbed in an attempt to rid himself of his dangerous considerations. After soaping his shoulder-length black hair, he rinsed the strands before stepping out of the wooden tub. He made haste to wipe away the moist droplets of water and quickly donned the carefully arranged clean clothes.

Still restless, he decided to visit Titan in the stables and leave the master bedchamber with all its temptations behind. If distraction didn't help with his demons, he would go for a vigorous ride to clear his head. Since he was a firm believer in a well-set course, he was hopeful a positive outcome could be had.

On his way through the room, he noticed the day was almost over, and night would soon be upon them. At the twin windows, he shut the hinged windowpanes to keep out the night chill coming off the ocean. The day was milder than most, so there would be no need to close the wooden shutters tonight.

When he walked by the master bed, Richard slowed his steps. He leaned over the mattress, adjusted the blankets around Katherine's small shape and swept away a rebel curl from the side of her delicate face. Her chest rose and fell in an easy rhythm. When his eyes fixed on her slightly parted red lips, he could almost taste their sweetness.

He shook himself out of his tempting contemplations, and with every ounce of strength he possessed, he turned and walked away.

~Chapter Twenty~

Richard faded in and out of a half-sleep. The heat from the hearth's embers warmed his face as he reclined in a chair with his long legs stretched out before him. A whimper cut through the usual noises of the night, yet he sensed no real danger, so he kept his eyes closed.

Hours ago, he left his bedchamber for the sanctuary of the stables. Unable to find the tranquility he craved, he engaged in a groundbreaking ride to the Connor cottages. Once there, he accepted an invitation for dinner, but the meal didn't distract him from his unwanted thoughts.

While he observed Thomas and Helen together as man and wife, his ache grew stronger. Everywhere he looked, he saw images of Katherine's sweet face, laughing at his jesting or blushing at his teasing. After only a short stay, he excused himself and returned to his bedchamber where he found a tormented peace, the woman causing his unrest only a few feet away.

A muffled noise came from the direction of the twin windows. One of the glass panels must be ajar; a cool draft caressed the back of his neck. In the distance, he heard the pounding of the surf slapping against the cliffs below.

He slowly opened his heavy-lidded eyes and glanced over his shoulder to the narrow, cushioned seat below the windows. Long before he saw his wife curled up in a ball in the corner, he knew who was breaking the room's silence. Her soft, sad noises mingled occasionally with a lone sniffle.

Richard's stomach knotted. His throat tightened. What did he know about weeping women?

Absolutely nothing.

He had never been around one for more than a few seconds. He avoided females with complaints. In the past, he managed to evade trouble.

His first instinct was to sneak out of the room and leave the woman to her misery, but this was not just any lady, this was Katherine. He hated to see her sad.

Noiselessly, he left the comfort of his chair and made his way to stand at her side.

***

Deep in her own thoughts, Katherine startled when a heavy hand landed upon her shoulder. She had hoped not to arouse a slumbering Richard, but luck was not on her side.

Earlier, when she woke from an unsettling nightmare, she was too upset to stay alone in the oversized bed. The window seat with its cool ocean breeze offered a safer haven, yet she underestimated the depth of her despair. When she saw her husband, the new Lord of Rosemont, sleeping in a chair because she was not worthy enough to share a bed, it reminded her of what a disappointment she was.

In the darkened bedchamber, her thoughts had drifted to the days before Lord Seton's takeover, and self-pity soon turned to self-loathing. Without warning, incredible guilt and misery racked her mind. To no avail, she tried to hold back her emotional turmoil, but her sadness knew no bounds. Her tears pushed forth, and the weeping began.

Now she would pay the price. For the man she had tried so hard to impress was standing next to her and was once again a witness to her failings.

She gazed out the open window and wiped her wet lashes with her long dangling tippets. Thankfully, the ocean breeze helped cool her heated cheeks.

"What ails you?" His hand lightly caressed the bare skin, just below the back of her neck.

She willed herself to ignore the tingling sensation his gentle touch elicited and instead focused on the moonlight glistening off the smooth waves of the ever-changing ocean. She didn't want to share her thoughts, but knowing him as she did, she knew he wouldn't go away without an answer.

"I guess I am sad. I never had a chance to tell my father and David, *Goodbye*."

"I believe there's more to your tears than that. Tell me," he insisted.

She cringed and silently cursed him for being so all-knowing. Why did he always press her for more? Why did he always pry? Why could he not just leave her alone to deal with her grief and guilt?

Out of the corner of her eye, she watched him take a relaxed position in the opposite corner of the narrow seat. He made a point to fold his arms over his chest as if he had all the time in the world. She hugged her knees together, pulling them against her body as a means of protecting herself from uncomfortable feelings she was sure would arise.

She pursed her lips and heaved an annoyed sigh. "Where do you want me to start?"

In a streak of moonlight shining through the windows, his face was visible. He arched a brow. "How about the beginning?"

She gave him one of her best-disgruntled looks. When he didn't flinch, she stared out over the water.

"I guess I could start on your father's last day at Rosemont," she said grudgingly.

"That will do."

She inhaled a deep breath of courage. "As we often did, around mid-morning, your father and I took a walk to the cliffs. I must have been quieter than usual because your father noticed right away that I was a little melancholy."

She pursed her lips and said with a hint of annoyance, "You know how he is when he gets a whiff of something; he is like a hound after a fox."

Richard smiled slightly and nodded.

Suddenly, it dawned on her; he was just like his father. *He's his father's son.*

"I mentioned to your father I was a little disappointed I never had a suitor for my hand in marriage, nor had anyone shown interest throughout the years."

She looked down as she twisted a long strand of hair around her fingers. "I worried maybe there was something wrong with me. That my time was past, and I was destined to spend the rest of my life with my family, here at Rosemont."

Katherine lifted her head and gazed out the window. Her cheeks flamed with humiliation for being forced to share her innermost thoughts.

"Your father assured me there was nothing wrong with me. He said he was sure it was an oversight. That many of the titled lords searching for a wife probably forgot I was available since I rarely traveled."

She stole a glance at Richard. His face was blank, and she couldn't tell what he was thinking.

"On our walk back to the castle, your father was overly quiet and preoccupied. When we reached the garden, he left me and went into the keep.

The weather turned cold. A few minutes later, I went up to my room to get my gloves. That's when I heard a heated argument coming from my father's bedchamber. Your father's voice was raised in anger. I did not mean to eavesdrop, honestly, I did not. Tis just that I had never heard your father use such a tone before."

"What were they discussing?"

"Me. Your father accused my father of being dishonest and unfair to me. He said he could no longer stand by while my father and brother misled me at every turn. He wanted to tell me the truth."

Richard leaned forward. "What truth?"

She wiped the moisture from the corners of her eyes and turned her head away from his view. "He accused my family of keeping me a virtual prisoner of Rosemont so I was available to see to their needs. Your father said they were selfish to deny me my right to find a husband and start my own family."

"What was your father's reaction?"

"My father said he would not part with me. He needed me here and could not bear to have me marry someone who would take me away." Her voice strained with emotion.

She stifled a sniffle with the back of her hand. "He told your father he did not regret turning away any suitors who showed up at his gate."

"Were you aware of what your father was doing?"

"I had no reason to believe he would do such a thing. I realize now that David and my father used elaborate ruses to get me out of the castle and far away if anyone came to call. More than once, they sent me out to care for a sick villager who did not appear sick. Father always had feasible excuses for his mistakes."

"How did you react when you found out?"

"At first, I was hurt and disappointed my family resorted to trickery to keep me close. I could understand some of my father's reluctance. After my mother died, he fell apart, so the running of Rosemont was left to me. By and by, over the years, he had almost no responsibilities, with David taking over most everything else."

"Tell me the rest." His blue eyes stared intensely.

Her eyes filled to the brim with tears. She gazed out over the water and hugged her knees even tighter.

"Your father said he was ashamed of my father and David for going to such lengths as spreading vicious rumors amongst the nobles that I had experienced a horrible kitchen accident and my face had been frighteningly disfigured."

She inhaled deeply to steady her shaky voice. "When I heard what they did, I was horrified. They wholly betrayed me. It was not enough for them to just turn away possible suitors. They made me undesirable to those who might be interested, blatantly lied to our peers, and tarnished my good name. Anyone coming upon me and seeing I am not disfigured would know my family lied and our name would be a disgrace."

***

Richard had heard the lies. The rumors had circled more than once. Lord de Grey's daughter wasn't to be considered for a wife due to the hideous scars marring her face. High ranking nobles weren't interested in a wife they'd have to hide away, even with a sizable dowry. They wanted a wife like Lady Elizabeth, one whose beauty was coveted by all.

"I was livid. I threw open my father's door and accused him of betrayal. I berated him for his selfishness and for treating me so poorly. I told him I never wanted to speak to him or David again. They could no longer count on me for their comforts, and I would go live at a convent. The two of them could rot at Rosemont for all I cared." Her voice rose with agitation.

He wondered if that was the plan she gave up when she was forced to marry him. He didn't think she would've made a good nun.

"I locked myself in my bedchamber. Your father came to my door. He tried to console me. I refused to listen. He left soon after. Both my father and David also attempted to make amends over the next few days. I stayed locked in my room, and their apologies fell on deaf ears. I had never been so angry. I hated them for what they did," she said harshly.

Richard watched her closely as he waited for the rest.

She shut her eyes to hold back the flood gates, but the tears pushed through and ran down her cheeks. He stopped himself from reaching out to wipe them away.

"Then I wished them dead," she wailed, covering her face with her hands. "I did. I said the words and meant them. I could not help myself. I fear their deaths fall on me alone."

Her shoulders sagged under the weight of her guilt.

"Their deaths are not your fault. You might've wished them dead in the heat of anger, but you certainly didn't mean it and are not responsible for them being murdered."

Katherine uncovered her face. "But I am. Do you not see? My father and David would never have let Lord Seton through the gates if not for me."

She pleaded with him to understand. "They would have sent him on his way like they had done so many times before. They were trying to appease me because I was so angry with them. They wanted to make things right, and it killed them."

"You need to stop taking responsibility for everyone's deaths and accept what happened as something out of your control. If your father and David hadn't let Lord Seton in, he would still have found a way to kill them. Murdering them was his intent all along."

"But…"

"There will be no more trying to convince me you are in any way responsible. Wishing someone dead does not make it so. I'll not allow you to wallow in guilt, not yours to bear. You did nothing wrong. You had every right to be angry at your family. Although your father and David went about it in the wrong way, they did what they did because they couldn't abide the thought of you leaving them."

Katherine brushed away the moisture under her eyes.

"What you need now is to end your turmoil. You were right in the beginning when you said you never said *Goodbye*"

Suddenly, it occurred to him what they had to do.

"Get up." He stood, grabbed her by her wrist, and helped her to her feet.

She blankly stared at him.

"Let's stop the nightmares. It's almost dawn. If we leave now, you'll have some privacy before the castle wakes."

Richard threw his leather tunic on over his white shirt and buckled his sword belt. He sat on the edge of the chair, donning one boot at a time, and then sheathed his sword and dagger. A lantern was lit with a stick from the fire.

"Put on your boots, get your cloak, and we'll be on our way." He retrieved his mantle and draped it over his shoulders.

When she didn't move, he seized her hand and led her to a bench at the foot of the bed where he made her sit. He put on her boots and tied them tight. Placing her hand in his again, he tugged her to her cloak hanging on a hook by the door. After wrapping the mantle around her shoulders, he pulled her hair out from beneath the wool before he gave the cords a quick tie. He then retrieved the lantern off the table, escorted her out of their room, and guided her along the blackened passage.

"Where are we going?"

"You'll see," he said.

As they made their way down the stone steps into the hall, their ears were assaulted by loud snoring. Many of the men-at-arms who traveled with them were bedded down on pallets along the walls.

Richard steered his wife past one man after another until they arrived at the double doors without waking a one. The blackness continued to encircle them as they made their way through the inner bailey, then the outer bailey, and finally to the wooden gate.

He ordered the guards on duty in the stone tower to open the doors, raise the portcullis, and let down the bridge. The men hurried to do his bidding. When all was done, he walked his wife over the drawbridge and into the eerie darkness, the one lantern's flame illuminating them in a small ring of light.

Katherine followed him without a word as they climbed the small hill on the side of the castle to the family burial ground. On top of the cliffs, he gazed out over the water. The silvery moonlight danced on the ocean waves, lighting up the clearing in a soft glow. The mounds of freshly turned earth were apparent, even in the muted haze.

He let go of his wife's hand.

"It's time to say goodbye."

He strolled over to a bench under a small tree and extinguished the flame from the lantern. It was better to not call attention to themselves, out in the open as they were, away from the castle's protection. Dawn would soon arrive. At the moment, there was enough light to see into the shadows. He unsheathed his sword and gave Katherine his back. As he stood guard, he continuously scanned the tree line and surrounding landscape for any movement or anything alerting him to danger.

***

Katherine stood alone, staring down at the mounds of dirt. Someone, probably the priest, had erected crosses with the names of her father and brother carved in the softwood. Although she couldn't read the writing in the dark, she knew the names were theirs.

It finally dawned on her. Richard wanted to give her a chance to say farewell to her family in private, out of sight of prying eyes. He wanted to end her suffering.

The thought of facing her grief was terrifying.

Katherine fought off a strong urge to race back to the castle. She wanted to return to her father's bedchamber and hide under the covers. She wanted someone to tell her she was merely having a bad dream, and they were still alive.

Her vision blurred; wetness pooled in her eyes, threatening to cascade like a waterfall. She was scared. If she said goodbye, her family would be gone forever. They would really be dead.

Hot tears blazed a path down her cheeks.

They are dead.

After days of brushing aside her sadness, she finally had to pay her dues. Her trembling hands flew to her face, but it was too late, her suppressed emotions rose to the surface. Deep sobs burst forth. She sank to her knees between the two newly dug graves and sifted fresh dirt through her fingers as streams of tears poured over her cheeks.

Her emotions choked her as she silently told them how much she loved them…how sorry she was for her hurtful words…how she missed and forgave them. When she said everything she had to say, she finally found the courage to utter a whispered goodbye.

The sun began to rise. Day was breaking and with it came the morning light. She noticed Mary's fresh mound outside the family area, in a place set aside for those held dear.

Richard told her he'd take care of her beloved maid and he had.

On wobbly legs, she staggered to her maid's gravesite. Back on her knees, she openly wept as she said a few words over the old woman's final resting place. She patted the damp earth and thanked her longtime companion for the sacrifice of her life.

When she had nothing left to say, she rose from her knees and glanced over her shoulder at Richard, who remained vigilant. Her husband stood with his back to her, his mantle draped about his broad shoulders making him appear much larger.

A chill from the ocean breeze sent a shiver through her body. Her farewells were done. Although she was emotionally drained, the frightful darkness lifted from her soul. She was relieved. Her life could move forward.

Loose soil clung to her bare hands and she brushed away the dirt. Using the edge of her cloak, she wiped the lingering dampness from her face. She shut her swollen eyes and breathed in deeply of the salty ocean air, letting the freshness heal her shattered heart. When a peacefulness washed over her, she drew her hood over her head and made her way to her husband's side.

"The sun is coming up, and the castle is waking. Are you ready to return?" he asked, not looking her way.

"I am ready," she replied in a choked voice.

Richard returned his sword to his hip and adjusted his mantel. He set off down the hill toward the castle, so she followed on his heels.

Marcus watched them from the edge of the drawbridge, his sword unsheathed, the tip wedged into the earth. Once they were upon him, he nodded a silent greeting and fell in behind as they entered the castle.

Katherine, melted into the folds of her cloak, trying to make herself small. The castle people were stirring, a scattered few going about their morning duties. Her steps were quick. She hoped to make it into the keep without drawing too much attention.

Richard halted at the bottom of the stairs, one hand on the rail. She strode past him and climbed the steps leading to the Great Hall.

"We ride today to London. Be packed and ready to leave within the hour," he called after her, his deep voice breaking the silence.

Disoriented by his announcement, Katherine almost faltered. She regained her balance with the help of the rail and forced herself to continue up the last few steps. Moving without really seeing, she raced across the Great Hall and up to the second floor where her sanctuary awaited.

Finally, gaining the privacy of their bedchamber, she slumped onto a cushioned chair and removed her hood with trembling fingers. The meaning of his words sunk in. An ominous wave of foreboding washed over her and made her quiver.

Richard wanted to leave Rosemont as soon as possible. He was ready to be free of her. The moment was forewarned, but she had hoped for more time. He wanted an audience with the king, so he could end his unwanted marriage. He aspired to marry another.

She ruined any chance she had of winning his heart when she let her grief spill out. How could she have been so foolish to drop her guard? He didn't want anyone by his side who was weak and required constant attention.

Katherine resigned herself to her fate and decided not to waste her tears on a man that didn't want her. She would end their marriage with all the dignity she could muster.

Silently, she vowed to remain strong.

~Chapter Twenty-One~

Katherine stood over the washbasin and splashed cool water on her swollen eyes. A quick knock startled her.

She reached for a clean cloth. "Enter."

The door opened. Rosa stood in the entrance, her hands clasped at her waist. "Milady, your husband sent me to help you prepare for your journey. He said he would take a cart for supplies, so you can pack a chest of your things if you want."

She wiped away droplets of water threatening to run down her neck. He wanted her to take what she needed because she wouldn't return to Rosemont.

Her newfound resolve faltered; dread rose like a ball in her throat and restricted her breathing until she swallowed the sentiment down.

"My clothes and traveling box are in my old bedchamber. I will pack myself. Gather a few strong men to carry my chest down when I am finished. I also need you to find Joyce, George, and Arthur so I may direct them in their duties while I am gone. Have them wait downstairs. I will join them, shortly."

After Rosa left, Katherine strode across the hall to her old room; a flickering candle guiding her steps. She pushed the weighty door open slowly, so as not to wake Owen. The thick drapes were closed against the early morning light, blanketing the room in darkness. At the foot of the bed on the floor, Matilda slept on a pallet.

"Lady Katherine, is that you?" Owen called in a weak voice.

She lifted the candle in the direction of the knight. "I am sorry I disturbed you."

"Not at all. I'm glad to see you," he said hoarsely.

She strolled to the window, blew out her candle, then drew back the drapes to let in the morning rays.

Matilda stirred.

"How are you faring?" she asked Owen, who was propped up on pillows in her old bed.

"I've felt better. I have a headache like no other." A hint of humor sounded in his tone.

"I am sure you have." She went to his side and placed the palm of her hand on his forehead, then ran her fingers along both sides of his face. "Tis good you are without a fever. You are awake and alert, also fine signs of healing."

She pressed a cup of water to his lips.

After quenching his thirst, the knight said, "Please forgive me, Lady Katherine. I fear I failed you yesterday."

She returned the cup to the side table. "Nonsense. Why do you say such?"

"I was unable to protect you from Lord Seton."

"Well, none of us could have foreseen his cowardice. It was no one's fault he attacked from behind and without warning."

"Marcus tells me you were put in harm's way, and your life was in grave danger. I'm sorry for not taking better care of you."

"You did just fine. Things would have turned out a lot worse if you had not made your way to the wall to call out to Richard. I thank you for that."

The tension vanished from the knight's face. "I heard he saved your life and then put to death Lord Seton. I'll do better protecting you the next time you need me."

"I hope there will not be a next time. I am afraid I have endured more than enough danger in the past week to last a lifetime," she teased.

Matilda rose from her pallet. Although the maid's face remained bruised and swollen, a small flicker of purpose smoldered in the depths of her eyes.

Katherine nodded to her in greeting. "Sir Owen, since you are on the mend; I will leave your care in Matilda's very capable hands. I travel with my husband to London this morning, and we may be gone for a while."

Surprise crossed the knight's face. "I wish I were going with you."

"I can tell you are an adventurous soul," she said amiably. "Matilda, since Sir Owen is awake, go fetch him something to break his fast. He will need his strength to heal."

"Yes, milady," the maid said and left the room.

"Richard asked me to gather my things, so we can be off." She opened the lid of a small trunk against the wall and began removing clothes and personal items from her wardrobe. After folding them, she stacked them neatly at the bottom of the leather-hinged chest.

Owen observed her with quiet interest. The man's health was much improved. She would've been reluctant to leave if his condition had taken a turn for the worse.

Two burly servants arrived to carry her chest down to the waiting cart.

"Arthur, our healer, will make sure you mend nicely, without pain. Rest and do not do too much, too soon. Matilda will stay with you and take care of your needs. Do not hesitate to ask for what you need; it will be yours. I am not sure when I will see you again, but I will pray you recover well."

"Thank you, Lady Katherine. Godspeed."

She gave him a warm smile before leaving.

***

Less than an hour later, Katherine emerged from the family chapel and made her way across the Great Hall to the double doors leading outside. While breaking her fast earlier, she spoke to the castle servants about their duties in her absence. Not sure when she would get another chance, she sought out the new castle priest to put her mind at ease before her journey.

Finished with her preparations, she stood on the keep's landing and scanned the inner bailey. The men and their mounts were waiting. She recognized the knights who would join them as William's three and two of Richard's own. The knights wore light chainmail. Their armor, extra weapons, and supplies were loaded in the cart along with her wooden chest.

Richard stood beside Titan as he talked to Peter, his knight-in-charge, who would stay behind to run Rosemont in her husband's absence. Marcus held the reins of her saddled mare, along with the reins of his stallion. Her mood improved when she realized she'd be riding her palfrey. She made haste down the steps to her mount.

"Good morning, Sir Marcus. I see you will ride with us," she said brightly, glad to have the older knight as a companion on their journey.

"I would be amiss if I didn't see our quest all the way through."

"No matter why you are here, tis good to have you with us." Katherine rubbed her horse's velvet muzzle, and her mare mouthed her open palm. She ran her hand down the muscular neck and entwined her fingers in the silky mane.

"My mare is well?"

"Aye, Lady Katherine, she's sound and ready to carry your weight," Marcus replied.

"I am anxious to ride her." She wrapped her arm around the mare's neck and gave her horse an affectionate pat.

One of Richard's knights pushed his way past Marcus's large frame. "Lady Katherine may I be of service and help you mount?"

"Yes, Sir James, I believe you could," she said, surprised by the man's show of gallantry.

***

Richard turned in time to see his youngest knight drooling over his wife and regretted agreeing to let him ride along. He left Titan with Peter and rushed to her side.

"James, find your horse. I will assist Lady Katherine." He moved the eager young man out of the way with his bulk.

James didn't seem daunted and flashed a broad smile at his wife before he stepped aside.

"It's a good thing Owen is better for I surely wouldn't have wanted to be left behind." Marcus chuckled.

Richard shot Marcus an icy look.

Marcus snickered as he heaved himself up onto the back of his charger. "I foresee that our travels will be very entertaining."

Shaking his head in defeat, Richard lifted Katherine onto the saddle. She gazed down at him from atop her palfrey, and he caught a bit of sadness on her sweet face.

"Come, I'll have you ride by my side. Someone has to make sure you don't get into trouble. I'm not sure I ate enough food this morning to do any damsel rescuing, so you will need to behave," he said lightheartedly, attempting to draw out a smile.

When her eyes twinkled in response, a rush of warmth flowed through his veins. He studied her closely and noted she had recovered from the early morning hours. Even though her face remained puffy, a light pink hue had returned to her cheeks.

He did the right thing by taking her to the graves, although when he heard her gut-wrenching sobs, he questioned his sanity for putting her through such heartache.

Richard swung up on Titan and easily sat his seat while his high-spirited stallion pranced, muscles rippling with anticipation. He nodded farewell to Peter and then made sure his wife was at his side.

"Ready?"

Katherine nodded. She took up her reins and smiled broadly when she had to control her excited mount.

"We ride!" he roared over his shoulder to his men, who let out a collective hoot of approval.

The couple led the riders in a steady canter, two by two, through the outer bailey and over the drawbridge. Castle dwellers and villagers alike lined their path and cheered them on their way, wishing *Godspeed* to their new lord and lady.

Upon arriving at the edge of the woods, the horses slowed their pace to a brisk walk for the trailing cart.

***

Katherine delighted in the beautiful day and the miles flew by quickly. Each knight took his turn riding out front, scanning for anything amiss. Their constant attention to safety made her feel well-protected. She willed herself not to think too deeply about the past few days, or what might lie ahead. She would just take pleasure in the sunny weather and the ever-changing scenery. Her little mare's lively gait was enjoyable as the young palfrey tried to keep up with the larger horses.

She stole sidelong glances at Richard as he rode upon Titan. Power and strength radiated from both man and beast. Her husband's back remained straight and his head held high. Big calloused hands clutched softly to loose reins, so as to not distress his horse. His dark wavy hair and short-cropped beard added a ruggedness that made him so handsome her heart pounded uncomfortably. She found herself so drawn to him that she struggled with unresolved yearnings. Unfortunately, she had to keep reminding herself that her desires would remain unfulfilled, for he didn't return her affection.

Around noontime, the riders came upon a huge clearing with a narrow stream running on the outskirts. In the center of the field, an oak tree stood alone. By the water, Richard signaled the knights to dismount.

She reined her mare alongside Titan. "Would you mind if I raced my mare across the grass to the tree and back? Since your father gave her to me, I have longed to find out how fast she can run. He said they bred her for speed. I just want to see if it is so," she pleaded, batting her eyes for effect.

He glanced at Marcus, who was preparing to dismount and asked cheerfully, "What say you, Marcus? Katherine wants to test her mare. Is the animal sound enough for a sprint to the tree and back?"

"As well as she's ever going to be. I see no harm in giving the mare her head." Marcus chortled.

"I guess I wouldn't be opposed, especially if I were to ..." her husband began.

She kicked her palfrey into an explosion of motion.

"… race you," he called after her.

She urged the mare into a ground eating gallop and sunk low over her horse's neck. When she slackened the reins with outstretched arms, her animal sprinted into the wind. The sound of Titan pounding the earth behind her made her push her little mare to quicken her pace.

She smiled when the animal gave her even more. *This is heaven.*

At the moment, there was only her and her horse. They were one. Nothing else mattered. Nothing except, of course, beating Richard and Titan. The warhorse's heavy breathing sounded from behind, she sank even lower over her horse's neck.

***

Richard knew Katherine could ride; she rode with the boys many times when they were younger, but he had no idea how skillful a rider she was until now. A few lengths ahead, she adeptly maneuvered her horse over the rough terrain.

Golden hair and unfettered gowns billowed behind her, making her appear as if she had wings and could fly. When she rounded the tree, a look of pure joy shown on her pretty features. Suddenly, he realized she was indeed gaining ground, so he coaxed Titan into a faster stride after cornering the tree.

The two horses were neck and neck when they reached the imaginary line the knights erected. When the horses crossed the finish, cheers went up, along with a good deal of back-slapping.

After they ran past the onlookers, his wife brought her horseback down to a high-stepping prance. The mare protested the slower pace by rearing up, which made her grin grow even larger. Once the mare's front hooves were again firmly on the ground, she patted her horse's silky neck.

"Easy, Velvet," she soothed.

He rode up beside her. "Velvet? You named her?"

"I guess I did." She laughed. "Did you see her fly? She raced like the wind and had the smoothest gallop, like floating on air."

"I believe I won," he stated smugly.

"I think not. I could have sworn Velvet crossed the line before your massive beast." She swung her horse around and headed back to their party.

"We had a disadvantage. You started before us," he complained.

"'Tis not my fault you were slow to react to your own challenge."

"The words never crossed my lips before you were already gone; besides, poor Titan carried a heavier load."

"I cannot help that my horse is a little faster than yours," Katherine boasted. She leaned over her mare's neck and caressed both sides, giving Richard a clear view of rounded breasts spilling forth over her low neckline.

His face blanched and loins hardened. He inhaled and exhaled a couple of unhurried breaths to slow down his wildly beating heart. As he fell in behind his wife, he struggled to gather his wits.

Since this morning, he tried remaining indifferent to her nearness in order to protect himself from his longings. As the miles passed, his resolve grew more and more difficult. He kept telling himself he only had to stay away from her one more night but dreaded the torture the next few hours would bring.

Katherine reached the circle of knights first and reined in her horse. "Sir Marcus, tell me I won."

"Now, you know I'm bound by my oath to tell the truth," the knight said with a chuckle.

She gazed at Marcus longingly, hope shining in her eyes.

The older knight's face lit up in a wide-toothed grin. "The truth of it is, I would have to say Lady Katherine's mare won by a hair."

Collectively, the knights on the ground let out snorts of amusement as they took turns slapping Marcus on the back and pushing him around.

Unable to contain her pleasure, his wife threw back her head and let out a peal of laughter. "I knew it," she exclaimed, making the surrounding men smile at her unrestrained pleasure.

"Better luck next time," she teased.

Richard raised his brow at Marcus and received a noncommittal shrug in return. He dismounted and reached for his wife. Instantly, he was taken aback by the potency of their touch. Fire burned his fingertips. As her body slid down his to stand beside him, he shuddered from the assault.

James brought him out of his bothersome reactions when he asked if he could do the honors of walking out his wife's mare. She gave the young knight a grateful look as he took Velvet's reins.

"Enough of this play. We'll never make it to London if we don't make haste. Katherine, come sit, share a bite to eat, and rest. We still have many miles to go before we camp for the night."

His desire to get to London became much more powerful as a deep sense of urgency tore at his gut.

~Chapter Twenty-Two~

Katherine's excitement grew to spine-tingling heights as the group of riders crossed the River Thames by way of London Bridge. Once across the swift-moving river, she and the band of knights rode into the heart of the city. Never had she beheld a town such as London. She craned her neck, not wanting to miss a thing.

Whitewashed houses made of weathered timber and hardened clay lined the narrow streets. Hundreds of shingled and thatched roofs dotted the horizon. Puffs of thick black smoke swirled from legions of rooftop chimneys, painting the sky a hazy gray.

Townsfolk of all shapes and sizes eyed the mounted party with open curiosity while scurrying back and forth in front of the riders. On both sides of the thoroughfare, a busy market skirted the group's path. The noise rose to deafening levels as merchants hawked their wares.

Katherine, seated upon Velvet's back, kept pace alongside Richard while they maneuvered through the maze of people. Her nostrils flared in distaste when she caught a whiff of the repugnant stench rising from the drainage channels running along the street. She covered her nose and mouth with a piece of her tippet to ward off the foul smell. Down the alleys, dogs and swine vied for piles of waste left behind. People walking past, over the uneven cobblestones, paid little notice of the mangy animals foraging for food and went about their business as if the sight was not unusual.

As the riders moved deeper into the city, the crowd grew larger, the hustle and bustle more frenzied, and people showed less interest in the riders, making it harder to cut through the throng.

She worried about causing someone harm if they failed to move out of her way, so she reined Velvet in, falling back behind Titan. Marcus and Godfrey took positions on either side, letting Richard lead the way.

Walking side by side, the warhorses loomed over her small mare, squeezing the fine-boned palfrey between them. Alarmed by the crush, Velvet pranced and threw her head about in protest. Katherine stroked the mare's neck and used soothing words to settle the young animal.

When screams of terror rang out from the street directly in front of the mounted party, Katherine jerked her head up and looked around for danger. Without warning, Richard halted his horse, causing her mare to ram into the back of his charger.

As Katherine worked to calm Velvet, she glanced up in time to witness a handful of scared townsfolk plow into Marcus's stallion while attempting to get out of the way of a runaway destrier. The older knight's horse shifted sideways, slamming into Velvet, causing her palfrey to stumble. As the mare dropped to her knees, Katherine lurched forward with a shriek.

Richard grabbed her under her arms, lifted her off the saddle and onto his lap. She let go of the reins and watched her unburdened mare easily right herself when Godfrey took hold of the bridle and yanked her horse's head up.

Katherine exhaled a deep breath, for once again, she was safely seated in front of her husband. Godfrey passed Velvet to Miles, who led her mare to the back of the cart where there was room for the animal to move.

Behind them, James caught the rider-less destrier and bowed with devilish delight to a cheering crowd. Nestled in the security of her husband's arms, she smiled at the young knight's brazen performance before she turned her attention back to the street ahead.

"Needed to be rescued again, did you?" Richard breathed in her ear, laughter ringing in his voice.

"That was not my fault," she insisted while wiggling her bottom to find a comfortable position.

"You sorely abuse me, for I've never shared Titan so much with anyone else," he complained good-naturedly. "Riding together has become quite a habit of yours. One might think you seek it out."

"I do not," she protested overly loud.

***

Richard found her reaction amusing. He enjoyed having her in his arms and had missed her soft touch. Inhaling deeply of her fresh scent helped lessen the rank odor wafting upon the light breeze.

"I have never seen the likes of such a place. I am not sure I like the commotion, and I definitely am not fond of the smell." She held a piece of cloth under her nose and breathed in and out through her mouth.

"Once we leave the main road, the odor will be more tolerable. The worst is behind us," he said.

"Are we almost at your father's place?"

"His townhouse is around the next corner. The Tanners take care of the property for him. I sent them a message we were coming. Avery Tanner has a leather shop on the ground floor, and he lives in the back with his family. They've been in my father's employ for a great many years. The arrangement works out well for everyone. Some of the other nobles haven't been so lucky and have left dishonorable people in charge of their holdings. They've returned to their homes to find nothing left."

"Why do the nobles need their own houses in town? I thought the nobility stayed at the Palace of Westminster when in London."

"Many of them do, but only if you're invited to do so by the king or queen, and then you never know where you might be told to lay your head. Sometimes King Edward and his family aren't even in residence, as the royal family often spends time at Windsor Castle. It makes more sense to have your own house, so one can come and go as one pleases. I was a boy when my father found this property. Back then, my mother enjoyed a few months a year at court."

The group of riders left the main road and turned onto a side street. Richard slowed Titan's pace in front of a three-story building. Over the thick, dark door hung a wooden sign with a big piece of leather tacked onto the planks. Two multi-paned windows on either side of the entrance displayed the shop's wares. A tall fence surrounded the property on three sides.

"We have arrived." He turned Titan down a small lane running alongside the house toward the back of the building.

The knights followed him to a stone stable with a thatched roof abutting the back fence. The stable housed a few horses, a milk cow, pigs, sheep, and chickens. There was a row of empty stalls, and one was filled with hay. A wagon stood against the side of the fence, as did a small wooden cart.

Mistress Tanner stepped out of the house. "Sir Richard, welcome home. Come rest. Your meal is simmering over the fire. It'll be on the table directly."

"Good to see you, Mistress Tanner. Did I ever tell you that you're the best cook this side of the Thames?" he teased.

"Every time you grace me with your presence." The woman smiled wide, dimples indenting her fleshy cheeks.

He dismounted and reached for his wife. "May I introduce you to Lady Katherine?" He lifted her off his horse and gently placed her feet on the ground.

The rotund woman's face brightened with warmth. "Good to meet you, my lady." She presented Katherine with an awkward little curtsy. "Sir Richard explained everything in his letter. If you need anything, let me know and I will fetch it for you."

"Thank you," Katherine said.

Mistress Tanner turned his way. "As you requested, we've hired a few servants for your stay. I'll make sure your personal belongings are delivered to your bedchamber. In the meantime, you and your men are welcome to withdraw to the common room. I would be happy to fill some tankards while you wait for your meal."

With a glance, he sent silent instructions to Marcus who barked out orders. The courtyard suddenly filled with a flurry of activity as knights alighted, stable boys grabbed horses, and servants hurried to unpack the cart.

"I need to send a missive to the king. I'm looking for an invitation to court tonight. Could I find paper and ink in Avery's shop?"

Mistress Tanner rested meaty hands on her rounded hips. "Most certainly. When you're finished, he can hire a messenger to run your request to the palace."

"I shall seek him out posthaste. Would you show my wife to our bedchamber so she may freshen up?" He smiled affectionately at the gray-haired woman he had known since his youth.

"I'd be honored. Come, Lady Katherine, I'll see to your comfort," Mistress Tanner said.

***

Katherine's jaw tensed at the sight of Richard's back when he hurried toward the house. He intended to solicit an invitation to attend court this very evening.

An eerie chill of dread traveled up her spine and she shivered. Her husband wanted to get rid of her as soon as possible. He couldn't even wait until tomorrow; instead, he wanted her gone immediately.

After they stood before the king and were granted permission to dissolve their marriage, she would need to leave London directly. How could she stay once she was cast aside? Hopefully, Marcus, Godfrey, and Miles would agree to escort her back to Stamford. She had run out of precious time.

Katherine reluctantly followed Mistress Tanner into the house. Preoccupied with having failed to win her husband's heart, she trailed behind, her feet weighted down with apprehension.

When she stepped through the doorway of the third-floor master bedchamber, she stopped to stare. The huge post and beam room was warm and inviting. Multi-colored rugs rested upon the wide-board wooden floors. A canopied four-poster bed with tied back forest green velvet curtains took up almost a whole wall. The mattress was piled high with feather pillows, wool blankets, and fur pieces. Two small tables stood on either side of the bed. On them, a pair of oil lamps made ready for the night's darkness. Across the way, two stuffed chairs faced a beautifully arched stone hearth. A few cold logs were stacked and ready for a warm fire. In the corner, a wooden tubbed peeked out from behind a curtain.

Four small windows along the outside wall looked out over the city of London. The Palace of Westminster was clearly visible in the distance. The beauty and majesty of the king's residence drew her notice. What would it be like to experience such magnificence up close? She brushed a loose tendril away from her face and sighed heavily. If Richard had his way, they would be amid its splendor in no time.

"Lady Katherine, please, make yourself comfortable. Call me if you need anything. I'd like to make your stay pleasant. I can't begin to tell you how nice it is to have a lady gracing our rooms. Not since Lord Weston's wife, Lady Sarah, has there been another woman under this roof. How we missed the fair lady after she passed. There was none sweeter," Mistress Tanner gushed.

"My mother and Lady Sarah were the best of friends, so I will have to agree with you about her character."

To hear Richard never had a lady overnight was a relief. It would've bothered her deeply to imagine her husband spending tender moments alone with another woman in this very bedchamber.

Her trunk arrived with the help of two young men. Left alone, she used the clean basin of water to wash away dirt and grime from the day's travels. She ran her fingers through her windblown hair but had little success taming the mess.

There was still time to change Richard's mind. The day wasn't over. They had yet to go before the king. It wasn't in her nature to give up without a fight, so she wouldn't. Not yet, anyway.

She opened her chest, rummaged through her clothes, and found her comb nestled at the bottom. Sitting on the edge of a chair by the cold hearth, she dragged the ivory teeth through her tangled locks. After she had straightened her hair, she tied a braided strand from each side of her face onto the back of her head to keep flyaway hair from her eyes. A quick peek in the mirror confirmed she was indeed presentable.

Refreshed, she made her way back down to the common room on the second floor.

The smooth-timbered chamber welcomed her with a roaring fire. A big kettle of stew simmered over the open flames, tended by one of Mistress Tanner's daughters. She knew it to be so, for there was no mistaking the round face, bright eyes, and dimples.

Richard was absent, but his knights sat on benches around the trestle table. The weary men held tankards of ale in their hands and appeared to have eagerly quenched their thirst, for their eyes glistened from the potent drink.

"Mistress Tanner, your food smells delicious," she proclaimed. The tantalizing odors made her stomach growl.

The older woman beamed with delight. "Sir Richard said you liked wine, so I made sure we had a few small barrels on hand. Can I get you a cup?"

"Yes, that would be nice."

"Lady Katherine, come join us." Marcus retrieved a soft chair from in front of the fire and put the seat next to him, at the head of the table.

She made her way to the offered chair and nodded her thanks. When Mistress Tanner handed her a full goblet of wine, she took a sip and let the warm fruity liquid slide down her throat.

"How do you like London, my lady?" Marcus asked.

"To tell you the truth, this is all new to me. London is the first city I have ever laid eyes on. The only other town I have visited is home to the Copper

Stallion Inn, and I am afraid it is quite tiny in comparison. I am a little intimidated by the noise, crowds, and smell, and can say with utmost confidence my little mare feels the same way I do."

Marcus chuckled. "I, too, prefer the country over such a large town."

The knights sitting around the table gave their own grunts of agreement, eager to be part of the conversation. She smiled at their friendly faces. After days of spending time together, she now had an easy rapport with these knights, just as she had with her father's men, the ones who were now gone.

The wine worked its magic, and her taut muscles relaxed.

"Sir Marcus, have you ever been to the Palace of Westminster?"

"Aye, my lady, many times. As the second son of the former Earl of Warwick and brother to the new earl, I'm often invited to the festivities at the palace and Westminster Hall when I'm in London."

Katherine had no idea Marcus was related to such a lofty family. There was much she didn't know about the men who rode with Richard, except that they were good and loyal men.

"I fear I am a little nervous. I am not sure what to expect when I arrive at court. I am not sure how to behave properly and hope I do not do anything to cause disgrace."

"Set your mind at ease, my lady. You'll be fine. Richard has been there many times and will guide you through easily enough," Marcus assured her.

"What do I do if I find myself in King Edward's or Queen Philippa's presence?" she asked timidly.

Godfrey rose from his chair. "I've been there a few times myself. If the king and queen arrive, the men lower their heads and bend at the waist like this." He demonstrated the technique. "The ladies do it a little differently." Godfrey stood before James; he gave the knight a few exaggerated flirtatious blinks, hiked up pretend skirts, bent his knees to drop down very low, and respectfully lowered his head. The knights at the table whooped with laughter when he almost tumbled over.

James, always vying for attention, jumped up from his seat. "Come, Lady Katherine, let me help you practice."

The young knight presented her his open hand, along with a big grin that flashed across his young face. A dimple on each cheek peeked out from under his sparse beard. "I'll pretend to be the king, and you can be the ever so fair lady waiting in line for my audience."

Mistress Tanner chuckled behind her hand, her eyes flashing in merriment. Light-headed from the wine, Katherine accepted his hand with a giggle and rose to her feet.

"Why, thank you, Sir James. I would be honored to use you for my schooling."

***

Richard reached the top of the second-floor landing and stopped short when a roar of laughter exploded from the common room. He stayed in the shadows behind the doorway and quietly observed his wife entertain his men. Katherine's golden hair tumbled around her shoulders. Her surcoat clung to her fine figure so snuggly, it left little to his imagination. He wet his lips. It'd be best to keep some distance between them.

James held her hand lightly as she attempted a very low curtsy. Graceful and poised, her movements were fluid until she lowered herself too far and lost her balance. Marcus caught her arm and prevented her from toppling over. After apologizing, she insisted she would try again and again until she succeeded.

In the darkened corner, he reflected on her endless determination and fortitude.

The room was suddenly alive with well-meaning suggestions and encouragement. Big men moved swiftly off the wooden benches as each showed his wife how a lady should curtsy to the king and queen. Mistress Tanner and her daughter couldn't contain their amusement at the men's antics, and tears from laughter rolled down the women's cheeks until they swiped them away with the back of their hands.

His wife presented the men with a few more awkward attempts before she executed a perfect curtsy. Hoots of approval rang out, making her face turn bright red. She bit at her bottom lip from all the attention. His knights slapped each other on the back as if she'd accomplished a feat of daring. She then showed off her newly acquired skills by performing the bob, again and again, using each of his men as the king, not favoring one over another. Richard grinned at her playfulness as he watched, unnoticed by most.

Out of breath, she took her seat and reached for another sip of wine. "Now that I have mastered my curtsy, what else can you tell me about court?"

"The ladies are dressed in rich colors of very fancy finery," Miles exclaimed. "And they cover their hair with barbettes and veils, or wimples if they are old."

The men at the table muttered that what he said was true.

She frowned. "I had not considered I might be underdressed. I brought my best. I hope it is good enough for his majesty and the queen." She hesitated a moment while her brows furrowed and lips tightened. "The women cover their hair? Does everyone cover their hair?"

"Those who are married do, my lady," Miles replied.

"Mistress Tanner, would you know where I might obtain a hair covering for tonight?"

"Yes, my lady, not to worry yourself needlessly. I think a hair covering can be arranged." Mistress Tanner glanced toward Richard in the darkened entryway and gave him a pointed look.

Without drawing anyone's attention, he backed away from the doorway and silently headed down the stairs to speak with Avery.

***

"The guests like to dance at court. Do you dance, Lady Katherine?" Godfrey asked.

She took a big sip of wine and beamed. "I am happy to say my brother did indeed teach me to dance. Hopefully, the dances have not changed much."

"Oh, no, my lady. I'm sure they remain the same," Godfrey assured her.

Marcus stood from his seat. His green eyes twinkled in mischief. He held out a hand and made a gentlemanly bow. "Lady Katherine, may I have the pleasure of a dance before our meal is served?"

"Sir Marcus you honor me with your invite. You certainly must be a brave man to desire to take on my clumsy attempts at dancing. For although I said I was familiar with the dances, I did not say I was any good at them. I am warning you now, for I fear for your toes."

"My lady, I'm ready and willing to take my chances." Marcus boyishly grinned.

"Then I am yours." She held out her hand.

Marcus took her fingers in his big hand and assisted her to stand. "Miles, Mr. Tanner's lute is leaning in the corner. I'm sure he wouldn't mind if you were so kind as to display your skills and pluck us a song. It'd be much appreciated."

"I know just the tune." Miles retrieved the lute as the other men pushed the trestle table, benches and chairs against the wall to make room.

Once the music began, the tall gray-haired knight with the laughing green eyes led her easily around the room. His movements were smooth and effortless, making it easy for her to keep up as he was well-trained in his dance steps.

"Sir Marcus, I am truly impressed by your dancing abilities. I am afraid you put me to shame."

"Lady Katherine you're very free with your praise, but I'm sure you're mistaken. For none could put you to shame," Marcus said.

Her face heated with the compliment. When she turned her head, she caught a glimpse of those in the room watching them with cheerful smiles. The men tapped their hands and feet along with the music, enjoying themselves immensely. She took pleasure in their company. She'd miss them when she returned to Stamford. Maybe when she visited Lady Elizabeth at Hammerstead, she'd see a few of their friendly faces from time to time.

Marcus spun her around in a few tight circles. "I've had quite a bit of practice in my day. My father insisted his children were proficient in our steps. He loved to entertain."

Katherine giggled and threw back her head. She closed her eyes, secure in the skills of her partner and enjoying the heady experience of being whirled around. Marcus made the circle bigger and then slowed to almost a stop. Suddenly, an alarm rang out in her mind when a thick arm grabbed her about the waist and Marcus's light touch was exchanged for a more possessive one that guided her through the moves.

Startled by the change, her eyes flew open. She looked up at Richard's handsome face. He smiled ever so sweetly as he gazed down at her. When she peered into the sparkling blue depths of his bright eyes, a shiver rippled through her body, leaving a tingling in the pit of her stomach. He drew her close against his hard body and she inhaled deeply of his masculine scent. Her legs wobbled and went weak. Afraid of disgracing herself by plummeting to the wooden floor, she made a deliberate effort to concentrate on each step as he twirled her with ease around the room.

She could no longer recognize anyone else in the room, although she knew the men were still amongst them. She vaguely remembered the hoots of delight when her dance partner changed, but at the time the sound didn't make sense.

Time stood still and she chided herself for her foolish reactions when her husband was about. She wished she could treat him with the same indifference he showed her. Why couldn't she steel herself against how he made her feel?

The song finished too soon. Cheers and clapping from their onlookers resounded off the walls. Richard gave her a gentlemanly bow, attached to a mischievous smile and twinkling eyes. She presented him with a dainty bob in return. More hoots rang out. Embarrassed by the attention, she kept her eyes downcast as she spun in her tracks and made her way back to the safety of her chair and goblet of wine.

Mistress Tanner announced their meal, and the knights quickly returned the furniture to order. Servants stood between the big men to place trenchers on the table. Richard took a seat on her left.

Katherine swept away a wayward curl from the side of her face. She breathed deeply and focused on taming her errant emotions. Her earlier vow of not giving up was remembered, so she turned her attention to her husband and pursued a line of safe conversation.

"You dance quite well," she remarked.

"I've had my share of practice," he chuckled.

"I hope I am not to be considered one of your most unskilled partners?" she said, ignoring his boast.

"On the contrary, my lady. You, by far, are one of the best." He leaned in close and whispered in her ear. "Even when your legs weakened and you fairly turned to jelly in my arms, you were still better than the rest." He sat back, arms across his chest and smiled smugly. "Now that I think about it, I guess I do bring forth such a response quite often when engaged with the fairer sex."

The nerve of him to flaunt her flaws and brag about the many women he had held in his arms while flashing a brazen smile. How insufferable. "You are far too bold with your comments, sir, especially since you are mistaken about my reaction to your nearness. My legs are just overly fatigued from days on horseback. I am sure I cannot say why a lady would find herself weak in your arms." He was so aggravating; she didn't understand why she bothered with him.

"Yes, I'm sure your legs are just fatigued. Nothing else," he snickered, giving her an all-knowing sidelong glance.

So much for trying to win his heart. He stroked her ire, and she wasn't sure she could bring herself to be flirtatious and captivating at the moment. She reached into the trencher they shared and took her fill of food. She was so disgusted with him; she ate in silence, forsaking any friendly banter they might have engaged in.

A short time later, a royal messenger arrived with a message from the king.

"We leave tonight for Westminster Hall. King Edward will hold court there. You should return to your bedchamber and get some rest. It might be a long night," he said with too much enthusiasm.

Katherine wasn't sure what she could say to change his mind. Her shoulders sagged in defeat. She had hoped for more time in his company, yet doubted it would happen. If only she hadn't let herself get so bothered by his teasing, maybe she could've used their moments together more wisely.

She finished her wine and rose from her chair. "Mistress Tanner would you be so kind as to have a bath readied?"

"Your tub is already filled. It's just waiting to add the hot water, my lady."

"Thank you. I shall retire to my room then." She nodded a good day to the men seated around the table, and they returned the gesture in kind. As she ascended the stairs, the room grew jarringly quiet with all eyes upon her, as if they knew her association with them was coming to an end.

When out of sight on the top of the landing, the noise rose again to a normal level. With a heavy heart, she made her way to the privacy of her bedchamber, where she would count down the minutes until she was gone.

~Chapter Twenty-Three~

Katherine entered the master bedchamber and slowly closed the wooden door. She leaned heavily on the firm surface and let her tired body melt against the sturdy frame. Her head pounded with confusion. Was Richard only being nice to honor their agreement, or was there something more? Was he smiling at her because he enjoyed her company or was he just in good spirits at the prospect of reuniting with the lady he left behind?

Yesterday on their journey to London, he'd sent her so many conflicting messages. Once their exciting race was over, his easy rapport faded. Without warning, his demeanor changed. He ignored her very existence. A wall of cold indifference rose whenever she cast her eyes upon him.

The group had stopped in a clearing for the night and the men set up camp. After sharing a meal, she was escorted to her tent, where she found a pallet of soft fur coverings arranged in the corner. As she stretched out on the makeshift bed, she had high hopes her husband would eventually come share her quarters.

She heard him outside the tent, sitting around the fire talking in muted tones and laughing with his men. One by one, the knights took their leave to find their resting places. She strained to listen for any sign he was on his way to her bed. Time moved forward, but he never joined her. After hours of hoping, she finally succumbed to a restless sleep and awoke in the morning, alone and dejected, knowing he preferred the company of his horse to that of his wife.

Katherine laid across the oversized bed and buried her face in the soft fur pelts. Inhaling deeply, she noticed they lacked the usual masculine scent that clung to the fur lining on the inside of Richard's mantle. How she loved to curl up with his aroma.

In a melancholy mood, she stroked the smooth surface, basking in the silkiness as she eased her misery.

A knock on the door startled her from her reflections, and she sat up quickly. "Enter."

Mistress Tanner walked through the doorway, followed by three well-dressed women, their arms loaded with baskets of material and trim. "Lady Katherine, may I introduce you to Madame Beauchamp and her assistants?"

The three women bobbed in unison.

Katherine swung her legs off the side of the bed and stood. Her eyes narrowed as she offered the visitors a small, rigid bow and a nod.

"Madame Beauchamp stitches very elaborate gowns for the nobility." Mistress Tanner explained. "She does excellent work and is quite sought after. Sir Richard hired her to help you get ready for your visit to Westminster Hall tonight."

"He did?" *Why would he spend coins on finery when she was returning to Stamford on the morrow?*

"Come, Lady Katherine. We have very little time before this evening, and we have much to do." Madame Beauchamp eyed her boldly. "I have something that just might do, but we need to get you measured right away."

She stood in the middle of the room as the three women flew at her in a whirlwind, touching and twirling her in all directions. Mistress Tanner observed from the edge of the commotion, smiling merrily.

"Normally we would have had to cut and sew from a new bolt of cloth, but there was another young lady, a little heavier and taller than you, who ordered some fine gowns but can no longer use them. I believe we can make a few tucks here and there," Madame Beauchamp explained. "All will be lovely for tonight."

Katherine remained statue-still and let the women fuss over her as she tried to figure out why Richard would show her such courtesy. Deep down, she was afraid to get her hopes up.

***

Hours later, Katherine stood alone in her room admiring the royal blue, heavy silk brocade surcoat. The afternoon flew by in a furor of activity and everything came together in perfect order.

She ran her hand across the silky-smooth material with the little peaks and valleys of the raised design. Never had she seen anything so grand. The outer tunic laced up the front. The rounded neckline was low and edged with white ermine. The snug sleeves of her surcoat, trimmed in the same soft fur as around her neck, ended above her elbows, where the longest tippets she ever laid eyes on, hung almost to the floor and swung back and forth with the slightest movement. A pale azure silk kirtle lay beneath, hugging her silhouette and peeking out from a slit running down the front of her surcoat.

The undergarment fit like a second skin and covered her arms to her wrists. Fine leather slippers peered out from the bottom of her gown. Her hair was washed, dried, and the top was arranged elegantly under a dainty white barbette and veil, with the remainder of her soft waves cascading down her back.

Through her pursed lips, she slowly blew out a chest full of air. There was no reason to postpone their trip to Westminster Hall. No longer could she use the excuse of being underdressed. Madame Beauchamp assured her the newly acquired attire would rival any lady's clothing at court.

It was time. She needed to be brave.

She grabbed her richly adorned girdle, slung the belt low around her curved hips, and fastened it securely. She retrieved her mother's dagger and studied the jeweled hilt. Her mother used to tell her each jewel represented a good memory. Her mother was long gone. It was time to replace each of her mother's memories with good ones of her own. She ran the tips of her fingers over the precious stones. Unfortunately, tonight's memory might not be one she wished to remember. She sheathed her dagger and headed toward her future with all the dignity she could muster.

At the top of the stairs, she heard the raised voices of the men below. When the knights finished their meal, they had remained in the common room enjoying each other's company. Gathering her courage, she grabbed onto the handrail, straightened her back, and descended the wooden steps.

Immediately, her eyes were drawn to Richard standing by the fire with Marcus. He was a picture of perfection dressed in a navy velvet doublet, fastened down the front with wooden toggles, and gathered at the waist with an ornate belt and dagger.

Instead of the commanding knight, he had transformed himself into every bit a dashing lord. As their eyes met, she forgot to breathe. When he smiled, his whole face lit up, the warmth touching the corners of his eyes. She slowly expelled the air from her lungs and returned a small smile of her own.

When her foot hit the bottom step, she was accosted by James, who knocked over his chair in a rush to get to her side. He stood directly in her path and executed a gallant bow. "Lady Katherine. May I be the first to say that I have never laid eyes on a lady more beautiful."

The knights seated around the room raised their glasses and cheered "Hear, hear."

She touched the palm of her hand to her burning cheek.

Richard instantly made his way to her side and forced the smaller man out of the way. "James, go sit down before you make a nuisance of yourself. Come, Katherine, our carriage waits." The room vibrated with good-humored whoops of laughter as her husband presented her with his arm and she held it lightly.

Mistress Tanner sat in the corner wearing an ear to ear grin that made her cheeks swell to almost bursting.

On her way by the hearth, Katherine caught Marcus staring at her in wide-eyed wonder. She tilted her head and gave him a slight nod in greeting. He flashed her a white-toothed grin.

At the doorway leading down the stairs to the ground level, she let go of Richard's arm and turned around. To the occupants of the room, she bestowed upon them the most perfect curtsy she could muster without toppling over. The room exploded in applause and roars of approval. She twirled around to face her husband, whose brow was cocked inquiringly.

"We practiced earlier when you were downstairs. I just wanted to prove to them I could execute one with poise."

"Well done, then. You were perfect," he said in a husky voice as he grabbed their cloaks off the pegs and wrapped her fur-lined mantle around her shoulders. Taking her hand, he escorted her down the darkened steps leading to the back door. She willed herself to ignore the jolts of lightning pulsating through their clasped hands and instead concentrated on one step at a time.

She paid little heed to the chill in the air during the bumpy carriage ride over the uneven stones. Being in such close quarters with Richard had her heart pounding unnaturally fast. She looked out the window, hoping to change the direction of her thoughts, but to no avail.

For years, she had dreamed of no other than the tall, handsome man seated on the opposite bench. During all of Matilda's colorful stories, it was Richard she'd envisioned holding her in his arms and kissing her so hungrily she forgot who she was.

Now, here he was, so close, yet so far away. She battled an urge to throw herself across the aisle, wrap her arms around his neck and proclaim her love.

Katherine swallowed hard. She wouldn't resort to making a fool of herself. She still possessed some pride. He hadn't made his intentions clear, but since they were wasting no time in getting to Westminster Hall, she guessed he was eager to meet up with the lady he left behind.

The carriage passed shop after shop and house after house. A great many townsfolk still walked the streets and gave way to the matched pair of high-stepping horses pulling their carriage. She stole a glance at Richard and found him staring at her with a detached gaze, deep in thought. Not able to read his stoic face, she had no idea what he was thinking. His somber mood sent a shiver of alarm up her spine.

She cleared her throat. "I wanted to thank you for the gowns. They are lovely and much appreciated."

"My pleasure," he responded absently.

She frowned at his lack of emotion. "You know I have never been far from Rosemont, nor have I attended a social gathering such as this. Please warn me if I do something I should not."

"You'll be fine."

Their carriage barreled through a set of fancy iron gates and stopped at the bottom of the steps leading to Westminster Hall. A footman helped her alight, and she waited for her husband to join her. Together, they made their way up the stone risers and through the lavishly carved doors.

As Katherine entered the hall, she pulled her cloak tighter. So awed she was by the magnificence of the room she fought an urge to spin around and leave, not sure she belonged. Never had she beheld such grandeur. The hall was the largest room she had ever laid eyes on. The elaborately painted ceiling rose to heights that made her dizzy when she looked up to admire the scenery.

They handed their cloaks to a waiting servant. Without her armor of protection, she crossed her arms over her chest and gawked at the hundreds of richly dressed nobles circulating among their peers. The noise rose to thunderous levels as the guests' voices echoed off the soaring ceilings and walls.

Richard motioned her to follow and led her through the crowd with barely a glance back. He studied those in attendance, obviously trying to find someone in particular. She closely trailed behind him and tried to catch a glimpse of anyone drawing his attention. How she wished she were taller, for she couldn't see over anyone's shoulders and had no idea who he was setting his sights on. When he stopped abruptly in the center of the room, she walked into his broad back and gasped.

"I found someone I want you to meet. Follow me," he said, practically shouting over the din.

She had no choice but to obey, falling into step behind.

Her husband took her to a group of high-backed chairs close to an outside wall. She was sure sitting in one of the cushioned seats rested the oldest woman in England. There were so many wrinkles sagging from the woman's face it looked like her skin was melting off. Some wisps of hair sneaking out from beneath her wimple matched so perfectly to the stark white of her headdress you could not discern one from the other without a closer inspection.

Richard stood before the elderly lady sitting alone. "Lady Margaret, it's good to see you again," he almost yelled.

The woman scrutinized Richard's face. When Lady Margaret recognized who spoke her name, she gave him an open-mouthed smile revealing a few missing teeth. "Sir Richard, my boy, you honor us with your presence."

He squatted down, so he was at eye level with the woman. "I hope all is well with you."

"A few pains here and there, but I still live, much to the disappointment of some of my relatives."

"I want you to meet my wife, Lady Katherine." Richard turned to Katherine. "May I introduce you to Lady Margaret, the Countess of Wakefield?"

Katherine gave a low curtsy and a respectful nod in greeting.

Surprise crossed the old woman's weathered face. "Sir Richard, you got yourself married? There will be a lot of sad young ladies at court once they hear the word."

"Could you spare a few minutes of your time and keep Lady Katherine entertained while I attend to some pressing business?"

"You young men are always rushing off for one reason or another. I am afraid my days of lively conversations are well past, but your wife is more than welcome to sit with me a spell and take in the sights."

"Are you leaving me?" Katherine asked in a shrill voice.

"Only for a short while. Sit and enjoy the goings-on with Lady Margaret. I'll return to you directly." He gestured for her to take the seat beside the Countess of Wakefield.

Katherine sat on the edge of the chair and watched her husband's back as he pressed through the crowd and out of sight. An uncomfortable pang jabbed at her belly. Without him at her side, she was very much alone. She gave a slight, tight-lipped smile to Lady Margaret.

"Do not fret, my dear, he will be right back." Lady Margaret reached over and gave her clenched hands a gentle little pat. "Now, tell me a little about yourself and how you came to capture the very elusive Sir Richard Weston."

***

Richard leaned heavily against one of the massive ornamental pillars in Westminster Hall. On the outside, he appeared relaxed, yet inside, he was like a caged animal ready to spring. From his vantage point he watched closely, the woman he had searched for and finally found. As he hoped, Lady Alice was in attendance this evening.

What a relief.

It was her habit to come to court almost every night. He couldn't fathom what he would've done had she not shown up. Surely, he would've made a fool of himself barging into her family's townhouse without so much as an invite. Since she was surrounded by friends and family, he waited in the distance for a moment when he could get her alone.

"Where's Lady Katherine?" Marcus asked from behind, his voice tinged with concern.

Richard spun around to find Marcus standing at his shoulder. A perplexed look contorted the knight's bearded face.

"I left her in the company of Lady Margaret. She'll be fine." He glanced back at Lady Alice.

"I'm not sure I understand you anymore. Why would you leave Lady Katherine with someone older than dirt? By the way, what are we doing in London when you should be at Rosemont with your new wife?"

Marcus was one of his closest friends. Since the older knight had followed him thus far without question or complaint, Richard owed him an explanation.

"I'm afraid things have gotten complicated. When last in London, I found myself attracted to a certain lady. I decided I would lease one of Lord Marten's estates and return to London to ask for her hand in marriage. Then I rescued Katherine. Suddenly, everything changed. When I heard the king's edict that I was to immediately wed her to keep her safe, I became furious. My mind was set on a different course. In the heat of the moment, I vowed to God and my father that I wouldn't consummate my marriage until I returned to London and set eyes upon the woman I left behind. I figured if I still felt strongly that the other suited better, I could petition the king to dissolve my marriage to Katherine. So, here we are, breaking my vow and sealing my fate."

Marcus blew out a quiet whistle. "No wonder you've not been yourself this past week and hell-bent to get to London."

"It was a stupid vow. I regretted the words the minute they left my tongue. It's time I finish this. The sooner I break my vow; the sooner I can return to Rosemont."

"Which lady in the crowd is the one you seek?" Marcus asked.

"She stands next to her father, Lord Cromwell. Lady Alice is the tall one with the dark hair."

"She looks a lot like Lady Elizabeth," Marcus noted.

Richard stared hard at Lady Alice. "Except for her green eyes. Otherwise, she does resemble William's wife. I think the similarity is what drew me to her in the first place. After witnessing William's happiness, I envied him his new life. I suppose I hoped Lady Alice would be like Lady Elizabeth and make me as content as he seems to be."

"If I'm to understand you correctly, you are here to break your vow and decide who would be the better wife. Maybe I can help you with that," Marcus volunteered good-naturedly.

"I believe I've already made up my mind, but I'm curious as to who you would choose for me?"

"I can be very astute when it comes to women," Marcus said playfully. "Let me help you pick the right one." He studied the lady in question. "Something tells me Lady Alice likes to be the center of attention; she likes social gatherings and the company of high-ranking nobles. Life at court and in London is all she knows. She spends hours getting ready for each event, with servants doting on her every whim."

"I think you're right," Richard said with a chuckle.

"Somehow, I cannot imagine Lady Alice tolerating pain or escaping captivity. I doubt she'd race through darkened caves or crawl over dangerous rocks, alone, in the blackness of the night. I can't see her facing life-threatening outlaws wielding only her dagger for protection. She'd probably complain if she were to ride a horse any distance and wouldn't care for her animal if injured, just demand a new one. I can't imagine her protecting a peasant child, or even talking to people, not of her standing. She'd be hysterical if attacked by other knights on horseback. I doubt she has any idea how to run a keep and the people in it. She wouldn't care for your knights if they were harmed, never mind fight for their lives. Her complaints would be numerous, unlike another, who complains not at all."

Richard gaped at his friend.

"Most of all, Lady Elizabeth wouldn't like her. She'd instantly see through her shallow exterior and would never offer the friendship she has already extended to Lady Katherine. Lady Alice might look like Lady Elizabeth, but it's actually Lady Katherine who's more like her, although in a different, yet very appealing package."

Richard closed his mouth. He had never heard Marcus speak so many impassioned words before. His head reeled with all Marcus said.

"The way I see it; you only have one choice. You should break your vow as quickly as possible and set things right with your wife. A man's life shouldn't be so complicated it wears on his mind. Take me, for instance. I'm on my way to find the widow, Lady Abigail Wykeham. We have an understanding that when I'm in London we spend time together. No ties. No complications. Just the way I like it." He slapped Richard's shoulder with a heavy hand. "Good luck, my friend. I'll see you tomorrow morning."

Richard gave Marcus a nod of thanks. Lady Alice was now standing alone. He started across the room. It was time to break his vow.

~Chapter Twenty-Four~

While awaiting Richard's return, Katherine fidgeted in the cushioned chair next to the Countess of Wakefield. Lady Margaret wanted to know more about her, but Katherine was reluctant to reveal too much. After sharing that their families were close and she had been acquainted with Richard since childhood, their conversation waned.

When an awkward silence followed, the two women returned to perusing the colorfully dressed nobles strutting around the room.

Servants arrived with drinks. Katherine selected a goblet of wine to calm her quivering nerves. Lady Margaret took one also. They raised their glasses to one another before tasting the fruity liquid. Small groups of inquisitive guests gathered within view of their chairs and cast curious glances her way. They whispered in barely audible tones, as they tried to figure out the new face in the crowd.

Uncomfortable with the attention, she gulped down her wine and asked for another. Suddenly, she remembered her family's lies about her distorted face and lowered her head in shame. What if someone asked her about the rumors and discovered her family started them? Her throat tightened. She didn't want strangers to judge her.

Katherine looked at Lady Margaret to help divert her wayward thoughts; however, her hopes were dashed for the elderly woman dozed peacefully with an empty wine glass tipped in her hand.

Again, she shifted in the chair and asked a passing servant for another drink. The cup barely touched her fingertips before she drained it.

Too late she realized she shouldn't have drunk so much wine. She felt lightheaded and when she turned her head the room moved uncharacteristically.

A woman's high pitch laugh behind Katherine caused her to glance over her shoulder. Was she the butt of someone's joke? Seeing the woman's mirth wasn't directed at her, she chided herself for being so jumpy.

Where's Richard? What's taking so long?

When Katherine shifted back, she startled at the sight of a young man with a sparse beard, standing directly in front of her. Richly dressed in a forest green satin brocade tunic, his attire spoke of wealth and noble lineage.

He bowed before her in the manner of good breeding. "My lady, I'm so glad to have found you. I've come to retrieve you, posthaste. I'm afraid there was an accident and your presence is needed."

She nearly toppled her empty glass when she hastily put it down. Her hands flew to her gaping mouth. "Oh my, is it Richard? Is he all right?" she asked, afraid to think the worst.

"Yes, my lady, it's Richard. He would like you to follow me."

"Of course. First, I must tell Lady Margaret what has happened."

"Please, don't rouse the Countess. She'll be ashamed for having fallen asleep. As soon as she wakes, she'll know you left to join Richard. She's a very astute woman."

Katherine nodded. *He's the only person I know here.*

The young man gave her his arm and she rose from her seat. Her heart hammered in her chest.

Please, God, let Richard be all right.

The two walked through the double doors leading to a stone terrace. As Katherine stepped through the doorway, the chill of the night took her by surprise. She breathed deeply of the fresh night air and struggled to clear her befuddled head.

"Richard is outside?" She furrowed her brow. *Why would he be outside?*

"Yes, my lady. He awaits your company." The man's hand landed upon the small of her back and pushed her forward down the steps into the dark torchlit garden. Once her soft leather slippers touched the grass, her head cleared of the wine. She stopped short in her tracks.

"He is not down here … is he?" Her voice trembled.

The man pressed her up against a wooden fence with the length of his body. He grabbed hold of each wrist, preventing her from removing her dagger.

"I must confess. Your Richard didn't send me," he said impishly as if sharing a naughty secret with a mischievous playmate.

Katherine fought against him. In the dim torchlight, she discerned an evil smile and his eyes glistened with excitement.

She jerked her head toward the people who stood on the other side of the terrace's double glass doors, still opened slightly. Her throat tightened. They couldn't see out into the darkness from Westminster Hall. She wanted to scream, but no one would hear her cries over the noise inside.

"What do you want with me?"

"Do not play coy. I'm sure you are well aware of your allure. I fear you're a gifted enchantress and have cast your incantations over me. I find myself so drawn to your beauty that I need to taste you. You'll tease me no more, for now that we're alone I'll take my fill." The man leaned down to steal a kiss.

She turned her head from his unwelcome advances and pressed her lips tightly together.

"Don't make me hurt you," he whispered gruffly in her ear. He held both of her wrists in one hand. With his free one, he forced her face forward.

His eyes told her he intended to hurt her whether she cooperated or not. She resisted righting her head, but her strength was no match against his. The man made her yield to his will. As he leaned in for a repulsive kiss, she waited until his breath touched her mouth and then bit his bottom lip.

"Owww!" the man hollered. He covered the wound with his hand.

She yanked against his hold, freeing a wrist. With all the power she could muster, she recoiled her arm and slapped him across his face.

"You little bitch," the man snarled. "How dare you strike me. You'll pay for your insolence."

Before she could grab her dagger, he captured her freed wrist and again held both wrists in one hand. Taking a big step back, he brought up his arm to return the slap.

Preparing for the stinging blow, she shut her eyes and held her breath. The seconds moved forward, but the jolt didn't come.

"If you do not release my wife, you will die," Richard growled in a deadly voice.

Her eyes shot open. Richard held the man's arm in mid-swing and the tip of his dagger pressed threateningly against the man's throat. Richard's steely gaze bored into the young noble.

The man, sensing her husband's lethality, released her. "I want no trouble," the man stammered and stepped back.

"Behind me, now," Richard ordered.

She wasted no time following his command. Once she was safe, she peered around his frame and read fear in her assailant's pinched face.

"You've chosen the wrong woman." Richard sheathed his dagger, wound his arm back and punched the man in the face so hard he landed on his backside.

Her assailant howled in pain and covered his bloody face with his hands. "You… broke… my nose," he screamed through garbled words while spitting out blood and a broken tooth.

"You're lucky I didn't kill you. If you ever come within sight of my wife again, I'll finish the job. Now get out of here."

The man rolled away, found his feet, and hurried off through the garden.

Richard turned abruptly, giving her his broad back. His body remained rigid, and he took weighty steps while climbing the stone stairs to the terrace.

She caught a glimpse of his expressionless face. A cold breeze brushed against her skin, sending a shiver of dread through her body. He was livid. His anger radiated like a hot poker in all directions.

Stepping livelily, she followed in his wake. "Forgive me. I should never have left Lady Margaret's side. She dozed off. The man said you were sending for me…that there had been an accident. I had no idea what he wanted until he pinned me against the fence."

***

"Did you not ask where he was taking you before you left with him?" Richard should never have left her alone to fend for herself. He couldn't believe she'd be so naive as to follow someone on their say-so alone. She didn't belong at court without an escort. The woman was far too trusting and innocent. Some men believed they were above the ideals of chivalry.

Katherine stopped short. "Like I said, I thought you needed me, and I rushed to do your bidding."

He turned to face her. There was a distinct change in the pitch of her tone; she no longer sounded apologetic. She rested her hands on slender hips, straightened her back stiffly and pointed her chin defiantly. Through squinted eyes, she sent him a look that shot daggers at him. God, she was beautiful in this fiery state. He would never tire of her ever-changing emotions.

Masking his true feelings, he met her gaze with bored indifference. He wanted to hear what she had to say.

"I did not ask to be left alone among these people and in a place, I am unfamiliar with. You have no cause to be angry. If anyone should be furious, tis I, for I know why you left me behind."

"You have no idea where I went." He raked fingers through his long locks. How would she know he went to see Lady Alice?

"You think not. I am not as slow-witted as you believe me to be. I know you went to meet up with the lady you wanted to wed…before you were forced to marry me."

Richard's body tensed, but he quickly regained his composure. "Maybe I did," he said with annoyance to cover the wave of guilt twisting his stomach in hundreds of little knots. He should've told her the truth before now, but he had no idea she had any notion of Lady Alice. He should've told her about his impetuous vow and how he suffered from such a declaration. How his impassioned words had kept them apart.

***

Katherine huffed her disgust. Richard didn't refute it. He didn't deny that he still cared for another woman. Her profound heartache left her with an unimaginable gush of emptiness that turned her numb.

This was the moment she had dreaded, yet couldn't put off any longer. She was tired of hoping he would want to stay married. She had to think about her future.

Better to speak the words sooner than later. Later she might not have enough strength to accept their parting.

A shroud of deep sadness besieged her.

Katherine strode past him, her eyes downcast. She leaned her hips against the waist-high stone wall bordering the terrace. In the hazy light, she gazed absently over the hedges encircling their enclosure. Through the small opening from the double glass doors left ajar, she observed lavishly dressed nobles mingling about in the well-lit room. Music drifted out into the yard; however, the pretty tune in the background failed to lessen the seriousness of the moment.

Katherine crossed her arms over her chest like a shield as she blinked back threatening tears. "I know why we are in London. I also know why you have not consummated our marriage." She paused to find the right words. "I am eternally grateful for all you have done. You rescued me from sure death, agreed to marry me and protect me from Lord Seton, avenged my family and seized Rosemont back from my enemies. I will forever be indebted to you. As your reward, I would like to give you what you desire most."

She bit her lower lip. Her hand dropped to her side and she stroked the hilt of her mother's jeweled dagger. She wanted to get her next words out without faltering. "I will give you your freedom. We can go to the king as soon as feasible and petition to dissolve our marriage. I will swear to my purity, and you will be free to marry another."

***

Richard's head fogged. What did Katherine say? She wanted to dissolve the marriage. It couldn't be. Not now. He sucked in a breath of cool night air to clear his head. Yes. He had thought to end their forced union at first, but not anymore. Why did she want to leave him?

"Of course, Rosemont and her people are yours. You have earned them. My father would approve. Do not worry about me. I intend to live with your father. He will see that I am well cared for. I am sure he could help me find a well-suited husband," her voice fell flat.

Richard's head pounded. This isn't what she wanted. This is what she thought he wanted. She was sacrificing herself for what she thought he desired.

He grabbed his wife by her shoulders and spun her to face him. She refused to make eye contact so, he tilted her head up. In the depths of her eyes, he saw pain and anguish. "You seem well versed in my desires. I wonder, what do *you* want?"

She swatted his hand away.

He stood deathly still so she could think.

Katherine's expression changed from misery, to defeat, and then to defiance. It appeared her feelings were hurt. She thought he cared naught for her. He knew she was considering a lie to preserve her dignity. After all, her pride was at stake. In the faint light, her face hardened with determination. She uncrossed her arms, placed open hands on her hips, and readied herself to answer.

Then, at the last moment, her countenance changed. Her eyes softened, as did her features and stance.

He waited expectantly.

"Do you really want to know what I want?"

"Indeed, I do."

She locked eyes with his. "I want you. I want you to be my husband in all the true senses of the word. I want to bear your children, to spend my life with you, and to grow old with you. I have loved you forever, and that will not change, no matter what happens here today."

Richard's breath caught in his throat as if another knight had punched him in the stomach. His heart pounded so rapidly it was in jeopardy of bursting.

Her wide, sparkling eyes begged him to go easy with her heart.

How could he not?

He smiled impishly as he placed his calloused hands on each side of her face. Tilting her head to one side, he leaned down and brought his parted lips to her full, soft ones.

***

Katherine hadn't expected such a response. She closed her eyes and savored the feel of his gentle hands cradling her head. Shockwaves coursed through her body with the touch of his warm supple lips pressed against her own. Her racing heart pounded in her ears. His mouth covered hers hungrily, searching its depths. She became powerless to stand. Her arms snaked over his velvet doublet and wrapped around his thick neck. Without much thought, she clutched at his long hair, caressing the silky strands. As his arms wrapped around her waist to hold her upright, her body arched against his, in an effort to remain as one.

***

Pleased by her response to their first kiss, Richard wished to tease her with headier experiences. He lifted her and set her on top of the stone wall without breaking their embrace. His hands lightly stroked up and down her back. As he stood between her opened legs, his mouth left her sweet, succulent lips and pecked a path of gentle kisses across her cheek to her earlobe. He nibbled on the soft, delicate bulb as he breathed with fiery passion in her ear.

When he felt quivers of excitement course through her body, a wicked smile turned up the corners of his mouth. He then kissed a tender trail down the side of her neck to the top of a rounded breast.

When he reached the fur edge of her gown, she let out a muffled moan and grabbed the top of his head, pulling him into her soft bosom.

Richard, unprepared for her passionate response, suddenly understood his need to maintain a semblance of control. He hastily rubbed his beard across the bare skin above her beautifully shaped breasts, the ones that had tantalized him mercilessly over the past few days, and gave them each a quick peck. With some regret, he pulled away to gaze into her gleaming, bright eyes.

She looked more than a little bewildered.

"You were wrong, Katherine." Leaning forward, he placed a cheek against the side of her face. "What I most desire, is you. There is no other. Nor will there be another, as you've ruined me for all time," he whispered in her hair while inhaling her intoxicating lavender scent.

***

Did Katherine hear him correctly or was she dreaming?

She broke their embrace so she could study him. "There will be no dissolving of the marriage?"

"Definitely not. Rosemont is ours together, as it should be. And, to ease your mind, we'll spend just enough time being polite before we return to my father's townhouse and see to some unfinished business. After we are together as man and wife, there'll be no question that our marriage is true." He sent her a carnal stare.

Her face warmed under his gaze and she laid the side of her head against his velvet doublet. A giant smile stretched across her face. She wrapped her arms tightly around his waist and heaved him against her, as she breathed in his masculine scent.

Tears of joy ran down her cheeks.

***

Richard lifted her chin. "There now, what do we have here? Tears again? Tell me you aren't saddened by this turn of events."

"Not at all," she choked out, "these are happy tears."

"Since your tears are always flowing, even when you're happy, I'm going to have to find a hauberk that doesn't rust." He squeezed her tight and then kissed the top of her forehead.

"I never cried until I met you. You turned me into a blubbering girl." She wiped away the last of the moisture with the edge of her tippet.

"Why I get blamed for everything is beyond me," Richard joked, as he, little by little, loosened his hold. He stroked her silky hair hanging down her back and reveled in their closeness.

He knew he'd need to distance himself soon, well aware of the unleashed desire still burning through his veins and hardening his loins. He disengaged himself from their embrace and sat down next to her on the edge of the stone wall.

"I'm afraid you haven't acquired the best choice for a husband, for I fear I haven't always treated you well and I'm sorry for that. I let my anger, and frustrations get in the way."

She rested against him. "I have borne your moods well and bear you no ill-will."

"I owe you an explanation. Before I rescued you, I had set a course in my head. I intended to return to London and ask for the hand of a lady I had met. When the king ordered me to wed you instead, I became angered because my course was altered without my consent. In a heated temper, I made a vow to God that I would marry you, but not consummate the marriage. At the time, I thought it was only fair to at least wait until I was face-to-face with the other lady again, and if I still desired such a union, I'd be free to ask the king to dissolve our marriage. I had no idea you'd change my mind so quickly."

***

Katherine's curiosity was piqued. "When did your feelings for me change?"

Sitting on the wall, Richard draped his arm around her back, and he gently stroked up and down her arm. She snuggled into his side, basking in their proximity.

"I knew I was in trouble the minute you took your place next to me on the steps of the church. As a knight, I take my vows seriously, no matter how impulsively the words are voiced or how unfortunately foolish they may be.

That's why I behaved so badly and tried to keep my distance. You're far too tempting, and I was easily captivated by your womanly charms."

Katherine smiled. She had no idea she possessed womanly charms but made a note to find out which ones worked, so she could use them to her advantage in the future.

"I've cast my eyes on the lady in my past. I've no desire to pursue her any further. My vow to hold you at bay no longer binds us. There's nothing left to keep us apart. I fully intend to live up to my marriage vow and make you my wife in every way," he said, pulling her closer.

She couldn't wipe the smile from her face. Her dreams had come true.

Richard rose from his seat and chuckled in good humor. "What say you, wife, shall we join the festivities? Now that the music has started, I could whirl you around the dance floor a time or two before we beg our leave. I wouldn't be opposed to showing you off to the less lucky husbands."

She raised her hand to stifle a giggle.

Without warning, he swept her off the wall and into his chest. His lips claimed hers with sweet tenderness. Her arms encircled his neck, and her body melted in response.

When her feet hit the ground, he steadied her before letting go.

"That, my lady, will have to last you until tonight," he teased.

~Chapter Twenty-Five~

Richard held tight to his wife's hand as he walked through the terrace doors and back into Westminster Hall. He fought an urge to grin like a young squire who had lost his heart to the lady of the castle.

Earlier, after explaining his new marital status to Lady Alice, he'd made haste to return to Katherine's side. With his vow finally broken, he was no longer bound like a chain to his heated words. There was nothing left to prevent him from claiming his wife.

Unfortunately, when he returned to where he left Katherine, all he found was Lady Margaret fast asleep in her chair. At the sight of his wife's empty seat, an ache of dread had squeezed across his chest.

She should've been where he'd left her. It was only by chance he spied the terrace doors slightly ajar and a sense of foreboding sent him out into the night.

Now that the immediate danger was over, Richard inhaled deeply to calm the rising anger gnawing at his insides. He took full responsibility for his wife being waylaid by a cowardly knave and wouldn't make the same mistake twice. He was not going to leave her alone again.

He weaved her toward the dance floor, around a maze of small groups of nobles. King Edward and Queen Philippa were not in attendance yet, however the room was full of guests already enjoying the evening. He dropped her hand and snaked an arm around her back, letting his fingers stroke her ribs as he guided her forward.

Lively conversations mixed with music made the hall echo in a cheerful din. Tonight, he and Katherine would start over. No more foolish vows hung over their heads. He intended to lavish his wife with so much husbandly attention that her head was going to spin with pleasure. When she was at the point where she could take no more, he would escort her back to their room and--

Without warning, Katherine halted. His arm tightened around her stiff body. Since she refused to budge, he had no choice but to stop and stand at her side. He glanced down. Her face was as white as her veil. With his fingertips, he swept away a loose tendril and placed it behind her ear. When she looked up, he flinched, for in the depths of her clear blue eyes, he saw a silent scream of terror.

"What ails you?" His muscles bunched into hard knots, and he reached for his dagger.

"Do you hear it?" Her face pinched as she listened intently.

"Hear what?"

She stroked her dagger. "A very distinct, high-pitched laugh. It is the same laugh I heard at Rosemont. The man who gave Lord Seton orders to kill my father and brother is here."

He scanned the room, looking for a man laughing. "Are you sure? Where's the sound coming from?"

She listened harder and pointed through the crowd. "Can you hear it? He is still laughing. Do you see him?"

He strained to pick out a man's sharp laugh. His height allowed him to look over the field of bobbing heads. Finally, his eyes rested on a nobleman just arriving with a few other men.

"Is he still laughing?"

She shifted her weight from side to side. "No, he just stopped."

"Come, I want to get closer so you can put a face to the laugh." Richard gripped his wife's arm, but when he tried to move her forward, she pulled back.

"I do not know if I can. What if he recognizes me?" she said, wringing her hands.

"I'll be by your side. We won't let him see you. I want you to look at him from behind a pillar." He guided her head up and gave her a reassuring smile. "Trust me."

***

Katherine's resolve to run from the well-lit hall melted away. She trusted Richard. No harm would come, as long as he was near.

This evil man scared her. He had showed himself to be powerful. A nobleman formidable enough to order the deaths of those she held dear. If what she overheard was true, he had ordered the deaths of many others as well. The man needed to be identified and stopped. Richard was right; she had to attach a face to the laugh. She needed to know her enemy.

Richard led her to one of the ornamental columns used to break the enormous room up into sections. "We'll wait here until he laughs again. When he does, I want you to look around the pillar. I believe he's one of the nobles at the far end of the table. After you pick him out, describe him to me, so I may know him, also."

She stood with her back pressed to the rounded pillar. Her husband hovered over her, enclosing her in an envelope of safety. He gazed down, his sapphire eyes twinkling mischievously.

"What are you thinking that has you smiling so?"

"I'm thinking my wife has her back against a column, which makes her an easy target for a stolen kiss."

"You would not dare embarrass me in front of all these people," she said under her breath.

He let out a dejected sigh. "I suppose my adoration will have to wait."

She held back a knowing smile, for the grown man acted no better than a child.

Abruptly, the frightening laugh broke through her musings. Other sounds ceased to exist. The air grew stifling. Her muscles tensed and turned to hardened rock. It took all the courage she could muster to crane her neck around the side of the pillar and take a look.

The men stood where Richard said they would be. The group of gray-haired nobles were dressed in rich finery, their moods jovial. Her husband's heavy hand came down upon her shoulder; his reassuring touch calming her waves of fear. She matched the sickening laugh to a well-worn face. When the man spoke, she recognized his voice and knew without question he was the one.

She returned to her secluded spot and rested heavily against the column.

"You know which one?" Richard asked.

"With certainty. He is the tall one on the right wearing the gold brocade tunic."

Richard looked around the pillar. His brows drew together, and his jaw muscles tightened. "As I thought. It's time to go."

He grabbed her upper arm and guided her toward the entrance.

"Do you know who he is?" She breathed out the words as she practically ran to keep up with his long stride.

"Yes, but we'll not discuss matters now. We'll wait until we're somewhere safe. There are too many eyes and ears here," he said, without slowing his pace.

Back at the front doors, they retrieved their cloaks. They summoned their carriage and stepped out into the night.

Katherine inhaled the crisp air, welcoming the icy chill sliding down her throat. She let her body unwind, now that the danger was past. Richard assisted her into the carriage and took a spot on the opposite seat. He tapped on the door to direct the driver to move along.

"Who is he?"

"He's a high-ranking lord, under the king's protection. There's nothing we can do about him tonight. Let's wait to talk about him later. Right now, other things are occupying my mind."

She made out his outline in the dim lantern light and swore he looked like he could devour her in one pounce.

"Come here," he said in a deep guttural voice.

Leaning across the aisle, he seized her about the waist and yanked her abruptly onto his lap. He removed her head covering and ran his hands through her thick curly hair.

"I like your hair down…like this." His hands made their way under her cloak and onto her back. He drew her to him and captured her lips with his own.

She moaned into his mouth and wrapped her arms over his shoulders, pressing her breasts to his chest. She reveled in the feel of his moist lips pressing against hers and let out a little gasp of surprise when his tongue flickered in and out of her slightly open mouth. Intimate warmth and sweetness mingled together like a fine smooth wine.

His big hands slid into the opening of her surcoat, stroking up and down her ribs, over her tight satin kirtle. Acutely aware of his faintest touch, she experienced every new sensation with frank wonder. His hands traveled ever so slowly up her outline, journeying over the supple mounds of her breasts, teasing her senses with unfamiliar yearning.

As his thumbs glided over hard peaks, he stopped long enough to give a gentle rub. A jolt of lightning coursed through her body and pulsed between her thighs. Her head snapped back as she shuddered in pleasure. He searched her mouth again, exploring deeper and deeper.

An unknown need rose from fathomless depths within her. Frantically, she clawed at his back and pulled him closer. She needed him against her; needed them to be as one. Weighted down by cumbersome garments, she impatiently tugged at her cloak. She was on fire and had to disrobe before she was ablaze.

Richard withdrew his lips. "Slow down, Katherine, we're almost home."

His tormented voice broke through her stupor. *He wanted her to stop.*

"My apologies. I do not know what came over me." She untangled her limbs from about his body and moved with haste to sit on the seat across the way. Heat rose from her inflamed cheeks. She placed her hands on her lap.

How could she behave so wantonly, no better than a harlot?

Of course, he was entirely to blame. Had he consummated their marriage when he was supposed to, she wouldn't be acting like a rutting animal.

She traded her unaccustomed passion for growing irritation, which helped return her to her senses.

***

Richard regretted the loss of her close company, however, the tightness in his loins reminded him of the rightness of their separation. Locked together any longer would've put him in a dangerous place of no return. He wasn't accustomed to wanting a woman so badly. He wasn't sure he could control his desires and didn't want their first time together to be in a carriage rocking over cobbled stones.

He looked across the aisle. In the hazy light, his wife looked dejected. She didn't know how much he enjoyed her unabashed responses.

Richard leaned forward and captured her clasped hands lying in her lap. He brought them to his mouth and brushed his lips softly over her knuckles. "God smiled down upon me the day I rescued you."

He heard her sharp intake of air and grinned. She sounded pleased with his words.

The carriage stopped at the stables in the back of the townhouse. Richard helped his wife alight, and the two of them walked up the steps together.

"I'll need to speak to my men for a few minutes before I join you," he said.

The common room was dark, with only three lanterns burning. Before entering, Richard took off his wife's cloak and hung the mantle on a peg by the door.

"Do not be too long, husband, for I will be waiting impatiently for your return to our bedchamber," she said in a silky whisper. Not waiting for a response, she spun on her heels and hurried across the room to the stairs.

His breath caught in his throat as she dashed away. Her boldness made him stiffen with yearning. He never expected such an invitation from his innocent wife. He licked his dry lips and shook his befuddled musings out of his addled brain.

He reminded himself that arrangements needed to be made. London was not a safe place for Katherine. *She knew too much.*

Godfrey and Miles were stretched out on overstuffed chairs in front of the fire. Each knight flashed him an all-knowing grin as they peered around the wings of their seats. His own smile grew, tugging at the corners of his mouth.

Richard took possession of an empty chair and sat on the edge. He stared at one man and then the other. "We have a problem."

The seriousness of his topic made his smile fade into the night.

~Chapter Twenty-Six~

Katherine floated into the bedchamber, her steps barely touching the ground. Richard wanted her for his wife. They would share their lives together.

She opened her arms and spun in circles until the dizziness made her stop. With a giggle, she fell back on the bed and stared unseeingly at the canopied top.

All of her life she had dreamed of this moment.

The fire in the hearth roared and the logs popped in protest. She couldn't dally; he would come to her soon. She sat on the edge of the bed and removed her shoes and stockings. The tales of Matilda's conquests came to mind and she lit a small lantern on the bedside table. She wanted to gaze upon his face, wanted to lay her eyes upon every inch of his breathtaking body.

Barefooted, Katherine made her way to stand in front of the open hearth. She unfastened her girdle and placed the belt and dagger, on the table. Her trembling fingers unthreaded the front of her surcoat. The garment fell in waves from her body.

Hundreds of times over the years she had envisioned this night. It was always Richard's face she saw when Matilda shared her stories. She wanted to savor their coming together. Her hunger for him subdued any virginal fear. He teased her enough with his kisses and caresses; she wanted more.

Unlacing the sides of her satin kirtle, she slid the tight-fitting material down and stepped out of the garment when it pooled at her feet.

The door opened slowly.

When Richard entered their bedchamber, a ripple of excitement lurched in her stomach. The door barely closed before his eyes filled with warm passion as she stood in front of him in only her chemise.

She forgot to breathe when his gaze floated leisurely over her curves. From the carnal way he stared, she knew her body was outlined provocatively against the glow of the fire, the same way his body had been in the cottage in the woods.

His eyes never wavered as he placed his dagger, leather belt and sword on a nearby table. "You're beautiful," he said in a gruff voice.

Her heart pounded to an ancient rhythm. His words of praise fogged her mind. When he smiled tenderly, she crossed the room, her arms raised, inviting him to her.

The open neck of her chemise spilled from her shoulders and lodged halfway down her outstretched arms. The cool air danced against her skin, heightening her senses. Tingles rose to the surface.

When a few feet away, she stopped, dropped her arms to her sides and let the sheer garment slide from her naked body and fall to the carpet. Her heart swelled as the sharp intake of his breath cut through the silence of the room. No shyness emerged to make her want to cover up. She had waited too long.

Taking a few more steps forward, she stood before him, unfastened his velvet doublet, one toggle at a time, and removed the surcoat. Her hands roamed over his white linen shirt.

Richard stared at her intently, without moving, letting her have her way as she memorized the hills and valleys of the rock-hard muscles below the thin material. Her restless fingers made their way to his long silky locks of hair. She swept her slender fingers through the soft waves, grabbed the back of his head and drew him to her. While standing on tiptoes, she opened her mouth slightly and met his warm, sweet lips with zeal as she pressed her soft body into his hard one.

Her excitement grew as his broad hands journeyed over her naked skin. His hands dropped lower and he caressed her rounded buttocks as if he were memorizing their shape. His tongue teased the recesses of her mouth, searching deeper and deeper, introducing her to new sensations. He pulled her hips against his hard bulge and held her there.

For a second, the connection was startling, but then, her ardor grew and heat settled between her legs.

Needing him closer, she grabbed the bottom of his linen shirt and with the palms of her hands on his bare skin, she caressed a slow path up the fully exposed muscles of his torso, drawing the material along as she went. Halted by his shoulders, she broke off their kiss, he leaned forward, and she yanked the cloth from his arms and over his head.

She let the material tumble to the floor. Her fingers clasped the back of his thick neck. She guided his head down and captured his lips to resume their impassioned kisses. Her naked breasts pressed against his unclad chest. When her budding nipples rubbed against his unclothed muscles, a deep moan rose in her throat as a jolt of pleasure flowed through every fiber of her being.

Although hazy with passion, she was aware of him gently guiding her toward the bed. He lifted her feet off the ground and laid her on her back on top of the mattress. When he broke his embrace, and his mouth moved away, she clung to him to keep him from withdrawing.

He unwrapped her arms from around his neck. "I'll not go far," he said in a hoarse, husky voice.

Katherine stretched like a cat, with her arms overhead, and ran the backs of her hands across the soft fur pelts covering the bed. She took a deep cleansing breath to right her spinning world.

Her husband was so close she could almost touch him as he doffed the rest of his clothes and boots. She shut her eyes. Flashes of light like the stars in the sky illuminated the blackness. Every inch of her skin screamed for his touch. Warm fluid pooled in her loins.

In an instant, he returned, lying alongside her, flesh against flesh. One of his muscular legs entangled with one of hers. She squirmed under his weight, craving his heaviness. He kissed her thoroughly with fierce possessiveness, while his battle-worn hands tenderly caressed and committed to memory every inch of unclothed skin. His fingertips traveled across her stomach, down her legs, behind her sensitive knees and back up her inner thighs, making her yearn for more. He explored every place but one, and her need grew beyond her understanding.

Fervently, her hands imprinted their own tracks upon his body, enjoying each silken touch over the bulges and indentations that composed his hardened muscles.

His tantalizing kisses retreated from her mouth and made their way down her neck and over the plump mounds of her breasts. The short-cropped hairs on his face joined in exciting her senses as they prickled her bare skin. His gentle lips captured a hardened nipple and sucked softly.

A moan escaped her throat.

The tip of his tongue flicked her sensitive nub, sending a lightning bolt through the center of her body. It exploded deep within her core. Her eyes rolled back in her head and her nails dug into his back.

A growing hunger clawed at her innards. She wriggled under his heavy arm and leg.

He lifted his head, and she locked eyes with her husband's dark blue orbs. In their depths, his passion smoldered, ready to burst into flames at the least provocation. Heat soared in a special spot below her belly. His head dropped, and he renewed his focus on her chest, using his lips to trace a path to her other breast as his hand worked its way across her stomach.

Her body responded to his tongue teasing her nipple to a firm peak. She twisted under him, and she let out a faint whimper when, at the same time, a thick finger found the opening between her legs.

Moist with need, her body arched, and she tugged on his back, urging him closer.

She was beside herself with want. As his fingers delved in and out of the slick, wet opening between her legs, her body gyrated all on its own, seeking out the exquisite sensations building inside. His tongue licked and played with the hardening peaks of her breasts and with every gentle touch the underlying flames in her loins promised to explode.

His mouth captured her lips for a scorching kiss that curled her fingers and toes. His breath came out in short pants, and his eyes were dark with desire. Using feathering kisses, he worked his way across to nibble at her earlobe. With a heavy breath, he exhaled slowly in her ear. "I will go easy, but this will hurt," he said in a throaty voice.

"I know, but please, don't stop," she begged.

Katherine welcomed his weight on top of her, however, he didn't burden her with his complete heaviness. He spread her legs wide and slid his hard member into place between them. She wrapped her limbs around his hips and drew him toward her.

When he penetrated her outer sanctuary, her innards erupted with quivering tremors as she was brought to the edge of a fiery awakening. His throbbing manhood slid into her and their entwined bodies moved together until he came upon resistance.

She tugged at him to continue but soon lost herself in savoring the sweet recesses of his mouth while his thumb rubbed a sensitive nipple. When she could stand the onslaught no more, she let out a groan that turned into a whimper of pain as he plowed ahead against her woman's barrier.

A tear trailed down the side of her cheek and her husband kissed the wetness away.

"Do you want me to stop?"

She heard the concern in his voice. When he turned his head to gaze upon her, his face was taut. "No. The pain is all but gone."

In truth, it was, for how could any pain remain when she could see how much he cared for her?

He kissed her senseless until her passion resumed to fully aflame. Soon, their bodies again moved in a harmonized rhythm, his shaft plowing deeper and deeper into her core.

Katherine matched him thrust for thrust, in their sensuous dance, until her body arched at the pinnacle of heightened arousal and exploded in ecstasy. An array of bright lights burst forth in front of her eyes. A satisfied moan escaped through her slightly parted lips.

He gave an all empowering plunge at the sound of her pleasure, and his body shuddered over hers. His loud groan echoed in the room.

She melted into the fur pelts on the bed as his body did the same. He took the brunt of his weight through his arms as he leaned down and kissed her lips so tenderly as if savoring a sweet morsel. He then moved on to kiss the top of one full breast and then the other before rolling off to the side and draping a heavy arm across her waist.

"Did I hurt you badly?" he whispered as he drew her so close their bodies molded together as one.

"What is a little pain when the ending was so grand?" she sank deeper into the depths of her husband's body, enjoying the warmth of his naked skin. "Any discomfort is already forgotten."

His warm lips kissed the side of her forehead. While his face remained nuzzled in her hair, he inhaled deeply and let out a little sigh.

She snickered. "What are you doing?"

"I'm taking in your scent. You drive me crazy with the smell of lavender. It follows you wherever you go and lingers in places you've been. It's very enticing. I have been sorely abused these past few weeks."

"May I remind you that you brought all of this on yourself? If you had just agreed to the marriage and not been so against it, we could have avoided being distant for so long."

"Aye, things could've worked out better." He nestled his face into the nape of her neck until she giggled.

"Then again, this is not so bad. Tis a good thing we have put the past behind us because I do not think I could have gone another day without you." Her cheeks heated with the admission and she burrowed further into his embrace

He chuckled. "I'm glad we rushed to London to break my vow. I wouldn't want it said I'm in the habit of denying my wife the attention of her husband." He rolled her onto her stomach, into the mountain of fur pelts on top of the bed.

"Do the wounds still pain you?"

She laid the side of her head on a pillow and tucked her hands beneath, giving him the full expanse of her backside. She knew he referred to the three long scars on her back. "The pain has subsided. I stopped wrapping them yesterday."

He pecked butterfly kisses along a scar. "Let me see if I can guess when your feelings for me changed," he said playfully. "I bet it was when I charged down the hill on Titan, sword drawn, and rescued you from those outlaws in the woods?" He raised an invisible sword in the air and waved it around.

Katherine chortled into the pillow. "Wrong."

"It must've been when I fought off those knights on horseback." He pressed a few gentle kisses on the next wound. "It was my bravery that set your heart aflutter."

"No, not then." She giggled.

His lips moved on to the next scar and brushed his lips against the raised surface. "Then it must've been when I won the day and saved you from Lord Seton?" he said merrily, the breath from his words tickling her back. "You were so impressed with my skills; you couldn't help but claim me as your own."

She chuckled. "Not even close."

"Tell me," he insisted mischievously as he traced the scar end to end with a soft touch.

She shivered from the sensation. "It was our last summer together at Rosemont. My brother teased me. You stepped in front of him and threatened to thrash him if he continued. That was when my heart was lost."

His hand roamed her lower back and cupped her rounded buttock. "That's a long time to harbor feelings for someone," he whispered, gently stroking her naked bottom.

Her breathing shallowed and a tingling sensation sprung up again between her legs. "I happen to be a very patient woman," she boasted.

"From what I've seen of you tonight, you're not that patient." He chuckled as he turned her onto her side and dragged her back into his chest. His hand snuck around and cupped her naked breast.

"Maybe I just knew being with you was my destiny," she said, basking in the pleasure of his hands upon her.

"I suppose we can't fight destiny." He gave her breast a gentle squeeze. "Now that you have worn me out, what say you if we close our eyes and get some rest? Tomorrow will be a busy day."

Katherine hid her disappointment that their joining had ended, but the hour was late. She closed her tired eyes and let her body melt into his embrace.

"Goodnight, husband." His reference to tomorrow made her worry. Something weighed heavily on his mind, however, she could tell he didn't want to ruin the moment.

He leaned across her body to extinguish the flame of the oil lamp. On his way back, he turned her head and placed a sweet kiss upon her lips. He yanked on a fur to cover their naked bodies and rested his cheek against her hair.

He sighed in her ear. "Goodnight, wife."

***

Katherine came awake slowly and stretched from corner to corner in the oversized bed. She threw off the haphazard covers and let the cheerful rays from the early morning sun warm her naked skin. Memories of last night's burning passion turned the corners of her mouth into a smile.

She relived some of the more colorful moments and was not sure which one of the two of them demonstrated a stronger need for the other. Never had she felt so alive. Every caress of his fingers had her body crying out for more. She snickered softly; no wonder Matilda had her way with so many men.

At the moment, she sorely missed her husband's presence in their bed. She rolled to his side and inhaled deeply. His woodsy male scent remained. He must be downstairs with his men.

She sat upright and drew her knees to her chest. He would be working on setting a course for the day. Now that the man responsible for the deaths of her family was identified, he would want to share this information with someone.

Katherine wanted to be part of whatever he decided. She didn't want him to leave her out.

Excited about being in his company again, she jumped out of bed with renewed energy. She grabbed her chemise off the floor and slipped the material over her head. A new set of clothes hung from a peg on the wall. The purple damask surcoat wasn't decorated as ornately as the garment she wore last night, yet it was still finer than anything she had brought from home. She slipped on her new clothes and combed out her tangled hair.

The door opened without a knock. She whirled around. Her husband walked in with an all-knowing swagger and a boyish grin on his handsome face. He appeared very pleased with himself.

"Do not tell me I married a lazy woman. It's almost the middle of the day and you're only now getting out of bed. For shame, woman. Is this how your days will be when we return to Rosemont?" He chuckled.

To assure herself that his claim was untrue, she glanced out the window. It was still early morning. "I would be up and about even earlier if my husband had not seen fit to wear me out well into the night with his ardent attentions. Mayhap, if he showed less attention, I would have a quicker step."

"Yes, but having such a passionate wife causes one to strive to excel. So you see, you are surely to blame." He gave her an impish little bow.

She giggled at his play on words.

He grabbed her around the waist, leaned down, and planted a thorough kiss on her mouth, which made her knees go weak. "My lady, you look ravishing today. If we had no pressing matters to attend, you can be assured we would be in bed right now and I would be enjoying your sweetness."

She placed her arms around his neck to help her remain upright. "What are these pressing matters you speak of? Would they have anything to do with the man we saw last night?"

"That they do," he said, running his hands along her sides.

"You were upset when I pointed him out. Who is this man?"

"Come, sit by the fire and I'll explain." He guided her to the twin chairs in front of the low burning embers. They each took a seat. "His name is Lord

Mortimer. He's a very powerful man. As the king's cousin, he has the king's ear and stands in line to the throne."

Katherine gasped. Accusing a member of the royal family of treason was not done.

"I am sure what I heard was a plot against the king," she insisted. "Lord Seton and Lord Mortimer thought I was passed out from the pain. The two of them talked in hushed tones, but I overheard what they discussed. Lord Mortimer said it was imperative Lord Seton find a priest to marry us, and once the deed was done, he was to send a missive to the king telling him that he came upon my family killed by outlaws, that he rescued me from certain death and felt obliged to marry me for my own protection. Lord Mortimer would speak to the king on his behalf, encouraging King Edward to see the benefit of rewarding the man who had rescued Lord de Grey's daughter with Rosemont. From the way he spoke, I could tell he had done this a few times in the past."

"With all the deaths over the last few years between the plague and the war with France, many of the nobles have lost many of their immediate family. It would be easy enough to find the ones with an eligible daughter and only a few relatives, if any, left to protect her. Once the family was out of the way, who would raise the cry if the king rewarded the noble who rescued the poor girl with the family's holdings, especially after marrying her?"

"Only she is not being rescued, she is being imprisoned by her family's murderer. After a short time, if the man given the estate no longer wants her as a wife, she is put to death and no one is the wiser." Katherine cringed because such was her fate had she not escaped.

"If this has been happening for years, Lord Mortimer is strategically placing men loyal to him all over England. In essence, he's raising an army to rise up against the king."

"If King Edward is unaware of this conspiracy, it could mean the end of his reign." She squirmed on the edge of her seat.

"We have a bigger problem." He squeezed her hand. "You're the only witness tying Lord Seton to Lord Mortimer. The only one who escaped. Your life is in great danger."

"I had not thought about that."

"Lord Seton would never have alerted Lord Mortimer to your escape because that would have made him appear incompetent. Lord Mortimer is probably awaiting word from Lord Seton as to when he should speak with the king. If the king hasn't shared the contents of my father's letter with anyone, there's still a chance no one but the king knows about your escape or our marriage. We're the only ones who know about Lord Seton's death and that we reclaimed Rosemont. My missive to the king yesterday was just for an invite. I didn't divulge any particulars."

"So, we are safe for the moment, if no one knows who I am or that we have married." Katherine brought trembling fingers to her lips. "Oh, no," she wailed. "What about last night? Everyone at Westminster Hall saw me and they also saw us together."

"I don't think anyone recognized you. Don't forget, they expect Lady Katherine de Grey to be grossly disfigured."

"How could I forget?" she said dejectedly.

He squeezed her hand. "It might've worked in our favor. Last night, Lord Mortimer didn't look like a man worried about being found out. We may have a little more time."

"Time for what?"

"I hate to do this to you, but we're in a dangerous position here. Lord Mortimer will eventually find out you live, and he will try to kill us to make certain we don't talk. If we say nothing about our suspicions, there is a good chance King Edward and his family will be overthrown and killed. If we choose to go to the king with our speculations, he could accuse us of disloyalty against the royal family and we could be imprisoned or worse. I need to know where you stand."

She brushed a tendril out of her face with a shaky hand. Richard was right; they were in a bad position. There was no question about what to do. "We have to go to the king with our worries, lay them before him, and hope for the best. You know as well as I do that, as loyal subjects to our sovereign, it is our life for his. How could we live with ourselves if anything happened to him?"

"I needed to hear the words from your lips before we moved forward. I will send a message to King Edward to ask for a private audience. Marcus and our knights are aware of what's at stake. They'll protect us from Lord Mortimer."

"What do we do now?" she asked.

"We go downstairs so you can break your fast. Then we wait to hear from the king."

~Chapter Twenty-Seven~

Katherine sat on the edge of a high-backed chair and fidgeted with her wedding ring as she and Richard waited for an audience with King Edward. The antechamber at Westminster Palace was elegantly decorated in rich gold tones. Tall windows with brocade drapes took up an entire wall and offered a spectacular view of a well-tended small garden. Carved moldings framed doorways and windows. The soaring ceilings had colorful battle scenes painted on them. The room appeared formidable and fancier than anything she had ever seen before.

Her nerves were twisted in a ball from days of apprehension about the possibility of her marriage being dissolved. Even though the uncertainty had passed, a foreboding remained. The king could be angered by accusations against his cousin. He could lock Richard and her away and keep them apart forever.

Will I ever see him again?

The more her thoughts wandered, the more her fingers fussed.

Richard patted the tops of her hands. "King Edward is a fair man. He'll hear us out."

Katherine nodded.

The heavy metal door banged open.

She flinched.

"Sir Richard. King Edward will meet with you now." A tall, gangly man, dressed in the king's colors stood at attention in the doorway and beckoned them forward. Two armed guards stood on either side of the door.

Richard led her into a richly fashioned room. It was smaller than expected…more intimate. Colorful jeweled boxes were on display in an oversized cherry cabinet with fancy curved legs.

King Edward sat behind an elaborately carved desk, elevated on a raised dais. His majesty appeared older than she imagined. His snow-white beard and shoulder-length hair framed his kind green eyes.

"Sir Richard Weston. It's good to see you again. I received an urgent message you needed to speak to me in private. We don't usually go through such a ceremony, so you have piqued my curiosity. Who do you have with you?" King Edward's interest changed once he noticed her.

Richard bowed deeply. "Your majesty. I have brought my wife, Lady Katherine, Lord de Grey's daughter." His voice was low and formal with a hint of pride in his tone.

Katherine inhaled deeply to still her pounding heart before she executed a perfect curtsy.

King Edward cocked a brow. "Lady Katherine, a pleasure to meet you. I received Lord Weston's missive explaining your hardship. My condolences for the deaths of your father and brother. They were good men and will be sorely missed. I'm delighted you're in good health after escaping from Lord Seton. Come, sit, both of you. I want to hear all about what took place."

Richard ushered her to a pair of seats in front of the massive cherry desk. "Your majesty, we came here to warn you about a possible conspiracy underfoot."

King Edward entwined his fingers and rested his hands on the desk. "Is this the reason for a private meeting?"

"Yes, your majesty, I'm not sure who can be trusted."

"Tell me everything," the king said gravely.

As uncomfortable as it was to tell King Edward about a family member plotting against him, Richard left nothing out. He described the details of the past week in an organized manner.

The king listened intently without interruption, his face solemn.

When Richard finished the recounting, King Edward turned to her and implored. "Are you certain, Lady Katherine? Positive, this man you speak of is Lord Mortimer?"

"Yes, your majesty. I would stake my life on it. I have no doubts," she responded with confidence.

"It's possible. I have given permission for a few marriages and have granted several estates over the past year arising from such stories. There is a pattern. But you lack real proof of an underlying conspiracy and that Lord Mortimer is behind such a plot. You never saw his face. I need something more substantial. I cannot accuse my cousin of high treason without more proof."

She shivered at the king's impassioned words and understood his anguish. "Your majesty, if I may be so bold, I have an idea to get your proof."

King Edward leaned forward over his desk. "What do you propose?"

Richard scowled.

"I could draw him out. If he is not aware of all that has happened at Rosemont, we might have a chance to trick him into acknowledging his participation."

"I doubt he knows. I haven't shared the information of Lord Weston's missive with anyone. What do you suggest?"

She sat forward, ignoring Richard's displeasure. "I could send him a letter stating I have escaped Lord Seton's imprisonment. I will inform him I am aware of his role in the takeover of Rosemont, along with other estates, and I will only keep quiet if he meets with me and hands over enough coins to see me free of England. I believe he will understand greed."

"What would stop him from killing you right there at the exchange?" Richard questioned worriedly.

"I will mention in my missive that four letters detailing all of what I know will be left with various people around London. Should I fail to return for these letters; they will be shown to the king on my behalf." She sat back on her chair.

"So, if Lord Mortimer arrives and pays you to keep quiet, it will seal his guilt. If he doesn't show or arrives without money to pay for your silence, then he probably had nothing to do with it," King Edward said.

Richard shook his head. "I don't like it. Too many things can go wrong."

"I can appreciate your hesitancy, but your wife's idea makes perfect sense. We need to confirm we have the right man. I want no doubts. Let us strike before he has time to flee, or worse."

"Your majesty, what do you propose?" Richard asked.

King Edward rang a bell.

The double doors opened. The tall man stood at attention in the center of the doorway. "Your majesty?"

"Send for Prince Edward immediately."

The man nodded and closed the door.

King Edward sat back and crossed his arms over his chest. "I will ask my son to join us. I'm sure we can figure out a way to keep Lady Katherine safe while we uncover a possible traitor."

"As you wish," Richard said through clenched teeth.

***

It was late afternoon and the warm rays of the sun were starting to wane. A bite of cold spring air floated on a breeze. Katherine sat in the carriage and drew the sides of her cloak together, partially to ward off the chill, but mostly to chase away her fears. The message had been sent. Now all they had to do was wait to see if Lord Mortimer arrived.

Richard and Prince Edward had agreed on a quiet place, just over a bridge outside of town near some old ruins. James was dressed as the carriage driver, for he was the smallest of the knights. Richard, Prince Edward, and the rest of the men hid in the woods across the road and behind a crumbling stone wall. Lord Mortimer was to take his carriage and not to bring any guards other than his driver.

She heard the familiar clopping of horses' hooves striking wooden planks as Lord Mortimer's heavy carriage rolled over the bridge. Although Richard and his knights surrounded her, it didn't help her quivering stomach.

She would have to face Lord Mortimer alone.

Richard gave her a long list of instructions to follow, and she kept repeating them in her mind. She had to keep her hood over her head, in case Lord Mortimer saw her with her husband last night. She had to get Lord Mortimer out of his carriage and meet her halfway on the road so those watching could witness all that transpired. She was not to let him get within arm's length. Once she received payment, James would quickly escort her out of the way, then Lord Mortimer would be seized and brought before the king.

All she had to do was be convincing enough for a few minutes, until, by his actions or admission he gave proof he was indeed part of a conspiracy against the king.

She put up her hood and waited for James to help her alight. When situated safely on the road, the knight let go of her arm and stepped in front of Lord Mortimer's team of horses so the other carriage was positioned in the right spot.

The coach door creaked open. She held her breath and stood her ground. An air of arrogance surrounded Lord Mortimer when he stepped down from the swaying carriage. His black eyes were piercing, and she knew he was trying to intimidate her.

"Lady Katherine." He spat out the words as if they were poison on his tongue.

"Lord Mortimer. So we meet again." She rose to her full height and held up a hand. "You can halt right there. No need to come closer. It would make my driver nervous, and I cannot be responsible for your health if he fears for my safety."

Lord Mortimer stopped a few feet away. "You picked a good place to meet. Private and out of the way."

"It will do. Do you have the money?"

"Mayhap." He patted his tunic. "Was there ever a wedding?"

"Sorry to disappoint you, but it never happened."

"How did you manage to escape?"

"I am quite capable when motivated. I will not go back to Lord Seton. The man is revolting. Unfortunately, I now find myself in a quandary. I am left with no other option except to seek your assistance. I need funds to leave England, and as I see it, you owe me." She struggled to keep her voice from cracking.

"What assurances do I have that you will not spew filth about me? Or that you will not return for more money?"

"By filth, do you mean your plot against the king, where men loyal to you take over estates all over England and then rise up as one? Once I receive my coins, my letters will not be sent. I intend to leave England's shores, with my driver's escort. He will be paid handsomely for his silence. I will not have any cause to seek you out again. I give you my word. There is nothing left for me here; you have managed to see to that."

Lord Mortimer took a step forward. "I need more than your word."

"Kill me and you will regret your actions. I have planned well for such an event. Should any of your men follow me, I will flee and not pick up my letters, which will put you in jeopardy. My advice to you is this: give me what I ask for and let me go." Her hands trembled. She clasped them together to stop them from shaking.

Lord Mortimer withdrew a large pouch of coins from inside his richly embroidered tunic. He took another step closer.

She steeled herself from stepping back. "That's far enough. Toss it over."

As he made a move to lob the bag, the half-ajar carriage door flew open and a young man placed a pointy-toed shoe on the top step, sword drawn.

"Uncle, it's a trick," he yelled.

She stared into the face of her assailant from last night. His lip was torn, and his nose was red and swollen. A scream stuck in her throat. She reached for her dagger.

Lord Mortimer didn't question the validity of his nephew's statement. Instead, he lunged at her, grabbed the hand going for her dagger, and yanked her toward him. At the same time, he dropped his coin purse and unsheathed his dagger. Before she could fight him off, the cold tip of his steel blade bit into her throat and all she could do was pull on his arm wrapped across her chest.

James reached for her, but the driver of Lord Mortimer's carriage pulled a small crossbow from undercover and let the arrow fly, hitting the young knight in the shoulder. The force knocked James off his feet and onto the ground. Behind her, she heard the driver fall from his seat, and she could only imagine that he suffered from the same fate.

The two teams of horses stamped and shook their heads to protest the commotion. However, draped in their taut harnesses, facing each other on the narrow roadway, the animals could do nothing more than stand their ground.

"What's the meaning of this? Explain yourself," Lord Mortimer yelled to his nephew. He stood with his back to his team and used Katherine as a shield while they moved in front of the carriage door.

The young man's eyes bulged in anger as he dropped behind them, sword at the ready. "I don't know what lies this whore told you, but this is Sir Richard Weston's wife. She's the one that caused me all the problems last night." He grabbed the top of her hood and snatched it off.

She glared at him.

"Come out or I'll kill her," Lord Mortimer shouted.

Richard was the first to show himself. He threw down his sword and put his hands in the air. Prince Edward and his knights followed his lead and came out from their hiding places.

"Let her go," Richard said. "It's over. Lord Seton is dead. Rosemont is mine. The king knows of your deception. There's no hiding from this."

"This is not over. Roger, get my coin bag," Lord Mortimer ordered.

She stole a glance at James, who had propped himself up against one of the carriage's wheels and held tightly to the shaft of the arrow still lodged in his shoulder. His apologetic eyes implored her to forgive him.

"We're leaving and no one is going to follow us." Lord Mortimer took small steps with Katherine pressed against him. "Bring me two horses. Do it now, or so help me I will kill her."

Richard gave Marcus a nod. The knight disappeared into the woods.

"Go easy with Lady Katherine. Remember, your fight is not with her," Prince Edward pleaded.

"Is it not? If it were not for her, I would've executed the perfect takeover of your father's crown. I would have the ultimate power and you and your family would all be dead. Everything was falling into place. It wouldn't have been much longer." Lord Mortimer pulled her closer, his fingers biting into her arm. "But then I had the misfortune of running across this one's path. Roger, stay close. They'll not rush us while we have the girl. Sir Richard won't do anything to jeopardize his wife's health. It's written all over his face."

Katherine stared into her husband's dark eyes as Lord Mortimer made her side-step to the end of the carriage. She had let her husband down. Again, she had put herself in danger. His jaw tensed with barely suppressed anger, and her heart went out to him.

"I'm impressed by your tactics. The king must've wanted proof of my deceit. It almost worked. Lady Katherine was extremely convincing. I had no reason not to believe her. It's a good thing I agreed to bring Roger with me before I left." Lord Mortimer pushed her along for a few more steps.

Marcus led Titan and his own stallion out of the woods and onto the road. He handed the reins to Roger and stepped back.

"You have our horses, now let my wife go," Richard ordered.

"She comes with us as our hostage. If anyone follows, I won't hesitate to cut her throat. Actually, it would be a pleasure."

Katherine cringed.

"If anything happens to her, I will hunt you down and disembowel you while you plead for your miserable life," Richard stated.

"Whether it comes to that or not, is up to you." Lord Mortimer studied the horses brought to him. "Fine animals. These will do nicely. Roger, Lady Katherine and I will ride together on the black; you can have the other."

She was surprised by Marcus's selection of horses. It seemed odd he would willingly offer Titan and his stallion unless he had a good reason. While her captor was distracted, she dropped her arm slowly toward the dagger at her side.

"That will get you killed," the older man growled in her ear while he pressed the point of his steel dagger deeper into her neck. She froze when she felt a pinch.

He unsheathed her dagger and tucked the blade in his belt. "I think you'll be more compliant without temptation."

Roger held the two horses by the reins, nose to nose, facing each other. His sword remained drawn. Lord Mortimer nudged her forward, his dagger now pressed menacingly into her ribs. "Step on the back of the carriage and sit on the saddle. Remember, any wrong move and I will gut you like a pig."

She locked eyes with Richard, who gave an ever so slight nod of his head for her to do as the man said. His eyes then darted to Titan and back. All the knights surrounding the carriages stood stone still as if any slight movement would put her in further jeopardy. She struggled against feeling helpless and at the mercy of the man responsible for her family's deaths. Her heart pounded in her ears. She needed to remain strong.

Purposefully, she untied her cloak at her neck and hiked her skirts to her thighs so she could step unhindered onto the back of the carriage and then slide onto the saddle. Lord Mortimer remained on the ground with the sharp tip of his dagger pressed to her waist with every move.

"If you know what's good for you, you will remain still while I get up behind," he said, lifting his leg for the stirrup.

She instinctively knew what Richard wanted her to do. To prepare, she wrapped her hand in Titan's long mane, sat forward in the saddle, and leaned over the horse's neck. A barely audible whistle floated on the wind from where her husband stood. She squeezed her thighs, urging Titan forward. He took a few steps toward Richard, pushing against Roger as he went.

"Halt," Lord Mortimer called, hopping on one leg, unable to hoist himself onto the moving animal.

Roger, observing his uncle's predicament, yanked down hard on Titan's reins.

At the unspoken command, the stallion sat back on his haunches and came up with his front legs, striking out. A sharp hoof hit the young man in the head. He let out a strangled cry, and his body crumpled to the ground.

While Titan stood on his hind legs, Katherine held on tight to his mane and swung her leg over the warhorse's back to the opposite side, away from her captor.

Lord Mortimer frantically pulled at her cloak in an attempt to bring her back, but since she'd untied the cords at her neck, the garment fell from her shoulders. As all four of Titan's legs returned to the road, a burn pierced her forearm before she let go and dropped to the ground on the other side of the stallion, far out of reach of the king's cousin.

***

Richard couldn't believe his eyes. Without a word Katherine had understood what he wanted her to do. Lord Mortimer would never have allowed her to live. Richard couldn't let his wife leave with the king's cousin, or her fate would've been sealed. They had only one chance.

He felt relieved when she stood on the road, his horse between her and her abductor. Marcus rushed forward, scooped her up, and delivered her across the road out of harm's way. Roger's body jerked on the ground, mortally wounded by Titan's hoof to his head.

Richard whistled and his stallion trotted over, leaving the king's cousin at the mercy of the knights surrounding him.

Lord Mortimer had not foreseen such an escape. He stood alone, dagger in hand, mouth agape.

"Lord Mortimer, you are under arrest for treason," Prince Edward proclaimed.

"I will not rot in my cousin's dungeons." He picked up Roger's blade and moved toward Prince Edward and Richard.

Richard stepped in front of the traitor with his sword drawn. He wanted to hurt the man who put his wife in harm's way…the man who wanted her dead.

He held the hilt of his weapon in both his hands. Lord Mortimer came at Richard with all he had. The man was no fighter and swung with abandon, the sword too heavy for his weak muscles.

Richard fended off a few thrusts before he found an opening and plunged the point of his blade into the man's heart.

When the body hit the ground, Prince Edward put a hand on Richard's shoulder. "You were right. My father's cousin was a traitor and deserved to die here today. The king will know of your valor."

Richard bent down and wiped the blood off the sharp edge of his blade on Lord Mortimer's silk tunic before he placed the sword back in his belt. He removed Katherine's dagger from the man's belt and put the small knife in the top of his boot. "It's not I who deserve such an honor, it is my wife. She's the one who uncovered this treachery and was willing to die for the truth. She's the one who has shown true valor."

"That she has," Prince Edward remarked.

Richard looked for her; however, the carriage blocked his view. Out of the corner of his eye, he saw Miles and Godfrey caring for James's injury. The other knights surrounded the dead on the ground.

He pushed through the circle of men and went around the carriage. The blood drained from his face. Katherine sat on the ground with Marcus leaning over her, wrapping his wife's arm with a cloth.

Richard sprinted up the small incline and knelt beside Marcus.

"Katherine, are you hurt?" he asked, hovering over her.

She gazed up lovingly into his eyes. "Only a scratch where Lord Mortimer cut me with his blade before I broke free."

"Let me see." He pushed Marcus aside and began unwrapping the bandage.

"Leave it be until we get back to the Tanners." Marcus gave him a pointed look. "We can have a physician attend the wound and maybe give it a few stitches to stop the flow. Right now, the bandages will help."

Richard sighed and let Marcus rewrap the bandages. He picked up her other hand and squeezed it. "I should never have agreed to put you in such danger. I don't know what I was thinking."

"Tis not your fault. I can be quite convincing when I want to be. What happened to Lord Mortimer and his nephew?"

"Both dead and unable to harm you ever again." He removed her dagger from the top of his boot and handed her the hilt.

She gave him an approving smile and sheathed the dagger in her girdle.

"You were very brave and did the right thing when you put Titan between you and Lord Mortimer."

"I could not imagine you giving up your horse so readily. I figured there was a reason for your generosity."

"Both of our horses have been trained to come when called. If Lord Mortimer and Roger did somehow get away from us, there was always the chance we could call our animals back. Thankfully, Lord Mortimer chose Titan as his own."

Prince Edward joined them. "Lady Katherine, are you well?"

"Just a gash on her arm from Lord Mortimer's dagger. We'll take my wife back to our townhouse and fetch a physician for her and James," he said.

"We have loaded the dead into Lord Mortimer's carriage and are returning to Westminster to inform the king. I'll send one of my men ahead and ask for my father's physician to meet you at your home. It's the least I can do." Prince Edward bowed. "Lady Katherine, the crown thanks you for your loyalty and courage."

"My honor, Prince Edward," she said.

The prince walked away. Marcus went to collect the horses. Richard bent down and scooped Katherine up in his arms.

"What are you doing?"

"I'm carrying you to the carriage."

She touched the side of his face and giggled softly. "I can walk; my arm is injured, not my legs."

"I beg you. Do not deny me an opportunity to hold you close after I almost lost you," he pleaded.

She wrapped her arms around his neck and melted into his chest. He gently kissed her lips until she was breathless. As he turned toward the carriage, she nestled her face in the nook of his neck.

Relief flooded his body.

~Chapter Twenty-Eight~

"Why have you stopped?" Richard halted his mount alongside Katherine, who had reined in her gray-speckled mare at the edge of the tree-line. In the distance, Rosemont sat regally on the rocky cliffs overlooking the ocean.

"Because I don't believe I have ever seen anything so beautiful and I want a moment to take it in. A few days ago, I was not sure I would ever return, but now here I am."

"This is your home. This is where you belong. Here with me." The huskiness in his voice surprised him.

She nodded. "Of that I am sure."

"Come, wife, I'll race you to the drawbridge."

Before the words rolled off his tongue, she had galloped off. He squeezed his thighs around his horse's sides and prepared for an explosion. Titan, accustomed to chasing after his wife's little palfrey, needed no urging. Without hesitation, his warhorse's massive legs sprang to life, easily tearing up the ground.

As the couple rode neck and neck, his spirits soared. In a few short days, his life had changed completely, all because of the woman riding like the wind at his side.

She was a vision with her long, honey-colored hair billowing behind her and determination painted on her lovely face. He knew in his heart he would never tire of such a sight.

When they were almost at the drawbridge, he sat back on Titan, asking him to slow his pace. His charger tossed his head in protest before reluctantly backing off, letting the mare win the race by a nose.

Katherine threw back her head and cried out in triumph as she worked to calm her excited mount. "Looks like I have won again."

"So you have," he agreed wholeheartedly, caught up in her delight.

At the edge of the drawbridge, the pair waited for the five knights to join them.

Thankfully, James's injuries were not such that he had to be left behind. His youngest knight led the way to the castle in a thunder of hoofbeats, the men's moods jovial as they laughed at his and Katherine's antics. Once all the riders were together, congratulations were freely given to his wife, with a hint of amusement in their voices.

They all set off in a collected canter over the drawbridge and through the outer and inner baileys. Welcome calls rang out from the guards in the gatehouses and those on the battlements. He noticed extra care was taken to make sure the castle inhabitants had been protected while they were gone.

The riders halted in front of the keep. Richard dismounted. "I wonder how Peter fared in our absence. I might have been amiss leaving him with such a great responsibility of running Rosemont so soon after we reclaimed the estate from Lord Seton."

"We did leave rather quickly," she said.

Richard gave his wife what he hoped was a devious look. "At the time, there was an urgency. I needed to get you to London as quickly as possible to break my foolish vow or I was going to go mad."

"You just wanted to bed me, I think," she teased, her cheeks turning rosy.

"That's what drove me," he heartily agreed. "And it was worth it."

Katherine buried her burning face behind her hand. He could tell she was secretly thrilled by the compliment.

Richard helped her off her palfrey. Purposefully, he let her body slide down the length of his and left his hands lingering about her waist. His eyes rested with longing on the soft mounds pressing enthusiastically against her low-cut velvet gown, threatening to spill over the top. A whiff of lavender teased his nostrils, causing them to flare, and he breathed in deeply, not willing to part with the sweet scent too soon.

Suddenly, a need to be alone with his wife cropped up. Taking her small hand in his, he guided her up the stone steps to the double doors of the keep. When she stole a glance toward the garden where her maid had been displayed, just a few days before, he squeezed her hand.

"Don't think about it. Your maid's death was not your fault. She sacrificed herself to save your life."

Katherine flashed him a grateful smile. "I know. I miss her so much. It will not be the same without her."

The doors stood wide open, welcoming in the afternoon light. As they stepped into the dim hall, they heard a loud bellow.

"It's about time you showed up," a voice boomed from the vicinity of the hearth.

"William?" Richard called out in surprise. He drew Katherine along as he made his way to the chairs by the hearth. When he reached William standing before the fire, he slapped his friend on the shoulder and then braced himself to receive an even harder smack in return.

"I got tired of waiting for you to send for me, so we took it upon ourselves to make our way to your fathers, only to find you left without me," William said accusingly.

Richard smiled warmly and nodded silent greetings to Lady Elizabeth and Emma, who both stood next to William. He glanced back at his friend. "Sorry. I didn't have time to send for you, so I borrowed your knights instead."

"Sure, take my knights and let them have all the fun. Leave me pacing the halls at Hammerstead, waiting for a call to arms," William complained with good humor.

"You never leave your wife's side anymore. I was getting worried you might be too old to butt heads. Next time, I promise to save some fighting for you."

"You better. Peter was good enough to fill me in on all that took place. I'm glad the siege was successful, and Lord Seton is dead. Good riddance to him."

"I'm sorry about Owen being harmed," Richard apologized, his voice tinged with guilt.

"I heard Lady Katherine saved his life when she distracted Lord Seton from finishing the job." William gazed down at Katherine and gave her a nod of approval. "I will be forever indebted to you."

Richard smiled proudly. Her face flushed a rosy red as she accepted his friend's declaration.

William placed a big hand on Richard's shoulder. "He's upstairs, healing nicely. Seems he's quite smitten with the girl taking care of him. He can't keep his eyes off her. He says she has a heart of gold and a quick laugh. I'm worried he might not want to come home to Hammerstead."

"In that case, maybe you can take James in exchange for Owen. All he does lately is look at my wife and drool. It's quite annoying." Richard chuckled.

William threw his head back and roared with laughter. "Now you know what I've been going through for the past year. It is pure agony being married to a beautiful woman." He glanced at his wife, who gave him a piercing look. He sent her a playful wink and received a slight smile in return.

***

Katherine bowed to Elizabeth and Emma standing quietly at her side. "Elizabeth, I am so happy to see you. You too, Emma."

"No formalities here." Elizabeth wrapped arms around Katherine's shoulders and pulled her close.

Katherine was delighted by such a warm welcome and gave her friend a big hug in return. "I have much to tell you."

"I guess you do. You have married," Elizabeth stated.

She exchanged a thoughtful smile with Richard. "That would be the truth."

"Then I guess congratulations are in order," Elizabeth said.

"Tell me, old man, how does it feel to get caught?" William teased Richard, whacking him on the back.

"William, do not start trouble with the newly married, or you will be sharing the hay with your horse tonight," Elizabeth threatened playfully.

"I'm sure, as a newly married man, you feel the same as me. The word 'bliss' comes to mind. *Pure heavenly bliss*," William boasted with exaggeration, making the couples laugh loudly.

"Is no one going to bother welcoming an old man?" Lord Weston whined good-naturedly from a high-back chair in the corner.

Katherine covered her mouth with her hands. "Lord Weston, you are here too?" she shrieked with joy.

"I came to see for myself how things are going," the gray-haired man said, as he stood and opened his arms so she could go to him. "Are you well, daughter?" he asked in a whisper, his arms hugging her tight.

"Aye, I am. It was a bumpy ride. However, things have turned out favorably."

"I always had faith they would. And, if the truth be known, it did not hurt that I prayed, also." Lord Weston chuckled.

***

Richard shook his father's hand. "It's good to have you here, Father." He scrutinized the older man from head to toe. "You look healthy. I take it your gout is better. I hope you were able to ride without too much discomfort."

Lord Weston cleared his throat. Nervously, he fiddled with his short beard. "Funny thing about my ailments. They cleared up overnight. Right after you left. Suddenly, I was able to ride again. It must've been a miracle."

"You don't say," he said dubiously.

Marcus and Peter walked through the double doors and made their way to the group standing around the sitting area.

"How did you make out in my absence?" Richard asked Peter after the men had greeted everyone.

"All is as it should be. We are patrolling the surrounding countryside. A few of Lord Seton's men returned and they were dealt with. The people of Rosemont have been easy to work with. The Connors have been a big help with the villagers, and the healer has been vigilant about caring for Owen."

"That's good news. Well done." He gave Peter a hearty slap on the shoulder.

Marcus's green eyes twinkled in merriment as he spoke to William. "Did you miss me in my absence?"

"I didn't even notice you were gone," William jested, teasing his senior knight.

"I can tell you, my head is fairly spinning, after all, I've been through in the past few weeks. Remind me never to leave Hammerstead again and go off on a jaunt with Richard, for I fear my old body couldn't take any more excitement." Marcus chuckled.

"Was it really that bad?" William asked with fervor, encouraging his knight to continue.

"Did you even realize what you were sending me into? I had to battle knights in full armor on horseback, bear witness to a marriage, jump into cold water to save a damsel in distress, sleep in the pouring rain, crawl over sharp rocks on the side of a cliff, sneak through darkened tunnels, battle more knights, play nursemaid to a friend, travel to London, watch Lady Katherine uncover a plot against the king, and then to top it off I had to stand by as King Edward granted Richard the title of Earl of Rosemont for saving the kingdom. I don't think I can take any more excitement. I'm ready to go home. My chair by the fire is looking better and better all the time," he rambled on, smiling brightly when hoots of congratulations rang out echoing off the walls, drowning out his last words.

William was the first to speak. "The Earl of Rosemont. The king bestowed on you the title of Earl of Rosemont?"

"My wife figured out Lord Mortimer was behind Lord Seton's acquisition of Rosemont, and she tricked the man into admitting to his treachery. King Edward was so pleased that Katherine uncovered his cousin's plot to take over England and so amazed by her unwavering loyalty, he wanted to reward us."

Richard smiled at her. "I'm no longer just a lord of the manor, but a titled lord."

Lord Weston sat back down on the chair with a thud. "My second son, an earl. I would never have imagined it. God has certainly smiled down upon the two of you."

"That he has," he agreed.

"I hope you don't expect me to call you, *Your Excellency*, anytime soon," William joked.

"I think this news calls for a toast," Elizabeth suggested.

The men seconded her motion. Servants rushed for tankards of ale and food.

Katherine guided Elizabeth to the chairs closest to the hearth to share what happened after leaving Hammerstead. She was so excited, she chatted nonstop, oblivious to anyone else in the room.

William questioned Marcus about his exploits over the past few days, and before long, the green-eyed knight had William and Peter bursting with laughter.

Richard cringed when he heard his friends' unrestrained laughter, sure their merriment was at his expense.

He strode over to his father, who sat quietly in the corner and hauled up a chair, so he could face the older man.

"Congratulations, son. I'm very proud of you."

He absentmindedly accepted his father's praise. "I have to tell you, Father, I'm a bit confused," his voice purposefully low.

"What about, son? Maybe I can help."

"When Katherine and I had an audience with King Edward, he appeared surprised we were man and wife. For a moment, I had the distinct feeling I was not the husband he expected."

"Really?" his father said incredulously.

Richard was not impressed with the older man's attempt at looking surprised. "Tell me, Father, exactly what did the king's message say? You know, the one that supposedly ordered me to marry Katherine."

His father fidgeted in his seat. "Well, I read the letter quite fast. I'm an old man, and I don't remember things as I should."

"You can't squirm your way out of this. I won't accept your *old man's* excuses. You're as sharp as your dagger. I want to know what King Edward's missive said."

His father wrung his hands in his lap. "The letter said he wanted the Weston and de Grey families united. The king wanted to make sure his new ward was safe from those who would use her as a pawn. Rosemont was to be reclaimed and Lord Seton punished. His majesty wanted Rosemont in the hands of someone loyal and trustworthy."

Richard leaned forward on the edge of his seat. "Father, tell me who King Edward actually wanted Katherine to marry."

His father expelled a deep sigh. "King Edward might have wanted Katherine to marry me. There, I said it. Are you satisfied? Since I was the titled lord and unmarried, he thought we would make a good match."

Richard's face tensed. His father had lied.

"Katherine's like a daughter to me. I would never have been a proper husband. The king didn't actually name me. It was implied. She always cared for you. That's why I never pushed your brothers to wed her. I was waiting for you to be ready for marriage. How could I not chance the king's wrath?"

"You made me believe the king ordered me to marry her. You made me think a marriage between us was what the king wanted, even after I told you I had feelings for another. You manipulated me."

"I only said the king wanted the Weston and de Grey families united. You just assumed you were the one he spoke of."

Richard's eyes narrowed. His father was right; he never questioned who the king wanted for a husband, just believed it was him.

His father gripped the arms of the chair. "I saw a chance for two people I hold dear to make a life together. I watched her grow over the years. I know what kind of woman she is. You could never find another like her, but you were too blind to see. The opportunity presented itself and I took it. I'm sorry if I tricked you into doing something you were against."

He sat back in his chair. Katherine was to have married his father. If his father hadn't tricked him, she would've been his father's wife. The image of their union provoked discord, and he quickly erased the vision from his mind.

His face grew stiff and his lips taut. He didn't like to be manipulated, especially by his father, who seemed to do it so well. But his father knew that sometimes he had to be hit over the head in order to see what was right in front of him.

Richard glanced over his shoulder at his wife, who was in deep conversation with Lady Elizabeth. He caught her eye, and she bestowed on him a look of pure love. Warmth flowed through his body as his heart lurched.

His father sat erect, no doubt steeling himself for Richard's angry explosion. There were no regrets dancing in his father's eyes, just a belief that he had made the right decision.

"Thank you, Father. I think I can live with your meddling. After all, I'm content with what came from it." He laid a gentle hand on his father's knee.

"Really?"

Richard met his father's blue eyes and nodded.

Servants arrived with trays of food and ale. He went to sit next to his wife as the group gathered about the couple. Tankards and goblets were passed.

William did the honors. "A toast to the new Earl of Rosemont and his beautiful wife, Lady Katherine. May your lives be blessed with much happiness and prosperity. May you always be surrounded by good friends and family. May Richard not have to sleep in the stables with Titan too often."

A resounding, "Hear, hear," along with wild merriment rang out amongst the well-wishers.

He took up his cup. "A toast to good friends and family."

"Hear, hear," was once more cried in unison.

***

A few hours later, Richard stood with his wife next to the stone wall along the cliffs. A light breeze teased at their clothes and hair. As they leaned against one another's sides, they gazed out over the ocean, inhaling the salty air.

"I never tire of the ocean. It is so untamed and has such an undeniable appeal," Katherine gushed.

Without giving his wife warning, he turned her toward him, reached under her arms and sat her on top of the half-wall. She shrieked in surprise. He grabbed her waist and worked his hips between her legs until his chest pressed against her well-endowed breasts.

"It sounds like you're describing me in our bedchamber." He laughed.

"Someone will see us," Katherine cried in feigned horror, but made no attempt to move away. Easing her arms around his neck, she entwined her fingers in his long hair.

"Let them; I care not. I am the Earl of Rosemont and can do anything I wish," he boasted with playful arrogance.

She giggled.

He leaned in and captured her moist, pliant lips in an all-consuming kiss. His wife dragged him closer and a whisper of a moan escaped her throat. From deep within, he found the strength to break from their kiss before things became too heated. His forehead rested against hers, while he waited for his breath to return.

He gently caressed the side of her face with his fingers before drawing back so he could stare into the depths of her bright eyes where passion smoldered under the surface. "Are you happy?"

"Overjoyed," she purred.

"Are you glad about the way things turned out?"

"I am very happy for us, although I wish my family were here to share in our joy."

"I know you miss them." He brushed a wayward tendril out of her face and put the hair behind her ear. The corners of his lips curled up in a slight smile when he caught a whiff of a flowery scent.

"I miss them a lot." She paused and then continued. "This might sound strange, but I believe that somehow my mother has been watching over me these past days." She unsheathed her jeweled dagger and held the knife lovingly in her hands, palm up, as she presented the blade to him.

"My mother gave this to me on her deathbed. Her words to me were, *May my dagger bring you great strength and courage in a time of need.* I felt her presence come through the dagger the day I slashed Lord Seton's face after he killed my family. Since then, whenever I needed strength and courage, all I had to do was stroke my dagger, and I was provided with what I needed."

He took the dagger and ran his hand over the jewel-encrusted hilt. "It was an act of God that the steel was sharp enough to cut through Lord Seton's chainmail, giving you a chance to escape." He handed the blade back. "It was also fortunate the dagger lay on the floor within reach when I needed a weapon to avenge your family."

"It gives me comfort to think my mother watches over me." She returned the dagger to her sheath.

"I hope you're right. Since I met you, I noticed you have a gift for finding trouble. Maybe if we join forces and protect you together, we may be able to keep you safe." He chuckled.

"You better. I plan on being your wife for a long time to come."

"I would have it no other way," he said, his heart almost bursting as he leaned in for another kiss.

~The End ~

<u>Many Thanks</u>

Thank you for reading *Dagger's Destiny*. I hope you enjoyed my Medieval adventure as much as I enjoyed writing it.

If you took pleasure in reading this book, help other readers find my story by writing a review on your favorite retailer site, on your Facebook page and/or on other reader platforms you frequent. And, please don't forget to tell all your friends who may be interested!

Visit my website and sign up for my newsletters at: <u>www.karen-muir.com</u>
Friend me on my Facebook page at: <u>www.facebook.com/karenmuir.writer</u>

Also, feel free to contact me on either platform to chat about writing, or to leave a comment.

Dagger's Destiny is part of a Medieval series where some of your beloved characters will have reoccurring roles. We'll find out how William and Elizabeth became a couple. There will also be stories revolving around Richard's three brothers and William's little sister, Emma. I will be working on these stories in the near future.

I recently finished the first book in a Western series about four brothers on a ranch in Montana, in 1886. *Fated Beginnings* is now available!

Best Wishes,

Karen Muir

<u>*About the Author*</u>

"Historical Romance Writer"

Yikes, is that really me? Where in the world did that come from? If you asked me years ago what I saw in my future I would never have said, "I see myself as a writer.". Writing is hard. It takes a lot of thought. It's time consuming.

And, I love it!

My journey began quite differently than most other writers. I didn't grow up writing. I didn't spend day after day locked in a room pressing pen to paper.

For as long as I can remember when my head hit the pillow, I dreamed.

I dreamed about people I didn't know and the lives they might have led. Scenes evolved and aligned themselves in perfect order. Beginnings and endings became clear. Stories emerged. Soon I had a handful of stories taking up space in an already crowded head. There was nothing else to do but write them down, if just to make room for more adventures, pushing their way in, vying for a spot.

I've found it's much easier to dream than to write. In order to share my stories with those who might enjoy them, I studied the craft of writing and joined my words together until I finished my first manuscript. I cannot begin to convey my delight when *Dagger's Destiny* was finally complete.

As I continue on my quest to share my stories with readers who enjoy them, I've embarked on the journey of self-publishing, in the hope that I may touch, in some small way, the lives of those around me.

With Warmest Regards,

Karen Muir

www.ingramcontent.com/pod-product-compliance
Lightning Source LLC
Chambersburg PA
CBHW031945110726
47902CB00001B/301